It's time to unlock . . .

THE SECRET

Kathryn Hughes was born in Altrincham, near Manchester. After completing a secretarial course, Kathryn met her husband and they married in Canada. For twenty-nine years they ran a business together, raised two children and travelled when they could to places such as India, Singapore, South Africa and New Zealand. Kathryn and her family now make their home in a village near Manchester. *The Secret* is Kathryn's second novel, the first being the Kindle Number One bestseller *The Letter*.

Stay in contact with Kathryn by following her on Twitter @KHughesAuthor, or find her on Facebook at www.facebook.com/KHughesAuthor.

By Kathryn Hughes

The Letter
The Secret

Praise for

THE LETTER

'A wonderful, uplifting story' Lesley Pearse

'Autumnal Sunday afternoons were invented to read heart-tugging novels like this' *Red*

'This moving love story had everyone talking . . . Get set to be hooked' *Look*

'A moving story of love, loss and hope' *Bella*

'A beautiful story . . . I didn't want to put it down' *Reviewed by Fran*

'Chrissie and Tina's story is one that will stay with me for a long time' *Jaffa Reads Too*

'You will find it hard to put down. I cried buckets of tears reading it' *Books With Wine And Chocolate*

'A beautifully told, tragic tale . . . restoring your faith in the kindness of strangers and the strength of the human spirit to rise despite adversity' *Ajoobacats Blog*

'Beautifully written and incredibly poignant. You cannot fail to fall for this story' *The Last Word Book Reviews*

'The story kept me gripped . . . A breath of fresh air, and just what I needed after a long day in the office'
Here.You.Me

'I don't think I can put into words how beautiful this book is . . . *The Letter* is a touching tale of love and loss in two different time periods. I was engrossed by both Tina and Chrissie's stories and went through every emotion under the sun whilst reading, from sadness, to anger, to joy. *The Letter* is absolutely stunning' *Samantha Kilford*

'I loved it and regard it as one of the finest stories I have ever read' Joe4sure, *Amazon,* 5*

'It is beautifully written with characters who are totally believable. I got lost in their story and my heart broke for them over and over' ShellyB, *Amazon,* 5*

'I loved this book. The storyline caught, actually GRABBED my attention from day one. I shall keep an eye open for everything she writes' Jenny R, *Amazon,* 5*

'This book was a sheer joy to read, and I cried at the end. Wonderfully romantic with beautiful characters . . . Enthralling and well-written' Marianne I, *Amazon,* 5*

'WOW! What a moving book! I loved every second of *The Letter*' Lauren T, *Goodreads,* 5*

'This must be one of the best books I have ever read, without exaggeration!! It is written impeccably, as if every single word was chosen carefully and positioned in the right place. You just cannot stop reading it' Daveprp, *Amazon*, 5*

'I have finished reading this book with tears in my eyes but a smile on my face. This is the first book I have read by Kathryn Hughes and I sincerely hope it will not be the last' M. I. R, *Amazon*, 5*

'This is one of the best books I have read. It's not very often I get emotional or cry when I read a book but this brought me to tears . . . An absolute delight to read; you won't regret it' Filopastry, *Amazon*, 5*

'I recommend it to anyone who has some time and a heart ready to be tumbled into a washing machine of stirring and emotional weepiness' *A Creative Girl Nadia*

'Wow, what a powerfully emotional story . . . I just loved all the twists and turns' Emma, *Amazon*, 5*

'One of the best books I've ever read' Lynne, *Goodreads*, 5*

'*The Letter* by Kathryn Hughes is both beautifully written and incredibly poignant. You cannot fail to fall for this story' John, *Amazon*, 5*

'Moving smoothly between two generations, the families linked in heartbreaking ways, this book had me spellbound and totally occupied my thoughts. I loved it' Eleanor T, *Amazon*, 5*

'I have read quite a few great books in the past couple of months . . . *The Letter* beats them all hands down! A page-turner from the very beginning and no dull moments! This is the best book I have read for a long time' Victoria, *Amazon*, 5*

'With twists and turns, this is a wonderful, page-turning read. Could not put it down' Emma H, *Amazon*, 5*

'Just brilliant, but be warned, once you start reading you won't want anyone interrupting you' Veronica T, *Amazon*, 5*

'I read a lot of books but it has been some time since I read a book as good as this' L. K. C, *Amazon*, 5*

'This is one of the best books that I have ever read' Cheryl W, *Goodreads*, 5*

'I couldn't put it down. So beautifully written. I feel like I'm a better person for reading it' Ms Z. O. O. A, *Amazon*, 5*

'The best book I've read for a long time!' bookfan, *Amazon*, 5*

THE SECRET

Kathryn Hughes

headline
review

First published in Great Britain in 2016
by HEADLINE REVIEW
An imprint of HEADLINE PUBLISHING GROUP

Cataloguing in Publication Data is available from the British Library

ISBN 978 1 4722 2999 1

Typeset in Garamond by Palimpsest Book Production Limited,
Falkirk, Stirlingshire

Printed and bound in Great Britain by CPI Group (UK) Ltd,
Croydon CR0 4YY

MIX
Paper from
responsible sources
FSC
www.fsc.org   FSC® C104740

Head   ewable and
recyc   ell-managed
forests   manufacturing
proces   al regulations

For my Mum and Dad

If light is in your heart
you will find your way home.

Rumi

1

June 1975

She had first married Thomas Roberts in the school playground when she was five years old. The ceremony had been days in the planning, and when the time came she'd worn one of her mother's net curtains fashioned into a makeshift veil and topped with a halo of daisies, and everybody agreed that she looked just like a real bride. Thomas presented her with a little clutch of hand-picked wild flowers he had collected on his way to school, and they'd stood hand in hand as little Davy Stewart officiated. Davy's speech was impaired by a crippling stammer, and his jam-jar glasses magnified his eyes to the size of a bush baby's, but he was a choirboy and the closest thing they had to a vicar.

Mary smiled at the memory as she turned to one side and admired her profile in the full-length mirror. She ran her hand tenderly over the swell of her belly, admiring the way it jutted out from just beneath her breasts and formed a perfect dome. She placed her hands in the small of her back, leaned forward and studied her complexion for any signs that she might be blooming. The bootees she had bought from Woolworths, a neutral lemon colour, lay on the dressing table. She buried her nose in the wool, but without little feet to warm them, they smelled new and sterile. At the sound of her husband clumping up the stairs, she thrust the bootees back in the drawer and just managed to whip out the pillow from under her dress before he opened the bedroom door.

'There you are, love. What're you doing up here?'

She bashed the pillow back into shape and laid it on the bed. 'Nothing, just tidying up a bit.'

'What, again? Come here.' He pulled her close, nudged her blond hair to one side and kissed her on the neck.

'Oh, Thomas, what if I'm not pregnant?' She tried to keep the whining note out of her voice, but she'd tasted disappointment so many times before that it was becoming difficult to remain positive.

He grabbed her round the waist with both hands and wrestled her on to the bed. 'Then we'll just have to keep trying.' He burrowed his face into her neck, and she detected the familiar lingering smell of coal dust in his hair.

'Thomas?'

He propped himself up on his elbows and gazed into her face. 'What?'

'You will hand your notice in if I am pregnant, won't you?'

Thomas sighed. 'If that's what you want, Mary, yes, I will.'

'I can't look after a baby and run the guest house by myself, can I?' she reasoned.

Thomas gazed at her, a crease of worry lining his forehead. 'It'll be tough, though, Mary. I mean, we've just had a thirty-five per cent pay increase. It's a lot to give up, you can't deny that.'

'I know, love, but it's such a dangerous job and you hate the long commute to the pit.'

'You're not wrong there,' he conceded. 'What time's your appointment at the doctor's?'

'Three.' She stroked a finger down the side of his cheek. 'I wish you could come with me.'

He kissed her fingertip. 'So do I, Mary, but I'll be thinking of you and we can celebrate when I get home, can't we?'

'I hate it when you have to work the night shift.'

'It's not exactly a barrel of laughs for me either.' It was said with a smile that removed any hint of rancour from his words.

As he sat on the bed to pull his boots on, Mary snuggled up beside him. 'I love you so much, Thomas.'

He reached for her hand and laced his fingers through hers. 'I love you too, Mary, and I just know you're going to make a cracking mother.'

Ever since their official wedding night, three years ago, they had been trying for a baby. Mary had not envisaged it being so difficult, and at thirty-one years of age, she was all too aware that time was running out. She was born to be a mother, she knew it, had always known it, and she could not understand why God was punishing her in this way. With each passing month, as the familiar dragging sensation crept into her stomach and the cramps took hold, a little more of her optimism had ebbed away, and her yearning to have a baby had become ever stronger. She was longing to be woken at four in the morning by a screaming infant, would relish having a bucket of terry nappies festering away in the corner of the kitchen. She wanted to look into her baby's eyes and see the future. Most of all she wanted to see her Thomas with his strong arms tenderly cradling his baby – boy or girl, it didn't matter – and to hear him being called 'Daddy'.

She would stare too long at babies in the street and glare at mothers who shouted at their children. She had once pulled out a tissue and wiped the nose of a little kid when his useless mother seemed oblivious to the long candles of snot the child was trying to reach with his tongue. Needless to say, her interference had not been appreciated. Once, on the beach, she'd come across a young boy sitting by the shoreline all alone, taking in the deep, juddering sobs that all children did when they had been crying too much. It turned out he'd dropped his ice cream on the sand after only one lick and his mother was refusing to buy him another. Mary had led him by the hand to the ice cream van and bought him a 99, his beaming face all the thanks she needed.

Her mothering instincts were never far from the

surface, and she was becoming more and more desperate to nurture a child of her own – hers and Thomas's. As she listened to her husband moving round the kitchen downstairs, getting ready for his shift, she prayed that today just might be the day when her dream would start to become a reality.

It was shortly after lunchtime when the train pulled into the station, its screeching brakes causing Mary to cover her ears. Thomas picked up his duffel bag and heaved it on to his back. He hated saying goodbye just as much as she did, but he always tried to remain upbeat. He held her in a bone-crushing embrace and rested his chin on her shoulder. 'I'm sure it's going to be good news at the doctor's, Mary. I'll have my fingers crossed for you.' He tilted her chin and kissed her lightly on the lips. 'And I give you my word that I'll hand my notice in the minute that little one comes along.'

Mary clapped her hands together, her eyes widening in delight. 'Really? Do you promise?'

He made the sign of a cross on his chest. 'I promise, Mary.'

'Thank you.' She kissed him on his stubbled cheek. 'Oh Thomas,' she sighed. 'Parting is such sweet sorrow.'

'Eh?'

'*Romeo and Juliet*.'

He shook his head. 'Sorry, you've lost me.'

'Oh Thomas,' she laughed, thumping him playfully on

his shoulder. 'You're such a philistine. Juliet tells Romeo that their sorrowful parting is also sweet because it makes them think about the next time they'll see each other.'

'Oh, I see.' He frowned and wrinkled his nose. 'Makes sense, I suppose. He knew what he was talking about, our Bill.'

He stepped on to the train, closed the door and pulled the window down so he could lean out. He kissed his fingers and pressed them to her cheek. She held his hand in place, struggling to stop the tears she knew he hated so much. 'You take care now, Thomas Roberts, you hear me?'

She wagged her finger in his face and he responded with an emphatic salute. 'Yes, boss.'

The guard blew his whistle and the train eased its way along the platform. Mary ran alongside for a few paces, Thomas waving his white handkerchief and dabbing at his eyes. She knew he was teasing her and she couldn't help but smile. 'I'll see you in a couple of days,' she shouted, as the train gathered speed and retreated into the distance.

The doctor's waiting room was crowded and stiflingly hot. The woman sitting on her left held a sleeping baby, who, by the smell of things, had recently filled its nappy. The man on her right roared a sneeze into his handkerchief and followed it with a violent coughing fit. Mary turned away and flicked through a well-thumbed magazine. It was fifteen minutes past her appointment time and she had chewed her way through two fingernails. At last the receptionist bobbed her head round the door. 'Mary Roberts? The doctor's ready for you now.'

Mary looked up from her magazine. 'Thank you.' She rose slowly from her seat and knocked gingerly on the doctor's door. The minute she entered the room, however, all her apprehension dissipated. The doctor was sitting behind his large mahogany desk, but he had rocked back in his chair, his hands clasped together on his lap, a knowing smile on his lips.

She decided to take the scenic route back to the guest house. A bracing walk along the seafront would put colour in her cheeks, and a lungful of the salty sea air would clear her head. She found she didn't really walk, though; it was something between floating and skipping, and by the time she arrived home she was light-headed and breathless. She played the doctor's words over and over in her head. 'I'm pleased to tell you, Mrs Roberts, that you are indeed pregnant.' Finally, after three years of heartache, false alarms and crushing disappointment, they were going to be a family. She couldn't wait to tell Thomas.

2

It was the incessant ringing of the telephone in the hall downstairs that wrenched her from her deep, dreamless sleep. She was groggy and disorientated as she glanced across at Thomas's side of the bed; there was nothing there but an empty space. She ran her hand along the cold sheet, confirming that he had not been sleeping there, and as her mind began to clear, she remembered he was working the night shift. She glanced at her bedside clock as the numbers flipped over to read 3.37. The first lump of dread settled into her stomach; nobody called at this time for a chat. She scrambled out of bed and thundered down the stairs, not caring that she might wake her guests. She snatched up the clunky black receiver, her breath coming in short fitful bursts. 'Hello, Mary Roberts speaking.'

'Hello, Mrs Roberts. I'm sorry to wake you.' The disembodied voice sounded thick and rough, as though the speaker needed to clear his throat.

'Who is this?' All her saliva had evaporated and her tongue refused to cooperate. Black dots danced before her eyes in the gloom of the hallway, and she placed a steadying hand on the banister.

'I'm ringing from the colliery.' He paused, and Mary heard him struggling to take a deep breath. 'There's been an explosion, some miners are trapped and I'm really sorry to tell you that Thomas is one of them.'

Instinctively, one hand went to her stomach and she closed her eyes. 'I'm on my way.'

After pulling on the first thing to hand, Mary hurriedly scribbled a note for Ruth. The young girl had worked for her for a year now and was more than capable of serving breakfast to the guests. As least that was what Mary told herself, because she didn't have time to think about the amount of china the girl dropped or the number of times she left the bacon under the grill too long. A less patient employer would have sacked her long ago, but Ruth was the sole breadwinner in a family comprised of her asthmatic widowed father and her younger brother who could only walk with the aid of calipers. Mary had never had the heart to add to her problems.

The rain lashed the pavement as she pulled open the car door, silently praying for the engine to start. The stench of oil rose from the sodden carpet in the footwell. Their old Vauxhall Viva had never been the most reliable vehicle. It was more rust than pale blue, and the exhaust chugged out the sort of obnoxious cloud of black smoke more commonly seen belching out of a chimney. Mary managed to coax the engine into life on her fourth attempt, and made it to the colliery in just over an hour.

She could barely remember the journey, but knew she'd exceeded all the speed limits and dreaded to think whether she had bothered to stop for any red lights.

A small crowd had gathered on the pit banks, the men standing with heads bowed, silent in the rain, just watching and waiting. The sky had taken on an apricot hue as dawn broke over the horizon, the only sound coming from the winding shaft as it slowly pulled up its grisly cargo. A collective gasp emerged from the crowd as two bodies were retrieved from their tomb. Mary rushed forward, but then felt herself being pulled back.

'Let them do their job.' A sombre-looking man in a hard hat with a torch on the front gripped her shoulders. His eyeballs and teeth stood out from his coal-blackened face, and a trickle of blood ran from a deep cut just below his left eyebrow. He was evidently one of the lucky ones.

'What's taking so long?' implored Mary.

'There've been a number of explosions down there, love, but you can be sure everybody wants them miners brought up just as much as you do. We're all pulling together.' His deep cough sounded as though he was going to bring a lung up, and he snorted the resulting globule of black phlegm on to the ground beside Mary, who could not conceal her disgust. 'Sorry,' he apologised. 'You waiting for your husband?'

Mary nodded. 'Thomas Roberts. Do you know him?'

'Aye, I do. He's a good man, and a strong one at that. He's not afraid of hard work either. I wouldn't be surprised if a promotion's in the offing.' He placed a reassuring hand on her arm and nodded towards the bank. 'The chaplain's over there. If you believe in that sort of thing, it might help you to pray.'

A few members of the colliery band had arrived and began to play hymns, but the mournful tunes only added to the despairing gloom and Mary wandered off to a quiet corner to wait for news. She wasn't sure praying would do any good. Surely if there was a God, there wouldn't have been an explosion in the first place? Still, it couldn't hurt. She clasped her hands together and closed her eyes while she mouthed a silent prayer for the safe return of her husband, making all kinds of promises in return that she knew she would never keep. She tried not to think of Thomas trapped beneath her feet, deep in the bowels of the earth in a place that was surely as terrifying and inhospitable as hell itself.

The rain had eased off and the sky was beginning to clear, yet deep within her chest she felt it. A loud rumble of thunder exploded in her ears and she looked up at the sky. The crowd on the pit banks surged forward as one, but the firemen coordinating the rescue held their arms wide and prevented them from advancing.

'Please, can you all stay back. Come on now, everybody, please move back.' The fireman's tone was firm but kind.

Mary rushed over and joined the throng, suddenly wanting the comfort of others in the same position.

An old man in a shabby donkey jacket removed his

cap and clutched it to his chest. He turned to her and shook his head. 'Did you hear that?'

'The thunder, you mean?'

'That wasn't thunder, lass, it was another explosion.'

'Oh God, no.' She grabbed the stranger's arm. 'They will get them out, though, won't they?' Her voice dropped to a whisper. 'They have to.'

He attempted a smile. 'We can only hope and pray. Who are you waiting for, love?'

'My husband, Thomas.' She patted her stomach and added, 'We're expecting a baby.'

'Well that's right nice for you. My lad's down there, our Billy.' He motioned with his head. 'His mam's up on the bank, in a right state she is. We lost our Gary in a motor-cycle accident last year and she still hasn't got over that.' He paused and shook his head. 'This'll finish her off, this will.' He stole a glance towards Mary's stomach. 'When's your babby due, then?'

'Oh, I've only just found out that I'm pregnant. Thomas doesn't even know yet.' She felt her chin wobble and the words caught in her throat as she began to shiver. 'He's my life. I'm not sure I could bear it if anything's happened to him. I've loved him since I was five years old. I can't lose him now.'

The old man held out his gnarled hand. 'Name's Arnold. What d'yer say we get through this together, eh, lass?' He pulled out a hip flask and offered it to her. 'A nip of brandy will warm you up, erm . . . What's your name?'

She shook her head to the brandy. 'I'm Mary, Mary Roberts.'

Arnold took a swig from the flask, wincing as the brandy hit the back of his throat. 'I'll tell you something, Mary,' he said. 'Them miners down there deserve every penny of that pay rise; dirty, dangerous work it is.' His bitter tone exposed his simmering anger. 'But what can you do? Mining's in our family's blood. Our Billy was born with coal dust in his hair.'

Mary wrapped her arms around herself. 'I hate it too, but Thomas has promised to resign when the baby comes along. We run a guest house, you see, so I need him to be around.' She stared down at her freezing feet. In her hurry to get dressed and leave the house, she had slipped on a pair of sandals, and now the mud oozed up between her toes.

The winding shaft creaked into life once more and the crowd fell silent. The two firemen who brought the cage to the surface exchanged a look, and then one of them turned to his commander and shook his head.

'No!' Mary screamed. 'Is it my Thomas?'

She tried to run, but Arnold held her tight. 'Mary, love, come on now, you're best off not looking.'

It was mid-afternoon by the time a watery sun finally broke through the clouds, and still Mary shivered. Her back ached and her stomach grumbled, but the thought of food only made her want to retch.

The chief fireman, his face blackened and expression

grave, removed his helmet and ran his hand through his plastered-down hair. He put a loudhailer to his lips. 'Can you all gather round, please?'

The crowd fell silent and shuffled forward a few steps. Mary clung on to Arnold.

The fireman cleared his throat. 'As you all know, there have been a number of explosions in the main shaft, about two thousand feet down. It's estimated that there are still around eighty miners trapped behind a fire in the main section. We've made some progress, but it's clear that the fire has taken hold.' The crowd drew its breath as one, halting the fireman's delivery momentarily. He held up his hand for silence, before continuing in his solemn tone. 'The air in the shaft is carrying carbon monoxide in dangerous quantities.' He licked his lips and swallowed hard. 'It is believed highly unlikely that anybody could survive in such conditions.' The loudhailer gave a long, piercing whistle, and Mary covered her ears.

She suddenly came over all hot and was afraid she might faint. Her hands clutched her stomach as she turned to Arnold. 'What's he talking about?'

Arnold wiped his eyes, then stared unblinkingly into the distance. 'I think he's trying to tell us our boys are dead.'

Mary's knees buckled and she sank down on to the mud. 'No,' she wailed. 'Not Thomas, not my Thomas.'

It was another four hours before the search was officially called off. With fears for their safety, the rescuers were

14

withdrawn from the mine and the foreman advised the waiting families to go home for some rest. As the crowd began to dwindle, Mary sat down stubbornly on the muddy bank and wrapped her arms around her knees. There was no way she was leaving Thomas just when he needed her most. She felt Arnold gently squeeze her shoulder. 'Come on, lass, up you get. You'll be no good to anyone sat here, and you've got that babby to think of.'

It was late evening by the time she arrived home. Ruth, bless her, had done an admirable job with the breakfast, cleared away all the pots and made up the rooms. She was sitting at the kitchen table reading the paper when Mary walked in. 'Oh, Mrs Roberts. What can I say? I heard it on the radio. They said there were no survivors.' She stood up and reached her arms out to her employer.

Mary ignored the gesture; any sign of kindness was sure to tip her over the edge. 'I'm just going up to my room, Ruth. Thank you for all you've done today. I'll see you right.'

Alone in their bedroom, she opened the wardrobe and took out one of Thomas's shirts. She pressed it to her nose, forcing the scent of him into her nostrils. She wanted to drink him in, to be forever ingrained with his familiar smell. She stripped off her clothes and put the shirt on. It was far too big now, but it brought her a degree of comfort to know that in a few months it would fit her perfectly. She would nurture Thomas's baby and make sure he or she knew what a brave man he was, and how much he'd been looking forward to being their father.

As exhaustion took hold, Mary lay back on the pillow and closed her eyes, but it was only a few seconds before images of Thomas choking behind a wall of fire had her on her feet and running to the bathroom. She splashed cold water over her face and stared at her reflection in the mottled mirror above the sink. Her cheeks were streaked with lines of muddy tears and her eyes were bloodshot, little pillows of fat underneath. She began to fuss over her flattened hair, momentarily thinking that it would not do for Thomas to see her in this dishevelled state. She stopped and gripped the edge of the sink. She had no idea how she was going to carry on without him, how she was going to bring their baby up all by herself. It was all she had left of Thomas now, but it was the most precious thing. She wondered if it would be enough to see her through the dark times ahead.

She woke up a few hours later, sprawled on top of the bed, still clad in Thomas's shirt. Her mouth was dry, her head throbbed and the stench of smoke clung to her hair. Her left arm dangled over the edge of the bed and fizzed with pins and needles. It was several seconds before she remembered that her life was never going to be the same again.

She padded to the bathroom and stood with her back to the toilet as she hitched up the shirt. She pulled down her panties, stared at the red stain in the crotch and screamed.

3

March 2016

A bright shaft of sunlight penetrated the leafless trees and bounced off the gold name plaque on the cherrywood casket. Beth formed a peak with her hand to shield her eyes and blinked away the temporary blindness. She crunched the frost on the grass beneath her feet as she squinted at the other mourners, their heads bowed, many of them dabbing at their eyes. She pulled a tissue out of her sleeve and pressed it to her mouth, stifling the scream that threatend to shatter the sombre gathering. The vicar handed round a box of soil and Beth took a handful and tossed it gently on to the coffin. The sound of the earth thumping on the hard wood echoed the pounding in her head. She had loved her mother so much, but it should not have ended like this. There was still so much that had been left unsaid, and now it was too late.

The vicar's words sliced through the chill March wind, his white vestments billowing around him and his lacquered comb-over standing comically on end.

'For as much as it has pleased Almighty God to take

out of this world the soul of Mary Roberts, we therefore commit her body to the ground, earth to earth, ashes to ashes . . .'

Michael gripped her hand more tightly in a gesture of solidarity, and she welcomed his reassurance. Not for the first time, she wondered where she would be without her husband's unstinting support. They were both helpless now, though, and the one woman who could have come to their aid was buried as deep as the secret she took with her.

Jake was sitting up in his hospital bed, a jigsaw spread out on the tray before him, when Beth and Michael returned. They had not had time to change, their dark clothing contrasting conspicuously with the bright, sterile ambience of the ward.

Beth leaned over the bed and kissed her son on his forehead. 'We came back as quickly as we could.'

Michael engaged Jake in one of their complicated hand-shakes that had taken weeks to perfect and ended in them both clicking their fingers and bumping their fists together. 'How's my big fella?' He ruffled the boy's hair.

'Look, Daddy!' Jake patted the completed puzzle. 'I've finished it and the nurse said it's for seven-to-eight-year-olds and I'm only five.' His huge chocolate-coloured eyes sparkled with delight.

Michael turned the tray round to get a better look. 'You're such a clever boy, Jake. I'm so proud.'

'Was Nana's funeral good?'

Michael glanced over at his wife. 'Well, it was all right, I suppose. You wouldn't have liked it, though. Too long and boring for you, son.'

'I wanted to come. I loved Nana and I would have liked to go to the party after.'

Michael laughed. 'I wouldn't call it a party, Jake. There was no pass-the-parcel or jelly and ice cream.'

Beth squeezed on to the bed next to Jake. 'I know you loved Nana, and she loved you too, but it's important for you to get better. It's freezing out there and we don't want you to catch your . . .' She left the sentence unfinished and busied herself with clearing away the jigsaw before changing the subject. 'Anyway, your tea will be here any minute, Jake. Can you remember what you're having?'

Jake squeezed his eyes shut and thought for a moment. 'No, but I bet it's that lumpy mashed potato again.'

Michael laughed. 'You don't know how lucky you are, son. I didn't have a real spud until I was about seven years old. My mum used to think mashed potato came out of a packet, and that was when she bothered to cook at all.'

Beth and Jake exchanged a knowing glance before they both took up their imaginary violins.

Michael reached beneath the sheets and tickled Jake under his ribs. 'Yes, all right, you two, very funny.'

The laughter was brought to an abrupt halt by the sound of Dr Appleby clearing his throat. The consultant nephrologist stood at the end of the bed with a clipboard in his hand. 'Sorry to interrupt. How are you feeling today, Jake? You certainly look a lot better. Perhaps we need to think about getting you home soon.'

Jake scrambled to his knees and bounced on the bed. 'Yeah! I want to go home, can I, Mummy?'

Beth placed a calming hand on his shoulder. 'Careful, Jake, you've got to take it easy, remember?' She turned to Dr Appleby. 'Really, Doctor? You think he may be ready?'

'Jake's about to have his tea now. Why don't you come with me to my office and we can have a chat?'

The inside of Dr Appleby's office was as familiar to Beth and Michael as their own living room. Although he surrounded himself with apparent chaos, evidenced by the towering stacks of files and endless used coffee cups, they trusted him completely with the health of their only son.

'How did your mother's funeral go, Beth?'

Beth was touched by his thoughtfulness.

'As well as can be expected, I believe the phrase is.'

The doctor pulled down his reading glasses from the top of his head and ran his hands through his thick white hair. Beth noticed his neatly trimmed fingernails. She did not know his age but guessed he could not be far from retirement. She pushed the thought to the back of her mind.

'Mmm . . . quite. Well, as you know, Jake's procedure went very well yesterday and I'm happy that the catheter is firmly in place. He has a small cut just below and to the right of his belly button, which obviously has a dressing on at the moment.' He consulted his clipboard again. 'His blood test results were good; the creatinine level has reduced, although his blood pressure is a little on the high side, but that's to be expected in a boy with his condition.'

Michael leaned forward and put his elbow on the desk between them. 'When will dialysis begin then, Doctor?'

'We need to wait for scar tissue to build up around the catheter to keep it in place, and of course you two need to complete your dialysis training. He will have a few sessions in hospital beforehand and the dialysis nurse will go through everything with you in detail before Jake is discharged. The main thing to watch out for at this stage is peritonitis, an infection affecting the lining of the peritoneum. Again, the nurse will go through the signs with you and what to do if you have any concerns.' He put down his notes and steepled his hands together. 'I realise how difficult this is for you. Jake's a robust little boy, all things considered, but as I've said before, you need to prepare yourselves for the fact that he will now need a transplant. From the day he was born we all feared it might come to this at some stage, but I know that doesn't make it any easier for you.'

Beth shook her head. 'Whatever it takes, Dr Appleby.'

'Of course. Now, a kidney transplanted from a living donor works better than one from a cadaveric donor, and they last longer, but as you know, neither of you is a match, so we maybe need to think about casting the net a little wider.'

He spoke in such a low, measured tone that it was difficult for Beth to hear him clearly. Her eyeballs were dry and itchy behind her contact lenses and she longed to rub her balled fists into them to bring some relief. She knew it wasn't fair to ask her next question, but before she could stop herself she blurted it out. 'Can you move him up the waiting list?'

The doctor's response was firm, but gentle. 'The waiting list is not a queue, Beth. You don't wait your turn and then get the next available kidney.'

Beth felt her face redden. 'I'm sorry, Dr Appleby. I just feel so helpless.'

'I understand your frustration and I'll try to reassure you. Children and young adults are given priority to some degree, but it really is a case of finding the right patient for the right kidney. We owe that to both the donor and the recipient. As you can imagine, demand far outstrips supply, and we need to minimise the number of rejections. In the meantime, the peritoneal dialysis will do the job of the kidneys.'

Michael shook his head. 'Poor kid. And he'll need to have this every night?'

'I'm afraid so, Michael. However, you'll be surprised

by how quickly he adapts. I never cease to be both amazed and humbled at the way some children cope. This will be a way of life for him and for you now, and the support you show each other will go a long way to making this as painless as possible for Jake.'

Beth noticed Michael biting at the skin around his thumb. Worry was etched on to his face and she tried to remember the last time she had seen him laugh. Not the little chuckles they both shared with Jake to keep his spirits up, but a proper stress-relieving belly laugh. The kind of spontaneous expression of unadulterated joy that most people took for granted. Even in the subdued lighting of Dr Appleby's office, Michael looked older than his forty-six years. His hair was still thick and mostly dark, but grey was beginning to creep in at the sides, and the lines around his eyes seemed more pronounced. 'Distinguished', her mother used to call him, but Beth knew this was just a fancy word for 'old'. She reached out and took his hand in hers.

He gave her a reassuring glance before continuing. 'We know Jake is getting the best care possible, Dr Appleby, and we are grateful.' He pursed his lips and added emphatically, 'Truly grateful.'

A beam of light illuminated the small office as a nurse stuck her head round the door. 'Dr Appleby, will you . . . Oh, I'm sorry, I didn't realise you were in a meeting.'

'It's all right; I think we're almost finished here.' He stood up and shook hands with both Beth and Michael.

'Please call any time, day or night, if you are worried about anything, anything at all. You're not on your own here; we'll get Jake through this together.'

Once outside in the corridor, Beth had the usual urge to return to her son. She could not remember the last time she had simply walked anywhere without a feeling of dread pulling her towards her destination. Michael called after her.

'I'll just get us a couple of coffees.'

She turned and waved her hand in agreement as her high heels clacked along the freshly mopped floor. She saw the hazard notice that had been put out warning people about the possibility of slipping but did not slow her pace. Her right foot shot out to the side in a way that would have been comical in other circumstances, but she managed to stay upright and continued her march forward, leaving a long black skid mark on the otherwise pristine floor. Somehow she had kept her balance, kept going. That was all she needed to do, she told herself; that was all she needed to do.

Jake was sitting up in bed, sipping his orange juice, a clean plate on the tray before him.

'You ate it all then? What did you have?'

'Fish and peas and that mashed potato but I squashed the lumps out with my fork, and then it was apple crumble with ice cream but the apples were too hot and I burned my tongue.'

Beth peered into her son's mouth. 'Oh dear, well I can see you've had ice cream. Strawberry, was it?' She took a tissue out of her sleeve. It was already a crumpled mess, but she dabbed it on her tongue and then wiped away his pink moustache.

Michael returned with the coffees. She took the cardboard offering, but as usual it was hot enough to melt iron, so she set it on the bedside cabinet out of harm's way.

'Do you want me to stay with Jake tonight, love? You look done in.'

She let her head loll back on Jake's pillow and closed her eyes. Michael had noticed her exhaustion now so there was no need to pretend any more. 'If I could just close my eyes for a few minutes I'll be all right.' She knew this was not true. Even if she slept solidly for the next twelve hours she would still feel drained when she woke up. Her reserves of physical and mental energy were severely depleted and she had no idea how she was ever going to fill them again. With a monumental effort she raised her head and spoke to Jake.

'Would you like Daddy to stay with you tonight?' It was a rhetorical question and she did not need to wait for an answer.

'Yeah, Daddy!' He clapped his little hands together as though he was welcoming Michael on to the stage. 'Daddy's the best.'

Beth heaved herself up off the bed and reached her arms out to her son. 'Come on then and give me a kiss.'

Jake pulled himself into a kneeling position and wrapped his toothpick arms around her neck. His small body felt warm but fragile and she was afraid to squeeze him too tightly. She slid her hand up inside his pyjama top instead and gently scratched his little back with her long fingernails. It was how she used to get him off to sleep as a toddler, and he still enjoyed the sensation now. She rocked him from side to side, remembering how simple, happy and uncomplicated their lives had been before Jake's devastating diagnosis.

Her thoughts turned again to her mother. She really had loved Jake too. He was her only grandchild, and to say she'd doted on him would be an understatement. She'd bored her friends rigid with stories about him, she'd kept a photo of him in her handbag that she shoved into people's faces at every opportunity and she'd bestowed on him the greatest gift of all – her time. As long as Jake was with her, the pots would go unwashed and the house-work could wait. So why Mary had withheld information that could potentially have saved Jake's life was something Beth would never be able to understand, a mystery her mother had taken to her grave.

4

The house was in complete darkness when Beth arrived home. She flicked on the hall light and squinted as her eyes became accustomed to the sudden brightness. In the kitchen, the fragrant scent from a bouquet of flowers delivered that morning filled the room and masked the antiseptic smell of the hospital that seemed to have taken up residence in her sinuses. She had stipulated family flowers only. She picked up the card and read the touching words again. *I'm so sorry for your loss, Beth. Your mother was a truly wonderful woman and I know how much you will all miss her.* It was typical of the sender to think of herself as family.

Her throat tightened again as she fingered the stem of a long white lily. Naturally, when a person died nobody had anything but praise for them, nothing but heartfelt platitudes, superlatives and compliments. She glanced over at the rows of cards adorning the mantelpiece and the windowsills. Cards that had arrived from all over the country, many from people Beth had forgotten about or did not even know at all.

The kitchen was eerily silent. Beth could not remember the last time she had been alone. She listened to the hum of the fridge freezer and the ticking of the old station clock over the fireplace, an anniversary gift from Michael. She had admired it in an antique shop in Harrogate on one of their weekends away and he had driven back there days later all the way from Manchester to buy it for her as a surprise. She poured herself a large glass of Sauvignon Blanc, slumped down on the sofa and kicked off her shoes. It only took a few sips before she became light-headed and remembered she had not eaten for several hours, not since the funeral in fact, and even then it had only been a couple of triangles of a curling ham sandwich and half a tomato. She heaved herself up, wincing as her unshod foot connected with something sharp embedded in the rug. It was a piece of Jake's Lego. He loved his Lego, and Michael would spend hours with him building castles and houses and cars; anything Jake wanted, Michael was able to conjure up, much to the delight and admiration of his son. Beth was convinced it was because Michael was an architect; it also didn't hurt that Lego had been his favourite toy as a child and his own father had taught him to build practically anything out of the little plastic bricks.

The doorbell sliced through the silence and she jumped, causing wine to slosh over the side of her glass and down the front of her blouse. Elaine was standing on the doorstep without a coat, a pair of furry slippers on her feet. She hugged her arms across her chest and bounced up and down in an apparent effort to keep warm.

'I saw the light on. How is everything?'

Beth opened the door and beckoned her in. 'Go through to the kitchen.'

'Thanks, I'm bloody freezing.'

'Michael's staying with Jake tonight. I was just about to go up for a bath.'

'You look knackered. I'd have a drink if I were you.'

'You'd have a drink whoever you were. Go on, there's a bottle open in the fridge.'

Elaine topped up Beth's glass and poured one for herself. 'I didn't see you leave the wake.'

'We just slipped out quietly. I wanted to get back to the hospital. It's good news, though: the doctor thinks Jake will be able to come home in a couple of days.'

Elaine took a gulp of her wine. 'That's grand. He's a fighter, that little lad of yours. I can't wait for him to start kicking his football over the fence into my garden.'

Beth smiled. 'Thanks for coming, Elaine. You don't know how good it is to just do something normal for once.'

'If there's anything I can do, you only have to ask.'

'He's going to need a transplant, you know.'

Elaine shuffled uncomfortably in her armchair. 'Well I'm not sure I'd be able to help with that. I mean—'

Beth snorted on her wine. 'I'm not asking you to donate a kidney, you fool. It's one thing asking a neighbour for a cup of sugar, but body parts? For goodness' sake, Elaine.'

'That's a relief. Oh, sorry, that sounds awful. What I meant was—'

'Elaine, please stop now. You're off the hook. He'll go on the waiting list, but the doctor says we need to start thinking about other family members who might be a match.' She took another sip of wine, her empty stomach grumbling in protest. 'But that's the problem, you see. Our family is so small. Neither Michael nor I have any siblings. Michael's father is dead, and he's more or less estranged from his mother, but in any case she's abused her body with drugs and alcohol her entire life. And my mother has just died and either couldn't or wouldn't tell me anything about my father, even though she knew her grandson's life depended on it.' Beth had only ever felt love and deep affection for her mother, but now she couldn't keep the anger out of her voice. She drained the rest of her wine in one gulp.

Elaine fell silent for a moment, circling her finger round the rim of her wine glass. She looked as though she was mulling over a particularly difficult conundrum. 'What do you know about him?'

'My father?' Beth shook her head. 'That's just it, absolutely nothing. It's never mattered until now. I can honestly say that growing up without a father has not affected me in a negative way at all. Not consciously, at least. I had a brilliant childhood and I loved my mother so much. Because it was just the two of us, we had a special bond. Oh, we've spoken about my father fleetingly over the

31

years, but all she would ever say was that it was a mistake and she didn't love him, but that didn't mean she didn't love me, and I believed her. It was only when we found out we weren't a match for Jake that I pressed her for more information. Just a name would have been a start. With the internet and everything these days, it's relatively easy to trace people.' She stood up and refilled their glasses. 'By then, though, it was too late. She'd had her stroke and couldn't talk any more. She died a few days later.'

Elaine wandered over to the mantelpiece. 'What about all these cards?'

'What about them?'

'Do you know who they're all from?'

'Some, but not all.'

Elaine raised her eyebrows theatrically. 'Seems to me like a good place to start.'

Beth felt her heart inflate with hope as she jumped up from the sofa. 'God, Elaine, you might be on to something here.'

She sifted through the cards one by one. There were seventy-two of them in total, and by the end she had two piles, one of which contained just two cards of interest. They sat cross-legged in front of the fire, Beth filled with a vigour she had not felt in a long time, her exhaustion temporarily forgotten.

She held up the first card. 'Okay, this one says: *I was*

very sorry to read of your mother's passing. I have many happy memories of the times we shared together and I know she will be missed by all who loved her. With kind regards, Graham Winterton.'

'Have you ever heard that name before?' Elaine enquired.

Beth wrinkled her nose and tried to think. 'It does sound vaguely familiar, yes. I'll have to ask Michael. Let's have a look at the other one.'

She picked up the remaining card. It was larger than most of the others, with a picture of lilies embossed on the front. 'Lilies were my mother's favourite flower. Do you think he knew that? Could this be a cryptic clue?'

'Don't get too carried away, Beth. Half of them have got lilies on. It's the flower of death, you know. What does it say inside?'

Beth opened the card and read the words aloud carefully. '*Words cannot express the sorrow I felt when I saw the notice in the paper to-day. Although I had not seen your mother in a very long while, we were close once and to learn of her passing has truly saddened me. I will always remember her with fond affection. With my sincere condolences, Albert Smith.*'

Elaine clasped her hands to her head. 'Aargh, no! Smith? Well, that narrows it down a bit.'

Beth turned the card over, looking for further clues. The envelope had already been carted off with the rest of the recycling, which was annoying, as a postmark would have been useful. She brought it up to her nose and inhaled the cardboard smell. She studied the writing. A fountain pen had been used, and the handwriting was small but neatly joined. He had also hyphenated the word 'today', a sure sign that he was of a similar age to her mother, who had been taught to do the same. 'Albert Smith,' she said aloud.

She shook her head. 'I've never heard of him before, so in a way that makes sense. It's going to be a name I've never heard, because we never spoke about him.'

'Smith,' Elaine said again. 'That's a shame, that is. He couldn't have been Albert Waverley-Pemberton, could he?'

'Who's he?'

'Well, no one, I just made it up. What I meant was it would have been better if he'd had an obscure name that would have made him easier to trace.'

Beth sighed and gathered up the cards. 'It's a long shot anyway, Elaine. And what would I say if I did find him? *Hi, I'm Beth, your long-lost daughter. My son needs a kidney, how are you fixed?*'

'Hmm, when you put it like that . . . He might be too old, anyway.'

'That's possible, I suppose, although you can be a living donor up to the age of eighty if you're in good health. My mother was seventy-two; he may be a little older or a little younger. Plus he might have gone on to have more children, in which case I'd have half-siblings who might have a compatible blood group and tissue type. It's all about creating a well of hope for Jake, rather than demanding people surrender their organs to a complete stranger.'

'Have you been through your mother's things yet? You know, documents, papers, that kind of paraphernalia? There might be something there.'

'I'll do it soon, but it's not a task I'm relishing, to be honest. She threw out a lot of stuff when she moved over to Manchester, but hopefully she kept hold of anything that was important.'

Beth picked up the empty wine bottle and carried it over to the recycling box. 'I'm going to go up for that bath now, Elaine, if you don't mind.'

Elaine clamped her arms around Beth's shoulders. 'You do that, poppet, and I'll be round again tomorrow with one of my casseroles.' She placed her cool hands on Beth's cheeks. 'You need building up, you do.'

As Beth finally submerged herself in the hot water, she closed her eyes and let the calming Jo Malone bubble bath work its magic. She had tipped in a huge indulgent dose, almost emptying the precious bottle, but she supposed she deserved it. She had buried her mother today. The two of them had barely gone a day without speaking to each other, and yet so much had been left unsaid. She thought about the cards she had received, the flowers, all the people at the funeral. They were right. Mary had been a good woman and a loving, protective mother. Beth could scarcely believe that she was never going to see her again. As the tears spilled over once more, she pinched her nose and slid beneath the surface of the water.

5

After a few days at home, Jake was already looking much better. The colour had returned to his cheeks and his energy levels had risen to the point where he wanted to go outside and kick a football at the fence.

'I think it's too cold for that, love. Why don't you stay inside and play?' reasoned Beth.

Jake sighed and slumped on to the sofa. 'But I'm bored in here all the time. I want to play outside. I need to practise so I'm as good as the other boys and I'll be picked first.' He folded his arms across his chest, a deep frown signalling his annoyance. 'I don't like it when I'm the last one to be picked.'

Michael intervened. 'It's a good sign, Beth. We can't wrap him in cotton wool for the rest of his life.' He knelt down so he was level with Jake's face. 'Come on then, little man. Just for a while.'

Beth resigned herself to the fact that she was beaten. 'Okay then, but not the hard ball; use the sponge one.'

Jake wrinkled his nose, then scrambled up from the sofa and ran to the hall to pull his trainers on, muttering something about the sponge ball being for babies.

Michael took Beth's hands in his. 'He deserves to lead as normal a life as possible, love.'

'I know that, but I can't help wanting to protect him. He's so vulnerable.'

'He's doing fine. As long as we look after the catheter site, make sure it's kept covered, and don't overdo things, I think he'll benefit from some fresh air.'

She knew Michael was right. He always was, and not in an annoying way either. 'All right,' she relented. 'But I'll just take his temperature again first.'

'Beth! You only took it ten minutes ago. It's fine.'

'You heard what Dr Appleby said. A raised temperature could be a sign of peritonitis. We need to be vigilant.'

Michael shook his head. 'Go on then, if it makes you feel better.'

She scuttled off to get the thermometer as Michael called after her, 'Never mind about my raised blood pressure, will you?'

Beth settled herself in front of the patio windows overlooking the garden. The daffodil bulbs she had planted in the tubs during the winter were now paying dividends. Jake was well wrapped up in his duffel coat, scarf, hat and mittens. Michael had protested that the poor lad could hardly move, but she was insistent, and as she watched them kick the ball to each other, she relaxed a little. She picked up her notes from the hospital and began to read them for the umpteenth time. She had not revised for her A levels as meticulously as she studied these instructions, but she was determined that by the time Jake began his dialysis at home, she and Michael would know exactly what they were doing. There was a lot to learn, but most of their training had taken place on the ward. Working as a freelance food stylist, Beth was able to pick and choose jobs to suit herself, which enabled her to devote plenty of time to her son. Michael had his practice to run, though, and however much they wished they could both be there for Jake twenty-four hours a day, the bills still had to be paid.

She was so engrossed in the notes that she didn't hear them come in again after fifteen minutes. She looked up to see Michael with Jake in his arms and was on her feet in a second. 'What happened? Is he all right?'

Michael laid his son down on the sofa and arranged a cushion under his head. 'He's fine. He just felt a bit light-headed, that's all.'

Beth felt his forehead. 'I knew you shouldn't have gone outside, but would you listen?' She turned to Michael hovering behind her. 'Ring the doctor, now.'

He placed a reassuring hand on her shoulder. 'Beth, I told you, he's fine. You've got to stop overreacting to every little symptom.'

Jake struggled with the toggles on his duffel coat. 'I'm hot, Mummy. Please can I take this off now?'

Beth fumbled with the fastenings. 'Michael, quick! Help me get this thing off. He's burning up.'

'I'm not surprised. Eskimo Nell goes out on to the frozen tundra with less clothing on.'

She ignored him and managed to relieve Jake of the bulky coat. 'Do you feel nauseous?'

Jake frowned. 'What does that mean?'

Beth could not hide her impatience. 'Sick. Do you feel sick?'

Jake shook his head. 'No, I feel fine now, Mummy.'

'Beth, will you leave the poor kid alone. You're smothering him.'

Jake raised his arms and hugged his mother tightly round the neck. 'I'm thirsty. Please could I have a drink of water?'

Beth jumped up immediately. 'He's thirsty, Michael. Do you think he's dehydrated?'

'For the love of God, Beth! No, I don't think he's dehydrated. I think he's thirsty, like he said. I'll fetch a glass of water.'

Beth knew her behaviour was driving her husband mad, and a less patient man might well have snapped. She could no longer remember a time when she did not feel anxious and sick to the stomach. She was so highly strung these days that she found it impossible not to overreact to every little setback. She had dropped a stone in weight in the last month alone, her hair was noticeably thinner and had lost its glossy sheen, and her green eyes were always ringed with dark circles.

Michael approached her from behind and massaged

her shoulders. He spoke gently. 'You need to try to relax, Beth. Look at the state of you. I don't think this constant worrying is doing Jake any good. You need to be more positive around him.'

She reached up and took hold of one of his hands. 'I know you're right, but I can't help it. I don't know what I would do if he . . .' She stopped abruptly as Michael squeezed her shoulder.

'I know it's difficult, love, but once he starts his dialysis at home, we can begin to move forward. The doctor said he'll be able to lead a relatively normal life once the machine starts doing the job of his kidneys.'

As Beth's thoughts turned once more to the possibility of a transplant, she remembered the cards she had received from Graham Winterton and Albert Smith. She retrieved them from the kitchen drawer and passed them over to Michael. 'I forgot to show you these. Do either of the names mean anything to you?'

Michael took the cards from her and studied each one. 'Graham Winterton? Yes, the name rings a bell. Wasn't he the chap who used to be her bridge partner, years ago?'

Beth took the card and read it again. Michael was right, and as her mother had only learned to play bridge in later life, that ruled out Graham Winterton. 'What about the other one, Albert Smith?'

Michael mulled it over. 'Albert Smith . . . Nope, can't say I've heard of him.'

Beth rubbed her hands slowly over her face and groaned. 'This is hopeless.' She slapped a hand down on the countertop. 'Right, that's it. I'm going over to Mum's tomorrow to sort through some of her things. I've put it off for long enough.'

An icy blast greeted Beth as she pushed open the front door of her mother's neat bungalow. The door resisted her efforts to open it because of the pile of post and free newspapers that had accumulated. The air inside was actually colder than that outside, and her nose immediately began to run. She dabbed it with a tissue, making a mental note to adjust the central heating to come on at least twice a day. She flicked the switch on the boiler and it roared into life.

Her mother had only lived here for a couple of years, but the place was ingrained with her very being. Her sheepskin slippers were arranged neatly side by side, and her lipstick was lying on the hall table. The last thing she used to do before leaving the house was to change her footwear and apply a smear of lippy in the hall mirror. Beth picked the case up and twisted it to reveal the pale pink colour her mother had preferred. It was worn nearly all the way down. Most people would have chucked it away ages ago, but Mary didn't believe in wastage. Even when she was down to the last sliver of soap, she would save it to stick on to the next bar. The washing-up liquid bottle always spent the final days of its life precariously upended on its lid in order to extract the very last drop.

Beth took her mother's favourite camel coat from the hook in the hall. She picked a couple of grey hairs off the collar and let them float to the floor. Then she closed her eyes, pressed the coat to her nose and inhaled the familiar White Linen scent. She put the coat back and headed into the kitchen, where she noticed an old biscuit tin on the worktop. She prised the lid off to reveal the last Victoria sponge cake her mother had ever baked, the once light and fluffy sponge now dry and covered with pale blue mould. She shuddered and replaced the lid. Clearing out the house would have to wait for another day, she decided. Right now all she was concerned with was finding any clues as to who her father might have been.

The bungalow was small, and Mary had had to be persuaded to throw out all sorts of junk when she moved to Manchester. 'You never know when it might come in useful' was her oft-repeated mantra, but when Beth had pointed out that she was only one boxful away from being the subject of a Channel 4 documentary, Mary had relented. Those potentially useful items had filled an entire skip. Now Beth stood with her hands on her hips and surveyed the lounge, crammed full with furniture that had looked elegant in the cavernous rooms of her old Victorian home but were out of place in the modern bungalow.

Her gaze fell on the old bureau; it was the obvious

place to start. She turned the ornate gold key and lowered the lid. Inside were four tiny drawers holding sewing items, paper clips, a couple of old Parker pens, a Swiss army knife and an assortment of foreign coins. Beth picked these up and jangled them in her palm. Although it was true that Mary's milkman was of Greek descent, she didn't think he would ever want paying in drachmas. She smiled and dropped the coins back into the little drawer, then closed the lid and turned her attention to the bigger drawers underneath. The top one was full of files and manila envelopes containing various insurance documents, a copy of Mary's will, and papers relating to the sale of her previous home. The drawer below housed her starched white tablecloth, napkins and a few unused candles. Rifling through her things like this felt incredibly intrusive, and Beth dreaded the day she would have to empty the rest of the house. As she rooted around at the back of the drawer, her hands alighted on a square tin that had evidently housed shortbread in a previous life. Her freezing fingers were stiff and uncooperative as she tried to prise the lid open, but it eventually gave way to reveal a jumble of photos.

She picked up the top one and studied the three figures standing on the steps of a bandstand. Her grandparents had both died before she was born, but she recognised them instantly as they stood behind her ten-year-old mother, all three of them beaming proudly. She turned the photo over; someone had written *Lytham 1954* on the back. There were a few photos of Mary with Thomas, her late husband, and lots of Beth herself playing on the beach. Some of the later ones were in colour, including Mary and Thomas's 1972 wedding photo. He was staring straight down the lens, but her mother was hanging on to his arm and looking up at him, laughing.

Beth smiled fondly as she rubbed her thumb over her mother's radiant face, frozen in time and with no hint of the heartache to come. She had often browsed through their wedding album when she was little, pretending that the handsome man with the cheeky smile and the chin-length wavy hair was in actual fact her father. Mary had told her so many wonderful stories about Thomas and what a caring husband he was. From the very first day they had met and he had offered to carry her books home from school, she had been smitten. Beth knew she had never really recovered from losing him at such a young age, so how she had ended up conceiving a baby just four months after he died really was a mystery. Any attempt to broach the subject, though, had been met with a dismissive wave of the hand.

Beth ploughed on through the photos, lingering over some, giving others just a cursory glance. By the time she reached the bottom of the tin, her legs had stiffened up and her back ached. Looking at all those memories had put her in a melancholy mood, and she was about to replace the lid when she noticed that the bottom of the tin had been lined with faded floral wallpaper, a pattern that she recognised from her childhood home. Half-heartedly she picked at the edge until the paper lifted up to reveal a handwritten envelope addressed to Mary stashed beneath. The top had been neatly slit open: she peered inside and took out an old newspaper cutting. The print was not as sharp as it might once have been, and the paper had a yellow hue to it, so she flattened it out carefully on top of the bureau. It was from the *Manchester Evening News* of Monday 26 July 1976, and the headline read: *Pub Outing Ends in Tragedy.*

Beth immediately felt her scalp prickle, and in spite of the chilly atmosphere, the heat rose steadily from her toes and broke out into a flush of anxiety across her chest. She could not imagine why her mother was hanging on to this newspaper article. She pulled out the accompanying letter and opened it gingerly. She recognised the hand-writing immediately, but the words did not make any sense at all.

By the time she had read it again, the juices had begun to flood her mouth and her head felt stuffed with cotton wool. She coaxed her shaking legs into a run and made a beeline for the back door. Her trembling fingers fumbled with the key, but she opened the door just in time before she vomited into the flower bed.

6

After gulping in deep, calming breaths of the chilly air outside, Beth returned to the kitchen and swilled her mouth out with water. She could still taste the bile at the back of her throat and tried unsuccessfully to snort it away. The earth had tipped on its axis and everything was suddenly different. Just as scientists were looking for a way to knock an approaching asteroid off course, thus avoiding a catastrophic collision with planet earth, this letter had altered the trajectory of her life. She felt utterly drained, like one of her mother's house plants that had been starved of moisture and was visibly wilting.

She stuffed the letter and newspaper cutting back into the envelope and tucked it into her handbag. She had a desperate urge to go home to her family. In spite of everything that was going on with Jake, she knew who she was at home. She was Michael's wife and Jake's mother. That was her identity, and she needed to be back where she belonged, back where there were no secrets or half-truths to muddy the waters of her very existence.

She slammed her mother's front door so hard that the glass rattled and something crashed to the floor on the other side. She started the car and pressed her foot down on the accelerator, causing the engine to rev loudly in protest. On the journey home, she drove faster than she would normally have done, and certainly too fast for one who could only see through a bubble of unshed tears.

The tyres gave a satisfying crunch on the gravelled driveway as she brought the car to an abrupt halt outside the front door.

She found Michael in the kitchen, sitting on one of their big squashy sofas reading a Famous Five book to Jake. In spite of everything, she smiled to herself. He loved those stories, and Beth was eternally grateful to Enid that she had been prolific enough to write twenty-one of them.

Jake looked up when he saw her standing there. 'Daddy's reading me *Five Go to Smuggler's Top.*'

'Ah, that's my favourite.'

Jake giggled. 'You always say that, Mummy.'

It was true. They were all her favourites, and it pleased her immensely that Jake enjoyed them as much as she had done as a child. Unfortunately, though, no amount of ginger beer was going to solve this problem.

'Michael, can I talk to you for a second?'

He removed his arm from around his son. 'Sure, what's up?'

She beckoned with her head, indicating that he should join her over by the island in the kitchen.

'Don't lose our place, Jake. I want to see how Julian's going to get out of this particular scrape.'

Beth fished in her handbag and thrust the envelope into Michael's hands.

'What's this?'

'I found it at Mum's.' Her measured tones belied her inner turmoil. 'Read it.'

Michael pulled out the newspaper article first. As he read it, his breathing became deeper and a vein pulsed in his temple.

Pub Outing Ends in Tragedy

A horrific motorway crash ended in tragedy on Saturday for the regulars of the Taverners pub in Manchester. They were returning from a day out in Blackpool when the driver lost control of the Ford Transit minibus they were travelling in. The unnamed driver and two other passengers died at the scene, and several others were injured. It is feared that the death toll may rise. The cause of the crash is not yet known, but one theory is that the recent scorching temperatures had melted a section of tarmac, which may have caused the vehicle to skid. Police are appealing for witnesses to contact them on 061 761 2442.

Michael finished reading and looked at Beth, his expression full of incredulity. 'What was your mum doing with this?'

'I have no idea, Michael, but wait till you read the letter I found with it.'

7

Harry Jones spent his days wandering the streets of Manchester, weighed down with the plastic bags that carried all his worldly possessions. The heatwave had dragged on for weeks now, with some parts of the country even having their water rationed, and standpipes were a common fixture in some streets. Harry hadn't come across any, though, which he thought was a pity, as he would have been grateful for somewhere to wash his feet. Life had not exactly treated him well, but he soldiered on, without bitterness or rancour. Living on the street for the past six years might have diminished his body, but his spirit was unbroken, and even at seventy-eight years of age he still clung to the hope that things could only get better. He was a proud man who had served his country twice, once in the First World War, when he had signed up despite the fact that he was underage, and then again in the Second, when, too old to fight, he'd worked for the engineering company that made the Lancaster bombers. Qualifying as an electrical engineer had been one of his greatest achievements. Not bad for a lad who had been born prematurely on a remote farm in mid-Wales with a misshapen head and a proclamation from the doctor that he would never amount to anything.

He'd not had a bad afternoon considering. He'd managed to get a spot on the pavement outside Rumbelows and watched through the window as Björn Borg won the Wimbledon men's final. Now, as he shuffled along the street, bent almost double by the weight of his bags, he noticed an abandoned supermarket trolley and his spirits soared. Maybe his luck was changing. Harry would never have stolen a trolley from a supermarket, but this one was just lying there looking a right eyesore. He would be doing everybody a favour if he removed it. He wrestled it from the bushes, grimacing as a long bramble caught on his arm and produced a scratch from which tiny droplets of blood appeared. He piled his bags into the trolley and laid his thick overcoat over the top. Of course he didn't need the coat in this weather, but it was useful to lie down on during the night, and it had served him well during his years on the streets.

Darkness was drawing in as he made his way to his chosen sleeping spot, struggling to keep the trolley, which had an irritating tendency to drift to the left, out of the gutter. The porch of the Taverners was one of his favourite places, and Selwyn Pryce, the landlord and a fellow Welshman, was most accommodating. Harry was careful not to take advantage of Selwyn's good nature, though, and tried to offer something in return, even if it was only collecting litter and used cigarette butts from around the pub, or pulling up the weeds from the cracks in the pavement.

It promised to be another sticky night, which would make sleep difficult. As he rounded the corner and the Taverners came into view, he could see the rather striking figure of Trisha, Selwyn's young wife, grappling with a punter who was refusing to leave. Harry chuckled to himself. Trisha was much better at getting rid of the stray drunks than her husband was, and it was no surprise that Selwyn had delegated this task to her. When she noticed Harry approaching, she adopted her familiar confrontational stance, with her hands on her narrow hips, her beautifully arched eyebrows raised and her tongue pushed firmly into the side of her cheek.

'Evening, Trisha.' He nodded politely as he drew level.

'Bloody hell, Harry! It's the third time this week you've bedded down here. Can't you find somewhere else to go?'

'The Midland's all booked up.'

She ignored his facetious remark and instead escalated her tirade. 'You take advantage of Selwyn, you do. You know he's a soft touch but it's not good for business having a tramp on the doorstep.'

Harry removed his coat from the trolley, spread it over the tiled step and slumped down. 'You're closed now, Trisha, and I'll be gone by opening time tomorrow,' he reasoned. He hated having to plead his case with this young girl who had barged her way into Selwyn's life, wrecking the landlord's marriage to the delightful Babs, and who now threw her weight around as though it was her name above the door and not Selwyn's.

Selwyn appeared in the doorway, still polishing a glass. 'What's all the shouting about, Trisha? I can hear you in . . . Oh, evening, Harry.'

Trisha threw her arms in the air and stormed back inside the pub. 'I don't know why I bother. I'm trying to turn this dump into a classy pub and you insist on having a dishevelled, filthy vagrant cluttering up the porch.' She slammed the door with such force that the glasses suspended from the bar rattled as she delivered her parting shot: 'And he stinks, by the way.'

Harry buried his nose in his armpit and inhaled deeply. 'Do I? I'm so sorry. It's the heat, very hard to keep cool, you know.'

Selwyn sat down beside him. 'Don't apologise, Harry.' He nodded towards the door. 'You know how she is. Would you like a bath?'

Harry roared with laughter. 'That's a belter, that is. Trisha would love that.'

Selwyn struggled to his feet and helped Harry up by the elbow. 'You leave Trisha to me. I'm still the boss round 'ere, you know.' It was not said with much conviction.

Trisha was behind the bar emptying the slop trays when

Selwyn entered with Harry in his wake. 'I've said he can have a bath.'

She stopped what she was doing and stared at Selwyn as though he had grown another head. 'A bath? Here? Well, of course, no problem, come in. Give me a minute and I'll pop a nice fluffy towel on the radiator for you, and I might even have some bath salts going spare.' She shook her head and carried on wiping out the trays.

Harry had picked up on the sarcasm, but Selwyn ploughed on regardless. 'I'm just helping him out, Trisha. Can't you show some compassion?'

'There's a water shortage, remember, Selwyn. You've seen the notices: "Save Water, Bath With a Friend".'

Selwyn turned to Harry and winked. 'I think she's offering to share with you.'

Trisha picked up a wet cloth and threw it at her husband, catching him squarely in the face.

Trisha had lived with the label of 'marriage-wrecker' for two years now. It hadn't bothered her at the start and it certainly mattered little to her now. After all, if Selwyn had been happy with Barbara, he wouldn't have looked once, let alone twice, at Trisha. It was mildly annoying that people seemed to lay the blame entirely at her door, but that was how small-minded the punters in the Taverners were. They conveniently forgot that it was their jovial landlord who was actually the adulterer, not her.

She sat at her dressing table and admired the reflection

staring back. She was twenty-six years old, in her absolute prime, and Selwyn was besotted with her. As well he might be, considering he was a forty-five-year-old bloke with an ex-wife and a teenage daughter and, though undoubtedly still a good-looking man, his best years well behind him. He really should count himself lucky that he was blessed with a nubile young wife. He wasn't nearly as attractive as her ex-fiancé, Lenny, but he was banged up in Strangeways for armed robbery. She'd promised to wait for him, of course, but twenty years was a long time and a woman had needs, and she hadn't meant to fall in love with Selwyn and his pub. Trisha was young, lithe and full of energy and looked the part behind the bar, with her huge bosom always threatening to escape the confines of her skimpy clothing.

She peeled off her false eyelashes and ran her fingers through her peroxide-blond locks. She leaned in towards the mirror to get a closer look, stretching the skin around her eyes with her fingers in order to eradicate what she thought were the first tiny signs of wrinkles. She turned to the left and patted the underside of her chin with the back of her hand. She hadn't noticed Selwyn leaning in the doorway, a look of quiet amusement on his face.

As he approached, she caught his reflection in the mirror and swivelled round on her stool to face him, letting her satin dressing gown fall open to her waist. Selwyn knelt down and planted a light kiss on her flat stomach. She ran her hands through his short curly hair as if inspecting it for nits.

'We need to get all this grey dyed out, you know.'

He straightened up and regarded himself in the mirror. 'Give over, you cheeky mare, there's hardly any there.'

She carried on as though he hadn't spoken. 'It's just the temples really. I'll get summat from Boots on Monday.'

She stood up and the dressing gown fell to the floor, forming a satin puddle at her feet. She placed her hands on her hips as Selwyn's eyes devoured her nakedness. He pulled her closer and grabbed a fistful of her long hair as he kissed her on the mouth. She pushed him away gently. 'Hang about. Not so fast, mister.' She nodded towards the landing. 'Get that filthy tramp out of my bath, and when you've done that, get down on yer 'ands and knees and give it a bloody good scrub with the Vim.'

He kissed her lightly on the forehead. 'You're all heart, you are. I'll just make Harry a brew and then I've got to feed Nibbles. I forgot earlier. I don't suppose you fed him, did you?'

'What do you think?'

There was no way she was going near his ex-wife's bloody rabbit if she could help it. Unless it was to 'accidentally' leave the cage door open. As far as Trisha was concerned, the animal was just another excuse for Barbara to visit the pub. Just because Barbara had been forced to leave the Taverners when she and Selwyn divorced and now lived in a flat without a garden, she thought it was acceptable to leave the rabbit behind for Selwyn to look after. His little cage was in the beer garden at the back of the pub. Well, maybe 'beer garden' was stretching it a bit. It was actually just a small patch of grass with a white plastic table and a Watney's Red Barrel umbrella stuck in the middle of it.

It wasn't fair, Trisha mused as she took a brush to her hair and savagely tugged away at the lugs. Selwyn was her husband now and Barbara could lump it. She could just about put up with his daughter, Lorraine, coming to visit; she wasn't that unreasonable. But Barbara was always hanging around the bar, laughing and joking with the regulars. Trisha was sure Barbara still considered herself the landlady, and the punters all loved her for some reason Trisha had yet to fathom. She was breathing deeply now and fought to control the anger that always manifested itself when she thought about Selwyn's ex.

She was sitting on the bed when Selwyn came back into the bedroom, rubbing his hands together. 'All done.' He pulled her hair to one side and caressed her shoulders.

She brushed his hands away. 'I've been thinking.'

Selwyn groaned. 'Oh no. I hate it when you start a sentence with those words.'

She ignored his remark. 'I want you to bar your ex-wife.'

'On what grounds?'

'On the grounds that she annoys me.'

'Trisha, half of my customers annoy you. I wouldn't have a pub if I worked on that logic.'

She tried a different tack as she reached up and began to undo his belt. 'Please, Selwyn. You don't know how it is for me having her hanging around all the time. I feel as though I have to share you with her, and I want you all to myself.'

Without taking her gaze off his face, she moistened her lips, slowly lowered his zip and tugged at the waistband of his jeans. As the blood began to leave his brain and travel elsewhere, he bent down and mumbled into her neck, 'I'll have a word with her tomorrow.'

She grabbed his face and forced him to look into her eyes. 'Promise?'

'I promise,' he sighed. 'Now come 'ere, you little minx.'

She took his hand and stroked the back of it, her eyes falling on the tattoo across his knuckles. Why couldn't he have just had 'love' and 'hate' like everybody else? Why did he have to have 'Babs', emblazoned like some everlasting memorial to their love? It was another irritation she would have to sort out to ensure that Barbara was removed from Selwyn's life for good.

8

Babs woke early on Sunday. It was one of those mornings where it seemed to take her brain an eternity to recall what day of the week it was. She rubbed the sleep from her eyes as she pulled the curtains and stared out at the blue sky, something everybody took for granted these days. She was actually fed up with the searing temperatures now and longed for a cool shower of rain to dampen down the dust and nourish the parched lawns. Not that she had a lawn to worry about any more. She had spent many happy hours weeding the tiny garden at the pub, making up the hanging baskets and tubs of flowers, all of which had brought her immense joy and satisfaction. The punters often complimented her on the abundance of fragrant flowers she had coaxed her petunias to produce, and she had even grown a prize-winning marrow once; only second prize, but the blue rosette was still hanging above the optics in the bar. Now gardening was another avenue of pleasure that had been blocked off since she'd divorced Selwyn. If only she could hate him for what he'd done to her, life would be easier, but nothing was ever that simple.

Babs had been in love with Selwyn since she was thirteen years old and he'd walked into her parents' pub in Salford looking for work. She had watched from her vantage point on the stairs as he introduced himself to her father. He was the most exotic-looking boy she had ever seen, with his glossy dark curls and impish grin. She could hardly tear her gaze away from his high cheekbones and olive skin. All the boys at school had pasty, spotty complexions with a curious bluish tinge that made them look as though they had spent their entire lives in a cave. She was mesmerised by his mellifluous Welsh accent, and when he'd spotted her peering through the banisters, he'd nodded his head, given a small smile and winked at her. Had she not been sitting on the stairs, gripping the spindles, her legs might very well have given way and sent her crashing to the bottom.

It was no surprise that her father and especially her mother had been charmed by his affable manner, and he'd moved into the pub a week later. Infuriatingly, though, he'd treated Babs like a little sister. He was only three years her senior, but back then it had seemed like a bridgeless chasm.

When he returned after completing his two years' National Service, the boy she had fallen in love with had become a man. He had grown at least four inches, and his body had filled out with muscle honed by months of hard physical training. His lovely curly hair had been shorn off, leaving him with a fuzzy style that only served to accentuate his refined features. It was fortunate for Babs, then, that she too had blossomed into a confident young woman who had prepared well for his homecoming. A talented seamstress, she had embraced the post-war 'make do and mend' philosophy and made herself a pretty floral dress from her mother's old summer curtains. The wide skirt emphasised her tiny waist, and she'd accessorised it with a red sash tied into a huge bow. A daring smear of her mother's red lipstick completed the transformation, and the day Selwyn walked back into the pub, he actually introduced himself to her as though it was the first time they'd met. From that moment on, he never treated her like his little sister again.

On their first date, he'd taken her to Belle Vue Gardens and persuaded her to ride the Caterpillar. She'd gripped on to his arm as the car gradually increased its speed around the wave-like track. When the canopy had swung over, plunging the riders into darkness, Selwyn had made his move and kissed her on the mouth for the first time. His lips stayed sealed to hers for the duration of the ride, and by the time the canopy lifted again she was dizzy and light-headed, though whether this was because of the motion sickness or her desire for Selwyn, she could not say.

But that was all in the past and it did her no good at all to dwell on it. She turned away from the window and padded into the kitchen. Selwyn had not simply broken her heart; she thought she might have been able to recover from a mere broken heart, one that had a crack in it that in time could be papered over. No, her heart had been shattered, and she knew without a doubt that it would never be healed.

Of course, it was not Selwyn's fault that that pneumatic hussy Trisha had thrown herself at him, smothering him with compliments and enticing him into a situation any man would find hard to resist. Selwyn might have been flattered and incredibly weak-willed, but he wasn't to blame. Nevertheless, Babs had made the impulsive decision to divorce him about five seconds after she found them in the cellar together, Trisha propped up against the wall with her legs wrapped around Selwyn's bucking torso. He'd had his back to Babs as she had slowly descended the cellar steps, her moist palms leaving a sheen on the wooden handrail, and had been oblivious to her presence, but Trisha had seen her all right and had given a small but triumphant smile over Selwyn's shoulder.

It was not in Babs's nature to hate anyone, but the sheer bitterness she felt towards Trisha was overwhelming sometimes, and she cursed the younger woman for turning her into someone she wasn't. Their strong, happy family unit had been torn apart by Trisha's selfish pursuit of her husband. Why she had had to pick Selwyn was anybody's guess. Trisha was a brash, blonde, big-bosomed strumpet who was never short of male admirers all desperate to get their hands on her ample assets. The injustice of the situation made Babs want to scream. Selwyn and Trisha were now ensconced in the Taverners, living it up as landlord and landlady, whilst Babs and her daughter Lorraine were squashed into this tiny ground-floor flat with its wafer-thin walls and threadbare carpets, the smell of hops from the local brewery constantly wafting through the open windows.

To make ends meet, Babs had been forced to take a job at the pickle factory, mercifully not on the production line itself, but in the sweaty office at the back, where she prepared the wages and fended off the unwelcome advances of her lecherous boss, Mr Reynolds. Every morning began with the stinging smell of vinegar assaulting her nostrils and making her eyes water in protest. Mr Reynolds was always asking her to retrieve some file or other from the bottom drawer of the filing cabinet, or dropping his pen on the floor and requesting she pick it up. It took Babs a week to cotton on that it was all a deliberate ploy that enabled him to take a peek under her skirt. Just sharing an office with him was an ordeal, what with his rampant body odour and the huge sweat stains under his armpits. Babs would not have been surprised to find mushrooms growing there. His shirts stretched over his bulging belly, and the folds of his neck and chin spilled over his collar. He was completely bald, his head pale and shiny, and his full lips were always wet. Spending eight hours a day holed up in the tiny office with him was certainly a test of endurance, but at least it paid the bills. She had, she told herself wearily, to be thankful for that.

She made her way down the corridor of their tiny flat and knocked tentatively on her daughter's bedroom door. Lorraine stirred beneath the sheet and called out, 'I'm awake, come in.'

Babs placed a cup of tea on the bedside cabinet and sat on her daughter's bed. 'Morning. How was last night?'

'Yeah, it was okay. We just stayed in and listened to Petula's David Cassidy records and talked and that. Her dad left us some Cherry B, so we drank it outside in the back garden.'

'You didn't drink too much, did you?' Babs smoothed her hand over Lorraine's long Titian hair. 'Your lips are still stained purple.'

'I'm eighteen, Mum!' Lorraine slumped back down on the pillow and closed her eyes. 'Just two bottles,' she confessed. 'But they're only tiny.'

Babs straightened up. 'Shall we go over and see Dad later? Maybe take Nibbles to the park after.'

'Yeah, if you like.' Lorraine stretched her arms over her head and let out an exaggerated yawn. 'Switch the radio on, will you, Mum?'

Babs fiddled with the dial on the transistor radio Lorraine kept next to her bed. 'I'll go and make breakfast. Are you getting up, or do you want me to bring it to you?'

Lorraine smiled. 'Thanks, Mum. I'll have it in here. Can you mix me up some Rise'n Shine too?'

Babs had just put the bread under the grill and was

whisking the orange crystals into a glass of water when a terrified scream pierced the air. She sprinted to Lorraine's room, expecting to find her daughter pinned beneath an intruder, fighting for her life. As she burst through the door, Lorraine was on the edge of her bed, clutching the radio to her ear, her Bambi eyes wide with shock.

'Breakin' news on Piccadilly Radio,' she gasped. 'Fire engines have been called to a fire at a pub in Talbot Road.'

'What? Talbot Road? Are you sure?'

Lorraine was frantic. 'Yes, Mum, that's what he said.'

Babs collapsed on to the bed and pulled her daughter into her arms. 'Oh God, no. Not the Taverners.'

9

Harry lay on the hard floor in the porch of the Taverners, shifting his position in an effort to get comfortable. His cheek was pressed against the tiles and he welcomed the sensation the cold slabs provided. His beard was itchy and he was desperate to use the toilet. He pushed his discomfort from his mind, closed his eyes and imagined he was lying on the crisp cotton sheets of his former home. During their thirty-two years of marriage, Elsie had changed the bed linen every three days. Harry had insisted this was not necessary, especially as the sheets had to be washed by hand and then put through the mangle. She would not be deterred, though. It was a compulsion, a habit, and one that only intensified when Harry presented her with a twin-tub for their silver wedding anniversary. Sometimes if he concentrated really hard he could smell the washing powder she had used and was transported back to happier times. This morning though, as he allowed his mind to drift, he noticed another smell, unfamiliar and out of place. His eyes began to sting behind his closed lids, and when he opened them, he saw acrid grey smoke swirling from under the doorway. In an instant he was on his feet and banging on the door.

'Selwyn, Selwyn.' He looked around in panic, but the place was so deserted the only surprise was the lack of tumbleweed rolling down the street. He tried again. 'Selwyn, Trisha. You need to get out, the pub's on fire.'

He picked up a large stone from the gutter and hurled it at their bedroom window. Mercifully, the glass shattered immediately and a plume of smoke rushed out into the clear morning air.

Oh God, the fire had reached their bedroom.

'Help, help!' Harry lumbered down the street as fast as his old bones would allow. He heaved open the door of the telephone box and dialled 999. The operator's calm voice focused his mind as he pleaded for the fire brigade to come and save the only friend he had left.

It took only ten minutes for the fire engine to arrive, but in that time Harry had managed to bruise his shoulder in his repeated attempts to barge the door down. He knew he stood no chance. The last thing Selwyn did at night was to draw the heavy bolts, top and bottom. He had been broken into on numerous occasions and he did not take any chances these days. Fortunately his precautions were no match for the fire brigade's battering ram, and the door yielded as though made of balsa wood. Harry had been ordered over to the other side of the street, where a small crowd had now gathered. The milkman had abandoned his float, all deliveries suspended as he watched the drama unfold. The chief fireman came across.

'Was it you who raised the alarm, sir?'

Harry clutched his injured shoulder. 'Aye. I noticed the smoke billowing out from under the door.'

'How many people are inside?'

'Selwyn, the landlord, and his wife Trisha.'

The fire officer frowned. 'That's three people, then?'

Harry was becoming agitated. 'Two. It's two. Selwyn *is* the landlord.'

The police had arrived and were beginning to move the onlookers further back. Harry stood on tiptoes, trying to see above the heads of the ghouls who were viewing the incident as welcome excitement in their otherwise dull lives. A ladder had been positioned under the bedroom window and a fireman sprinted up as though he was climbing his own staircase. He heaved open the sash and was immediately engulfed by black smoke. Harry could hear approaching sirens and prayed the ambulance was on its way. The fireman re-emerged at the top of the ladder with Trisha slung over his shoulder like a lifeless rag doll. Her nightdress had ridden up, and even though Harry did not think she was the type to wear underwear in bed, he was glad for her sake that she did. The ambulance crew jumped out and immediately took over. A mask was put over Trisha's face, which Harry interpreted to mean she was actually breathing. Another fireman shot up the ladder with the same ease as his colleague and reappeared minutes later with the unconscious bulk of Selwyn's body, making the return journey somewhat more arduous. Harry barged his way through the onlookers and staggered towards the ambulance. Selwyn had been laid on the pavement, his eyes closed and his face blackened.

'Is he alive?' he rasped.

A policeman took his arm and guided him back. 'Give them room to do their job. He's in good hands now.'

'Is he alive?' Harry shouted again. He knew he sounded hysterical, but he didn't care. He turned as he heard someone call his name. Babs and Lorraine ran towards him, their faces stricken with fear.

'We came as soon as we heard,' Babs panted. 'Where's Selwyn, is he okay?'

'Dad!' Lorraine screamed.

'They've brought him out and are working on him over there. They won't tell me anything.'

Babs approached the policeman. 'That man you brought out, I need to see him, he's my husband.'

The young officer frowned and slowly shook his head. 'Erm, I don't think so. We've already got his wife over there.'

Babs glared at him. 'Okay, if you want to be pedantic, he's my ex-husband. Now out of my way.'

She didn't wait for permission, but ducked under the tape and dropped to her knees beside Selwyn's body. 'Please don't tell me he's dead.'

At the sound of her voice, Selwyn turned his head towards her. 'Babs? Is that you?'

'Oh, thank God.' She reached out and grabbed his hand.

He spluttered and tried to sit up. 'Where's Trisha?'

Babs had not given Trisha a second thought, and her feelings of relief and affection for Selwyn were immediately sabotaged by his concern for his wife. 'They brought her out. She's fine . . . I think.'

Selwyn's voice was scratchy and weak. 'Would you go and find out for me?' He paused and squeezed her hand. 'Sorry to ask.'

Babs stood up and motioned to Lorraine behind the cordon. She was chewing furiously on her thumbnail. 'Dad's okay. Come and wait with him, will you?'

Babs could see Trisha laid out on a stretcher as she was funnelled into the back of the ambulance. She sprinted over and gazed down at the woman who had wrecked her life. Trisha's blond hair was tousled and her big blue eyes peeped out from her sooty face. As she saw Babs approach, she removed the mask. 'They . . . they tell me Selwyn's all right.'

Babs nodded. 'He'll be fine. He's smoked forty fags a day for the last thirty years, so his lungs are well used to it.'

Trisha coughed but managed a small smile. 'Has anybody remembered to bring Nibbles out? I know he's in the garden, but even so there's a lot of smoke.'

Babs clamped her hand over her mouth. 'Oh my God, I'd forgotten all about him, the poor little mite.'

As Babs ran to the nearest fireman and explained the situation in panicked tones, Trisha shook her head and replaced the mask over her face. 'Bloody rabbit!'

10

'How's Selwyn, then?' Petula asked as she bounced Nibbles on her knee, his pink eyes bulging at the up-and-down motion. The rabbit had come out of the fire relatively unscathed; although his hutch had been engulfed by the thick smoke, the only lasting sign he had been there at all was the fact that his white fur still smelled of bonfires four days later. Petula set him down on the scorched grass and he hopped into the shade of the empty bird bath.

Lorraine reached down and caressed the rabbit's silky ears. 'He's much better, thanks.'

'Where're they staying?'

'Some B and B Trisha knows in town. Listen, thanks for taking Nibbles in. Yer know how it is round ours with no garden and that.'

'S'all right, he's no trouble.' Petula paused and stared at her friend. 'Why weren't you in work today, Lorraine?'

'What? Oh, I . . . er . . . had a headache. I couldn't have coped with the sound of all the typewriters clattering away, and it's so stuffy in there at the moment. I'm sure there's not enough air for us all to breathe.'

'Did you ring in?'

'Well I was going to, but I couldn't lift my head off the pillow, let alone find the strength to walk to the phone box.'

Petula looked doubtful. 'Hmm . . . Seems you found the strength to go shopping, though. That blue eyeshadow's new, and I've not seen that top before either.'

Lorraine sighed and dropped her shoulders. 'Bloody hell, Petula, you're wasted in that typing pool. You should work for MFI.'

Petula shook her head. 'I think you mean MI5.'

'Well that then. Anyway, promise you won't tell Mrs Simmons? She's already got a right cob on with me.'

'Of course I won't. What d'yer take me for? But you need to watch it. Why don't you do a shorthand course like I did?'

Lorraine wrinkled her nose. 'Nah, I don't fancy that, it looks dead hard.'

'It'll help get you out of the typing pool. That's my aim anyway.'

'It's all right for you, Petula, your dad works there. He can make sure you get promoted.'

Petula narrowed her eyes. 'It's not like that. Dad would never give me any special favours, and I wouldn't want him to either. I want to make him proud of me. Since Mum walked out, he's done everything for me, and I intend to repay him on merit and not through nepotism.'

'Through what?'

Petula waved her hand dismissively. 'Never mind.'

Lorraine was aware that Ralph Honeywell had made sacrifices. He'd never had much of a social life. Being left with the nine-year-old Petula had certainly curtailed any opportunities in the romance department. He'd had to learn to cook, clean and do the laundry as well as holding down a full-time job. His priority had always been his daughter, and he'd been determined that she would not have her childhood blighted by having to assume the role of housekeeper.

'How long d'yer think it'll be before the pub's open again?' ventured Petula, changing the subject.

Lorraine shrugged. 'Dunno. Few weeks, I suppose. It was smoke damage mainly, nothing structural, thanks to Harry.'

'Hmm . . . Who'd have thought having a tramp camped out on your doorstep would turn out to be a blessing?'

Lorraine laughed. 'Well thank the Lord he was there. I can't bear to imagine what would have happened if he hadn't raised the alarm. Anyway, Dad's thinking of arranging a day out to Blackpool for everybody; you know, while the pub's closed.'

'Blackpool, eh? Shall we go?'

'It depends who else is going. I probably won't bother if it's just the oldies.'

'Oh come on, Lorraine, it might be a laugh, and we wouldn't have to hang around with the others. We could go to the beach, go swimming, take a picnic.' It was a rare spark of enthusiasm from Petula.

As she mulled it over in her mind, Lorraine slowly warmed to the idea. She gazed off into the distance. 'I might get Dad to ask Karl along.'

'The one that looks like Marc Bolan? Bloody hell, he's far too old for you, and in any case, he fancies your mum, I reckon.'

'No he doesn't, and he's only thirty-six.' Lorraine's words were caked with indignation.

'Yeah, but he's got a kid, hasn't he?'

'What's that got to do with the price of fish? He's divorced.'

'True. And he is gorgeous,' Petula conceded. 'Who else shall we ask?'

'Mum'll want to come, if only to annoy Trisha, and we can't really leave Harry out after his heroics.'

Petula snorted. 'Christ, it'll be more like an outing from the Darby and Joan!'

Lorraine struggled out of her deckchair and began to pace the small patio. She hopped from one foot to the other. 'Crikey, these slabs are still hot. Pass us me flip-flops.' She tapped her chin with her forefinger and frowned.

Petula lay back with her face up to the early-evening sun and closed her eyes. 'Oh God, what are you thinking? I know that look.'

'This could be just the opportunity I've been waiting

for to get Karl to notice me. If he sees me in my bikini, then surely he'll stop treating me like a little kid.'

'Lorraine, he's twice your age, and besides, where am *I* in this little scenario? Sat around like piffy?' She didn't wait for an answer but grasped her stomach and rocked forward in her chair.

'What's up?'

'Nothing, just the time of the month.'

'We could ask someone along for you too. What about Jerry?'

Petula looked up, her face set into a pained grimace. 'Jerry Duggan?'

'How many other Jerrys do we know?'

'Very funny, Lorraine.'

'Oh give over, Jerry's not that bad. I know he's a bit . . . strange, but he's harmless enough.'

'A *bit* strange?' Petula scoffed. 'His hobbies are bell ringing and plane spotting, for God's sake.'

'Well I think he's sweet,' countered Lorraine. 'You could do a lot worse.'

Petula heaved her ample frame out of the deckchair, casting a shadow over her friend. She placed her hands just above her hips and squeezed as though trying to accentuate her non-existent waistline. 'You don't think I could get anybody good-looking, do you, Lorraine?' We can't all look like you, you know, with your long hair and that figure of yours. You're like a flippin' whippet. I can't help it if I'm not.'

'Don't be ridiculous, Petula. Why are you being like this all of a sudden? I was only teasing you about Jerry. I know he's not your type.'

Petula seemed to relent. 'Well all right then, as long as you don't get any ideas about fixing me up with him. Now do you want a drink?'

Petula returned to the patio clutching two Coke floats. The ice cream had bubbled up and spilled over the edge of the glass. She passed one over to Lorraine. 'Sorry, it's a bit sticky.'

Lorraine reached up and took the glass. 'Ta. Jerry's all right really, you know.'

Petula tutted. 'Oh, we're still talking about him, are we?'

'He doesn't have many friends, and he is a good customer of my dad's.'

'You must be joking! He only goes in once a week for half a mild, which he makes last all night.'

'All right, *regular* customer then. Plus he brings his mum, Daisy, and she has a port and lemon.'

Petula puffed out her cheeks. 'But he's just so straight, Lorraine.'

'So what? That doesn't mean he can't have a nice day out. Don't be mean, Petula. I think he's lonely. He did have a girlfriend once, you know, but she cleared off to Australia.'

Petula grunted. 'I don't blame her.'

'You're not being kind. He was only three when his

dad died. Imagine what that must have been like for him.' Lorraine was warming to her theme now. 'And he was bullied at school. I remember Daisy telling Mum about his first day at the grammar school, when he got his head flushed down the toilet.'

Petula snorted on her drink, the Coke shooting up her nose, causing her to cough violently. 'Oh God, that's so funny.'

Lorraine stared flatly at her friend. 'Well I don't think it's funny at all. It gets worse actually, because on the way home he got jumped on and a gang of lads snatched his new leather briefcase, emptied it into a puddle and then stamped all over it.'

Petula clamped her hand to her mouth to suppress the laughter, but she was unable to stop her shoulders shaking. 'Oh dear, that's awful,' she managed.

Lorraine ignored her, determined to finish her story. 'Daisy had wanted to give him something special as a reward for getting into the grammar school, so she bought the briefcase for him on the never-never, even though she doesn't agree with buying things you can't afford. She ended up paying for it for months when it had been ruined on his very first day.'

Petula wiped her eyes with her fingers. 'Mmm, that is quite sad actually,' she conceded. She paused. 'Well, all right then, if you insist, let's ask Jerry and Daisy along.'

Petula's father appeared at the patio doors. Lorraine was used to seeing him trotting along the corridors at work, smart and purposeful in his brown corduroy jacket, a sheaf of papers tucked under his arm. Seeing him now, he cut an altogether different figure. He seemed diminished somehow, as though he didn't need to put on an act at home. His complexion resembled day-old porridge and he had dark circles beneath his eyes.

'Hello, Lorraine, are you feeling better?'

'I'm sorry?'

'You weren't in work today. I assumed you were ill.'

'Oh, er . . . yeah, I was. I'm much better now, though, Mr Honeywell, thank you.'

He winked at her as he flicked open the *Radio Times*. 'I suppose you two will be commandeering the television this evening for that racket you call *Top of the Pops*?'

Before they could answer, he shuffled off again, muttering something about paying the television licence but never being allowed to watch the damn thing.

'Is your dad all right, Petula?'

Petula slurped through her straw as she reached the bottom of the glass. 'He's got his pills, they keep him going.' She returned to the subject of the outing. 'How many's that then?'

Lorraine put her glass down and began to count on her fingers. 'Let's see, there's me and you, Dad, Mum, Trisha, Harry, Karl, Jerry and Daisy.' She clapped her hands and squealed. 'That would be nine of us. Eh, I'm getting excited now.' She stood up and playfully pinched Petula's cheek. 'Let's make sure we have a beltin' day out, shall we?'

11

Daisy Duggan was on her hands and knees polishing her front doorstep when she was startled by the loud crack of a stone being hurled at her lounge window. The yobs who had thrown it had obviously not seen her, though Daisy doubted it would have made much difference if they had. She picked up her broom and brandished it at the four loutish skinheads who were now laughing raucously at their hilarious prank.

'Why can't you just leave us alone?' she implored. 'What have we ever done to you?'

The tallest one stood his ground, hands on hips. 'Ooh, keep your hair on, Widow Twanky. We're only havin' a laugh.'

'Well I don't reckon much to your sense of humour. You could've broken that glass. Now please just bugger off and leave us in peace.'

She held the broom like a staff, more to steady her quaking knees than anything else, but her defiant stance seemed to do the trick and the boys moved along, no doubt looking for some other hapless victim to terrorise.

Daisy and her son Jerry always had a chippy tea on a

Friday night, followed by a drink in the Taverners. Jerry would pick up the fish and chips on his way home from Williams & Glyn's, balancing the bag precariously on his handlebars as he rode home. As she waited for him to return, Daisy slid the plates into the oven to warm. There was only one thing worse than eating your chips off a cold plate, Daisy always thought, and that was eating them straight out of the newspaper, unless of course you were at the seaside. Then it was acceptable.

She was startled by the doorbell. Jerry must have forgotten his key again. 'Oh Jerry, lad, you'd forget your head if it wasn't screwed on,' she said out loud as she made her way through the hall. How on earth he managed to remember all those mathematical formulae and equations, not to mention the chemical symbols, was anybody's guess. He'd won both the maths and science prizes at school in his final year, and he would have made a wonderful head boy. Unfortunately, the headmaster thought he was too eccentric and Jerry had had to make do with prefect. Still, she couldn't have been more proud. At twenty-one years of age, he was now on a training scheme with the bank and there was no telling where that might lead. With a lot of hard work, a bit of luck and a fair wind behind him, he might very well make a bank manager one day, a possibility that caused Daisy to beam with pride every time she dared to dream about it.

It wasn't Jerry at the door, though, it was Selwyn's daughter, Lorraine, and her friend, the big girl with the short pudding–basin haircut, that made her look like a medieval pageboy. Daisy couldn't recall her name. 'Oh, hello, Lorraine and . . . er . . .'

'That's Petula,' Lorraine offered.

'Of course. I'm sorry to hear about your father's pub, Lorraine. What a shock that must have been, but at least everyone got out. We shall miss our little drink there this evening.'

'Thank you, Daisy. I'll say it was a shock, but Dad and Trisha are on the mend. Anyway, while the pub's closed, my dad was thinking about arranging a day out to Blackpool on the twenty-fourth, two weeks tomorrow, and we wondered if you and Jerry would like to come along.'

'Well, I must say that sounds grand. Jerry's still at work but he should be home any . . .'

The sound of a bicycle bell halted the discussion as Jerry turned into the driveway.

'What's all this?' He propped his bike up against the fence. 'Good evening, Lorraine, Petula.'

Petula merely grunted in response, but Lorraine was more polite. 'Hi, Jerry. I was just asking your mum if you and she would like to come on a trip to Blackpool with a few of us from the Taverners.'

He pushed his glasses up with his forefinger and frowned. 'Blackpool? What for?'

Lorraine shrugged. 'We just thought it would be a laugh, and with the weather being so nice an' all . . .'

Jerry addressed Petula, who was staring intently at her shoes. 'Are you going?'

She didn't look up. 'Yep, thought I might.'

He turned to Daisy. 'Do you want to, Mum?'

Daisy reached up and ruffled her son's hair as though he were a twelve-year-old. 'Why not?' She tugged at the hem of his woollen tank top. 'And who knows? We might be able to wrestle you out of this thing.'

As Jerry lay on his bed later, he thought he could well do without this trip to Blackpool, especially if Petula was going. She was rather moody and monosyllabic these days and he was sorry Lorraine had ever introduced him to her. He couldn't say they were exactly friends, but they had gravitated towards each other one evening in the Taverners, both finding themselves alone at the end of the night. Jerry had never been interested in any other girl since Lydia had left, and he wasn't remotely interested in Petula either. In fact the first time he set eyes on her, he thought she was a man until she turned round to face him, and even then he wasn't sure.

He clasped his hands around the back of his head and stared at the ceiling. Just over two years had passed since Lydia had left with her family on an assisted passage to Australia. Of course she hadn't wanted to go, but she was only sixteen and her parents had refused to leave her behind. He reached inside his bedside drawer and pulled out the familiar dog-eared photo taken in his back garden the day before she'd sailed out of his life. Her light brown hair was cut into a chin-length bob and she stood smiling at the camera with her head cocked coyly to one side and her hands linked in front of her midriff. She was such a sweet girl, and absolutely perfect for Jerry: his mother always said jokingly that they were not spoiling another pair. Jerry knew people thought he was a little strange – he'd put up with tormenting bullies all his life – but Lydia understood him. She didn't mind that he rang the bells at church, or that he tucked his trousers into his socks when he rode his bike. She thought it was sweet that he still wore jumpers knitted by his mother and refused to don the latest flared jeans, which would be forever getting caught in his chain. She liked his short-back-and-sides haircut, which he maintained despite the fact that his peers were growing theirs to absurd lengths.

Lydia had begged Jerry to go with her to Australia, but there was no way he could leave his mother alone. Lydia had understood. His loyalty and affection for Daisy was one of his most endearing qualities and made Lydia love him even more. On the day of her departure, Jerry had accompanied her to Southampton by train, and as they'd rattled inexorably towards their destination, their fingers entwined for the whole journey, he'd not been able to shake the feeling that he had made a terrible mistake and should have bought a one-way ticket after all.

Now, as he clutched her photo to his chest, he heard a tapping on his bedroom door.

'Come in, Mum.'

Daisy entered brandishing a mug of tea. 'I've brought you a brew, love.' She sat down on the end of the bed. 'What've you got there?'

He passed Lydia's photo over. Daisy had seen it a thousand times before. She smoothed her thumb over the black-and-white image.

'You still miss her, don't you, Jerry?'

'Every day, Mum.' He tried not to show it, especially to his mother, but sometimes he couldn't be bothered to pretend. It was too exhausting.

'Jerry, I'm going to say this one last time and then I'll not mention it ever again.' She stood up and tenderly swept his fringe to one side. 'Go to Australia. Go and be with the love of your life. You'll end up regretting it if you don't.'

'I can't, Mum, it wouldn't be fair on—'

'Shh, don't say it, Jerry. I don't want all that guilt laid at my door. You have my blessing, I want you to go.'

'But—'

'But nothing, Jerry. Lydia wants you, doesn't she?'

'Of course she does.'

'Well then, what's stopping you? On second thoughts, don't answer that.'

'I appreciate what you're trying to do, Mum, but you forget I've inherited your stubborn streak. You're stuck with me, I'm afraid.'

Daisy gazed around her son's bedroom and her eyes

rested on the posters that adorned the walls. Not of a favourite football team or Olivia Newton-John, as most boys had. No, her Jerry had one poster of the solar system and another of the periodic table. Was it really any wonder he didn't have anything in common with other boys of his age? He cocooned himself in this tiny room most nights, poring over Lydia's letters no doubt, writing back to her with God only knew what news. Apart from work, the pub on a Friday night and church on Sunday, he never did anything. He must have run out of bell-ringing stories long ago.

The tears threatened but she pasted a smile on her face that kept them at bay. 'True love only comes along once in a lifetime, Jerry. In fact some unfortunate people don't experience it all. You and Lydia are lucky. Please don't throw it all away because of some misplaced loyalty to me. I can't live with that burden.'

Jerry reached up and took her hand. 'You really think I should go, don't you?'

'You're like a bird that's had its wings clipped, Jerry. You're being stifled here and you deserve to soar. You need to think about yourself for once. I'll still have my life here. I've got Floyd, my two jobs, and the church, which incidentally I know you only go to because of me. You don't even believe in God, not with your science brain.'

He nodded and smiled. His mother was no fool. 'Maybe I don't believe in God, but I believe in the comfort your belief brings you, and that's good enough for me.'

'Think about it, Jerry . . . please.' She leaned down and kissed him on the cheek. 'That's the last I'll say on the matter. 'Now, I'm going downstairs to give Floyd his cuttlefish.'

There was no doubt Daisy was fond of her budgie, but Floyd was hardly a substitute for a son, Jerry reflected. Despite her best efforts, the daft bird had never uttered a single word. According to Lydia, budgies were as common as sparrows in Australia, and not confined to cages either. They were free to soar, not like poor old Floyd with just a mirror and a bell to entertain him.

Now Jerry had the chance to fulfil his potential, a chance to be with the girl he loved, all with his mother's blessing. He would go with Daisy on this trip to Blackpool and make sure she had a good time. It was the least she deserved.

It only took a few minutes for him to make his decision. He heaved himself up off the bed, sat down at his desk and pulled out his pad of thin blue airmail paper.

12

It was 7.30 in the morning when Babs and Lorraine arrived outside the Taverners. The redecorating of the pub was almost complete and Selwyn hoped to reopen on Monday – nearly three weeks after the fire. Babs looked resplendent in her short lime-green shirtwaister with the white butterfly collar, always a favourite of Selwyn's. She had made it herself on her trusty Singer sewing machine, a gift from Selwyn on her fortieth birthday, two years ago, just before Trisha had ruined everything. Her shoulder-length auburn hair was bouffant on top, flicked out at the ends and kept away from her face with a floral headband. She had been a little too liberal with the Aqua Manda, though, and Lorraine had flapped her hand in front of her face as she'd walked through a cloud of the orangey scent that morning. 'Flippin' 'eck, Mum, who are you trying to impress?'

Babs was a little too quick to defend herself. 'No one, don't be so daft.'

They each carried a huge striped beach bag bulging with towels, changing robes, bikinis, a picnic lunch and a couple of flasks. They set the bags down on the pavement as they waited for the others to arrive. The temperature was already climbing, and it promised to be another day of relentless heat.

Lorraine nudged her mother. 'Look out.'

Babs stared down the street at the two familiar figures approaching arm in arm. 'Bloody hell, what's she come as?'

Trisha tottered alongside Selwyn on platform heels, totally unsuitable for a day on the beach. She was wearing a microscopic pair of frayed white shorts and a checked cheesecloth blouse tied just above her tanned midriff, the see-through white fabric allowing everybody a glimpse of her bright pink bra. With her wide-brimmed floppy hat and oversized sunglasses, she looked like a film star being escorted by her minder.

As they drew level, Selwyn greeted Babs with a kiss on the cheek. 'Morning, love. Glad you could come.'

Babs flashed him a smile. 'Wouldn't have missed it for the world. Morning, Trisha.'

Trisha removed her sunglasses and nodded. 'Morning, Barbara . . . Lorraine.'

The awkward silence was broken by Harry rounding the corner with his shopping trolley. A wide grin cracked his face. 'Morning, all.' He was wearing a shabby grey suit, with a shirt and tie. If you ignored the yellow stain down the front of the shirt, the bobbles of lint on the jacket and the fact that he was wearing odd shoes, he had scrubbed up rather well.

'You look very smart, Harry,' ventured Babs, though she couldn't imagine why he would want to dress so formally for a day trip to the seaside.

He looked her up and down and gave a low apprecia- tive whistle, then doffed his cap in an exaggerated fashion. 'And I could say the same about you, Babs. That's a pretty dress, is that.'

'I'm glad you could come along, Harry,' said Selwyn. 'We'll never be able to thank you enough for raising the alarm and saving our lives.' He nudged his wife in the ribs. 'Will we, Trisha?'

'What? Oh, no, sure. Cheers, Harry.' Trisha blew a cloud of grey smoke over her shoulder.

'Where's Don with that flippin' minibus, Dad?' asked Lorraine.

Selwyn glanced down the road. 'He should be here any minute. Stop fretting, our Lorraine. Anyway, we're not all here yet. Who are we waiting for?'

'Petula, but I can see her coming now,' said Lorraine, as she spotted her friend lumbering down the road. 'And then Jerry and Daisy, and there's one more.' She rubbed her chin as though she had forgotten the remaining member of the party.

Babs smiled in quiet amusement at her daughter. 'Karl. We're still waiting for Karl.'

Lorraine turned to her mother. 'Oh yeah, that's right, Karl. I couldn't remember for a second there.'

Karl stirred, rolled over and reached out to bash the top of the alarm clock with his hand. The persistent ringing stopped and he groaned as he remembered what day it was. He couldn't think why he had agreed to go on this blessed trip to Blackpool. He knew Lorraine carried a torch for him and he would never want to hurt her feelings, but she was just a kid. Her mother, Babs, however, was undoubtedly a looker. She was possibly a little too old for him, and clearly still in love with Selwyn, but Karl never shied away from a challenge.

He inspected himself in the mirror, looking first right and then left at his profile. Working as a postman meant he often had afternoons off, and the result was a deep tan the colour of a coffee bean. There was no time to shave, but nevertheless he splashed some Hai Karate on his bristled cheeks and sprayed on some deodorant. The many hours he spent tinkering with his motorbike meant he was never really able to mask the smell of engine oil, nor get the grime out from under his fingernails. He looked at the clock and realised he was going to have to skip breakfast. He pulled on his denim flares and a clean tight white T-shirt that showed off his muscled torso, and fastened his shark's tooth pendant around his neck. He grabbed his keys, and as he opened the front door he was startled by his witless ex-wife, finger poised ready to ring the doorbell.

'Bloody hell, Andrea. What're you doing here at this time? You look awful.'

Their son came out of his hiding place in the ginnel. 'Boo!'

Andrea tucked a greasy strand of hair behind her ear and nodded towards the young lad. 'I need you to mind 'im. I've got summat on.'

Mikey surged forward and wrapped his arms around Karl's legs.

Karl glared at Andrea, his deep breaths failing to quell his anger. 'I can't, I'm goin' out for the day.'

The little boy craned his neck to look up into Karl's face. 'Aw, Dad, please. You said we could have a go at fixing the exhaust on the bike.'

Karl ruffled Mikey's sandy hair. It had clearly not seen a comb this morning. 'I'm sorry, kid, we'll have to do it tomorrow.' He felt a rush of affection for his son as he gazed into his innocent little face, but he was determined not to make this easy for Andrea.

Andrea turned to leave. 'Come on then, Mikey, you'll just have to stay on your own. I'll leave you some cereal.'

Karl grabbed her arm. 'Wait. You can't leave him on his own. He's only six years old, for God's sake.'

Andrea shrugged. 'You haven't left me any choice, have you?' She pulled her arm away. 'Come on, Mikey, your dad's too busy today.'

Karl was all too aware he was being manipulated and seethed quietly. He would never let Andrea leave Mikey on his own and she knew it. 'Okay, he can come with me,' he relented.

Mikey pulled away from his mother and ran back to Karl. 'Thanks, Dad.'

'Go inside for a second, kid. I need a word with your mother.'

With Mikey safely out of earshot, Karl unleashed his fury on Andrea. 'You can't keep doing this, you know. If you want me to have him full time, then fine, I'll go for custody, but you can't just drop him off when you feel like it at a moment's notice. I do have a life of my own. You know I love that kid, but he needs stability and routine, and if you can't provide it, then I will.'

Andrea faced him defiantly. 'You lost, Karl, face it. The judge didn't believe I was the feckless mother you made me out to be.'

'Andrea, you have no maternal instincts whatsoever. You're a terrible mother.' He threw his hands in the air. 'And don't think I don't know about all the fellas you have back either. Mikey talks about a different "uncle" every bloody week. This situation needs sorting out once and for all. I'm going to my solicitor on Monday.'

He slammed the door shut and stood in the hall, breathing hard. His son deserved better than that man-eating, weed-smoking waste of space, and he was determined he was going to get it.

Mikey was in the kitchen, helping himself to orange juice. 'Mikey?'

'What? Am I in trouble, Dad?'

Karl shook his head. 'No, kiddo, you're not in trouble. Come 'ere.' He held out his arms and Mikey pressed himself against the familiar contours of his father's body. 'How would you like to live with me permanently?'

Mikey pulled away and looked up at his father. 'Really, can I?'

'Well, it'll need sorting out with the court, but if that's what you want, kid, then I'm going to try and see that it happens.'

Mikey looked doubtful. 'But what about Mum? She'll be on her own and she's no good at looking after the house and stuff. She needs me.'

Karl sighed. 'You're a good 'un, Mikey, but it's not your job to look after her; she's supposed to look after you.' He glanced up at the kitchen clock. 'Anyway, never mind about all that now. How do you fancy a trip to the seaside?'

By the time they arrived at the Taverners, Karl was breathless, having had to run all the way with Mikey on his back because the little lad couldn't keep up. He let Mikey slide to the floor and then peeled his own soaking T-shirt away from his skin.

The minibus had just pulled up outside, and Don, the driver, climbed out clutching his stomach. Selwyn tapped his wristwatch. 'About time, Don, we'd almost given up on you.'

Don groaned. 'Sorry, Selwyn, I can't do it. One of you lot will have to drive, I've got the Earthas.'

Mikey looked up at his dad. 'What's wrong with that man? What're the Earthas?'

Trisha tutted. 'The Eartha Kitts . . . you know, the sh—'

'Er, thank you, Trisha,' Karl interrupted, placing his palms over his son's ears. He bent down to address Mikey. 'He's got a bad stomachache, that's all.'

Don bounced from one foot to the other. 'Seriously, I have to go. I'll leave the bus here and one of you can drive. I'll sort it with the insurance.' He threw the keys to Selwyn. 'Sorry, got to dash.'

Selwyn addressed the glum-looking group assembled on the pavement. He dangled the keys in front of them. 'Any volunteers?'

'Well, I've not driven for years and my eyesight's not what it used to be,' said Harry.

Daisy put her hand up as though addressing a teacher. 'I don't have a driving licence, Selwyn, sorry.'

Trisha lit another cigarette and stared at Babs. 'And I won't survive this little jolly unless I can drink, so that rules me out.'

'Trisha, we'd all like to have a drink. Stop being so selfish,' snapped Selwyn.

'Don't take that tone with me, Selwyn Pryce. This isn't my fault, you know.'

Selwyn shook his head. 'No, nothing ever is.'

Babs nudged her daughter and suppressed a giggle. 'Looks like this trip is going to be more fun than I first thought.'

Jerry stepped forward and held out his hand. 'It's all right, Selwyn, I'll drive,' he offered.

'You?' Selwyn could not hide his astonishment. 'I didn't know you could drive. I mean, you go everywhere on yer bike.'

Daisy vouched for her son. 'Actually, he's a very good driver, Selwyn. Passed his test first time, he did.' She smiled at Jerry and rubbed his back.

Petula whispered to Lorraine. 'Obviously not as green as he's cabbage-looking then.'

Selwyn offered a grateful smile. 'If you're sure, Jerry, that would be grand.'

Trisha crushed her cigarette out on the pavement. 'Well thank Christ for that. Now can we get a move on?'

Selwyn pressed the keys into Jerry's hand. 'Thank you, lad. That's got us out of a hole, and I'm sure we all appreciate it.' He glanced round at the group and raised his eyebrows. They all muttered their thanks and broke out into a muted round of applause.

Daisy puffed out her chest and beamed with pride. She removed Jerry's glasses, breathed on both lenses and gave them a good polish on the hem of her skirt. 'Don't worry, everybody. You'll be in safe hands.' She placed the glasses back on Jerry's face. 'Thanks, son, I'm proud of you. Now let's get this show on the road.'

13

Jerry climbed into the driver's seat and familiarised himself with the controls. Admittedly he had never driven a Transit van before, but apart from the two-foot-long gearstick it didn't feel that much different from a car. He ran his hands over the fake-wood panelling on the dashboard and adjusted the seat so that he could reach the pedals. He didn't particularly enjoy driving in the way that some young lads did. It was a means to an end, and as long as he could ride his bike to work, there didn't seem much point in shelling out for a car. With petrol at seventy-seven pence a gallon, he could think of better things to spend his money on.

He could hear the arguing going on in the back about who should sit where. There were two bench seats running along the length of the minibus, which faced each other and made for convivial conversation. At least in the driver's seat he was afforded the luxury of a seat belt. The black plastic seat was already hot and sticky.

He wound the window down to let some air in and heard Daisy laughing as she chatted to Harry on the pavement. He hadn't seen his mother looking so happy in a good while. Even in her mid-forties her hair was still jet black, and her latest perm had now grown out sufficiently so that it fell in soft curls about her face. She had pinned it back on one side with a fancy plastic clip, and judging by the wasps that now circled above her head, she had been liberal with the hairspray. It saddened him that she had never found another husband after his father had passed away. Eighteen years was a long time to be on your own. Not that there hadn't been admirers over the years; the bread man had been particularly attentive, often slipping in a couple of cream buns from time to time by way of endearment. Then there was the chap who came to collect their pools money, who had more hair growing in his ears than on the top of his head. He made his mother laugh, though, but although they had sometimes gone out for a drink together, it had never turned into anything more serious.

Jerry leaned out of the window. 'Mum, why don't you and Harry come and sit in the front with me?'

The last thing he needed was Lorraine and Petula climbing in beside him. That was one distraction he could well do without. He was only doing all this for his mother anyway. He could hear Petula groaning as she heaved herself up into the back. Lorraine gave her a shove from behind and she fell on to her knees as the others piled in behind her. Jerry turned round to address his passengers. 'All aboard?'

Trisha had ended up sandwiched between Selwyn and

little Mikey and she did not look at all happy about it. Karl was seated opposite his son and next to Lorraine, who had her right leg pressed up against his although there was really plenty of room.

Trisha indicated Mikey with her thumb. 'Karl, please tell me buggerlugs 'ere is not going to play with them things all the way to Blackpool. He's driving me nuts already and I swear I'll end up wrapping them round his neck.'

Karl reached over and took the Klackers off Mikey. 'Best leave them for now, eh?'

Mikey shrugged. 'Sorry, Dad.'

Karl stared at Trisha. 'Happy now?'

Jerry turned the key in the ignition and flicked the wipers to clear the ladybirds off the windscreen. They must be suited to the hot weather, because their numbers had taken on biblical proportions in recent weeks. It took him several attempts to start the engine, but eventually after much coughing and spluttering it came to life, resulting in a cheer from the passengers in the back.

Babs was seated opposite Selwyn, and as she crossed her bare legs their knees brushed for a second. He smiled at her and lowered his eyes. Trisha took out yet another cigarette and offered the packet around. Selwyn accepted one, and as Trisha held the lighter to the end of it, he tenderly cupped her hand in his. She stroked his cheek and laid her head on his shoulder. Babs shifted awkwardly in her seat and turned to Karl, who was seated further along the bench. 'Are you still playing in your band, Karl?'

Petula and Lorraine were seated between them, so he craned forward to answer. 'Yeah, sure. Could always do with a few more gigs, though.'

'Why don't you ask Selwyn if you can play in the pub one night?' she suggested.

Selwyn took a huge drag on his cigarette and shrugged. 'Don't see why not. What do you think, Trisha?'

Babs bristled. Why did he always have to defer to her? It wasn't her name above the door.

Trisha thought about it for a second. 'It might work, yeah. What are you called again?'

'Hundred Per Cent Proof.'

'How did you come up with that?' asked Lorraine, dying to be involved in the conversation. Disappointingly, Karl had barely acknowledged her presence so far.

'Well, me and the lads were sitting round one night thinking about names and that when Georgie said that the Bay City Rollers used to be called the Saxons. They wanted a new name so decided to throw a dart at a map of the USA, and wherever it landed that would be their new name. There's a place called Bay City in Michigan and that's where the dart landed. Georgie thought we should do the same, but we only had a map of Manchester, so we stuck that up and the dart landed in Burnage.' Karl shrugged. 'I mean, it's not exactly rock 'n' roll, is it?'

Lorraine burst out laughing and placed her hand on Karl's arm. 'That's so funny, but how did you end up with Hundred Per Cent Proof?'

Karl looked down at the hand now resting lightly on his forearm. 'I said it was a hundred per cent proof that Georgie was an idiot, and we all agreed he was, so the name stuck.'

'Dad, I'm hungry. Mum forgot to give me any breakfast,' Mikey piped up.

They all turned and stared at the sound of the plaintive little voice. Karl patted his pockets. 'I'm sorry, kid, I've not brought anything. I'll buy you some chips when we get to Blackpool.'

Babs reached under the seat and delved into her beach bag. 'He can't have chips for breakfast, Karl. Here, have one of our egg butties.' She passed the soggy offering over to Mikey, who opened up the little triangle and peered inside. The pungent aroma of boiled egg pervaded the air, competing with the cigarette smoke. He wrinkled his nose.

'Don't be so picky, Mikey,' admonished Karl. 'What do you say to Babs?'

Mikey took a huge bite and mumbled his thanks as crumbs spilled on to his lap. He peered at the bite mark he'd left in the sandwich and gingerly picked something out. 'This butty's got grass in it,' he exclaimed.

'That's not grass, it's cress,' Karl tutted. 'Just get it down yer.'

Trisha nudged Selwyn. 'Have you seen the speed Jerry's going? We've been trundling along in the inside lane for most of the journey. It'll be dark by the time we get there.'

'Leave him alone, Trisha. At least he offered,' said Babs.

Trisha ignored her. 'Tell him to get a move on, Selwyn,' she ordered.

Selwyn leaned over and tapped Jerry on the shoulder. 'Would you mind putting your foot down a bit, Jerry lad?'

Lorraine glanced over at Petula. 'You're quiet. What's up?'

'Me? Nothing. It's just these bench seats are so uncomfortable. My back's killing me.'

'Well, not long to go now. What d'ya wanna do first?'

Petula shrugged. 'Pleasure Beach?'

'Good idea. We don't want to be throwing up our lunch. Those egg butties smell bad enough before they've been eaten, never mind them coming back up again.'

'Lorraine!' scolded Babs. 'Don't be so disgusting.'

Lorraine ignored her mother and turned to Karl. 'Do you want to come with us?'

Karl hesitated. 'Well, it depends on what Mikey wants to do really.'

Mikey clenched his little fists and bounced them up and down on his knees. 'Yeah, can we, Dad, can we, please? That'd be dead good that. I love fairground rides. I want to go on the big dipper and the ghost train.'

Karl winced. 'Not my idea of fun, but I'll stand and watch if the girls take you on.'

A piercing shriek rang out from the front seat. 'Look out, Jerry!' screamed Daisy. As he slammed on the brakes, the passengers on the bench seats concertinaed up against each other and the bus veered crazily from side to side. Car horns blasted their impatience as the vehicle weaved from the middle lane to the outside lane and back again, with Jerry fighting to control it.

The whole episode had lasted mere seconds, but all of them were shaken up. Trisha was the first to speak. 'Jesus Christ, Jerry, what're you playing at? Are you sure you've got a driving licence?'

'It's all right, Jerry,' Babs placated. 'No harm done.'

Jerry wiped the sweat from his forehead with the back of his hand. 'Sorry about that, folks. That car just pulled right out in front of me. Is everybody all right back there?' He turned to have a look behind him.

'Keep your eyes on the road, Jerry,' implored Daisy.

Babs leaned forward to address Selwyn, keeping her voice to a whisper. 'You could have driven us, you know.'

'I was just thinking that myself, but better he gets to know the controls on the way there whilst it's still light. He'll be fine for the journey home.'

Trisha fished her compact out of her handbag, flipped open the mirror and blotted her nose. 'Hopefully we'll be too pissed to care on the way home anyway.'

Selwyn patted her knee. 'It was a close call but we got

away with it, so let's just enjoy the day, shall we?' He left his hand resting on Trisha's bare thigh, his thumb gently caressing the soft flesh. Babs longed to flick it away and tell him to stop being so insensitive. It gave her some satisfaction to see her own name still tattooed across his knuckles, but it wasn't enough. Trisha didn't know how lucky she was to have a husband like Selwyn, and sooner or later Selwyn would come to his senses. When he did, Babs would be waiting with open arms.

14

The Sands were already filling up by the time they eventually arrived in Blackpool. Lorraine felt confident that Karl was beginning to notice her. She'd seen him gazing at her long legs on the bus, and he didn't even move away when she 'accidentally' pressed her thigh against his.

They all assembled on the promenade and leaned over the railings. Rows of blue and white striped deckchairs stood along the seafront, and a couple of toddlers in flowery bathing suits and swimming caps dashed in and out of the waves, shrieking as the brown foamy scum swirled around their ankles.

Selwyn clapped his hands and addressed the group. 'Right then, let's 'ave a team photo. Jerry, you've brought a camera, I see.'

After a few moans of protest, Jerry had them all lined up against the railings, smiling dutifully for the camera. Trisha plumped her hair up and pouted down the lens. She turned her body in to Selwyn's and raised her knee so that her upper leg crossed his stomach. He in turn placed his hand under her thigh and pulled her close. When the shutter came down, he was gazing into her cleavage. Babs pointedly looked the other way. Little Mikey stood in front of Karl and giggled as his father squeezed his neck and made him squirm. Daisy linked her arm through Harry's, as Lorraine and Petula urged Jerry to get on with it.

'All done,' he announced, replacing the lens cap.

Trisha took hold of Selwyn's arm. 'Let's go and get a lager and lime. I'm gasping.'

Selwyn glanced at his watch. 'It's not even ten o'clock yet, Trisha.'

A look of genuine puzzlement creased her brow. 'What's that got to do with owt?'

'Me and Petula are going to the Pleasure Beach first, and Karl's coming with us, aren't you, Karl?' Lorraine grabbed hold of Mikey's hand. 'We're taking this young man on the rides.'

Karl held his palms aloft. 'Yep, sounds good to me. You'll come too, won't you, Babs?'

Lorraine tried to hide her disappointment. She loved her mother, of course, but she'd never envisioned having to compete with her for the attentions of a man. Why Karl was so obsessed with Babs, she couldn't comprehend.

Babs nodded and took hold of Mikey's other hand. 'I don't have any better ideas, so why not?'

'Okay, it looks like that's settled then,' announced Lorraine. 'Us five will go on the rides first and then we'll head down to the beach after that.'

'Daisy, Harry, Jerry, what do you want to do?' asked Selwyn.

Jerry pulled out a notebook from his back pocket and consulted it. 'I'd like to go to the Doctor Who exhibition.'

Trisha whooped with feigned joy. 'Oh yes, me too. Can I come with you, Jerry?'

He looked at her in surprise and took a tentative step forward. 'Of course, Trisha. It would be my pleasure. I'm quite knowledgeable about the programme, so it would be like having your own personal guide.'

Trisha stared at him open-mouthed and shook her head.

'She's just teasing you, Jerry,' Selwyn explained. 'She doesn't want to go to the exhibition really.'

Jerry slipped his notebook back into his pocket. 'Oh, I see, it was a . . . a joke, then?'

Harry clapped him on the back. 'I'd love to come with you, Jerry, and I'm sure your mum would like to as well.'

Daisy nodded her agreement.

Lorraine was impatient to get going. 'Can you lot stop dithering for a minute and let's decide what time we should all meet up later.'

'A fellow licensee of mine has a great pub further down the prom,' said Selwyn. 'He does a grand scampi in the basket, so I propose we meet there around six. It's called the Ferryman, you can't miss it.' He took hold of Trisha's hand. 'Is that okay with you, love?'

'Anywhere that serves alcohol is fine by me, Selwyn.' She looked pointedly at Babs as she kissed him on the cheek.

The Pleasure Beach was buzzing as they made their way through the entrance, the music so loud that all Lorraine could feel were the bass notes throbbing in her ribcage. The atmosphere was one of carefree excitement, although the whiff of hot dogs and onions, mixed with the sweet smell of candyfloss, was somewhat nauseating.

Lorraine and Petula walked ahead with Mikey in between them. They held his hands as they swung him in the air on the count of three. Lorraine glanced behind to check Karl was watching. She'd worked out that the best way to get to Karl was through his son. If Mikey liked her, then Karl was sure to take more notice. Frustratingly, though, Karl was deep in conversation with Babs, carrying her beach bag and hanging on her every word. Honestly, her mother could be so selfish at times. Babs was way too old for Karl, and besides, she was still in love with Lorraine's dad. Everybody could see that, except Selwyn, of course.

They came to the carousel, and although it looked tame to Lorraine, Mikey was excited and asked his dad to take him on.

'I can't, kid, I'm sorry,' said Karl. 'I'll be sick with all that round-and-round motion. I feel a bit queasy just looking at it.'

'I'm the same,' said Babs. 'I don't mind going up and down, but round and round, no way, I'd definitely throw up.' She laughed as she took Karl's arm and guided him to a bench over by the fish and chip kiosk.

Lorraine glared at her mother before addressing Karl. 'But look at his little face. You can't let him down.'

Mikey stared up at Lorraine. 'You said you'd take me on the rides.'

Lorraine gritted her teeth. 'Yes, I know, but you'd like your dad to come with us too, wouldn't you?' The little beggar wasn't helping.

Karl shrugged. 'Fair do's, Lorraine. You did promise to take him on.' He bent down so he was level with Mikey. 'I'll take you to the arcade and the rifle range later. How about that?'

Petula stood with her hands in the small of her back, rubbing her aching muscles. 'Are we going on, or are we going to stand around all day debating the issue?'

Lorraine sighed. 'All right then. Come on, Mikey, it looks like it's just us.'

'Thanks, Lorraine, you're a doll.' Karl winked as he briefly touched her forearm. She wondered how her knees didn't give way on the spot.

Babs and Karl sat down on the bench and watched as the other three toddled off, Mikey running slightly ahead.

Babs smiled. 'He's having a great time, isn't he?'

'He's a good kid. I think the world of him, and he idolises me for some reason.'

'Don't be too hard on yourself, Karl, you're a great dad.'

'No, I've let him down. I should have fought harder for him. Andrea's a shocking mother and he doesn't deserve her.'

Babs frowned. 'Oh, go on. What makes you say that?'

Karl shuffled round to face her, his arm stretched out along the bench. 'She's not cruel or anything – obviously I wouldn't stand for that – but she's neglectful, you know. She only went for custody to spite me.' He dropped his gaze and scuffed at the ground with his foot. 'When he comes over sometimes it's as though he hasn't been fed for a week, poor sod. She lets him stay up till all hours, which he thinks is great, of course, but he needs discipline and routine. She seems to have a different bloke in tow every week and she never takes him anywhere. Not to the park or the pictures or anything. He loves coming to mine and is happy just to be with me as I tinker with the bike or strum away on the guitar.'

Karl's eyes brightened and his voice was filled with pride. 'He's such a good kid, and very intelligent too. I mean, God only knows where he gets it from. With some guidance he could be anything he wanted to be, and I'm so proud of him.' He stared at the carousel in the distance. 'Anyway, all that's going to change. I'm going to see my solicitor on Monday. I'm going to fight for him like I should have done in the first place. I'm going to do right by him at last.'

He took a deep breath and puffed out his cheeks. 'Look at me getting all soppy.'

'Not at all, Karl. He's your son and you should be proud of him.'

He changed the subject. 'How are things with you, anyway?'

Babs twirled a strand of hair in her fingers. 'What can I say? Same old story, still love Selwyn, still hate Trisha. You can't be bitter, though, can you?'

'Selwyn's an idiot. Everybody knows that.'

'Doesn't change anything, though, does it?'

A long piece of hair had escaped her headband, and Karl tucked it back behind her ear as he held her gaze. 'Babs, you're so—'

She put a finger to his lips. 'Shh, don't say it. It's one complication I can do without. Besides, you know our Lorraine fancies the leather pants off you.'

Karl groaned. 'And don't I know it, but nothing's going to happen, Babs. You've nothing to worry about there.'

'I'm pleased to hear it, Karl. Let her down gently, though, won't you? She's got it bad.'

'Of course. I don't know what she sees in an old geezer like me anyway. She's gorgeous. She could have her pick of the boys.'

'Unfortunately, boys her age don't measure up to a

handsome, bike-riding, guitar-playing god-among-men like yourself.'

'Steady on there, Babs, you'll have me blushing.'

Babs stopped laughing as she saw Lorraine and Petula returning arm in arm. They were both giggling about something as they approached the bench.

Karl was on his feet immediately. 'Where's Mikey?'

The girls stopped and stared at each other. Lorraine tried to keep the panic out of her voice. 'He said he was coming back to you. We went on twice but he said he felt sick and didn't want to go on a second time.'

Karl pushed between the girls and strode off towards the carousel. 'Mikey, Mikey!' He grabbed a passing kid, causing him to drop his toffee apple. 'Have you seen my son, a little lad about your age? He's wearing a checked shirt and brown shorts.' The boy was too busy scraping up his toffee apple to answer as Karl elbowed past him, continuing to call out his son's name. People were oblivious to him and his suffering, selfishly enveloped in their own enjoyment. He approached the uninterested lout who seemed to be running the carousel and grabbed him, by his collar. 'Have you seen my little boy? He was on this ride a few minutes ago and now he's disappeared.'

'Sorry, mate,' the youth replied, pushing Karl away. 'You'll have to be more specific. I've seen lots of kids in the last ten minutes.'

Karl ignored him and continued shouting. 'Mikey, where are you?'

He turned as he heard Lorraine running up behind him. 'Any sign?' Her face was flushed, and although she tried to sound nonchalant, her voice was an octave higher than usual.

'No, there's no bloody sign. What were you thinking, Lorraine? You were supposed to be keeping an eye on him. I swear if anything's happened to him I'll—'

Babs stepped in between them and took charge. 'Stop it, Karl. That's not helping. We need to focus. Let's spread out, he can't have got far.'

It only took a further two minutes before Babs found him, sitting on a bench, his little shoulders heaving up and down and his eyes puffy and red-rimmed. He stood up when he saw her approaching and wrapped his arms around her waist. She crouched down and hugged him hard, planting a kiss on his forehead. His left nostril had inflated a bubble of snot, which burst on her shoulder as she embraced him. 'I couldn't find you,' he mumbled into her hair. 'Dad said that if ever I got lost I should find a policeman, but he didn't say what to do if I couldn't find a policeman. Am I in trouble?'

Babs held him by the shoulders and looked at his grubby little face, now shiny with tears. 'No, Mikey, you're not in any trouble.' She pulled him close again and rocked him from side to side. He pressed his whole body into hers, soaking up her affection. 'Come on, let's go and put your dad out of his misery.'

Babs gripped Mikey's hand as they weaved their way

through the rides looking for Karl. There seemed to be twice as many people now, and Babs had to shove hard to make a passage through the throng. Mikey was the first to spot him, interrogating the customers in the queue for the ghost train.

'Dad!' yelled Mikey. 'I'm here. Babs found me.'

At the sound of his son's voice, Karl whipped round and Babs saw the tension instantly drain from his body. She let go of Mikey's hand and allowed him to run to his father. Karl dropped to his knees and held his arms wide. Mikey ran into them, almost knocking Karl off balance, and wrapped his arms around his father's neck. Neither of them spoke for a while until Mikey said, 'Dad, I can't breathe.'

Karl released his grip and instead held Mikey's face in his hands. 'I thought I'd lost you, kid.'

'I'm sorry, Dad.'

'It wasn't your fault, Mikey, it was mine. I'm never going to take my eyes off you now.'

Karl stood up and held his hand out to Babs. She took it and he pulled her close so he could plant a soft kiss on her cheek. 'Thank you, Babs.'

15

Lorraine emerged from under the changing robe wearing a skimpy polka-dot bikini, her razor-blade hip bones stretching the material tight across her midriff. She lay down next to Petula on the picnic rug. 'Are you going to take this off or what?' She tugged at Petula's peasant blouse. 'You'll never get a tan shrouded in that thing.'

They had managed to carve out a space for themselves on the overcrowded beach and spread out the rug. After the egg sandwiches and a cup of flask-stewed tea, Lorraine was ready for an afternoon's sunbathing. She stretched herself out and closed her eyes. 'I can't believe the way Karl reacted, can you, Petula?'

Petula looked up from the latest edition of her *Jackie* magazine. 'Mmm?'

'Are you listening to me? That flippin' Karl! The way he turned on me when Mikey went missing. He's not my bloody kid. I'm not responsible for him. I don't know why he had to bring him along anyway.' She pulled the straps of her bikini down over her shoulders in an effort to avoid tan lines. 'Anyway, I've gone right off him. Mum's welcome to him.'

When Petula didn't respond, Lorraine propped herself up on her elbows. 'Petula, have you heard a word I've said? You've barely spoken all day. What's up with you?'

Petula put down her magazine. 'I don't feel great, that's all. I've had this backache for a few days now, and no matter how many paracetamol I take, it just won't go.'

'Have you tried rubbing in some Fiery Jack?'

'I have, but it's a bit difficult to rub it on your own back, and I can't really ask Dad, can I?'

'Well try not to let it spoil our day. We'll be back in work on Monday, sitting in a stifling office with a mound of boring letters to type up, drinking coffee from that awful machine and fending off that lad from the post room – you know, the one with the lazy eye and the wandering hands. You'll be wishing you were back 'ere then.'

Petula gazed at Lorraine's red chest. 'Have you got suncream on?'

'Suncream? It's Blackpool, not Benidorm.' She rummaged in her beach bag. 'I've got cooking oil, though.' She tipped a dose into her palm and began to massage it into her shoulders.

Petula wrinkled her nose. 'It'll be like lying next to a greasy chip, and I can see you having to lather up with the after sun later.'

They both jumped as a line of donkeys ambled past, the one in the lead emitting a loud, impatient bray. The toddler on its back burst into tears and demanded to get off.

'Let's have a go on the donkeys, Petula.'

'Are you serious?'

'Come on,' Lorraine urged. 'It'll be a right laugh.'

Petula heaved herself up from the rug. 'Go on then, anything to keep you quiet.'

A man with a knotted handkerchief on his bald head was dozing in a deckchair beside them. Lorraine pulled on a pair of shorts and tapped him on the shoulder. 'Excuse me, would you mind watching our stuff for a while? We won't be long.'

They picked their way through the crowds of holiday-makers and approached the toothless man who appeared to be in charge of the donkeys. He had a battered leather satchel slung over his shoulder and a cigarette with an inch of ash hanging off the end stuck to his lips. Lorraine held out some coins. 'Two, please.'

He looked beyond the two girls as though searching for a couple of kiddies. 'You two, you mean?'

Lorraine linked her arm through Petula's. 'That's right, us two.'

The donkey man removed his cigarette and spoke out of the side of his mouth to Lorraine. 'I'm not being funny or owt, but yer friend's built like a quayside bollard.'

'She's not as deaf as one, though,' Lorraine hissed.

Petula turned to leave. 'Come on, Lorraine, it doesn't matter.'

Lorraine was undeterred. 'What about that one over there?' She pointed to a large mule who had his muzzle stuck in a bucket of oats, or whatever it was donkeys ate. His furry ears flicked back and forth constantly as he tried to rid himself of flies.

Donkey man seemed to relent. 'All right, but only because it's not in my nature to turn paying customers away.' He shouted over to a young lad who was busy snogging his girlfriend. 'Oi, Casanova! Put her down, will ya, and saddle up Boris.'

It took donkey man and his amorous assistant three attempts to get Petula on board Boris. She hoisted her long skirt up around her podgy bone-white thighs and heaved herself across the animal's back, then cast a nervous glance towards her friend. 'I don't think this is one of your better ideas, Lorraine.'

Lorraine sat astride a demure grey donkey and gathered up the reins. 'Nonsense, it'll be great fun.' She turned to the donkey man. 'Can we go off on our own along the shoreline?'

He looked doubtful, but then appeared to spot a business opportunity. 'I can give you half an hour, but it'll cost you more, and no trotting.'

With the deal done, they steered their mounts down to the sea and walked along side by side in the surf, Petula clutching handfuls of Boris's mane. She looked down at Lorraine. 'I feel like I'm riding a giraffe.'

'When we get out of sight of Hitler back there, we'll give them a little trot, shall we?'

'Ooh, I don't know, Lorraine, he said not to.'

'Come on, what harm can it do?'

Boris shook his head violently from side to side, causing his bridle to jangle, and Petula gripped the front of the saddle. 'You see, even Boris is telling us not to.'

Whenever Lorraine thought about what happened next, it seemed to be played out in slow motion. One minute they were both strolling along in quiet contentment; the next moment a lanky teenager kicked his ball a little too hard and it hit Boris on his rump with a resounding thwack. Boris jerked his head up in surprise, the whites of his eyes showing in alarm and his nostrils flaring. He obviously took umbrage at this assault on his rear end, because he took off at such a pace that poor old Petula was left clinging on round his neck as though her life depended on it.

'Petula, what the hell are you playing at?' shouted Lorraine. 'Pull him up, for God's sake.'

Lorraine slackened off the reins and kicked her own donkey into action as she tried to catch up with the runaway mule and its terrified passenger. The crowds parted as they saw the out-of-control animal approaching. Mothers grabbed their little ones and pulled them to safety. Lorraine urged her donkey forward, but its stumpy little legs were no match for Boris's, and Petula was getting further away, her screams growing fainter with each passing yard.

Eventually Petula could hang on no longer, and she slid sideways off the saddle, landing with a painful thud on the shingle. Boris had the grace to stop then, and by the time Lorraine arrived, he was nuzzling his former passenger, who lay on the ground clutching her back and moaning theatrically.

'Petula, are you okay?' Lorraine dismounted and knelt beside her.

'You were right, Lorraine, that was a good laugh. Done my back the world of good,' groaned Petula.

'I'm sorry. Here, let me help you up.' She pulled Petula into a sitting position, and as they both looked at their bemused mounts staring down at them, Lorraine tried to stifle the laughter she could feel building inside her. She bit down on her lip and looked away but was unable to stop her shoulders jiggling up and down.

'It's all right, Lorraine, you can laugh now. Let it out.'

She released a huge guffaw and lay back on the sand. 'Oh God, Petula, you should have seen yourself, bouncing up and down, elbows flailing, and then when you slid off, I thought I was going to wet myself.'

'Well I'm glad you think it's funny, and actually, Lorraine, I think I have wet myself.' She dabbed the sweat from her top lip and peered under her skirt. 'Yep, I hope you're happy now.'

'Oh dear. Well all that bouncing up and down would test anyone's bladder strength. Come on, let's get these two beasts back to the ranch.'

It only took a couple of hours for Petula's underwear to dry out on the sand beside her. As she pulled her pants back on under her skirt, she winced at the feel of the gritty crotch against her skin.

Lorraine's cheeks were glowing like sun-ripened apples, and a smattering of freckles fanned out across her chest. She began to gather up their things. 'Come on, we'd better go and find that pub now and meet up with the others.'

'Good, I'm starving.' Petula stood up and stretched her arms above her head. 'God, I'm stiff, and my leg's killing me where I landed on the ground.' She hoisted her skirt and pointed to the large purple bruise now blossoming on the back of her thigh.

'A couple of drinks inside you and you won't feel a thing.'

Petula bent down and picked up the rug. 'I'll just give this a shake. Shield your eyes.'

Lorraine covered her face as Petula flapped the rug, and a mini sandstorm peppered the back of her hands. She still had her face covered when Petula let out a resounding scream that startled everybody within a two-mile radius.

'Whatever's the matter now, Petula?' Lorraine's patience was being severely tested.

Petula bent over and clutched her hands across her stomach. 'I'm not sure,' she gasped. 'I just felt a rush of something down there, and then . . .'

Lorraine stared down at the ground beneath Petula's feet. She was now standing in a little puddle of wet sand, and as Lorraine moved forward to have a closer look, another gush of water was expelled from beneath the voluptuous folds of Petula's skirt. Lorraine took a startled step backwards and stared at her friend's stricken face, a mixture of horror and confusion. 'Jesus Christ! What's happening, Petula?'

16

The Ferryman's beer garden thronged with early-doors drinkers, some of them sprawled on the yellow lawn as they soaked up the last of the evening sunshine before heading into town for a night of drunken debauchery and mayhem. Daisy and Harry were sitting at a wooden picnic table with attached bench seats as they waited for the others to arrive. Harry had loosened his tie and laid his jacket on the rough seat for Daisy to sit on.

'You're so kind, Harry, thank you.'

'It's my pleasure, Mrs Duggan. I've enjoyed your company today.'

Daisy shook her head in exasperation. 'For the last time, Harry, please call me Daisy.'

She looked over at a rowdy group who were guzzling their drinks straight from the can. 'God, it's a rough pub is this. I've never seen so many skinheads with tattoos.'

'Aye,' agreed Harry. 'And the men are even worse.'

She noticed her son returning across the lawn, three pints of lager shandy clustered in his hands. A wasp buzzed around the sweet foamy glasses, and without a spare hand, Jerry tried to blow it away. 'Shoo, shoo.'

Daisy smiled to herself. If he'd had his hands free, he would have been flapping his arms around like a windmill. She called over to him. 'It's fine, Jerry, it's not interested in you, just the lager, that's all.'

He arrived at the table and plonked the drinks down. 'I hate them. A bloody nuisance they are. Anyway, I've found a nice spot for the minibus in the car park in the shade of a tree, so it shouldn't be too hot for the journey home.'

Harry picked up a pint and took a long, grateful gulp. He wiped the foam off his beard with his grubby handkerchief. 'Ooh, I needed that. There's nothing quite so refreshing as a lager shandy on a scorching summer's day, is there?'

'Coo-eee!'

They turned in unison to see Trisha teetering across the lawn. She wore a 'Kiss Me Quick' hat now instead of her floppy sunhat, and carried a diaphanous ball of candyfloss on a stick. Selwyn was trailing in her wake.

'How are we all? Have you all had a good day?' She squeezed on to the bench next to Jerry. 'Room for a little one?' Jerry shuffled along closer to his mother. 'Bit further, Jerry, we need to get Selwyn on as well.'

'And Babs and Karl and little Mikey,' ventured Harry. 'There was only this one table free, so we'll all have to squash up, I'm afraid.'

'Speak of the devils,' mumbled Trisha as she spotted the three of them approaching. Mikey was carrying a huge stuffed monkey, almost as big as he was. He thrust it into Trisha's face. 'Look what me dad won for me.' He beamed a gap-toothed smile and puffed out his chest. 'I'm going to call him Galen.'

'What sort of a name's that?' asked Trisha.

'You know Galen.'

Trisha shook her head 'Never 'eard of him.'

'He's in *Planet of the Apes*.'

'Oh right, yeah, fancy me not knowing that.' Trisha batted the monkey away. 'Where on earth are you going to put that thing anyway?'

Mikey ignored her. 'And my tooth came out on the big wheel.' He fished around in his pocket and pulled out the bloody tissue in which he had wrapped the prized tooth. 'I'm going to put it under my pillow tonight and the fairies will leave me five pence.'

Babs looked around the garden. 'Any sign of the girls yet? It's twenty past already. I hope they haven't forgotten.'

'You worry too much, Babs, love,' said Selwyn. 'They're eighteen, they can look after themselves. Now, can I get anybody a drink?'

'I'm all right with this one, thanks, Selwyn,' said Jerry. 'I want to be sharp for the drive home.'

'Of course. Anybody else? Babs?'

Mikey turned to Karl. 'Dad, am I allowed to eat this?' He held up a pink and white boiled-sugar lollipop the size of his own head. 'Mrs Duggan gave it to me.'

Daisy smiled apologetically, and Karl shrugged. 'Sure, your teeth are falling out already, what harm can it do?'

Mikey furrowed his brow and stuck his tongue into the gap where his tooth had been.

Karl laughed. 'I'm only joking. Of course you can eat it.' He rose from his seat. 'I'll give you a hand with the drinks, Selwyn. Mikey, you stay here with Babs.'

Babs looked at her watch again and drummed her fingers on the table. 'Where have they got to?'

'Oh will you stop fretting, Barbara. They've probably met up with a couple of lads and are having a whale of a time.'

'That's supposed to make me stop fretting, is it, Trisha? It's all right for you, she's not your daughter.'

Trisha picked off a clump of candyfloss and stuffed it into her mouth. It dissolved into a chewy mess within seconds. 'Actually, Selwyn and I are trying for a baby. I'd like a little girl.'

A tight fist clenched around Babs's heart. This was the news she had been dreading since the day Selwyn had married Trisha. The piece of paper they'd signed at the registry office that September day ten months ago was bad enough, but a baby would bind them together for ever. She couldn't stand the thought of Selwyn having a child with this woman. And what if it was a boy? Trisha might want a girl, but Selwyn had always longed for a son, and it still pained Babs that she had been unable to give him one.

Harry picked up the menus. 'Come on, ladies, stop bickering now and choose something to eat.' He handed round the little plastic cards, and Trisha swiped one off him. She scraped at a splodge of congealed tomato sauce with her fingernail. 'Disgusting,' she muttered. 'And look at these photos. As if we don't know what chicken-in-a-basket looks like. Where the hell has Selwyn brought us?'

'I think it looks all right,' reasoned Harry.

Trisha glared at him. 'No offence, Harry but when you're used to rooting round in bins for your supper, anywhere would look like the Savoy.'

Daisy patted Harry on the arm. 'Ignore her, Harry. I think she's had too much to drink.'

Trisha shook her head. 'Oh, believe me, Daisy, I haven't had nearly enough.'

Babs broke the tension when she spotted Lorraine weaving her way through the crowded beer garden. She stood up and waved her arms in the air. 'Oh, thank God, there she is. Over here, love.'

Lorraine quickened her pace when she saw her mother. She clamped her hands down on the table and breathed deeply, as though trying to calm herself.

'Have you been running, Lorraine? Your face is all aglow. I hope you've not caught too much sun.' Babs glanced around. 'What have you done with Petula?'

'She . . . she's . . . in the toilet. She's not . . . er . . . she's not very well, Mum. Can you come and see her?'

'Honestly, Lorraine, what have you two been up to now? I can't leave you alone for five minutes.'

Babs was totally unprepared for the sight that greeted her when she pushed open the door to the Ladies. Petula was on her hands and knees, howling like a wolf at the moon. Her hair was plastered to her face, which was shiny with sweat or tears, probably both. Babs placed her hand on Petula's back. 'Whatever's the matter, love?'

Petula blew out through her mouth in short, sharp bursts as though she were inflating a balloon.

Lorraine answered on her friend's behalf, her voice quivering. 'We think she's having a baby, Mum.'

Babs looked from one girl to the other, her mouth hanging agape as she struggled to form the words. 'You *think* she's having a baby? But . . . how . . . I mean, I didn't know she was . . . Oh, good God in heaven, whatever have you done, Petula?'

'Mum, calm down, that's not helping. We were on the beach and all this liquid came rushing out and—'

Babs immediately sprang into action. 'Oh my God, in that case her waters have broken, she needs to get to a hospital. Lorraine, go into the bar and use the payphone.'

Petula thrust her head back and grabbed Babs by the wrist. The manic look in her eyes told Babs she was serious. 'No!' she commanded. 'No hospital, please, I beg you. This will kill my dad.' She gasped as another wave of pain enveloped her body. 'I'm not kidding, it could finish him off.'

Babs knelt down beside her and spoke more gently. 'But I can't deliver a baby, Petula. I don't know what to do. I'm sure once your dad gets used to the idea, he'll come round—'

Petula let out another piercing scream. 'You're not listening to me. He can't find out. Now please go and fetch Daisy.'

Babs was confused. 'Daisy? What do you want her for?'

'She works at the hospital, she must have picked something up.'

Babs frowned. 'I thought she worked on the cheese counter at Fine Fare.'

Lorraine interjected. 'She has two jobs, Mum.' She turned to Petula. 'She only mops floors at the hospital, she doesn't deliver babies. We need an ambulance.'

'Aargh, this thing is killing me,' Petula wailed.

'Lorraine, do as she says and go and fetch Daisy. I don't think there's time for an ambulance anyway, and there's definitely no time for an argument.' Lorraine backed out of the door as Babs shouted after her, 'And bring my beach bag back with you.'

If Lorraine had briefed Daisy on the way back from the beer garden, it was not apparent from her astonished expression as she entered the toilets. 'What in the name of sanity is going on here?'

'Thank God,' breathed Babs. She nodded towards Petula. 'This one's having a baby, can you believe?'

Daisy scuffed her foot against a piece of chewing gum that was cemented to the tiles. 'On this floor?'

'The state of the floor is the least of our worries. Lorraine, get the beach towels out and lay one under Petula.' Babs looked at Daisy. 'Any ideas?'

'What, you mean she really is having a baby?'

Babs nodded. 'It's looking that way.'

'Well I'll go to the foot of our stairs.'

Daisy bent down so she was level with Petula's head. 'Are you comfortable on all fours, lovey? It'll help with the delivery, I think.'

'I'm fine, Daisy, please just get this thing out of me.'

'Okay, Lorraine, go to the kitchen and ask to borrow a pair of scissors. Babs, remove Petula's underwear and skirt, and the laces from her pumps.'

Babs expelled a cautious sigh of relief. Daisy seemed to know what she was doing. 'Have you lots of experience of this then, Daisy?'

'I saw someone do it on *Emergency – Ward 10* once. Now, has anybody rung for an ambulance?'

'No!' Petula gasped. 'Tell her, Babs.'

Babs shook her head at Daisy. 'She doesn't want her dad to know.'

'Well he might notice something when she returns from a day trip to Blackpool with a baby in tow.'

'I'm not taking it home, you daft bat. You'll have to

take it to a hospital or something.' She began to pant and dropped her head to the floor. 'I think it's coming. It feels like I need to go to the loo.'

Lorraine returned with the scissors and leaned against the inside of the door to prevent anyone entering. She stared wide-eyed at her friend's sweat-soaked body. 'How could you not know you were pregnant, Petula?'

Babs glared at her daughter and put a finger to her own lips. 'Not now, Lorraine, please.'

Daisy manoeuvred herself into position behind Petula's crouched frame. 'I think I can see the head. It won't be too long now. Babs, pass me the other beach towel to wrap the baby in. The main thing is to keep it warm.' She looked up at Babs and Lorraine. 'Let's hope it's a straightforward delivery.'

Babs was nervously chewing her thumbnail when a thought occurred to her. 'Petula, is this a full-term baby?'

Petula straightened up and rested on her knees, one hand in the small of her back. On her other hand she counted off the months on her fingers. 'Yes, it is. It must be. I need to lie down on my back, my knees are really sore.'

Somebody attempted to push open the door to the Ladies, and Lorraine leaned hard against it from the inside. She turned round and spoke into the wood. 'You can't come in, somebody's ill in here. Please go and use the Gents.'

She heard a fainting muttering of expletives as the

unwelcome visitor retreated down the corridor.

Lorraine was becoming more agitated. 'God, hurry up, I'm not sure how much longer I can keep people away. That one may have gone to fetch the management, for all we know.'

'You can't hurry babies along, Lorraine. We'll just have to be patient,' replied Daisy.

'I need to push again,' gasped Petula. She reached out and grabbed Babs's hand. 'Don't leave me.'

Babs smoothed her other hand over Petula's glistening brow and spoke in soothing tones. 'I'm not going anywhere. You're doing fine, love. It'll all be over before you know it, and then you'll have a lovely baby and all this pain will be forgotten.'

'Aargh!' roared Petula. 'Why will no one listen to me? I'm not keeping this bloody baby.'

Daisy placed a hand on the top of Petula's knee. 'Just pant for me, will you. When you feel the next contraction, I need you to push really hard for as long as you can.'

Petula allowed her head to fall back, wincing as it connected with the tiled floor. Her voice was now an exhausted whisper. 'Please, you don't understand. I can't keep this baby. My dad . . . Oooh, no, here comes another one.'

'Right, one last almighty push, Petula,' encouraged Daisy.

Lorraine recoiled and looked away in disgust as the baby's head emerged, its dark hair matted and covered in blood and white stuff. The rest of its body slithered out into Daisy's waiting arms. 'It's a baby girl, Petula. She's beautiful,' she gasped.

Babs craned to have a look, fighting back sudden unexpected tears. The room became eerily silent, as though Petula's screams had deafened them all, and Babs could not shake the sense of foreboding as she gazed at the baby's mottled-blue complexion. 'Why isn't she crying, Daisy?'

17

'What in heaven's name is keeping them?' Trisha was already on to her second pint of cider in the Ferryman and in addition to everything else she had drunk that day was in danger of collapsing into an alcohol-induced coma. 'I'll go and see what's up.' She stood too quickly and grabbed the bench for support. 'Oops.' She swayed on her feet. 'I think I need to get some food inside me, disgusting though it looks.'

'I'll go,' Jerry offered. 'Selwyn, would you mind ordering the chicken for me and Mum?'

He followed the signs for the Ladies through the crowded pub. The air was thick with smoke and the garishly patterned carpet was sticky beneath his feet. He was beginning to think Trisha had a point. He passed the jukebox and rubbed his temples as the music thundered through his eardrums like an express train. He found the toilets and knocked on the door. 'Mum, are you still in there? What's going on?' There was no reply. He tried again, a little louder. 'Mum, it's Jerry, open the door.'

He leaned against it and it gave way enough for him to poke his head round. He opened his mouth to speak again but a rough hand grabbed his collar from behind and pulled him backwards. 'Oi, pervert! What do you think you're playing at hanging round the ladies' loos?'

Jerry held his hands up in submission. 'I was just looking for my mother.'

'Then you're more of a pervert than I first thought. Go on, sling yer hook.'

Jerry stared at the man's shiny bald head and the folds of flesh around his meaty neck and decided it was best not to argue.

The door to the toilets opened and Daisy called after him, 'It's all right, Jerry. Petula's just been sick, that's all, we'll be out shortly.'

Daisy had the baby firmly swaddled in a beach towel. She had managed to coax her first breath out of her by rubbing vigorously on her little back. The cough and splutter, followed by a lusty cry, was a relief to them all, with the possible exception of Petula, who was refusing to even look at her newly delivered daughter. Daisy had tied the umbilical cord with Petula's laces and used the kitchen scissors to sever it. It had been surprisingly tough, a bit like cutting the gristle off a piece of meat. Babs and Lorraine were busy cleaning the place up. They had wrapped the afterbirth in a newspaper that Lorraine had plundered from a table in the bar, and Babs had found a cleaning cupboard housing a grim-looking mop that had seen better days.

Daisy rocked the baby from side to side. The little girl's eyes were squeezed tightly shut and she bore the angry expression unique to babies who had just been wrenched from the sanctuary of warmth and nourishment where they had spent the previous nine blissful months.

'It must be a shock being born,' mused Daisy as she gazed down at the infant's cross little face.

Lorraine looked pointedly at Petula. 'I'll say it was a shock all right.'

'Okay,' announced Babs as she finished mopping up. 'We need to decide what to do next.'

Petula attempted to stand on shaking legs. 'I need to go back to the bus and lie down.'

'And what about the baby?' asked Babs. 'I don't think you realise how serious this is, Petula. If you don't take her now, you'll regret it for the rest of your life.'

'Then I'll just have to take that chance, Babs. Please just leave her somewhere safe, where she will be found. She'll have a much better life without me.' She pulled on her skirt and blouse and looked around for her underwear. 'Where are my pants?'

Lorraine pointed to the newspaper parcel. 'In there, with the . . . you know . . . that huge piece of liver stuff. They were soaked anyway, you couldn't have put them back on.'

'She'll need something, though,' Daisy piped up. 'And a sanitary towel too.'

Babs rummaged in her beach bag and pulled out her

bikini bottoms. 'Here, these will have to do. They may be a bit tight but they should do the trick.' She turned to the machine on the wall and shoved in some coins. It spat out two sanitary pads, which she handed to Petula. 'Put these on.'

Lorraine stared at the blood-soaked beach towel now in a heap next to the newspaper. It had been carnage in here not fifteen minutes since, but at least the floor now looked cleaner than when they had entered. 'I'll just go and ask the kitchen staff for a bag or something to put this lot in.'

'And find out where the nearest hospital is whilst you're at it,' called Babs.

The baby began to murmur, and Daisy offered her the knuckle of her little finger to suck. 'The poor mite needs feeding. Petula, you're not being reasonable.'

'I've told you, Daisy, you can't make me keep her. Now please get out of my way.' She brushed past Daisy and made for the door, just as Lorraine returned.

'The nearest one is Blackpool Victoria, about three miles away,' she declared. 'Somewhere near the zoo.'

By the time Babs arrived back in the beer garden, she'd been gone for over an hour. The others had devoured their meals and a stack of empty baskets was balanced unsteadily on the edge of the table. Selwyn stood up and offered her his seat. 'What's going on, Babs love? Where are the girls?'

She slumped down on the bench and put her head in

her hands. 'God, I need a drink.' She squeezed Selwyn's arm. 'Could you get me a gin and orange, please, Selwyn?'

'He's not your slave, Barbara,' scoffed Trisha. 'Can't you get your own?'

'Can't you just shut up for once, Trisha,' snapped Babs. 'I've just about had enough of you and your snide comments and endless carping.' She turned to Selwyn. 'And make it a large one.'

'Where's Mum?' asked Jerry. 'Her chicken's gone cold here.'

'Oh, she's . . . helping Petula, who's been sick and feels faint. Daisy thinks it's sunstroke, so she and Lorraine have taken her back to the bus. She'll be fine after a lie-down, I expect. Don't worry, it's nothing serious.' Babs hoped her light, breezy tone sounded convincing enough.

Petula shuffled into position on one of the bench seats that ran along the side of the Transit and Lorraine arranged the picnic rug under her head. 'We'll never get away with this, you do know that, Petula, don't you?' Petula's lips were dry and cracked, her eyes were bloodshot and she gave off the odour of someone who had just run a marathon. She covered her face with her forearm, but Lorraine could still see her dimpled chin quivering, a sure sign that she was about to cry. She crouched down beside her and took hold of her clammy hand. 'How could you not have known?'

Petula shrugged, still refusing to look at her. 'I swear

I didn't know. I've had periods, and I've never been regular anyway. And I didn't look pregnant, did I?'

'I suppose that's true,' Lorraine conceded. 'But I only ever see you with your baggy clothes on. Surely you must have noticed something yourself?'

'I just thought I was a bit podgier round the middle. You know me, Lorraine, I'm not that fussed about my looks.'

The unspoken question hung in the air like a bad smell. Lorraine hardly dared to ask but she needed to know the answer. 'Petula,' she said gently. 'Who's the father?'

Petula groaned. 'Oh, I was wondering how long it was going to take you to ask me that. I can't tell you.'

'You mean you don't know? Jesus, Petula, how many lads have you slept with?'

Petula propped herself up on her elbow and looked Lorraine directly in the face. 'Of course I know! I'm not that much of a slapper, in spite of what you may think. I know we tell each other everything, but not this.' She slumped back down on the bench. 'What does it matter anyway, the baby's gone now?'

'But what if the father wants to keep it? You have to tell him.'

Petula gave a snort. 'Ha, that's hilarious. No way would the father want anything to do with the baby, or me for that matter.'

'You weren't raped, were you? That's it, isn't it? Did he force himself on you? Petula, you've got to tell the police. Your dad would understand if you'd been attacked.'

At the mention of her father, Petula sat up again. 'He's not well, you know. He tries to hide it from me, but you should see the amount of pills he takes every day. He's lost loads of weight, too. I'm really worried about him.'

'Please, Petula. I promise I won't tell anyone. Who is it?'

Petula gazed at her friend, as if trying to make up her mind. 'Do you swear on your life?' she said finally. 'On your mum and dad's life too?'

Lorraine shuffled uncomfortably. 'You know I don't like swearing on people's lives.'

'Suit yourself.' Petula shrugged.

'Oh, all right then, I swear.' She made the sign of a cross on her heart.

Petula adopted a serious tone. 'I mean it, Lorraine, you can't tell anybody, okay? Not even your mum. *Especially* not your mum.'

Lorraine nodded. 'Well?'

Petula puffed out her cheeks, her voice barely a whisper. 'You won't judge me?'

'For the love of God, Petula, just tell me!'

They both jumped as the back doors of the van were wrenched open and Jerry stood there with a puzzled expression on his face. 'Everything all right in here? We're just waiting for Mum to get back and then we'll be on our way.' He looked at his watch and then at the sky. 'Do you know where she went?'

Petula and Lorraine exchanged a conspiratorial glance.

'Er, Petula has been sick, so Daisy wrapped up her mucky clothes and that in newspaper and went to find a bin.'

Jerry wrinkled his nose in apparent disgust. 'Been drinking too much, have you?'

'Get lost, Jerry,' growled Petula. 'It's sunstroke, for your information.'

Daisy had already decided she was not going to take the baby to the hospital. Three miles was too far to walk, and to involve a taxi driver was an unnecessary complication. She strode along the front, cradling the sleeping baby close to her chest. She felt as though the accusing eyes of every passing stranger were burning into her soul. In fact, nobody gave her a second glance. She came to a row of Victorian-looking guest houses, all displaying the flashing neon 'No Vacancies' sign. The one on the end looked particularly well-kept. It was freshly painted in a rich cream colour, with a neatly mown lawn and sparkling white net curtains at the windows. The two steps up to the front door looked like they had been recently coated with the same Red Cardinal polish that Daisy herself favoured and now gleamed in the evening sunlight. The owner of this place was certainly house-proud, and with no further clues as to the occupants within, Daisy decided it would have to be enough.

As she hovered behind the gatepost, the front door opened and a woman Daisy guessed to be in her early thirties stooped and put down four freshly rinsed milk bottles. She straightened up and took a huge gulp of the salty air, then stood for a moment with her hands on her hips as she gazed out to sea. She had a kind face, but as she looked out over the gleaming water, her reflective expression hinted at something Daisy did not have time to speculate on.

Daisy hesitated once more, but with the baby beginning to stir again, she knew she needed to make a decision. She waited for a few moments after the woman had gone back inside, then hurried up the garden path, shoulders hunched, looking furtively left and right. She kissed the little girl softly on her forehead, drinking in her intoxicating scent one last time, before she carefully laid the precious bundle on the grass at the bottom of the steps. She hoped the gaudy beach towel was not too rough on her delicate skin.

'Goodbye, little one,' she sniffed. 'You have a nice life now. Your mother's not a bad person really. You just came along at the wrong time.' She raised her finger to the doorbell, pressed long and hard and then blew another kiss to the baby. 'Be lucky.'

She retreated down the path, skipped across the road, narrowly avoiding a passing tram, and waited in the bus shelter. She had a good view of the front door from her vantage point but was far enough away not to arouse suspicions. *Come on, open the door*, she willed.

She felt as though she had aged ten years by the time

the door was opened and the woman appeared again, a look of puzzlement creasing her pretty features. *Look down, please, look down*, Daisy urged from across the road. The woman shook her head, stepped back inside her hallway and began to close the door.

Daisy crept out from the sanctuary of the bus shelter and headed for the guest house once again. Everything was going wrong. She should have taken the baby to the hospital and faced the barrage of questions that would no doubt have been fired at her. This baby was nothing to do with her, and yet somehow she'd been left to clear up the mess. Petula had no right to put her in this position. She bounced on her heels as she waited impatiently for the road to clear and then sprinted across.

She stopped abruptly at the garden gate. The woman was standing on her step, cooing over the tiny bundle now safe in her arms, gazing in wonderment at the baby as she gently traced her finger around the infant's face. She looked up then, and their eyes met for a fleeting second, but it was still long enough for her to cast a quizzical look at Daisy before she turned and went inside, closing the door behind her.

Daisy breathed a sigh of relief. She had been forced to make a quick decision, but from what she had just seen, she had chosen well.

18

By the time Daisy arrived back in the beer garden, the others were packing up and preparing to leave. Jerry was herding them all together, fretting that he wanted to be on the road before it got dark. 'Mum! At last. Come on, we need to go.'

Daisy looked across at Babs, who stared intently at her drink, unable to meet her eye.

'Petula has been sick, so I took the newspaper and the stuff we used to clean the place up and put it in a bin further down the prom.'

'But your chicken's gone cold, Mum.'

'Stop fussing, Jerry, I'll take it with me. Now come on, let's get going.'

Trisha was slumped face down on the table, her head on her folded arms. Selwyn stroked her hair. 'Come on, you, time to go.'

She lifted her head, her bleary eyes ringed with mascara, and struggled to her feet with the aid of Selwyn's outstretched hand.

'For a publican's wife, she's not very good at holding her drink, is she?' Harry muttered to Daisy.

'As long as she doesn't throw up on the way home, I don't mind.'

Jerry called over to Karl, who was having a kickabout on the lawn with Mikey using a ball they had found hidden under the hedge. 'Time to go, I'm afraid, you two.'

Mikey gathered up the ball and tucked it under his arm. 'Can we take this with us, Dad?'

'It's not yours, is it, kid?' Karl reasoned. 'Why don't we leave it here for another little boy to play with?'

Mikey shrugged. 'Okay.' He kicked the ball back on to the lawn and took hold of Karl's hand. 'We can play lots more football when we go on holiday, can't we, Dad?'

'You bet we can. And there'll be loads of other stuff to do now that you're bigger, like swimming, abseiling, bike riding. We could even go pony trekking if you like.'

Mikey's eyes widened with delight and he beamed up at his father. 'It's going to be the best holiday ever.' He paused for a second and wrinkled his nose. 'Where is Butlin's, Dad?'

'It's in Minehead, remember? Where we went last year. It's a long journey, but worth it when we get there.'

'Is Mummy coming too, then?'

Karl hesitated and shook his head. 'No, not this time. It'll just be you and me.'

Mikey skipped along beside his father. 'I can't wait. It'll be dead good, it will.'

Jerry held the back doors of the Transit open and ushered everybody in. Petula had gone to sit up front in

146

the cab at Lorraine's insistence, because the seats were comfier and she would be less likely to feel sick. Lorraine clambered in beside her. 'You okay?'

Petula shook her head. 'Daft question that, Lorraine.'

'I know, sorry. I don't know what else to say. Look, I've managed to have a quiet word with Daisy.' She dropped her voice to barely a whisper. 'The baby's been found, so we know she's safe.'

Petula shrugged. 'Fine. That's good. Hopefully that's the end of it.'

'It's not the end, Petula, it's the beginning. I don't think you're going to be able to keep this a secret, you know.'

'Well *I'm* certainly not going to tell anybody,' she snapped.

Lorraine cast a glance at the others. 'Shh . . . Keep your voice down and think about it. Mum knows and Daisy knows, and there's bound to be a television appeal for the mother to come forward, there always is. You won't be in any trouble, Petula, but you may need medical assistance. That's what they always say when an abandoned baby is found, isn't it? They say they're concerned for the mother.' She took hold of her friend's hand. 'Anyway, you were just about to tell me who the father is.'

Petula closed her eyes and shook her head. 'Forget it, Lorraine. I've changed my mind.'

The Transit rocked from side to side as Jerry slammed the back doors shut. He hoisted himself into the driver's seat and squashed up next to Petula. 'Are you all right? You look terrible.'

She managed a small laugh. 'Thanks.'

He looked in his rear-view mirror at the passengers in the back. 'Right, is everybody okay back there?'

Trisha was slumped against Selwyn, her hat now covering her eyes. Selwyn pushed the rim of the hat up and kissed her on the nose. 'We need to get you home, Trisha love. I think you're ready for your bed.' He turned to Jerry. 'Thanks for driving, lad. Saved the day, you did.'

Jerry smiled and crunched the gears into reverse. 'I'm glad I was able to step in, Selwyn.' He looked at Daisy, whose head rested on Harry's shoulder. 'Mum's had a lovely day – we all have. Now you just relax back there and I'll have you home in no time.'

19

Mary often retired early to her private living quarters at the top of the house. Even if there were any guests still to return before bedtime, it wasn't a problem; they all knew that the front door key would be squirrelled away under the welcome mat. She sometimes waited in the guests' lounge and enjoyed a nightcap with them, just to be sociable, but it had been another day of sweltering temperatures, and the thought of a cool, shallow bath was just too much to resist. The intense heat made it so difficult to sleep these days; she had even taken to laying a damp towel on her mattress in an effort to stay cool. Even with all the windows flung open and the sea breeze wafting through the room, it was still stifling.

She stared out over the Irish sea, the water reflecting the clear blue sky, making it much more appealing than its usual colour of stewed tea. She smiled as she watched Bert collecting up his deckchairs, dusting off the sand and stacking them up along the railings ready for another bumper day tomorrow. He clapped his hands at two seagulls that were fighting over a discarded tray of chips. A line of donkeys trundled past, all tethered together as they made their way to their overnight pasture, tired from the exertions of ferrying sticky toddlers up and down the beach all day.

After her bath, Mary slathered on body lotion, popped her sponge rollers into her hair and slipped on her dressing gown. As she settled into her armchair to read, she heard someone trudging up the stairs. Her others guests had all departed after breakfast, so it could only be Albert. She recognised his faint tuneless whistle as he climbed the stairs.

Albert Smith had been staying at Claremont Villas for several years now. His job as a toy salesman often brought him to the town, where the myriad souvenir shops provided an outlet for his wares. Mary had always enjoyed his company, but now that Thomas was no longer around, Albert had become noticeably more attentive. It was impossible for Mary not to like him, though. He was an entertaining raconteur, full of amusing stories about his travels, and always had a trick up his sleeve. Quite literally, in fact, as Mary had often witnessed him pulling out reams of coloured handkerchiefs knotted together. He was an antidote to her sadness, and she really did look forward to his visits. In other circumstances his charismatic personality would have been hard to resist. He was wasting his time, though. Mary knew that Thomas would return one day. They said he was dead, but she had never had a body to bury, and until she did, a part of her refused to believe he'd gone for ever.

Over a year had passed since the accident, but images of Thomas's suffering still haunted Mary. She did not know if he had died instantly in the initial explosion, or whether he had been crushed to death, gassed by the afterdamp or burned alive in the inferno. Or maybe he hadn't perished at all. It had taken two days for the pit owners to come to the decision to seal the mine, thus entombing eighty miners for ever. Thomas's body had never been returned to her, and as far as Mary was concerned, there was no proof that he had actually died. The fact that the carbon monoxide readings from the shaft were so high that it was thought nobody could possibly still be alive was irrelevant. He could well have escaped uninjured, but dazed and confused, possibly with long-term memory loss. It was conceivable to Mary that he was alive somewhere with no recollection of his former life. It was this belief that sustained her, and without conclusive proof that her husband had been killed, her little flame of hope would never be extinguished.

As Albert reached the top of the stairs, she heard him stumble and curse under his breath. He was outside on the landing now, and Mary resisted the urge to call to him. He tapped lightly three times on her door.

'Mary? Are you in there?'

She pulled her dressing gown tighter across her body. 'Er, yes, Albert, I'm here. What is it?'

His voice was muffled by the thick wooden door. 'Mary, I've got something to tell you.'

She slotted her bookmark between the pages and laid the book down on the table beside her. 'It's open, Albert, come in.'

He turned the handle and cracked the door open a little, but remained respectfully on the other side of the threshold. 'I'm sorry to disturb you, Mary, but I've come to say goodbye.'

'It's okay, Albert. I know you've got an early start in the morning, but I've set my alarm. I wouldn't see you go without your breakfast.'

He looked down at the floorboards, unable to meet her eye. 'I'm going away, Mary. I've been transferred to our office in London . . . well, it's a promotion actually, but anyway, I don't know when I'll be back in Blackpool. I'm sorry.'

He seemed nervous as he fidgeted with the end of his tie and swallowed hard, and Mary had a sudden compulsion to comfort him. She rose from her chair. 'Come in, please, Albert.'

He glanced over his shoulder. 'Oh, I'm not sure that would be . . .'

'Please,' she insisted.

She was aware that she did not look her best and was surprised that this mattered to her. Her face was stripped of make-up, no doubt with a sheen of cold cream still visible, and her hair was tucked into an unflattering hairnet in order to secure her sponge rollers. They sat side by side on the edge of the bed and Albert took her hand in his. 'You're so beautiful, Mary.'

She smiled and squeezed his hand. It had been a long time since she'd heard those words.

Albert had undone his top button, loosened his tie and rolled up his shirtsleeves in an effort to stay cool. He reached out tentatively and traced his finger along the ridge of her collarbone. It was a bold move, but she did not recoil and instead slowly took his hand in hers and threaded her fingers through his. He leaned forward and softly brushed her lips with his own. 'You smell divine, Mary.'

An unexpected spring of sadness bubbled over as she reached out and touched his cheek. 'This is still Thomas's bed, Albert.'

'Oh Mary. You poor love.' He kissed her again, and after only a moment's hesitation, she responded. Long-forgotten feelings of desire were awakened, but as she pulled Albert closer, their embrace seemed awkward and unnatural. Thomas had fitted into her arms as comfortably as one jigsaw piece fitted into another. Albert propped himself up on his elbows and stared down at her face only inches away. 'Would you mind?' He rolled back her hairnet and carefully began to unwind the curlers. 'It's like making love to Hilda Ogden.'

Afterwards, as she lay in Albert's arms, she tried to push thoughts of Thomas out of her mind. She could not shake the feeling that she had been unfaithful to him. She really believed that Thomas was still alive, and with good reason. She had sat in front of the fortune-teller on the end of the pier on more than one occasion. Each time, as she'd exited the dimly lit, velvet-swathed room, she'd carried with her a different message of hope. Of course the fortune-teller had never been specific, but Mary knew what she meant. Her husband would return one day. Now she would have to live with the guilt that she had betrayed him.

20

Mary stared at her reflection in the bathroom mirror. She certainly looked the same – a little more flushed, maybe, and her hair was more tousled than she was comfortable with – but her heart was weighed down by shame. She should have been stronger and resisted Albert's advances. Albert wasn't to blame, of course; after all, she had invited him into her room. She cursed herself for being weak, but it had been so long since she had felt a man's touch. She could not imagine how she was going to explain this to Thomas when he returned. Would he ever forgive her, and did she even deserve his forgiveness?

She splashed cold water on her face and patted it dry with her face cloth. Maybe in the morning things would seem different. She settled herself back into her armchair and picked up her book, but it was a futile exercise; the words just swam in front of her eyes and made no sense. Naturally, Albert had wanted to stay with her for the rest of the evening, but she'd gently asked him to leave. She had a feeling the guilt was going to gnaw away at her until morning, and she didn't need him asking her if she was all right every five minutes. In spite of the fact that her room was far above street level, she could still hear revellers on the seafront, their merriment evident from all the laughter and singing that wafted in through the open windows.

She remembered then that she had forgotten to put out the milk bottles and inwardly cursed her absent-mindedness. As she descended the first flight of stairs and arrived on Albert's landing, she noted with relief that his door was firmly shut. The last thing she needed was him thinking she had come down for a repeat perfor-mance. She put the clean milk bottles on the step and inhaled a last blast of the warm sea air before closing the door again.

She had made it back up all three flights of stairs when she heard the doorbell, long, loud and impatient. With her other guests this weekend having departed this morning, she was not expecting anybody else. Not having had time to make up the rooms again, she had deliberately left the 'No Vacancies' sign switched on. It had been a bumper summer already and she felt she needed a little respite. She slipped her dressing gown off and replaced it with a housecoat; only a marginal improvement, but she couldn't be answering the door in her nightwear.

When she opened the door, she was surprised, not to mention mildly irritated, to see that there was no one there. Kids messing about, no doubt. As she began to close it again, she was stopped by a faint mewing sound coming from the bottom of the steps. She noticed a brightly coloured beach towel resting in the long grass; it appeared to be moving. Surely someone could not have abandoned a litter of kittens on her doorstep? Tiptoeing down the steps, she gingerly peeled back the towel and immediately withdrew her fingers as though she had been burned. 'What in heaven's name . . . ?' she whispered to herself.

She gathered the bundle up and stared down into the child's pink face. The baby opened its eyes, but it was obvious it could not focus. The moist mouth kept opening and closing like a little bird's when its mother returned to the nest with a juicy worm. Mary hastily went back inside, closing the door and bolting it before returning to the safety of her bedroom. By the time she reached the top floor, she was panting, a mixture of nerves and exertion. She laid the baby carefully on the bed and unwrapped the towel. A beautiful baby girl. It was apparent that some attempt had been made to clean her up, but her little body was still smeared with streaks of blood.

Mary discarded the gritty towel and fetched a warm flannelette sheet from the airing cupboard on the landing. Judging by the little knot of umbilical cord that still protruded from her belly, the baby had not been on this earth very long. Mary swaddled her tightly, the way her own mother had shown her with her baby dolls when she was little. Then, careful not to alert Albert, she made the journey down to the ground floor once more, and into the kitchen. At the back of a cupboard she found an old feeding bottle that had been left by a previous guest. Thomas had teased her about her inability to throw anything away, and now she was glad she had ignored him, though momentarily annoyed that he was not here to see she had been proved right. The bottle was cloudy with age but the yellow rubber teat still appeared to be intact.

Doing everything one-handed was proving cumbersome, so as she waited for the kettle to boil, she laid the baby down on the wing-backed armchair in the corner of the room. It was Thomas's favourite chair, the one he had collapsed into after a hard day's work down the pits. Beneath the antimacassar the fabric still bore the greasy stain of his Brylcreem. She poured some Carnation milk into the bottle and topped it up with boiling water. As she waited for it to cool, she planned her next course of action. She would give the baby a feed and all the cuddles and affection she had so far been starved of, and then she would take her to Blackpool Victoria Hospital.

After the baby had greedily taken the bottle, Mary took her back upstairs and ran a sinkful of warm water. She lowered the baby in and gently swilled away the last vestiges of afterbirth. She lathered up a bar of soap and massaged the suds into her matted hair. With a ball of cotton wool she wiped the stickiness from the baby's eyes and the ring of milk that had collected in the folds of her neck.

When the little girl was clean and dry, she laid her down in the bed. The same bed she had just shared with Albert, which now seemed a lifetime ago. She rummaged through her sewing box and selected a couple of safety pins. She took hold of the baby's ankles, lifted her slightly and slotted a towel underneath. With trembling hands, she folded the towel round her tiny body and secured it with the safety pins. As the baby dozed, her mouth made little movements, as though she was trying to talk. Mary traced her finger over the infant's perfect eyebrows and down the side of her cheek. It seemed a shame to wake her now. She would take her to the hospital first thing tomorrow.

21

As Daisy groped around with her hands, it took her a few seconds to realise she was upside down. The pressure on her eyeballs was so immense she was sure they were going to bulge right out of their sockets. The acrid smell of burning rubber funnelled up her nostrils and she felt a stickiness on her left thigh. She squinted through the translucent haze of the smoke and saw a livid gash that was oozing blood, thick and dark. Strange that she could feel no pain, she thought. She could not remember where she had been or indeed where she was going, but she was inside a bus that appeared to have been through the spin cycle of a washing machine.

That such chaos and devastation was accompanied by an eerie silence was even more unnerving. As the smoke in the bus began to dissipate, so did the fog in Daisy's memory.

They'd been to Blackpool, that was it. It'd been a nice day out, but there was something else gnawing away in the recesses of Daisy's subconscious. She felt sure it was important but struggled to recall any details. An approaching siren broke her concentration and she turned to the human form slumped on the floor next to her. Was it the floor or the roof? She eased herself into a sitting position and gently turned him over. Harry's eyes were open and she feared they had lost all capacity to focus, but there didn't appear to be a mark on him.

'Harry?' she coaxed. 'Are you all right?' Her voice sounded small and disembodied, as though it belonged to someone else. She loosened the knot on his tie and popped open his top button. 'Harry, it's me, Daisy.' She pushed two fingers under his collar and prayed for a pulse, but his skin was already cold and clammy. 'Oh Harry,' she whispered. His last day on earth might have ended tragically but at least it had been a day filled with joy and companionship. The thought that he was now safe in the arms of his beloved Elsie brought the faintest of smiles to her lips. She pulled his handkerchief out of his top pocket and placed it over his face. 'Sleep tight, love.'

Daisy's eyes were smarting from the smoke, but as she surveyed the bus, she noticed that the windscreen had completely shattered, leaving only shards of glass embedded in the rubber surrounding the gaping hole. It was then that she saw him, lying slumped across the seat, a piece of metal penetrating his shoulder blade and a deep gash across his forehead. The blood ran down into his eyes but he made no attempt to wipe it away. 'Jerry? Jerry, it's Mum. Talk to me, lad.' Why could nobody appear to hear her voice? She tried to struggle to her feet but something was pinning her down. She had no idea what. Maybe she was paralysed.

She gazed around the bus. The smell of burning rubber had been replaced by petrol fumes, which hung heavy and menacing in the warm air. There was a banging noise now, but nobody else appeared to notice. It all became clear then. She closed her eyes and let her head drop back against a cracked window. Of course she couldn't feel any pain. How could she have been so stupid? You couldn't feel anything when you were dead.

Trisha lifted her head but it immediately lolled back like a medicine ball on a spring, hitting the window with a resounding crack. The last thing she could remember was the screech of metal on tarmac as the bus travelled along a section of the motorway on its roof. It was almost dark now, but she could make out Barbara on the seat opposite, her left arm bent at an awkward angle round the back of her head. Her green dress had ridden up and Trisha could see her lacy pink pants. She also noticed, with some satisfaction, the other woman's dimpled thighs and the tell-tale signs of cellulite. How Babs would hate Trisha to see that.

With a monumental effort, she reached over and pulled Barbara's dress down. Then she turned to her husband and tugged on his arm. 'Selwyn, are you okay?' Her mouth was swollen and the words did not sound like her own. There was no response. 'Oh God, Selwyn, please don't be dead.' She laid her head against his chest and prayed for the rhythmic rise and fall that would tell her that her husband was still alive.

Lorraine stared at the place where the windscreen had once been. She could see the headlights of the cars on the opposite carriageway crawling by slowly to afford the ghoulish occupants a better look at the carnage in their midst. She was trapped, suspended by her seat belt, and the weight of her body straining against the strap made it impossible for her to unclip it. She flailed her arms about blindly. 'Mum, Dad, where are you? Are you hurt?'

Trisha's voice filtered through from the back. 'Are you all right, Lorraine? I've got your dad here. He's . . . well I think he's breathing.'

Babs stirred when she heard her daughter's voice. 'Lorraine, is that you?' She sounded as though she'd swallowed a shovel full of gravel.

'I'm in the front, Mum. I'm okay, but I can't find Petula.'

The blue flashing light illuminated the interior of the bus, giving them all a deathly pallor. Two ambulance men were crouched on the motorway ahead. Lorraine could not see what they were doing and she wondered what could possibly be more important than helping those still trapped inside the bus. One of them stood up, shook his head and motioned to his colleague. A young girl who did not look much older than Lorraine herself approached the figures, and as she drew level she clamped her hand over her mouth. Her colleague placed a reassuring arm around her shoulder before he took the sheet from her and placed it over something lying in the road.

It only took Lorraine a few seconds to put the pieces together. 'Oh no, not Petula,' she wailed.

Babs tried to turn to her daughter, but her arm was bent unnaturally behind her head and she could not dislodge it. 'Lorraine, what's the matter? Have you found Petula?'

'She's dead, Mum,' Lorraine sobbed. 'She's lying on the motorway up ahead. She must have been thrown through the windscreen.'

Babs closed her eyes as a vision of Petula's baby flashed before her. If they had been successful in persuading Petula to take her home, the little mite would surely have perished too. Whatever fate awaited her now could not be worse than the one that had befallen her mother. Babs was desperate to cradle Lorraine in her arms. She could hear her quietly sobbing for her friend and longed to comfort her.

The bus began to rock from side to side as a fireman wrenched open the rear doors. 'We'll soon have you all out. Now can anybody tell me how many passengers there are?'

Babs squinted into the beam of his torch and shielded her eyes. 'There are . . . were . . . ten of us.' She felt something grab at her ankles then, and instinctively drew her legs up. She peered down and looked under the mangled seat. The eyes staring back at her were filled with terror and utter confusion. 'Mikey! Thank God. Are you all right?'

'I think so, but me head hurts. What's happened?' He rubbed his fingers across his forehead and inspected them. 'I'm bleeding,' he declared. He prodded his tongue around his mouth. 'And I've lost another tooth.'

'The bus has crashed, Mikey, but the firemen are here and they're going to get us out. Everything'll be all right.' She reached down and took hold of his hand. 'I'm here, Mikey, I'll look after you.'

Babs could see he was trying to be brave, but it was impossible for him to ask his next question without his voice cracking. 'Where's me dad?'

22

As Albert hesitated on the doorstep the next morning, briefcase in hand and seemingly reluctant to leave, it was all Mary could do to stop herself from bundling him down the steps like a bouncer throwing a troublemaker out of a nightclub.

'Look, about last night, Mary,' he ventured.

Mary groaned inwardly. She did not have time for this. 'Albert, please don't say anything we'll both regret.'

He nodded gravely. 'I'll always remember you, Mary, and of course if I'm ever in Blackpool again . . .'

She began to shut the door. 'Yes, yes, be sure to look me up.' She made no attempt to hide her impatience.

He placed his flattened palm on the door, preventing her from closing it. 'I hope that what happened between us last night will help you to move on, Mary.' His tone was gentle but firm. 'Thomas is dead; he's never coming back.'

Mary chewed on her bottom lip and stared at her feet, unwilling to witness the pity in his eyes. 'I know,' she whispered finally.

Of course she didn't believe that, but it seemed to do

the trick, and Albert bade her a final farewell with a peck on the cheek. It was a relief to close the door on his retreating figure, and she hurried gratefully back upstairs.

The baby had slept peacefully next to her for most of the night, only waking once for a feed. Mary unwrapped the fleecy sheet she had swaddled her in and inspected the towel she had fashioned into a makeshift nappy. It was full of a black tar-like substance.

'Oh my goodness, little one. What have we here?' She reached for the tissues and wiped the infant's bottom carefully. 'I think we need to get you in the bath again before I take you to the hospital.'

Downstairs in the kitchen, with the little girl snuggled in her arms, Mary sat in Thomas's chair and leaned her head back. The upholstery was still ingrained with his essence, and she found a tremendous comfort from sitting in the chair where he had spent so many happy hours. She turned her head to the side and inhaled the smell of his pipe tobacco. She smiled as she recalled the number of times she had told him not to smoke in the kitchen. Now she couldn't get enough of the smell she had once impatiently wafted away with her tea towel.

She switched on the wireless and tuned into the news. She didn't know what she was expecting to hear, but it was a relief when there was no mention of an abandoned baby. Whoever had left her on Mary's doorstep did not appear to have changed their mind. There was news of a minibus that had crashed on the motorway between

Blackpool and Manchester, and she felt a fleeting sympathetic pang for the people who had lost their lives, but her attention was immediately drawn back to the sleeping infant in her arms.

'You're such a good baby. I wish my Thomas was here. He'd know what to do.'

She felt another prick of annoyance at Albert and once again cursed her own weakness for succumbing to his advances. Albert's belief that Thomas was dead had enabled him to seduce her, but he was not in possession of all the facts. As far as Mary was concerned, she had concrete evidence that Thomas was still alive. Only a few months after the accident at the pit, she had been to visit a spiritualist. She had not told the woman anything about her background, but had feigned desperation about her desire to hear from her beloved deceased husband.

The spiritualist had laid her palms on the table, closed her eyes and taken a deep breath as she rocked back in her chair. Her eyelids had flickered and her lips had moved as though she was muttering to someone. Eventually she opened her eyes and spoke to Mary. 'I'm getting someone coming through.' Mary had shuffled forward in her seat as the spiritualist closed her eyes once more and rubbed her temples. 'Yes,' she continued. 'I'm getting the name Bill or Billy.' Mary noticed how she opened one eye and peered at her for a reaction, but she remained impassive and the spiritualist was forced to continue. 'Wait, no, it's not Bill, it's Bobby; that's it, Bobby. Does that name mean anything to you?'

Mary had sat back in her chair as the relief washed over her. 'Yes, it does. We had a ginger tom when I was growing up. His name was Bobby.'

She had walked out with a huge grin on her face. She had dreaded receiving a message from beyond the grave, but this was all the confirmation she'd needed. Thomas's spirit could not materialise because he wasn't dead. Mary's own spirits had soared as she floated back to the guest house.

Mary decided to walk the three miles to Blackpool Victoria. The town was beginning to come to life again and the day promised to be another scorcher. The fresh sea air would do the baby good and put a bit of colour in her cheeks. As she waited at a zebra crossing, an old lady next to her beamed a gummy smile. 'Well would you look at that?' Her gnarled fingers peeled back the sheet framing the baby's face. 'She's beautiful – it is a girl, isn't it?'

After her initial discomfort at the unwelcome intrusion, Mary's heart swelled with pride. 'Yes, she's a girl.'

'Aah, that's lovely. How old is she then?' The old woman continued to coo over the baby, but Mary was becoming agitated. She pulled her closer to her chest.

'Er . . . a few days, not very old.'

'And you're out and about already? Well, I'm surprised, I am. You need to protect yourself, you know.'

Mary frowned. 'Protect myself?'

The woman sidled closer and lowered her tone. 'Yes, you need to take care of your . . . er . . . downstairs area. Did your midwife not tell you all this?'

It was beginning to sound to Mary like an interrogation; she was not about to discuss her private parts with a complete stranger. The cars had stopped for the two women to cross, and Mary nodded her thanks to the drivers as she scuttled over to the other side. The old lady was encumbered by a tartan shopping trolley but she arrived a few seconds later. 'What's her name?'

Dear Lord, will this woman ever give up?

'I'm sorry,' Mary apologised. 'I really must be getting along. It was nice to meet you.'

She left the bemused woman on the pavement as she strode purposefully towards her destination.

Her brisk pace had allowed Mary to complete the journey to the hospital in just under an hour. The baby had slept the entire time, no doubt comforted by the motion. As she stood outside the main entrance, Mary prepared to say her goodbyes to the little person who had been thrust into her life the day before. She tried not to dwell on what would become of her now; whether she would forever be affected by the knowledge that her own mother did not want her. Mary could not imagine a more devastating start to life, and her heart ached when she thought of the anguish this would no doubt cause the little girl when she was old enough to understand. There were many children who did not know who their real father was, but surely most knew something about their birth mother. This poor little mite would know nothing at all, apart from the fact that her mother hadn't loved her enough to keep her.

The baby began to stir as Mary made her way up to the entrance. There was an ambulance parked outside the main doors, its blue light still flashing. A medical team rushed out of the building and the back doors of the vehicle were flung open.

'Oh dear,' said Mary to the infant, who was now wriggling beneath the confines of the sheet she was swaddled in. 'Looks like we've come at a bad time.'

The baby gave a cough, took a deep breath and began to wail.

'Shh . . . there, there. We'll have you inside in no time. The nurses will take care of you. They'll put you in a nice hospital-issue babygro and leave you in your cot to cry yourself to sleep. If they have time, they'll give you a bath, perhaps a quick cuddle, and then there will be an appeal for the heartless mother to come forward.' The baby calmed down at Mary's soothing tone. 'And then, when she doesn't come forward – because let's face it, she doesn't want you or deserve you – you'll go into foster care and eventually be put up for adoption. Then you'll spend the rest of your life wondering who your real parents were and why they didn't love you enough.'

A swollen teardrop meandered its way down Mary's cheek and hovered precariously on her chin before plopping on to the baby's forehead. She turned and looked over her shoulder at the hospital, now some distance away. It had not seemed like a conscious decision, but Mary realised she was now making her way home again. This baby had been abandoned once, and she was not about to abandon her again.

23

Daisy lay in her hospital bed and stared at the bright light. She had read about this before, the long tunnel leading towards the warm, welcoming glow of heaven and God's waiting arms. She reached out blindly and her hands connected with the starched white coat of the doctor. He flicked off his torch and addressed his patient. 'Good morning, Mrs Duggan. How are you feeling?'

Daisy tried to sit up but her leaden arms and legs would not cooperate. 'Where am I? Where's my son?'

The doctor's face hovered only inches from hers as he spoke gently. 'You were involved in an accident last night. You have concussion and a nasty gash on your thigh. We'll be taking you for an X-ray later.'

'Where's my son? Jerry Duggan's his name. Do you know what happened to him?'

'Try to stay calm, Mrs Duggan. I'll find out for you just as soon as I've completed my examination.'

When he'd finished with his prodding and poking, all of which seemed intrusive and unnecessary to Daisy, she closed her eyes and tried to recall the events of the previous day. She remembered Jerry telling her they were nearly home; she'd been looking forward to her nightly mug of Ovaltine. Even in the sweltering temperatures she had been unable to break this habit. She remembered the loud bang and then the rolling sensation, over and over and over until she thought they would never stop. As the nausea took hold, she reached out for the glass of water beside her to quell the rising bile and noticed the doctor talking to another man who was wearing scrubs. She heard him mention Jerry's name. The surgeon ran his finger down his clipboard, glanced over at Daisy from beneath his long fringe and gave a barely perceptible shake of his head.

Mikey knew he wasn't in his own bed. The sheets were crisp and smelled clean, the pillow was firm, not lumpy, and the satin trim of the pale green blanket felt soft beneath his fingers.

'Are you all right, Mikey love?'

Not recognising the gentle tone, he turned to see who had just spoken and was surprised to see it was his mother. She had a huge stuffed monkey on her knee. Mikey's head hurt and he felt as though he was wearing a turban like his friend Mr Singh from the sweetshop. He fingered the crepe bandage that had been wound tightly round his head.

His mother patted the back of his hand. 'I've been so worried.'

He could not remember a time when his mother had

worried about him, so he knew it must be serious. He frowned, eyed his mother suspiciously, then reached out and took hold of one of the monkey's arms. 'Me dad won this for me at the fair. His name's Galen.' He remembered something then, and ferreted around under his pillow. His little hand found the tooth he had placed there the night before. He held it in his palm and stared at it for some time. 'The fairies didn't come,' he said eventually.

'The fairies? What on earth are you talking about, Mikey?'

'My tooth came out on the big wheel yesterday. I put it under my pillow for the fairies.'

'Oh Mikey, you daft beggar. You can't do that without telling anyone.'

Mikey stared at his mother. She looked the same but she sounded different. Her voice was softer, more gentle, but she seemed to be nervous about something and was fidgeting with her necklace. She put the monkey down, reached for a packet of cigarettes and placed one between her lips before remembering where she was. She pushed the cigarette back into its packet. 'Do you want some lemon barley water?' Without waiting for an answer, she poured a small amount into the glass beside Mikey's bed and topped it up with water. 'Here, drink this.'

Mikey pushed the glass away. 'I want my daddy. Where is he?'

His mother appeared unsure and flustered as she

pushed her chair back and hurried over to the nurses' station.

Mikey couldn't hear what they were saying, but he saw the nurse put down a funny-shaped bowl and pat his mother on the arm before approaching his bed. His mother followed in her wake.

The nurse spoke in the same gentle tones his mother had started using. 'Mikey, can you be a big brave boy? I've got some very sad news, but your mummy's here and we're all going to look after you.'

Mikey did not like the sound of this. He felt his chin begin to wobble and worried he wasn't doing a very good job of being brave. He took a deep breath and tried to force his lips into a smile. He nodded his head.

The nurse continued as his mother hovered nervously behind her. 'You remember the crash you were in last night? How you and some of the others were hurt?'

Mikey nodded again. He didn't know if he was expected to answer or not.

'Well, your daddy was very badly hurt, and I'm so sorry to have to tell you this, but the doctors were not able to save him.'

'Oh.' It was all he could think of to say.

'Do you understand what I'm saying, Mikey?' The nurse had hold of his hand now.

His small voice faltered and a single tear slipped down his cheek. 'You mean . . . my daddy's gone to heaven?'

His mother stepped forward. 'That's right, Mikey. Your

dad's died, but I'm here now and I'm going to take care of you, just as I've always done.'

The nurse patted her on the shoulder. 'I'll leave you to it now. You know where I am if you need me.' She offered Mikey a thin smile before she left them alone.

Mikey reached out to his mother. She only hesitated briefly before she enveloped him in her arms. He couldn't remember the last time she had hugged him, and her embrace was unfamiliar and awkward. He was suddenly fed up of trying to be brave, and he let the tears flow into her neck as she rocked him back and forth.

Babs was roused from her fitful sleep by the sound of Trisha arguing with a nurse. 'Please, you've got to let me see him, I'm his wife.' That woman could start a riot in an empty room.

The nurse was doing an admirable job of remaining patient under testing circumstances. 'As I've said before, Mrs Pryce, your husband is in intensive care at the moment and will be going to theatre later on today. He's in a serious but stable condition and you will be the first to know if there's any change.' She guided Trisha back to her bed next to Babs. 'I know it's difficult, but I promise we'll let you know as soon as there is any news.'

Trisha shrugged the nurse off. 'I don't need to get back into bed. I was only kept in for observation; now that you've observed me and seen there's nothing wrong with me, I should be able to go and see my husband.'

Babs intervened. 'Calm down, Trisha. Not everyone made it out alive, remember. We're the lucky ones, Selwyn included.'

This seemed to bring Trisha to her senses. 'Sorry. I'm just so worried about him. I do love him, you know, Barbara.'

'I know you do, Trisha. I love . . . I mean, I *loved* him too, and he's still our Lorraine's dad. We're all worried.'

She reached for the two painkillers the nurse had left by her bed. With her arm in a sling it was a difficult manoeuvre, and she was grateful for Trisha's help as her young rival passed her the tablets and a glass of water. Trisha nodded over towards Lorraine in the bed on the other side of Babs.

'She still asleep?'

Babs glanced across at her daughter. Her sun-tinged, freckled face made her look the picture of health, but she had suffered severe bruising to her chest caused by the seat belt. It was a small price to pay. Petula had not been wearing hers.

'Mum?' Lorraine fought to open her eyes. It was as though they had been gummed shut in some sort of sick practical joke.

Babs reached out her hand, but Lorraine was too far away to make any contact. 'I'm here, love.'

'Where's Dad?'

Trisha stepped forward and sat uninvited on the edge of Lorraine's bed. 'He's in intensive care. They won't let me see him yet, but as next of kin I'll be the first to know if there's any change.'

'He'll be fine, though, won't he, Mum?' Lorraine knew her mother wouldn't lie to her.

Babs adopted a cheerful tone. 'Course he will, love. You just concentrate on getting better yourself. You know how your dad worries.'

Lorraine stretched her arms above her head and struggled to take a deep breath. 'God, my chest hurts.'

A nurse appeared at the other side of Lorraine's bed and addressed the three women. 'Mrs Pryce?'

'Yes,' answered Trisha and Babs in unison.

The nurse consulted her notes. 'Which one of you is married to Selwyn Pryce?'

Trisha shot a triumphant look at Babs. 'I am.'

'In that case, can you come with me, please? The doctor would like a word and then we'll take you to see your husband.'

Trisha spread her fingers and ran them through her hair. 'Oh gosh, look at the state of me. Whatever will Selwyn think?' She belted the hospital gown tightly round her waist and leaned in towards Babs. 'Have I got anything between my teeth?' She pulled her lips apart in a rictus grin, and Babs caught sight of a piece of cabbage wedged between the front two.

'No, you're fine, Trisha, all clear.'

'Why do you think the doctor wants a word with her?' Lorraine asked when Trisha and the nurse had left the ward.

Babs turned her body so she was facing Lorraine in the next bed. 'I don't know, love. This whole thing is so awful, tragic . . .'

'I know. I can't stop thinking about poor Petula. This is going to finish her dad off. And then there's the baby. God, Mum, she would have been killed too if Petula had taken her home. Imagine being born and killed on the same day.'

Babs shuddered. 'I've thought of that too.' She reached out and tried to touch Lorraine once more. Lorraine returned the gesture and their fingers just about connected in the space between their beds. 'Lorraine,' ventured Babs. 'Karl didn't make it. I'm so sorry.'

Lorraine nodded and closed her eyes. 'I know. I heard you and Trisha talking when you thought I was asleep. Poor little Mikey, he's never going to get over this.'

They lay side by side in contemplative silence until eventually Lorraine spoke again. 'Mum, are you still awake?'

'I don't think I'll ever sleep again. Every time I close my eyes, I can just hear the sound of crunching metal and see bodies tumbling over each other and things flying round the bus and—'

'Petula was just about to tell me who the father was.'

Babs stopped abruptly. 'Oh, gosh, really? Why didn't she?'

'We got disturbed, but she would have told me eventually, I know she would.'

The conversation came to an end with the sound of the tea lady trundling along the ward with her trolley, the green china cups rattling on the metal trays. She stopped by Lorraine's bed and held up an enormous battered stainless-steel pot. 'Cuppa tea, my love?'

It was over an hour before Trisha returned to the ward. Babs knew that none of them was looking their best, what with the hospital gowns they'd been issued with and the lack of any cosmetics or hair products, but even so she was shocked at Trisha's appearance. Her face was chalky white, her eyes red and puffy and her bottom lip still bruised and swollen. Her hands trembled as she lifted a teacup that had been left on her bedside table.

'That'll be cold now, Trisha,' said Babs.

Trisha ignored her and swigged the cold tea down in one go. She wiped her mouth with the back of her hand. 'It's not good news, Barbara.' She slumped on the edge of her bed and rubbed her hands over her face. 'Selwyn has a spinal injury. They've still got some tests to do, but the early signs are that he could be paralysed.'

'Oh my God,' whispered Babs. 'That's just tragic news.'

Lorraine turned away and squashed her face into the pillow.

'I can't believe it, Barbara,' wailed Trisha. 'It's so unfair. I'm going to be married to a cripple.'

24

Every morning, the first thing Mary did after feeding her new daughter was to turn on the radio. It always produced an annoying whistle and a hiss before finally crackling into something coherent. The headlines as usual were all about the drought. Some parts of the country had now gone well over a month without rain. Mary hoisted the baby on to her shoulder and patted the infant's back as she gazed out over the bay. 'I don't know, water, water everywhere, and all the boards did shrink, water, water everywhere, nor any drop to drink.' She gave a small laugh and kissed the baby's ear. 'My Thomas used to love me reciting poetry. Oh, he pretended he didn't, wanted to come across all macho, but I could see it in his eyes.'

It had now been two weeks since the precious bundle had been abandoned on her doorstep, and with each passing day with no news about who might have left her, Mary's hopes had begun to rise. She had been left with no choice but to take Ruth into her confidence, though. Ruth had witnessed first hand Mary's grief when she'd lost Thomas's baby, though she did not share Mary's belief that Thomas wasn't dead. Mary had explained that the baby had been left on her doorstep by someone who'd known she would take care of her. Ruth had been too preoccupied cooing over the bundle in her arms to take it in.

'Ruth, do you understand what I'm saying?'

The girl had looked up at her employer, her creased forehead registering her confusion. 'You mean you're going to keep her?'

Mary swallowed uneasily but managed to reply with conviction. 'Yes, Ruth, I am. And if anybody asks, she's my baby, all right?' She took the little girl from Ruth and rocked her gently in her arms. The infant's eyelids fluttered open briefly and then closed again.

Ruth had stared at the two of them for a long time before she spoke again. 'Do you think Mr Roberts sent this baby?'

Mary gave a small laugh. 'Don't be so . . .' She stopped herself then. God bless Ruth. So simple, uncomplicated and naive. Of course Thomas hadn't sent her a baby, but it couldn't hurt to let Ruth think he had.

She smiled and placed a reassuring hand on the girl's shoulder. 'You know, Ruth, I think you might just be right.'

Last night, as Mary had finished bathing her, the baby's rosebud lips had stretched into a blink-and-you'd-miss-it toothless smile that Mary interpreted as a sure sign that the two of them were bonding. She had taken the decision not to accept any more bookings for the time being, and the neon sign continued to flash 'No Vacancies' as a deterrent to any potential guests. It would mean eating into the money she had received from the disaster fund, but she could not cope with running the guest house and looking after a newborn baby all on her own. Ruth tried her best, but the girl was a liability sometimes. Mary did have an elderly couple booked in this weekend, though, a long-standing arrangement that she did not have the heart to cancel. Mr and Mrs Riley had been coming to her on the same weekend for years.

She laid the baby down in the makeshift cot she had fashioned out of a drawer and placed it in the corner of the kitchen. She had made a nest of blankets to shield the sharp edges and lined it with a flannelette sheet. It would be perfectly adequate for a few weeks at least. As she heard Mr and Mrs Riley enter the dining room, she went to greet them and take their order.

'Morning, Mr Riley, Mrs Riley. Usual, is it?'

'Yes please, Mrs Roberts.' Mr Riley pulled a chair out for his wife. 'Beautiful day again, I see.'

'We've come to expect it now, haven't we? To be honest, I wouldn't mind a drop of rain to wash away the grime. Everywhere seems so grubby, doesn't it?' Mary placed the red plastic tomato holding the ketchup in the middle of the table.

'I must say,' remarked Mrs Riley, 'I'm surprised we're the only guests staying this weekend. Why do you have

184

the "No Vacancies" sign lit up? You're not full.'

Mary glanced towards the kitchen as she heard the kettle whistling on the stove. It gave her the perfect excuse to ignore the question. 'Ooh, the water's boiling, I must go and brew your tea.'

She leaned on the sink, taking deep calming breaths. Mercifully, the baby was sound asleep in the cot, the shrill whistle from the kettle evidently not enough to rouse her. If Mary had known she was going to face such awkward questions, she would have been better prepared.

She returned with the teapot, and Mrs Riley lifted the lid and began to mash the tea bags with a spoon.

'I've got my sister's baby with me for the time being. I'm looking after her,' Mary said.

Mrs Riley stopped mashing. Her apple cheeks glistened with perspiration. 'Oh, how lovely for you. I was just saying to Jack how lonely it must be for you since your husband passed away.'

Mary bristled. 'Well, there's actually no concrete evidence to suggest that he did—'

She stopped as she heard the baby crying in the kitchen. Half bowing, she backed out of the dining room. 'I'd better go and see to her.'

The strain of trying to hide the baby was beginning to tell, and now she had created this other ridiculous lie. She didn't even have a sister, for goodness' sake. She should have just come out with it and said the baby was hers. There was no way she could take a booking from Mr and

Mrs Riley again for next year. She would have to think of something more convincing, something that wouldn't involve making up family members who did not exist. Whilst it was true she largely kept herself to herself, especially since Thomas had gone away, her neighbours would surely notice a baby suddenly appearing on the scene. She didn't relish the prospect, but if anybody asked, she would have to say the child was the result of an ill-advised one-night stand with one of her guests. She shuddered at the thought, especially when she considered the timing. The baby must have been conceived in October 1975, just four months after Thomas's death. It was hardly the act of a grieving widow.

By the end of the weekend, Mary was exhausted. She'd always been fond of Mr and Mrs Riley, but now she found them a complete irritation. She was glad when she finally made up their bill and sent them on their way. They bid her a cheery farewell and a 'see you next year' as they trundled off down the crazy-paved path. *Not if I can help it,* Mary muttered as she gratefully closed the door.

She waited another two weeks before she made it official. There were a couple of awkward questions at the registrar's office about the identity of the father and where the birth had taken place, but fortunately the baby chose that moment to become especially fractious. Mary bounced the handle of the second-hand Silver Cross pram, but this seemed to make matters worse. The baby's face turned crimson and her little tongue vibrated inside her mouth like a piece of liver. 'She's due a feed,' Mary offered by way of explanation, struggling to make herself heard over the din. 'It was a home birth, twenty-fourth of July 1976.'

The registrar peered out from under her horn-rimmed spectacles. 'And are you married to the baby's father?' She waited, pen poised, for the answer.

'N . . . no, I'm not,' Mary spluttered as she felt the heat of embarrassment breaking out across her neck.

'I see. Well, is the father cooperating with the registration of the birth?' The registrar looked around the room for a suitable candidate.

'Er, no, he isn't. I—'

The registrar cut her off with two strokes of her fountain pen where the father's details should have been. When the ink had dried, she pushed the certificate under the glass and Mary grabbed it gratefully and fled the building.

As she strode along the promenade, the baby quietened down again and Mary began to relax for the first time since she had found her on her doorstep. She stopped and leaned over the railings, watching the little kiddies playing on the beach. The sands thronged with sun-burnished bodies and brightly coloured umbrellas; there was not a spare inch of sand to be seen. The sound of their excited chatter no longer stirred feelings of unful-filled maternal love. It had taken her thirty-two years, but at last she was a mother, and she had the birth certificate to prove it. Elizabeth Mary Roberts was her daughter.

She peeled back the brushed cotton sheet and gazed at the baby. 'Ah, bless you, little Beth, you're mine now and I'm going to make sure no one ever hurts you again. What a grand life we're going to have together.' She stroked the infant's cheek and was rewarded with a crooked smile. 'And one day your daddy will come home, and won't he be surprised to find he has a beautiful little girl?' Beth gurgled and kicked her chubby legs in delight. Mary laughed. 'Yes, you'll like that, won't you and he'll be the best daddy any little girl could wish for.'

25

The oppressive heat weighed Daisy down and made everything so much more difficult. She longed for the rains to come, ached to feel cool, dew-covered grass beneath her feet once more, to water the plants in her garden and nourish their brown crispy leaves. The whole country felt grubby. People had given up washing their cars and cleaning their windows. Buses and trains were covered with layer upon layer of grime. Rivers and reservoirs had dried up and now resembled the parched, cracked plains of Africa. She staggered down the street, leaden shopping bags in each hand, wondering how on earth people in Spain coped with this year in, year out. It was no wonder they needed a lie-down in the afternoons.

The plastic handles were cutting into her palms and the sweat on her neck beneath her hair was beginning to run down her spine. With no free hand to wipe it away, she hunched her shoulders, put her head back and swivelled it from side to side. She was looking forward to getting home and having a nice cool bath – no more than five inches, of course; she would not break the rules of the drought.

Four weeks after the crash, her physical scars were healing. The gash on her thigh was not as livid now, and she was able to change her own dressing. The emotional scars, however, would last a lot longer, probably a lifetime. Daisy was a battler, though. After all, what choice did she have? There were some worse off than she was. Poor old Selwyn was still in hospital with spinal injuries, and as for little Mikey, he'd had to cope with the devastation of losing his father at the age of six.

As Daisy drew closer to his house in Bagot Street, she could see the little lad sitting on the kerbside, rolling his marbles into a small hole outside his front door. The red-brick terraced houses all looked identical apart from the front doors. It seemed the occupants of this street were determined to outdo each other in the competition to see who could find the most garish colour. Daisy stopped outside Mikey's door, which was painted in a sickly shade of mustard, and decided it was a front-runner.

'Hello, Mikey.' She put the bags down on the pavement and rummaged around in one of them, bringing out a Curly Wurly. 'I stopped at Mr Singh's for a Jubbly, but he's run out, can you believe?'

Mikey reached up and took the chocolate. 'Thank you, Mrs Duggan.'

'You're welcome, love.'

She watched him struggle to open the wrapper before shoving it between his teeth. The front two were still missing, so it was an awkward procedure, but eventually he broke his way in.

'What are you doing here on your own, Mikey?'

Mikey's jaws were welded together with toffee and he tried to chew quickly so he could offer an explanation. 'All me mates have gone in for their tea, but I'm locked out.'

'Oh dear, that's too bad. Where's your mum, then?'

Mikey shrugged. 'Dunno. She said she would leave the key under the mat, but she must've forgot.'

Daisy noticed the way he devoured the chocolate bar. 'Mikey, when did you last eat?'

He scratched his head. 'Er, well I had some Rice Krispies for breakfast but there was no milk left so I had to eat them with me fingers, and then Kevin gave me half of his sandwich and some of his Monster Munch.'

'So you've been locked out all day then?'

Mikey nodded as he swallowed the last of the chocolate. He rubbed his woolly sleeve across his mouth.

Daisy sat down next to him on the pavement. 'Aren't you hot in that big jumper?'

He considered the question for a moment. 'Er, yeah, suppose I am a bit, but I've got no clean T-shirts.'

Daisy set her lips into a thin line of determination. 'I think I need to have a word with your mother.' She stood up and offered her hand to Mikey. 'Come on, I'm taking you back to Lilac Avenue and making you a proper meal.'

'But Mum'll be worried where I've got to.'

Daisy stared down at the little boy's innocent face. She didn't think Andrea McKinnon would spend a single second worrying about her son, but Mikey didn't need to hear that now.

'We'll leave her a note then.' She fumbled in her handbag, pulled out a pen and paper and scribbled a message. *Mikey's at my house. I'll bring him home later. No need to worry. Daisy Duggan.* She wondered if Andrea would detect the sarcasm.

Mikey had bolted down his food so fast that he now sat at the table fighting off hiccups.

'I told you to slow down.' As Daisy ruffled the boy's hair, she noticed the line of grime around the base of his neck. 'Mikey, when did you last have a bath?'

'What? Oh, Mum says we're not allowed.'

Daisy suspected it was the first time Andrea had obeyed a rule. 'It is allowed, Mikey. We still have to take care of ourselves, you know. I'm going upstairs now to run you one.'

Once he was clean and dry and dressed in one of Jerry's old T-shirts, Daisy joined him on the settee.

'Do you feel better now that you're all clean?'

'Yes thank you, Mrs Duggan.' He pulled at the T-shirt. 'It's a bit big,' he grinned.

'Why don't you call me Aunt Daisy? Mrs Duggan makes me sound so old, and I'm only forty-five, you know.'

192

'Forty-five! That's ancient. I thought me dad was old and he was only thirty-six.'

At the mention of his father, he looked down and fiddled with the hem of the T-shirt.

Daisy pulled him into her arms. 'He was so proud of you, you know. Whenever he came in the pub it was Mikey this, Mikey that, always telling us how well you were doing at school. Top of the class when it comes to sums, aren't you?'

Mikey nodded and rubbed his forehead. Daisy scooped back his fringe and peered at the scar beneath. Like her own, it was beginning to heal. It was anybody's guess how long it would take his heart to do the same.

26

Babs had been born to be a landlady, and there had never been any question that she would enter any other profession. She'd been brought up in pubs and it was second nature to her. Back behind the bar of the Taverners she felt at home both literally and metaphorically. Even the smell of the stale beer in the slop trays took her back to happier times. When Trisha had pleaded for her help to run the pub whilst Selwyn was in hospital, Babs had hardly been able to contain her joy, and took great delight in telling the slimy Mr Reynolds where he could stick his job.

Her arm was still in a sling, which made things slightly more difficult, but it was nothing Babs couldn't handle. Ordinarily she would have been in her element, back where she belonged, but the long shadow of what had happened four weeks ago cast everything in a very different light. Lorraine had moved back too, so an uneasy cessation of hostilities had been agreed upon and the three women tried to get along for Selwyn's sake. The news from the hospital was not great, but there were encouraging signs. Having been ventilated since the crash,

Selwyn was now able to breathe unaided, although he had yet to speak. To her credit, Trisha spent most of her time at his bedside and was vigilant in ensuring he had everything he could possibly need.

With the Taverners not yet open for the evening, Babs was taking the opportunity to catch up on the paperwork before the usual Friday-evening bun fight. She hunched over a small round table in the snug, enjoying the solitude. It had been almost seven weeks since the fire, but the smell of fresh paint still permeated the air, and the walls looked brighter with their new magnolia woodchip finish. She gazed up at the ceiling and wondered how long it would be before it was tarnished with nicotine stains.

An unfamiliar sound registered in her ears. She lifted the net curtain and peered through the rain-spattered glass, allowing herself a small smile. 'At last,' she breathed.

She ran her finger down a column of figures, mentally adding them up as she went along, pleased that she was still as sharp as ever. She heard the front door open and Lorraine sauntered in, her rain-soaked hair plastered to her cheeks. She threw her bag on the table and slumped in the chair opposite. Papers fluttered to the floor and Babs bent down to retrieve them. 'Watch out, Lorraine, I've spent ages sorting that lot out.'

Lorraine seemed distracted. 'What? Oh, sorry, Mum.' She scooped the papers off the floor and helped put them into some sort of order. Then she removed her soaking Afghan coat and hung it over a chair in front of the electric fire. 'Just my luck to get caught in the first shower we've had for months.' She flicked a switch at the side of the fireplace. 'I'll have to put one bar on to dry my coat, if that's all right.'

Babs stacked the papers into a neat pile. 'Fine. Where've you been until this time anyway?'

'I went to see Ralph – you know, Petula's dad. He's still not been back to work, so I thought I'd call round and see how things were.'

Babs leaned back in her chair, paperwork temporarily forgotten. 'Poor bugger, how is he?'

'Putting on a brave face, but he looks terrible, Mum. So pale and drawn, and he seems to have lost even more weight. His belt had run out of holes so he'd tied it in a knot instead.' She shook her head. 'He had Nibbles on his knee and was stroking him the whole time. It seemed to calm him, so I said he could keep him. Seems a bit cruel to ask for him back now.'

Babs patted the back of her daughter's hand. 'You're a good girl, Lorraine.'

'I felt awful, Mum. I kept thinking that I was going to blurt out that he had a granddaughter. I could hardly keep it in, but I know how determined Petula was that he shouldn't be told.'

'Hmm,' Babs mused. 'I wonder if it would bring him some degree of comfort knowing that part of Petula still lives on.'

'I did think that, but what about Petula's reputation?

She wouldn't want her dad to think any less of her, and she's not here to defend her actions now. She was so close to her dad and she could do no wrong in his eyes. I don't think I want to be the one to tarnish the memory he has of her.' Lorraine put her head in her hands. 'It's all such a terrible mess. I mean, I made her a promise that I wouldn't tell anyone about the baby, but I didn't know she was going to die then.' Her voice rose with the desperation of it all.

Babs chewed on the end of her pen and stared out of the window. 'How close?'

Lorraine lifted her head. 'What?'

'You said Petula and her father were close.' Babs raised her eyebrows. 'Unnaturally close?'

'God, Mum, you're not suggesting that Ralph . . . Eww, God, no, how could you even think that?'

Babs shook her head. 'I'm sorry, Lorraine. I'm just trying to find out why she couldn't tell you who the father was; why it was such a big secret.'

She hated seeing her daughter in such turmoil, so she changed the subject and tried to make her next question sound as casual as possible. 'Did . . . er . . . did Ralph mention the post-mortem?' Babs had been secretly dreading the authorities finding out that Petula had just given birth. An interrogation about what had happened to the baby would surely have followed, and she didn't think she would be able to stand up to such scrutiny.

'Yeah, he did, actually. Apparently she suffered a cata-

197

strophic head injury and the chances are she would have died going through the windscreen and not been aware of the car that hit her when she landed on the motorway.' Lorraine shuddered and blinked back the tears. 'It ran over her, Mum.'

Babs stood up and went round the other side of the table to embrace her daughter. Still seated, Lorraine hugged her mother round her waist, her hot tears staining Babs's skirt.

Babs pulled out a tissue from her sleeve and dabbed her daughter's eyes. She licked the tissue and rubbed away at the streaks of mascara coursing down her face. Lorraine managed a small laugh. 'I'm not five years old, Mum.' She gathered up her shoulder bag and stood to leave. 'Do you want me to start setting up the bar?'

'Please, love, if you don't mind,' Babs replied gratefully. 'I'm almost finished with this lot, but I don't think Trisha will be back for a while yet.'

Lorraine stopped at the door to the snug and turned back to her mother. 'Mum, don't you think it's weird that we haven't heard anything about the baby on the news?'

Babs had wondered the same thing and had even asked Daisy about it, but Daisy had assured her that the baby had been found safely and that the woman at the guest house looked a decent sort and was sure to have done the right thing.

'It was probably on the local news in Blackpool. Don't worry about it, Lorraine. I'm sure everything's fine.'

Babs put her finger to her lips as she heard the front door open again. Trisha appeared and stood there looking like a startled rabbit, unsure what to do next. Babs approached her carefully and touched her elbow. 'Trisha, what's the matter?'

She wrinkled her nose. 'Smells like wet dog in 'ere.'

Lorraine looked over towards her coat steaming by the fire. 'Sorry, it's my Afghan. I got caught in that shower."

Trisha stared blankly ahead. 'Oh, right.' She gave a quick shake of her head as if to clear it. 'Anyway, it's Selwyn. They've confirmed he'll never walk again.' She fished in her handbag and pulled out a piece of paper. 'I wrote it down so I wouldn't forget.' She flattened out the crumpled piece of paper on the bar and pointed to the word. 'That's it there. He has a C5 spinal injury, which means he's a quad . . . quadriplegic.'

Lorraine grabbed hold of Babs's arm. 'Mum, what does that mean?'

Babs looked at Trisha. 'Well?'

Trisha lifted the hatch and went through to the other side of the bar. She thrust a glass under the Gordon's Gin optic and drank it down neat and in one go. She repeated the process before answering. 'They're not sure yet if it's a complete injury, but he'll definitely not be able to walk again. He'll have no control over his bladder or bowels, and as for sexual relations, well, you can forget it.'

She downed a third gin and slammed her glass on to the bar. 'Why did this have to happen to me?'

'Trisha,' said Babs, horrified. 'It did not happen to you, you selfish mare, it happened to Selwyn.'

Trisha looked momentarily confused. 'What? Oh, yeah, well it's going to affect my life too, you know. I mean, where he's gonna sleep? How's he going to get up the stairs?' She threw her hands in the air. 'He'll be like a Dalek.'

As Trisha reached for the optic for the fourth time, Babs took hold of her wrist. 'That's enough now.'

Trisha snatched her arm away. 'This is still my pub, Barbara, and I'll decide when I've had enough.'

'Oh for pity's sake, will you stop arguing?' interjected Lorraine. 'We need to concentrate on Dad now, and you two falling out will be no help at all. You know he hates it when you argue.' She placed her hands on her hips and stared at the two women. 'Pack it in, both of you.'

Babs put her arm around her daughter's shoulders. 'She's right, Trisha. Let's try to get along for Selwyn's sake. It looks like he's going to need us more than ever now.'

27

The next day, Babs inched her way down the hospital corridor, each hesitant step taking her nearer to the shell of the man she'd once been married to. Trisha had refused to come, claiming that she was still in a state of shock over the prognosis and would be of no help to Selwyn.

Babs approached Selwyn's bedside and gazed at his sleeping form. His eyelids were closed but his mouth hung open and a small trickle of saliva had run out of the corner and stained the pillow. There were tubes and wires everywhere, and a bag of urine hung from the side of the bed. Babs knew that the doctors had explained the extent of his injuries to him, and her heart was filled with pity for the man she had never ceased to love. Seeing him lying there, forlorn and helpless, with useless limbs that would never cooperate again, she couldn't help thinking that those who had lost their lives in the crash were the lucky ones after all.

She covered his hand with her own, felt the warmth there and was immediately thankful that in spite of everything his big heart was still pumping the blood through his veins, keeping him alive. She smiled at her name tattooed across his knuckles. The blue ink had faded somewhat, but the intense delight and pride she had felt when he'd returned from the tattoo parlour had not. He had only been twenty years old and they had promised that day to love each other for ever. It was a pity that it was only she who had kept that promise.

She squeezed his hand, expecting him to stir and turn his head to look at her. When there was no response, she leaned into his face and whispered his name. With what appeared to be a monumental effort he forced his eyes open and stared at her. 'My mouth's so dry,' he rasped. 'Would you pour me some water, please, Trisha?' It was the first time she had heard his voice since the crash, and although it was hoarse and guttural, it confirmed once again that he was alive and that somewhere in this feeble body beat the heart of the man she had married.

She kissed him on the forehead, trying to hide her disappointment at his mistake. 'It's not Trisha, Selwyn, it's Babs.'

'Oh, Babs love, I'm sorry. I thought you were . . .' His voice trailed off, seemingly incapable of completing the sentence.

She poured a glass of water, popped in a straw and bent it at an angle so that Selwyn could drink without lifting his head. She watched his Adam's apple move up and down as he took long gulps, grateful that some muscles at least still worked. 'Wait here a minute,' she said, as he drained the glass.

He managed a weak smile. 'Don't worry, I'm not going anywhere.'

She cursed herself for her crassness as she made her way to the nurses' station. She returned with a warm, damp cloth and gently swabbed away the dried-on spit that had gathered at the corners of his mouth.

'Has it started raining yet?' he asked.

She was relieved to talk about something else, even if it was only the weather. 'We had a short, sharp shower last night, but nothing much really. Nowhere near what we need. It did rain at Lord's the other day, though, and stopped play for fifteen minutes. Everybody in the crowd cheered. And we have a new Minister for Drought, Denis somebody or other, but how on earth he's supposed to make it rain is anybody's guess. There are rumours that scientists have found a way to put ice seeds in the clouds, but that all sounds a bit far-fetched to me. I mean, have you ever heard anything like—'

'Babs.' Selwyn's voice stopped her relentless flow. 'I know what you're doing, love, but we need to talk about what happens next, so can you stop rambling on about the bloody weather?'

She knew he was right but could not keep the indignation out of her reply. 'You started it by asking me if it's rained.'

He closed his eyes again and she watched the shallow rise and fall of his chest. Thank God he was able to breathe without the aid of a machine. She delved into her handbag and brought out a little pot of Vaseline. She scooped her middle finger round inside it and smeared a globule of the jelly over Selwyn's parched, cracked lips. He opened his eyes again and smiled at the face peering down directly above him.

'Thank you, Trisha.'

Babs stamped a kiss on his lips, coating her own with Vaseline in the process. 'I've just told you, Selwyn, it's Babs.'

He seemed to find this funny, and his lips stretched into a thin smile. 'Sorry, Babs. It's the drugs, see.' He took a few laboured gasps before continuing. 'Trisha will leave me now, I expect.'

Babs slumped into the chair beside his bed, suddenly feeling exhausted. 'Don't be ridiculous, Selwyn. That girl loves you as much as you love her.'

He stared resolutely at the ceiling. 'You think she's going to stand by a cripple?'

'Of course,' Babs insisted. 'She's been here all the time since . . . you know . . . since it happened.'

Selwyn scoffed. 'Oh yeah, sure she has. She likes playing the grieving widow, does Trisha, accepting comfort from all those dishy doctors.'

'Selwyn!' cried Babs. 'Stop that. She's not a widow, you're not dead.'

She noticed a tear escape the corner of his eye and soak into the pillow. She had never seen him cry before and knew he would be feeling weak and ashamed, his masculinity eradicated to the point where he couldn't even wipe away his own tears.

She stood up and peered directly into his face. 'You're not dead,' she said again. She gripped both his shoulders and shook him forcefully. The bed squeaked with the motion and the bag of urine swayed from side to side. Her voice cracking with emotion, she managed to say it for a third, emphatic time. 'Selwyn Pryce, you are *not* dead.'

28

Daisy gazed out of the window and smiled as she watched the rain bouncing off the pavement. Heat was still in the air, though, and a fine mist rose from the tarmac, giving the road an ethereal quality. All summer she had longed for the day when the weather would finally break, and now it had. It was just a pity it was August Bank Holiday and Daisy had promised Mikey that she would take him to the Blue Lagoon outdoor swimming pool. It was one of his favourite things to do, but he had not been since his father had passed away. There was no way the worthless Andrea would ever have put herself out for her son. Now that the school holidays were coming to an end, it was going to be one last treat before he had to return to the classroom.

Daisy wrestled with the umbrella she had almost forgotten how to use and navigated her way through the puddles to Mikey's house a few streets away. As she turned the corner into Bagot Street, she could see him in the distance splashing about in the gutter. He shrieked with delight as he leaned his head back and tried to catch the raindrops on his tongue. She called to him, but the rain was so loud he couldn't hear her. The front door was flung open then and Andrea stepped out, yanking her son by his arm, clipping him round the back of his head and pulling him roughly inside.

Daisy quickened her pace, arriving breathlessly at his door a few moments later. She rang the bell and the door was opened immediately by Mikey.

'Hello, Aunt Daisy,' he beamed. 'I'll just get me stuff.'

He ran up the stairs as Andrea came to the door, a cigarette hanging from her lips. Her clothes hung off her scrawny frame and her lank, greasy hair looked as though it had not been washed for a fortnight. She had dark purple circles beneath her eyes, and if Daisy had not known better she would have thought she had been punched in the face. It would have been a stupid man to attempt such an assault, she thought ruefully, and one who no doubt would have come off worse.

Andrea's hands shook as she withdrew the cigarette and let it hang by her side. 'What time you fetchin' him back, then?' She swayed a little and grabbed the door frame to steady herself.

'I'll give him his tea and bring him back after that.'

Andrea took a sharp intake of breath. 'Ooh, any chance you could keep him for the night?'

Whilst Daisy loved having the little boy over to stay, this was his home and he needed to bond with his mum. There was a note of irritation in her reply. 'What, again?'

Andrea immediately took umbrage. 'Oh, leave it then

if it's too much trouble. It's just that I've got some mates coming round and he gets in the way.'

Mikey appeared with a rolled-up towel under his arm. 'Please, Aunt Daisy, I like it at your house.'

Andrea clipped him round the back of the head again. 'There you are, you see, the little bugger prefers yours to mine.'

Daisy sat next to Mikey on the bus and pulled a copy of *Whizzer and Chips* from her string bag. 'Here you are, love. I hope you've not got this one.'

Mikey's eyes scanned the front page, then he pressed the comic into his face and inhaled the fresh inky smell. 'Aww, thank you, Aunt Daisy, this one's my favourite.'

Daisy smiled fondly at the little boy. He was always so grateful for anything she gave him, whether material possessions or affection, and he was certainly starved of the latter.

He stuck out his bottom lip and blew hard through his mouth in order to lift his fringe out of his eyes. Daisy assisted him by smoothing his hair to one side. It was at least a couple of shades lighter than it had been at the start of the summer, and several inches longer.

'Do you think you should get your hair cut before you go back to school?'

He was engrossed in his comic and didn't seem to hear her.

'Mikey, do you want me to take you to the barber's?'

He looked up then and shrugged. 'Dunno, me mum said she was going to do it.'

Daisy was surprised Andrea had even noticed. 'Well, all right then, if you're sure.' She kissed the top of the boy's head and he gently leaned into her. Their relationship had morphed into something resembling that of a mother and son, and Daisy had become incredibly fond of Mikey. Andrea, in one of her more spiteful moments, had accused her of trying to fill the void left by Jerry, but if there was any void to be filled, it was the one left by poor Mikey's neglectful mother. Daisy just wished for his sake that Andrea was more attentive and caring, but as long as she had her fags and her weed she didn't care what happened to him. The poor little soul had lost his beloved father and Andrea really should be making up for that by showering him with love and affection, not palming him off on the first passing stranger. Mikey wasn't stupid, either. He knew only too well that his mother barely tolerated him.

Daisy noticed that he'd placed his comic in his lap and was now staring out of the window.

'What are you thinking, Mikey?' She stroked the back of his head.

He didn't turn round, but merely shrugged. 'Just thinkin' about me dad, that's all.'

'Oh Mikey.'

He turned to face her, his dimpled chin giving away the fact that he was about to cry.

'The last time I went to the BluLa was with him. He showed me how to dive in off the side and I was really scared but I didn't want him to think I was a chicken. Then he took me up on the high diving board but when we got to the top my legs felt funny and we had to walk all the way back down again. I thought he would be cross but he just ruffled my hair and held my hand all the way down.' He took a deep, shuddering breath. 'I wish I'd been able to jump off, Aunt Daisy, then he would have known I was a brave boy.' A large tear spilled down his cheek and he stuck his tongue out to the side to catch it. 'Why did me dad have to die?'

Daisy did not trust herself to speak. Instead she rifled through her handbag and pulled out an embroidered handkerchief. She dabbed her own eyes first before passing it over to Mikey.

She forced a note of encouragement into her voice. 'Tell you what, after our swim, why don't we go and visit your dad's grave in the cemetery?'

He looked doubtful, horrified even, at this suggestion. 'I don't know if I'd like that. It would be too spooky for me.'

'Well it's up to you, Mikey, but I think it would help you to see his final resting place again, and you could talk to him there.'

'Talk to him? Would he be able to hear me?'

Daisy nodded. 'Yes, I believe he would.'

He still looked doubtful. 'You'd stay close to me, though, wouldn't you, Aunt Daisy?'

She managed a small smile. 'I'll always stay close to you, Mikey, for as long as you need me.'

The weather had not put too much of a dampener on the afternoon; in fact, quite the opposite. It had been so long since the country had seen any rain that it was something of a novelty. The water at the Blue Lagoon was always freezing anyway, and it had taken quite a bit of persuading by Mikey before Daisy was able to descend the steps into the curiously green-coloured pool. Once she was immersed up to her neck, the cold snatched her breath away and she could well understand why Mikey's lips had turned blue. Her hair was itchy beneath the bright pink rubber swimming cap, and she wrinkled her nose in disgust as she scooped away a used plaster and a clump of hair from the surface of the water just in front of her face. Mikey had cheered up, though, and that was all that mattered to Daisy. She could endure swimming in this bacterial soup as long as he was happy.

Later, as they walked hand in hand through the cemetery gates, each clutching a 99, the sun decided to show its face once more. It was low in the sky now and it shone through the wet leaves of the trees, making them glisten. The day felt fresh and clean, as though it had been through a wash cycle and was now waiting to dry.

Mikey had bitten the end off his cone so that the melted ice cream had run down the inside and was now making its way down his wrist. Daisy pulled out her trusty handkerchief once more. 'Come here, you little rascal, you can't talk to your dad looking like that.'

Mikey allowed her to clean him up and popped the rest of the cone into his mouth. They had reached Karl's grave and Daisy put down her bags. 'I'll just be on that bench over there. You take your time.' She handed him the bunch of roses they had purchased at the cemetery gates. 'Be careful of the thorns now.'

She lowered herself on to the bench and watched as Mikey knelt down in front of his father's grave. She noticed that the soles of his trainers were almost worn through and made a mental note to buy him a new pair. He turned round and looked at her, puzzlement creasing his features.

'Go on, talk to him,' urged Daisy. She continued to watch as he gingerly laid the flowers on top of the grave. His voice was small and almost inaudible, but Daisy could just about make out the words.

'Hi, Dad,' he began. 'I've just been to the BluLa with Mrs Duggan, but I call her Aunt Daisy now. She's been kind to me since you . . . since . . . well, you know . . . since the crash.' He turned to look at Daisy again, and she nodded her encouragement.

'I don't know why you had to die, Dad. I've asked lots of people but nobody knows. Anyway, I climbed up to the top of the diving board today and this time I jumped off. I hope you were watching me and you think I'm brave. I'm sorry I couldn't do it last time.'

He stood up and traced the letters of Karl's name on the headstone with his fingers. Daisy noticed that the boy's shoulders were shaking, and she could hear his muffled sobs, but she let him be. He needed this time with his father. She got the feeling he was used to stifling his emotions at home. Eventually he took two steps back and paused one last time.

'I miss you, Daddy,' he said.

29

For the first time in weeks, Daisy was woken by the sound of her Teasmade. All summer she had tossed around on sticky sheets, unable to sleep in the empty house and always awake long before the machine started its gurgling and hissing. This morning felt different, though; her sheets were dry and a cool autumnal breeze wafted in through the open window. She was due for her shift at Fine Fare later, but she had offered to walk Mikey to school on his first day back. He was a resilient little lad all told, but the summer holidays, which had begun so promisingly for him, had ended in tragedy, and Daisy felt that today he could use a little extra support.

She pulled her tabard on over her head and stuffed her purse and keys into the front pocket before hurrying to Mikey's. When he opened the door, she took a startled step backwards.

'What in God's name have you done to your hair, Mikey?'

His bottom lip came out and Daisy immediately regretted her accusatory tone.

He ran his fingers back and forth over the stubble on

the top of his head. 'Me mum did it. She was only going to cut it at first, but then she found some crawly things so she said it all had to come off.'

Daisy pursed her lips. 'Did she now? Where is she?'

'Still in bed.'

Daisy pushed her way into the hallway and called up the stairs. 'Andrea, get yourself down here now.'

'It's no good, Aunt Daisy,' interjected Mikey. 'I tried to wake her before, but she's fast asleep.'

An uneasy feeling began to gnaw away at Daisy's insides. 'Wait here,' she commanded.

She took the stairs two at a time, arriving at Andrea's bedside moments later; it only took a few seconds more to establish the cause of the younger woman's apparent stupor. Eight empty cider cans had been discarded at the end of the bed, along with a vodka bottle that had been drained almost to the bottom. Daisy looked at the pathetic figure lying in the bed, the scrawny naked body tangled up in the grubby candy-striped sheets. She felt for a pulse and was almost disappointed to find one. 'Oh Andrea, you don't deserve that little kid, and he certainly doesn't deserve you.'

Mikey was sitting patiently on the bottom stair, chewing his thumbnail.

'Come on, love, your mum's still sleeping. Let's get you off to school. Have you got everything?'

He looked down at his scuffed shoes and Daisy tilted his chin with her forefinger so she could see his face. 'Mikey?'

His cheeks coloured a little and he looked away. 'She forgot to give me any dinner money.'

Daisy rummaged in the pocket of her tabard and pulled out some coins. He held out his hand like a Victorian street urchin begging in the street for a few measly crumbs.

At the school gates, Daisy stopped and let go of Mikey's hand. He'd been quiet all the way and Daisy had not been able to engage him in the usual chat. 'Do you want me to come in with you?'

He looked mildly horrified at this suggestion. 'No thank you, Aunt Daisy. I'm in Class Two now. I would look a right baby.'

He repositioned his satchel on his shoulders and without a backwards glance went through the gates, joining a circle of boys who were already engaged in the serious business of trading cigarette cards.

'I'll be back to collect you later, Mikey.'

He turned round and gave her a half-hearted wave, and Daisy hoped she had not embarrassed him. Of course he could walk home on his own – she was sure he had done it many times – but she had an overwhelming need to protect him. She was due for her shift at the hospital at five, so she would have just enough time to collect Mikey, give him some milk and a biscuit and return him to his mother before her labours would begin again. Her two jobs and the constant interaction with people had kept her spirits up over the summer. It would have been easy for her to descend into an all-consuming depression; it had almost happened once before when she had lost Jim, but back then she'd had little Jerry to care for, and he had given her a purpose, a reason to get out of bed in the morning. She might have been widowed but she'd still been a mother, she'd told herself. Now that she was alone, she realised Mikey was fulfilling the same role that Jerry had all those years ago, and she knew she needed Mikey as much as he needed her.

As she began her journey to the supermarket, she found herself walking behind a mother with a newborn baby in a pram. Her thoughts turned, as they so often did, to the baby they had left behind in Blackpool, and once again she speculated on what had become of her. There was little doubt that her brief life would have been snuffed out on the tarmac of the motorway had Daisy not abandoned . . . no, she chastised herself, not abandoned, *carefully placed* her on the doorstep of that guest house. She could have no regrets about her actions, she told herself. At least the child had a chance of life now, and that was surely for the best.

At 3.15, Mikey trotted through the school gates and thrust a painting in Daisy's direction.

'Careful, it's still wet,' he warned.

Daisy held it flat to avoid the paint dripping. 'It's beautiful, Mikey, you're so clever.'

He beamed up at her. 'It's of me and me dad on his bike. Look, that's me sat behind him on the back.'

Mikey had depicted Karl's face with two dots for eyes, and a deep semicircle representing a huge grin. Daisy felt unwelcome tears begin to prick. 'Your dad looks happy there, Mikey.'

Mikey's tone was matter-of-fact. 'Well, he's on his bike, isn't he? He was always happy on his bike. He was going to teach me to ride it one day.' It was said without bitterness or melancholy, and Daisy allowed herself to believe for a second that Mikey was going to be all right.

She glanced at his stained shirt. 'Look at the state of you with your dinner medals.'

'Me what?'

'Those food stains all down your shirt; dinner medals, we used to call them.' She wiped at them with her handkerchief. 'It's no good, I'll have to sponge them off properly when we get home.'

He skipped along beside her as they made their way home. 'Aunt Daisy?'

'Yes, love.'

'Will you be able to help me back my books?'

'Come again?'

'The teacher says we've to back our books in wallpaper to keep them nice. Me dad did it for me last year, so I don't know how to do it.'

'Ooh, I remember Jerry doing that. Of course, he was very good at it. He used to get the ruler out and measure everything so it was all perfect.' She looked down at Mikey. 'We'll work out how to do it together, eh? I've got some old Anaglypta somewhere that should do the trick. I'm not sure we'll have time today, though. I've got to be at work by five. Perhaps we can do it at the weekend.'

He stopped walking and his bottom lip came out. 'Am I not staying at yours for tea then, Aunt Daisy?'

'Not tonight, Mikey, I'm afraid, but I'm sure your mum will make you something nice. I gave her the recipe for my shepherd's pie the other day; perhaps she'll make that.' She pinched his cheek playfully and smiled down at him. 'Cheer up, lad. If you don't put that lip back in, all the birdies will come and sit on it.'

Mikey thought only naughty boys were sent to bed without any tea, and he struggled to imagine what he might have done to deserve such punishment. He'd had his milk and biscuits at Aunt Daisy's earlier, but he was still hungry – he nearly always was – and it was a good job he'd managed to force down his school dinner of lamb hotpot, though it wasn't like the one Aunt Daisy made. Hers didn't have globules of fatty meat in it that you had to chew for half an hour before they would go down. Lying on his bed now, however, his stomach rumbled at the thought of that watery stew with the doughy dumplings bobbing around in it. It wasn't as if he expected a delicious home-cooked meal when he got back from school – he wasn't that stupid – but his mother did usually manage to cobble together something edible. Sometimes she even pushed the boat out and heated up a Fray Bentos.

She didn't eat herself, of course. The only thing Mikey ever saw her put in her mouth was a cigarette. She sometimes rolled her own, and Mikey was fascinated by the way she sprinkled the strands of tobacco on the little bit of white paper, rolled it into a thin sausage and pinched it between her lips, all with one hand. It was quite a skill, he thought. Even his dad had had to use both hands.

He could hear her now clattering round in the kitchen, cursing as she slammed the cupboard doors. Something had obviously upset her and he was grateful for the sanctuary of his little bedroom. She hollered up the stairs, her voice rasping, 'Mikey, I'm just going to the offie, I'm out of cider.' She made it sound as though cider was a food staple, but maybe to his mother it was. He heard her open the front door before she added, 'You can come down now, I think you've had enough time to think. I'll pick you up a can of beans if you like.'

Mikey wasn't sure what he was supposed to have been thinking about, but he slipped out of bed and went downstairs to the kitchen, his bare feet sticking to the greasy lino. He opened the bread bin and pulled out the last slice; only the crust, complete with dots of blue mould. He picked them off, then stuffed the dry bread into his mouth. He wandered into the lounge and was surprised to see that his mum had made a fire. He couldn't imagine why she would need one on what was actually a rather mild evening, but she did seem to feel the cold. Typically, she had neglected to put the fireguard in place, so Mikey manoeuvred it into position, even though the hearth rug was already peppered with scorch marks.

It was well over an hour before she returned, looking bedraggled and unsteady on her feet, a bottle of cider tucked under each arm. She gave off a sickly-sweet smell that reminded him of Aunt Daisy's warm compost heap after she had tipped on the grass cuttings.

'Oh good, you've kept the fire going.' She knelt in front of it and unscrewed the bottle, taking a long gulp before offering it to Mikey. 'D'ya want a swig?'

Mikey shook his head. 'No thank you, I'm only six.'

She frowned at him as though this was news to her.

His stomach growled 'Did you get me beans?'

'What? Oh, bloody hell, no, I forgot.' She opened her little tin of tobacco. 'There's bread in the bread bin, have some of that.'

'I'm all right.'

'Suit yourself.'

Mikey climbed down off his chair and rummaged in the sideboard. He pulled out the old photo album and prised the pages apart.

'What yer doin' now?' slurred Andrea.

'I want to look at the photos of me dad.'

Andrea groaned and lay flat on her back on the hearth rug. 'Not this again. You need to get over it, Mikey. Your dad's gone.'

'I know that, but I like looking at him.' He studied a photo of Karl wearing a white cheesecloth shirt and black leather trousers, his foot up on a chair as he strummed away on his guitar, concentration etched on his face. 'He was going to teach me how to play the guitar. He was brilliant at it, he was.' He looked over at his mother for confirmation. 'My daddy could do anything, couldn't he?'

Andrea blew out a cloud of smoke 'Oh aye, he could do no wrong, your dad, he was bloody perfect.' She propped herself up on her elbows. 'Come 'ere.'

He knelt down beside her on the rug and she took the album off him. 'Shift that fireguard.'

The first stirrings of dread began to fill his empty tummy. Andrea peeled back the cellophane and took out the first photo. It was one of Karl holding Mikey as a baby. As he cradled his son, he beamed directly into the lens of the camera.

Andrea gave it a cursory glance, scoffed and then tossed it into the fire.

Mikey screamed. 'No, Mummy, please.'

The flames roared into life and licked at the image of his father, eating away first at his legs, then at little Mikey's sleeping form, until finally Karl's smiling face melted away.

By the time the last photo had been engulfed by the flames, Mikey's sobs had subsided, but his eyes remained puffy and his sleeve was streaked with snot and tears. Andrea slammed the empty album shut, the loud thwack making him jump. 'There, all gone.' She looked at Mikey's blotchy face. 'Oh, stop snivelling and go and make us a brew.'

By the time he returned with the tea, she was flat on her back again, one arm slung over her eyes. The scalding-hot mug wobbled in his hands as he held it above her. He thought about what she had just done. There were no photos left of his dad now, and Mikey would never get to see his face again. He tilted the mug so that a spot of hot tea dripped over the edge and landed on Andrea's chest. Just one flick of his wrist and the whole lot would pour out in a scalding torrent, melting her skin just like the flames had melted the photos. But Mikey knew he was better than that, and if his dad was watching him from somewhere, he would be disappointed in him. He bent down and placed the mug on the tiled hearth. By the time she woke up it would be stone cold. It would serve her right.

He trudged upstairs, flung himself on his bed and squeezed his eyes shut. He was relieved to find he could still see his dad in his mind's eye, a place his mother would never be able to reach. It was all he had left now and it would just have to be enough.

30

Christmas was usually Trisha's favourite time of year, a chance to indulge in a tipple of advocaat and lemonade garnished with a cocktail cherry on a little plastic sword balanced across the rim of the glass. She loved to hang a stocking for herself and Selwyn over the fireplace in the snug and leave a mince pie and a tot of whisky out for Father Christmas. At twenty-six years of age she knew it was ridiculous, but she'd wanted to keep up the traditions for when she and Selwyn had a baby of their own. Everything had changed now, though: there would be no baby and nothing was ever going to be the same again.

She was perched on a stepladder arranging silver tinsel around the picture frames and adding a sprig of holly to each when Barbara came downstairs.

'You're up early this morning, Trisha.'

At the sound of Barbara's voice, she wobbled on the top step and grasped the handle to steady herself. 'Bloody hell, Barbara, you frightened me to death.'

'Sorry, here, let me give you a hand.' She rummaged in the box of decorations and pulled out a paper chain. 'Oh look, our Lorraine made this in junior school.'

Trisha regarded the rather battered-looking effort. 'It's seen better days.'

Babs thrust it back into the box. 'You're right, time to throw it out maybe.'

'You could take it to Selwyn; put it up in his room. Be nice for him to have something to remind him of home.'

'Ah, that's a kind thought, Trisha.' She hesitated for a second. 'Er, perhaps you could take it this afternoon?'

Trisha busied herself with the decorations, not turning to look at Babs. 'I'm not going,' she replied flatly.

'Oh Trisha, please. He keeps asking for you. You've not been for days now.'

Trisha descended the steps and brushed past Babs as she picked up a duster and began to polish the bar with a vigour Babs would normally have approved of.

'You can take it, Barbara. It's you he wants to see anyway, not me.'

'You know that's not true. It just suits you to believe it, that's all.'

Selwyn was still in the spinal unit, and progress had been slow. He had not yet been lifted out of the bed, remaining flat on his back ever since that dreadful night in July. Every attempt to ease him into a sitting position had resulted in him feeling faint or throwing up. The bathing and toilet routine he had to endure, the endless rounds of bed-ridden physiotherapy, the pity in the eyes of the doctors and nurses had all served to erode his dignity, until all that remained was a shadow of the person he used to be.

'You're much better with him than I am, Barbara. I've seen the way you talk to him and keep his spirits up, as though everything's going to be all right.' She put down the duster and reached for a glass.

'It's only eight o'clock, Trisha, I'm not sure that's the answer.' Babs's disapproving tone only made Trisha more determined.

She took a swig of gin. 'Tell me then, Barbara, what *is* the answer, because I'm buggered if I know.'

'We just have to treat him the same as we've always done. True, his life is different now, but he didn't die, Trisha, and he still deserves to live the best life we can give him.'

Trisha picked up her tin of Brasso. 'I need more time, Barbara, I'm sorry.' She nodded towards the fireplace. 'Now, I'm going to make a start on them horse brasses.'

Babs left her to it and went into the kitchen to try and force down some breakfast. Her appetite was not what it used to be; she'd lost weight in the five months since the crash and her face held a careworn expression that still shocked her every time she looked in the mirror.

Lorraine popped her head round the door. 'I'm off to work now, Mum. See you later.' She kissed Babs on the cheek and slung her patchwork shoulder bag over her arm. 'By the way,' she added, 'I'm going to see Petula's dad on the way home, so I'll be a bit late.'

The mention of Petula always caused Babs to feel a frisson of foreboding. 'You're going to see Ralph?'

'Yes, he said he's got something for me. He's still not back at work, so I'll pop round on my way home. It's probably a small Christmas present or something.'

Lorraine had always had a soft spot for Ralph Honeywell. His overprotective ways had definitely driven Petula mad, but he was kind and thoughtful and had put his daughter at the centre of his universe. How Petula's mother could have walked out on such a close-knit family unit remained a mystery to Lorraine to this day. The evil cow had not even bothered to show up at Petula's funeral, and Lorraine would never forget how crushed Ralph had been when all she did was send a card expressing sympathy for his loss. *His* loss. As though it was nothing to do with her.

It was dark by the time Lorraine arrived at Ralph's, and the lounge curtains were drawn. She squeezed down the ginnel at the side of the house first in order to see Nibbles in the back garden. The rabbit climbed up at the mesh on his hutch when he saw Lorraine. She stuck her fingers through the holes and stroked his velvet nose. 'How are ya, big fella?' His pink eyes stood out like jewels against his white fur. She was pleased to note that the hutch was as fresh and clean as always, and he had a huge ball of straw to snuggle up in on this cold winter's night.

The front door was ajar, but Lorraine felt it was polite to ring the bell anyway. It was one of those that played a little jingle that seemed to go on for ever. When there was no answer, she pushed the door open and called into the hallway. 'Ralph, are you there? I rang the bell, but you mustn't . . .'

She stopped as she noticed a fat brown envelope on the hall stand. Her name was written on it in thick black felt-tip pen. She prodded the envelope all over and decided it contained a book. How kind of him to think of her at what must be a tough time of year for him.

Feeling like an intruder, she made her way along the hallway and into the kitchen. Ralph was evidently in the middle of cooking tea. The pressure cooker was on the stove and Lorraine recognised the smell of Petula's favourite hash. A jar of red cabbage stood on the side, its bright purple juice making a ring on the Formica. She pushed the door to the dining room open and heard the crackle of the record player as it scratched its way round the twelve-inch single, the music having long since stopped. She lifted the arm and replaced it in its cradle, then looked at the label on the record: 'I Couldn't Live Without Your Love'. Ralph had been playing his favourite song by Petula's namesake.

'Ralph,' she called out again. 'It's Lorraine, where are you?'

She returned to the hall and shouted up the stairs. Her patience wearing a little thin, she clutched the newel post and put her foot on the bottom stair ready to ascend. That was when she saw him. Or at least she saw the soles of his tartan carpet slippers, as his lifeless body swayed from the banister above her.

31

There hadn't seemed any point in splashing out on a turkey, so Daisy's Christmas dinner was not much different from her usual Sunday lunch. She bought a small chicken and some sausagemeat from the butcher's to make a nice stuffing. She planned to make some proper gravy too, maybe even adding a dash of port. There would be plenty of meat left over for her Boxing Day sandwich. She'd seen a recipe in her *Woman's Weekly* that involved drizzling honey over parsnips, and although it all sounded a bit odd to her she thought she'd give it a go, even though she imagined the roasting tin would be a bugger to clean afterwards.

She had desperately wanted Mikey to stay over on Christmas Eve so she could spoil him the next morning, but he was worried that Father Christmas would not be able to find him if he wasn't at home, so Daisy had promised to call round at his house and see him on Christmas morning. She'd already given Andrea his presents, and even though she was disappointed she wouldn't be able to see him open them, she had to respect the little boy's feelings. The first Christmas without his dad was bound to be tough.

She basted the chicken once more and turned the gas down low before donning her fur-trimmed hat and coat and making her way to Mikey's. Although there had been no snow, the weather was bright and the heavy frost that adorned the branches of the trees gave the day a certain Christmas-card quality. A robin pecked away at the ice in the bird bath, and long icicles hung like stalactites from the crack in the guttering.

She and Jerry had always had a drink in the Taverners on Christmas morning, whilst their turkey was roasting in the oven. Selwyn used to be especially jovial at this time of year, handing out free hot toddies and home-made mince pies to his customers. Even Trisha had embraced the tradition, and everyone overlooked the fact that her pastry was not a patch on Babs's and devoured the lardy offerings with feigned enthusiasm.

As Daisy turned into Bagot Street, she saw a group of children playing with their new toys. They were cosily wrapped up in new mittens and scarves, their faces glowing with the cold and their shrieks of excitement piercing the stillness of the morning air. She screwed up her eyes and tried to make out if Mikey was among them; she was saddened to see that he was not. One lad had obviously received a brand-new Chopper and was racing up and down the street showing off to his friends by doing wheelies. Mikey had always wanted a Chopper. His dad had said he was a bit too young but promised to buy him one when he was older. That job would now fall to somebody else.

Daisy did not want to knock on Mikey's door with sadness etched on her face, so she took a few moments to compose herself. After a few sharp raps, Mikey pulled the door open. He was still dressed in his pyjamas, a milk moustache on his top lip and his eyes red and swollen. He dangled Galen, his stuffed monkey, by his side.

'Happy Christmas, Mikey.' Daisy embraced the boy and kissed him on the top of his head, then held him at arm's length and scrutinised his face. 'Whatever's the matter? Have you been crying?'

Mikey nodded and swallowed hard. 'He didn't come,' he whispered.

'What? Who didn't come? What are you talking about? Oh no, you don't mean . . .' She pushed past Mikey and went into the lounge. His pitiful stocking was still hanging over the fireplace, completely empty. The pathetic Christmas tree, almost devoid of needles, nestled in the corner, with not a single present under it.

Daisy quelled the anger that was beginning to rise. 'Where's your mum?'

Mikey shrugged. 'Dunno. She was here when I went to bed, but then I heard her go out.'

'Please don't tell me you've been on yer tod all night?'

Mikey ignored the question. 'He didn't drink his milk, or eat his mince pie, and I used my own dinner money to buy the pie. Biffer was selling them in the playground on the day we broke up.' He pulled back the grubby net curtain and pointed at the children playing in the street.

'Looks like he did come, just not to my house. It must be because I've been naughty, like Mum's always telling me.'

'Mikey, you've not been naughty, don't be so silly.'

'Then why didn't he bring me any presents?'

Daisy had no immediate answer that would reassure him, but was determined to find out what possible excuse Andrea could have had for disappointing her only son on his first Christmas morning since losing his father. The whole thing beggared belief. 'I'm just popping upstairs for a second, Mikey. Wait here, will you?'

She was so incensed it was difficult to regulate her breathing. Andrea's bed had obviously been slept in, but as Daisy didn't think she was the type of person to make her bed every day, this was not conclusive evidence that she had slept in it last night. The ashtray on the bedside cabinet was overflowing, and two teacups were cemented to the surface, a grey mould covering the dregs.

Daisy began to go through the drawers; carefully at first, but then as her anger overflowed she recklessly pulled out Andrea's clothes and abandoned them in a heap on the floor. She eventually found what she was looking for on the top shelf of the wardrobe: the presents she had bought for Mikey that Andrea was supposed to have left under the tree. She tucked them under her arm and called out to him.

'Mikey, come upstairs now and we'll get you dressed. I'm taking you back to my house.'

By the time they had eaten their Christmas dinner, Mikey was in much better spirits. His hair had grown back since Andrea's hatchet job and the flimsy paper hat he wore kept slipping down over his eyes. He was especially pleased with the presents Daisy had bought him.

'Can we have a game of Buckaroo now, Aunt Daisy?'

'Of course we can, love.' She stood up to clear the plates away. 'Let's just listen to the Queen first, and then we'll play.'

Mikey scrambled down from his chair and carried his plate into the kitchen. He looked smart in the new jumper she'd knitted him. He'd chosen the pale blue wool himself and had spent ages going through the button box at Mrs Penny's wool shop before selecting three in the shape of little red postboxes in honour of his dad's job as a postman.

As the Queen's speech drew to a close, Mikey opened the Buckaroo and began to set it up on the coffee table in front of the fire. Daisy refilled her glass of sweet sherry and put her slippered feet up on the pouffe. It felt good to have a little kid in the house again at Christmas, and Mikey was so grateful for even the tiniest of things. She wished she could scoop him up and take him away somewhere his mother would never be able to hurt him again. Not that Andrea was violent towards him – Daisy would never have stood for that – but she was so wrapped up in her own squalid world that she didn't seem to notice her only son half the time. Mikey craved his mother's attention and her approval; any minute gesture of kindness on Andrea's part was seized upon by the little boy and seemed to keep him going for days.

Daisy proved to be hopeless at the game she'd bought Mikey. Every time she placed a piece of tackle on the stubborn mule, it kicked its back legs and sent Mikey into hysterics. It was worth losing just to hear his infectious laugh.

'Would you like to choose a chocolate off the tree, Mikey?' asked Daisy, after their twelfth game. 'Then perhaps we could play something else. What about draughts? My Jerry used to love a game of draughts. I could never beat him, though,' she chuckled.

'Yes please, Aunt Daisy, but you'll have to teach me first.'

'Ooh, a bright lad like you will pick it up in no time.'

He wandered over to the tree and picked his chocolate out with the same care and attention he had applied to choosing his buttons.

'Take as many as you'd like, Mikey. It is Christmas, after all.'

'Really?' He clutched a small handful as though they were the Crown Jewels and sat cross-legged in front of the fire as he unwrapped his booty one by one.

At the unwelcome interruption from the doorbell,

Daisy heaved herself out of her chair and found Andrea on the doorstep. Her hair appeared to have been washed for once but was frazzled at the ends, with long dark roots showing through. Her blue eyes contrasted with her sallow complexion and she had a huge cold sore on her top lip. She bounced on the balls of her feet as she fidgeted with her hair. 'He is here, I take it?'

Daisy caught a whiff of stale alcohol and pursed her lips. 'You mean Mikey?'

Andrea barged past, flattening Daisy against the wall. 'Come in, why don't you?'

Mikey looked up from his chocolate hoard as his mother burst into the room. 'Mummy, you're back. Where've you been?'

Andrea looked across at Daisy. 'Er . . . I've been to see a friend and I got . . . delayed.' She shrugged as she held out her hand. Mikey allowed her to pull him to his feet and then hugged her round her waist. She didn't return the show of affection but merely patted him on the head. 'Don't get soppy now, kid. I've been sorting out your present, actually.'

Mikey looked up at her, his furrowed brow displaying his disbelief.

'What? Don't look at me like that. Come on, it's outside.'

Daisy followed them out into the street. There, parked on the pavement, its handlebars at a jaunty angle, was the Chopper Mikey had coveted for so long. He screwed his eyes shut then opened them again, as though he could not believe what he was seeing. Andrea stood with her hands on her bony hips; she obviously considered herself a candidate for Mother of the Year.

'Well?'

'Is this for me?'

'No, it's for Daisy.' She cast a glance skywards. 'Of course it's for you, you daft 'apeth.' She took hold of the handlebars and flicked the stand up with her foot. 'Hop on, then.'

Mikey straddled the seat, but his feet would not touch the ground. 'I'm a bit too small.'

'Are you sure he's old enough for one of those, Andrea? I mean, he's not yet seven,' Daisy interjected.

Andrea glared at her. 'I know how old my son is, thank you very much.' She turned to Mikey. 'You'll grow into it, and we'll get Bill next door to lower the seat. Come on now, let's go home.' She lifted Mikey on to the seat and began to push him along the pavement.

'Mum, this is the best present I've ever had and you are the best mum in the whole wide world.'

Andrea cast a smug look over her shoulder. 'You see, he's chuffed to little mint balls, he is.'

Daisy called after him, but he was so wrapped up in his new present he didn't seem to hear her. She raised her arm and waved. 'Be careful, Mikey. I'll see you tomorrow.' He didn't turn round, but she remained on the pavement staring after them until they disappeared round the corner. 'Happy Christmas, love,' she whispered.

Alone in the living room, she began to pack away the Buckaroo. Christmas had not been so bad after all, but now, as the silence enveloped her, she was overcome with sadness. She thought she heard a sound then, coming from the kitchen, a clattering of china, and she looked towards the door, half expecting Jerry to pop his head round, offering her a cup of tea. Then she remembered, and as the self-indulgent tears threatened to spill over, she could think of no reason to hold them back.

32

Even with the lingering smell of turkey pervading the air and tinsel taped to the window frames, the hospital was a depressing place at this time of year. Trisha nodded to the nurses gathered at their station and felt a momentary spark of sympathy that they'd had to spend their Christmas Day in this godforsaken place. She stuck her head round Selwyn's door and prayed for the soft, shallow breathing that would tell her he was asleep and she would not have to endure another round of pointless, stilted conversation. Barbara and Lorraine had already been to visit him this afternoon, and now she had run out of excuses not to come and see him. It was her turn to play the dutiful, loyal wife.

As she tiptoed towards the bed, she caught her toe on one of the wheels. Reaching out to steady herself, she sent his water glass crashing to the floor. So much for a stealthy entry.

Selwyn lay flat on his back. 'Who's there?'

Trisha peered down at his face and smoothed her hand over his brow. 'It's me, Trisha.' She knew she should kiss his clammy forehead or – God forbid – his cracked lips, but she did not have the stomach for it. In the five months he had lain in this bed, he had not seen the light of day, and his skin was now thin and papery, the blue vein in his temple snaking its way into his mop of unruly hair, which nobody had bothered to trim.

At the sound of her voice, his face instantly changed from a mask of confusion to one of delight. 'Trisha, you came,' he croaked.

She sat down next to the bed and placed her handbag on her knee. She did not intend to stop long. 'Of course I came. Nothing would keep me from seeing you on Christmas Day, Selwyn.' Her words were spoken with a hollowness she could not be bothered to disguise. She wanted to love him, but in spite of what Barbara said, he just wasn't the same man she'd married. *In sickness and in health*. Whoever had thought that one up had clearly never been on a spinal injuries ward.

'Come and sit up on the bed, where I can see you.'

Trisha gave an involuntary shudder and reluctantly squeezed on to the bed next to his inert body.

'In my locker,' he breathed. 'There's something for you.'

She bent down and retrieved a small red foil-wrapped package with a white satin bow taped to the top. 'What's this, Selwyn?'

'Happy Christmas, love.'

She fingered the bow and picked at the Sellotape, gently easing the paper off. Inside was an exquisite gold heart-shaped locket, one that she had admired back in the summer and had coveted ever since. Selwyn had had it engraved on the back with the words *Trisha, you are the light of my life. Forever yours, Selwyn.*

She held the necklace up to the light and let the chain fall through her fingers. 'It's really beautiful, Selwyn, but how did you manage . . .'

'Babs got it for me. I'm so sorry, but there was no one else to ask.'

For a fleeting second, Trisha considered how painful that must have been for Barbara. Steeling herself, she stood up and leaned over the bed. She lowered her lips towards Selwyn's and allowed them to touch for the briefest moment. He parted his lips and tried to lift his head towards hers, but she recoiled from the stale smell of his breath and withdrew with barely concealed disgust.

'Thank you, Selwyn. I'll treasure it always.' She stuffed the necklace back into its box and thrust it into her handbag. 'Now, I really must be going.'

'What, already? You've only just got here. We need to talk about things. About what happens when I'm discharged.'

The thought of sharing her bed again with this old man who could no longer walk or control his bodily functions was abhorrent to her. However hard it would be for him to hear, it was time. 'I'm sorry, Selwyn. I can't do it. I'm no good for you.' After keeping her true feelings to herself for so long, she suddenly found she could no longer hold back. 'I know you'll think I'm a shallow, callous cow, but there's no point pretending. I'm not like Barbara, I can't love you like this.'

'Trisha,' he pleaded. 'You're still getting used to the idea. You'll come round, I know . . .'

'It's been five months, Selwyn. I'm not going to change my mind now. All our plans have gone out of the window. I'm only twenty-six. I can't be saddled with a man who cannot give me what I need.' She tried to soften her harsh tone. 'Look, I'm just being honest with you. It's the least you deserve. You never should've left Barbara. You two were meant to be together; you know it, she knows it, the whole damn pub knows it.' She gestured at his ramrod-straight horizontal body, like a grotesque mannequin unmoved since the night of the accident. 'The goalposts have shifted too far for me, Selwyn.' She picked up her bag and headed towards the door, pausing only briefly to take one last look at his helpless form. 'I'm sorry,' she whispered.

'Wait, Trisha, please don't go. I do still love you.'

His impassioned words failed to move her, and it was at that moment that she knew for certain there was no going back. Barbara was welcome to him.

33

It might have had something to do with the Babycham going to her head, or the reflective mood Christmas had put her in, or perhaps a combination of the two, but as Lorraine lay in her bed that Christmas night, she decided the time had come to read Petula's diary. She had already read the note Ralph had slipped inside the envelope.

I want you to have this diary, Lorraine. It's up to you whether or not you read it, but I didn't want it to fall into the wrong hands when I'm gone. I have no doubt that Petula's mother will come sniffing round afterwards to see what she can plunder. Thank you for being a good friend to my Petula. There's nothing left for me here now, so I'm going to say goodbye. I'm sorry you had to find me.

Look after yourself, Lorraine.

Sincerely, Ralph Honeywell

Her initial horror at finding Ralph's body had dissipated a little when she'd read the note. His final words before he'd climbed the stairs to end his life had been addressed to her, and tragic though it was, she regarded it now as an honour and a privilege.

She pulled the diary out from under her pillow and caressed the blue velour cover. She'd been with Petula the day she'd bought it down the market, and they had both been in hysterics when they'd read the gold-embossed words on the front. *Five-Year Dairy. 1975–1980*. The scruffy, black-fingernailed bloke running the stall had not been amused. 'What's so funny?'

Lorraine had managed to stop laughing just long enough to point out the mistake. 'Look, it says "Dairy" instead of "Diary".'

He shrugged. 'So? Do you want it or not?'

An old lady, almost bent double, had shuffled up beside them and peered at the diary closely. 'I'll take one,' she said.

Lorraine and Petula glanced at each other. 'Five years? Optimistic or what?' Petula had sniggered.

Lorraine smiled ruefully at the memory. How ironic that it was Petula who had only lived another eighteen months before her life was so tragically cut short. The old lady was probably still going strong.

There was a small brass lock on the side of the diary, but it was flimsy, and a quick jemmy with a butter knife was all it took for the pages to spring open and reveal Petula's innermost thoughts.

Lorraine thrust the diary under the covers as her mother poked her head round the door. 'Night, love,' Babs trilled. 'Trisha's still not back from the hospital, you know.' She pushed up the sleeve of her dressing gown and peered at her watch. 'It's gone eleven, what do you think that means?'

Lorraine sighed and pulled the candlewick bedspread up round her chin. 'I don't know, Mum, but she can't still be at the hospital, can she? They kick you out at eight.'

Babs drilled her fingernails on the door frame. 'Mmm, that's what I thought. I hope she's not had a tragic accident and is lying in a ditch somewhere.'

Lorraine caught the slight smile that played on Babs's lips. 'Mum, you're wicked!'

With her mother safely out of the way, Lorraine opened the diary and started at the beginning. She pressed the pages to her nose; they were ingrained with the familiar smell of Petula's house, a curious mix of patchouli oil and stale biscuits. It soon transpired that Petula had a disappointing habit of recording the minutiae of her life, and Lorraine felt a sense of guilt that she found her friend's ramblings so boring. By the time she'd reached March 1975, she was having trouble keeping her eyes open, and it was only at the mention of her own name that she became alert again. It appeared that the two of them had had some sort of argument that was all Lorraine's fault, obviously, and Petula was considering whether their friendship was worth continuing with.

*Lorraine can be such a pain sometimes.
I don't know why we bother staying
friends. I think we see too much
of each other. We sit next to each
other in the typing pool, her endless
chattering competing with the sound
of the typewriters, and it drives me
mad. My shorthand is coming on,
though, so hopefully I'll be transferred
out of that rat hole to an office of
my own. Oh, and the other day she
borrowed my David Cassidy record and
she gave it back scratched and covered
in nylon carpet fluff!*

Lorraine laid the diary down and stared at the ceiling. She closed her eyes and tried to think what she could possibly have done to incur Petula's wrath. It was mildly annoying that Petula had had the last word and Lorraine was not able to defend herself. As for the David Cassidy record, it'd had a bloody great scratch on it *before* Petula lent it to her.

She picked up the diary again and flicked through a few more entries, relieved to read that by April Petula considered they were friends again. Many happy nights in the Taverners had been recorded, with Trisha sneaking them drinks when Selwyn wasn't looking, as well as the time they got caught stealing pick 'n' mix from Woolies. They'd run down the street clutching their haul, with the spotty young shop assistant chasing after them in his new plat-form heels. Lorraine smiled to herself at the memory, but her heart was heavy with sorrow that they would share no more such escapades. Reading her friend's words only confirmed just how much she was going to miss her.

It was midnight by the time Lorraine reached October 1975. As she turned the page, she saw that the entry for Friday 24th was written entirely in shorthand. She stared at the incomprehensible mix of light and dark strokes, dots and dashes. She flicked through the rest of the diary, but it was only this one entry that had been written that way. By Saturday 25th, Petula was back to writing in longhand.

I've decided to try and forget about what happened yesterday. Everyone is entitled to make one mistake in their lives. Nobody is perfect, are they?

Lorraine stared at the words, wondering what on earth her friend had done. Petula had tried to persuade Lorraine to join her at night school to learn shorthand, but Lorraine had thought it would be a waste of time. She was quite happy being a copy typist and didn't think she would ever be able to master the seemingly illegible scrawl she was now staring at. She was in a quandary. Petula had obvi-ously not wanted anyone to read this entry and had taken extra precautions to ensure that would be the case. There was no way Lorraine would be able to find out what it contained. It wouldn't be fair to Petula and it was nobody else's business.

She turned out the bedside lamp and snuggled under the covers, but as usual, it was only seconds before the memory of Ralph's pendulous body swaying above her head had her reaching for the lamp again.

'Trisha didn't come back last night.' Babs cracked two more eggs into the Pyrex bowl and whisked vigorously. 'Do you think we should be worried?'

Lorraine smiled. 'Are you worried that she won't come back or that she will?'

Babs stopped whisking and untied her apron. 'I'm going to go down to the hospital.'

'Now? It's too early, Mum. At least finish your breakfast.'

'I'm not hungry. You have it.'

Babs pushed open the door to Selwyn's room, the usual apprehension at what she would find making her suck in her breath. When she saw that the nurse was giving Selwyn a sponge bath, she exhaled softly and leaned her forehead against the door, the sadness at entering this joyless room overcoming her. The woman had his pyjama bottoms off and was scrubbing away at his private parts with a vigour usually reserved for cleaning the bath. The accident had stripped him of everything, including his dignity.

Babs took a step into the room as she watched the nurse swab Selwyn down with her shot-putter's arms. There was no tenderness, no finesse, no love. 'I'll take over now, Nurse, if you don't mind.'

The nurse stopped and dropped the sponge into the bowl, soapy water sloshing over the sides on to the bed linen. 'It all right, darlin', I'm almost finished.' She glanced at the clock on the wall. 'Too early for visiting; what brings you here at this time?'

'Sister said it would be all right if I came to see my husband. Now, would you mind if we had some privacy.' It was all Babs could do to stop herself from bundling the woman out of the room like a drunk who had outstayed his welcome at the pub.

The nurse didn't seem to notice her irritation. 'If you're sure. I've done his bottom half, so you just need to do the top and give him a shave too if you like. He's not had one for days. He's letting himself go.' The nurse chuckled at her own inane remark as she left the room, leaving Babs silently fuming.

She approached the bed. 'Selwyn, it's Babs.'

'I know, love, I heard you.'

'How are you feeling?'

'You know I can't feel anything.'

'Don't be difficult, Selwyn, you know what I mean.'

'She's gone.'

'I know, I just sent her packing.'

'Not the bloody nurse. Trisha. Trisha's gone.'

249

Suddenly aware of his nakedness, Babs pulled the sheet over his body and sat down on the bed. 'Oh, I wondered why she didn't come back to the pub last night. I'm so sorry, Selwyn.'

'You can't blame her really, can you? I mean, look at me, no good to anyone. Maybe I was the selfish one asking her to stay. She's only a young girl and I can't give her a baby now. She needs to find someone who can.'

Babs took hold of his left hand; his gold wedding band was all he had left of his marriage now. She fought the urge to prise the ring off his finger.

He gave a mirthless laugh. 'Who would want to be married to me, eh?'

'Me, Selwyn. I want to be married to you. It's all I've ever wanted and nothing's changed.'

He continued as though he hadn't heard a word she said. 'I was clinging on by my fingertips, Babs, and now Trisha's stamped on them.'

Babs began to unbutton his pyjama top, slipping it gently off his shoulders. She lathered up her hands with the soap and massaged his chest, gently at first, but then more firmly, as though she were kneading dough.

She gritted her teeth, fighting to keep the despair out of her voice. 'Can you feel that, Selwyn?' She didn't wait for an answer, but pummelled her soapy fists into his body, willing him to respond to her touch. A solitary tear ran down the side of her nose and hung there for a second before she wiped it away, leaving a bubble of soap suds on her top lip.

Selwyn smiled, but his voice came out husky. 'I know I don't deserve you, Babs.' He paused and swallowed hard, his eyes now as glassy as marbles. 'But thank you.'

34

By the time January rolled around, Lorraine was more than ready to go back to work. Whilst it was true that things were a little calmer in the pub now that Trisha had moved out, she was sick of having to do shifts behind the bar, manage the cellar and even clean the toilets. Fishing out and replacing the eroded urinal cakes was above and beyond the call of duty as far as Lorraine was concerned, and Babs had finally agreed to hire some more staff to ease the burden.

As Lorraine walked to the office along the treacherous, icy pavements, she had a spring in her step that had not been present for weeks. She thrust her gloved hand into her pocket and pulled out the piece of paper she had carefully cut from Petula's diary. In spite of her promise to herself, curiosity had won the day and she was taking the entry into work to have it transcribed by old Miss Warbrick. Lorraine had offered no explanation for this request and none had been sought, but at the end of the day, when Lorraine knocked on Miss Warbrick's door, she could see from the one raised eyebrow on the secretary's face, and her questioning look, that Petula's scrawl had revealed rather more than either of them had bargained for.

'I've done my best with it,' explained Miss Warbrick. 'On the whole the strokes were good, although there were a couple of words I couldn't make out and I've guessed at a few more. Whoever wrote this did so carefully and precisely; it certainly wasn't written at speed.'

'Well, thanks for your help. I appreciate it.' Lorraine offered the box of Milk Tray she had bought, but Miss Warbrick stubbornly held on to the envelope.

'All the vowels were still present, you know, the dots and the dashes.'

Lorraine merely nodded. She didn't need a lesson in shorthand now.

Miss Warbrick gave a self-satisfied smile. 'I can take dictation at a hundred and fifty words a minute, you know.'

'Well, that's impressive. Now if I could just have it . . .' Lorraine reached out for the envelope, and Miss Warbrick pushed it into her grateful hand.

The pub was due to open again at six, and Lorraine was relieved to find the new staff setting up the bar when she returned. Her mother would still be at the hospital, so she had a little time to squirrel herself away and read Miss Warbrick's transcript. She thundered up the stairs and closed her bedroom door behind her. The fact that the secretary had put the note inside a sealed envelope only added to the tension as Lorraine slid her finger under the flap and pulled out the contents. Ever the professional, Miss Warbrick had typed out Petula's words flawlessly, and Lorraine settled down to read what her friend hadn't wanted anybody to see.

Went in the pub tonight with Lorraine. It was packed and Selwyn decided we could all have a lock-in. Lorraine had (persuaded?) me to try out some of her blue eyeshadow and she ended up doing my whole face, false eyelashes, lipstick, the lot. I thought I looked a bit like a (illegible) but some of the blokes in the pub said I looked nice. I don't think that's ever happened before! The old Cherry B was (illegible) as usual and I felt quite tipsy by the end of the night. Trisha asked us if we wanted to mix the Cherry B with cider, which she said was called a 'legover'. This turned out to be a very bad omen. Anyway, Lorraine was all over Karl, even though it's quite obvious he doesn't fancy her. It was (embarrassing?) actually and I decided to go home. Jerry was in the pub with his mother and they left at the same time so we walked home together. We reached their house first and Daisy went inside but insisted that Jerry walk me home the rest of the way. He didn't look too happy about it though.

My dad had gone to bed and the house was in darkness and for some reason I have been unable to (fathom?), I asked him in for a coffee. I'd always thought he was a bit straight but he was easy to talk to and he told me all about his girlfriend, Lydia, who'd cleared off to (Australia?). I felt a bit sorry for him and when he came to leave I gave him a kiss on the cheek. I'm still wondering what possessed me to do that. He's a bit smaller than me though so it felt more of a (illegible) gesture than anything. We were standing in the hall, our faces only inches apart, and he stroked my cheek and said I was beautiful. Ha, ha! Even allowing for the fact that he'd had a couple of drinks, that was stretching things a bit. (It's the last time I wear make-up, that's for sure.) The next thing I knew he was kissing me on the mouth, and even though I expected to feel revulsion, it actually felt really nice. In my limited experience I would say he is a good kisser even though it was obvious he was nervous. I was pinned up against the wall and felt his hand snaking its way under my skirt. He hesitated and looked into my eyes for a second as though seeking my permission and I was surprised by how much I wanted him to carry on so I did nothing to stop him. It is too embarrassing to go into detail here, but suffice it to say that it did feel good even if this was not how I'd planned to lose my virginity. It did spoil things a bit though when at the critical moment he called me Lydia.

Lorraine put the paper down and paced the room, running her hands through her hair. *Oh my God, oh my*

God. Petula had only gone and had sex with Jerry, of all people. They'd promised to tell each other everything, but Petula had always insisted she was saving herself for marriage and now it turned out the brazen little hussy had done it up against a wall with a lad who wasn't even her boyfriend. No wonder she'd written this entry in shorthand.

Lorraine slumped down on the bed, unable to shake the feeling of betrayal. She lay back on the pillow and stared at the ceiling, wondering how her friend could have allowed this to happen. Then, with a slow-dawning realisation, she began to count off the months from the date of the entry. When she got to July 1976, nine fingers were held aloft. Jerry was the father of Petula's baby.

When Babs returned from the hospital, she immediately took up her position behind the bar. Trisha had only been gone for just over a week, and Babs had slotted seamlessly back into her rightful position as landlady of the Taverners. She had always known Trisha was a shallow, superficial bitch who had taken Selwyn off her just because she could. She'd never loved him and had now proved it in spectacular fashion.

The early-doors drinkers were starting to congregate around the bar, pale blue smoke hanging in a fog above their heads as they supped their well-deserved post-work pints. At this time of the evening the clientele was made up entirely of men, most of them waiting for their wives back home to prepare their tea. After a few pints, many of them forgot they had a home, and Babs would often give them a gentle reminder, even though it meant turning down business. She'd just taken down the Christmas decorations and the pub looked spartan now that it had been stripped of its festive adornments.

Lorraine came through from the back and tugged at her mother's sleeve like an impatient toddler. 'Lorraine, I'm talking to Ken here, don't be so rude.' Babs turned back to Ken. 'Sorry, love, go on, you were saying about how your Sheila's taken to Tupperware . . .'

Ken took another swig of his pint. 'Costing me a fortune, it is. I mean, how many little plastic boxes does one woman need? Every time I open a cupboard door I'm hit by an avalanche of the bloody things.'

Babs laughed. 'Another pint?'

'Aye, go on then, you've twisted me arm. She's at another of them parties tonight, so I'm in no rush.'

Babs reached for the pump. 'There you are then, every cloud.'

'Mum,' persisted Lorraine. 'I need a word.'

'What is it, love?'

'Not here.' She motioned with her head towards the back room.

'I've got a pub full of customers, Lorraine. It'll have to wait.'

Lorraine lowered her voice to a whisper. 'I know who the father of Petula's baby is.'

Babs didn't flinch but calmly finished pouring the pint and handed it to Ken, froth spilling over on to the back of her hand. She took Lorraine by the arm and guided her through to the back.

'I've got a feeling I'm not going to like this. Come on, then. Who is it?'

Lorraine cupped her hand round her mouth and stage-whispered, 'It's Jerry.'

Babs's mouth hung open. 'Well I wasn't expecting that. Jerry Duggan, you mean? As in Daisy's son?'

'Yes, him,' hissed Lorraine. 'You realise what this means, don't you?' She waited for her mother to catch up.

Babs rubbed her face with her hands, then bowed her head. 'Oh my God. It means Daisy delivered her own granddaughter and then abandoned her on a stranger's step.'

'You've got it in one, Mum,' cried Lorraine. 'We have to tell her.'

Babs placed her hand on her daughter's shoulder. 'No, not yet. I need to think, Lorraine, don't do anything without me.' She turned and headed into the bar. 'I've got to get back to the pumps.'

By the time Babs rang the bell for closing, she had made her decision. This wasn't her secret to keep and Daisy deserved to know the truth. What she did with this information was up to her, but as far as Babs was concerned, she would have passed the baton and her own conscience would be clear.

35

Daisy was sitting at the kitchen table with Mikey, helping him with his times tables, although truth be told he was better at them than she was. His classmates were still grappling with adding up and taking away, but he was on his twelve times tables now.

It was taken for granted these days that she would collect him from school and give him his tea. The stuff Andrea had been feeding him was nothing short of a disgrace, like dried potatoes out of a packet that she mixed with hot water. There was no excuse for that; even Andrea was capable of peeling a spud. Daisy had thought the younger woman might have turned a corner last week when Mikey said she had made him cauliflower cheese, but it turned out she'd just boiled some cauli, bunged a Kraft cheese slice on the top and shoved it under the grill. No meat, no fish, nothing. It was little wonder the poor kid was just skin and bone, and Daisy had made it her mission to fatten him up.

Mikey ran his finger down the list of sums. 'I like the nine times table best, Aunt Daisy. What's your favourite?'

He was a strange little boy in many ways. Who on earth had a favourite times table? 'I don't know, Mikey, I've never really thought about it.' She placed the freshly made chocolate cake in the middle of the table. 'Do you want to spread the covering on?'

'Ooh, yes please.' He jumped down from the table and picked up the bowl of melted cake covering, sticking his tongue out in concentration as he carefully dipped the knife in and spread the glossy chocolate over the top of the cake. It ran down the sides and pooled on the plate. 'It looks yummy, Aunt Daisy. Thank you for making it for me.'

Daisy ruffled his hair with affection and passed him the hundreds and thousands. 'You're welcome, son.'

He sprinkled the tiny sugar-coated strands over the cake and admired his handiwork. 'Can I sleep here tonight, please?'

Daisy was taken aback by the sudden change in subject. 'Why of course you can, love. Is your mum off out again?'

'I'm not sure, but I don't like my bed at home. It smells, and it makes me itchy.'

'Does it?' She took hold of his arm and pushed his sleeve up. His skin was speckled with red spots, the tops raw where he had scratched them. 'Ooh, that looks nasty. I've got some calamine lotion in the bathroom cabinet. It's been there since our Jerry had chickenpox but I expect it'll still be all right.' She kissed Mikey on the top of his head. 'Let's go and put some on, and then we'll call round

260

at your mum's and let her know you're staying here tonight.'

Andrea answered the door in her underwear, the obligatory cigarette dangling from her lips, every rib visible through her translucent pale skin.

She didn't bother to disguise her disappointment. 'Oh, it's you. I thought you'd be bringing him back later.' She did not seem in the slightest bit perturbed by her state of undress.

Mikey stepped into the hall and hugged his mother's bony frame. 'I came first in the maths test today, Mum.'

'Did you? Right little swot, aren't you?'

Daisy pulled Mikey back and whispered into his ear. 'I think you're a very clever boy. Now run upstairs and get your pyjamas.' She turned to Andrea. 'He's staying at mine tonight and for the foreseeable future unless you sort his bed out. He says it smells, and he's covered in bites. You've got bed bugs, Andrea, and unless you clean this place up, I'm going to the authorities.'

Andrea laughed and blew a cloud of smoke in Daisy's face. 'No you won't. You want to see him taken into care? If what I've heard about those children's homes is true, he's better off here. His place is with me. I'm his mother.'

Calling in social services was the last thing Daisy wanted to do. Mikey needed to be nurtured in order to flourish and fulfil his exceptional potential, not shoved into a children's home where he would become just another kid, starved of affection and attention. She would not let that happen, and Andrea knew it.

'Just sort his bed out, Andrea,' she snapped through clenched teeth. 'His teacher collared me at the school gates the other day and said he's falling asleep in class.'

Andrea eased her out on to the street. 'Well he shouldn't be teaching then.'

She was just cutting into the chocolate cake when the doorbell rang. Daisy automatically glanced at the kitchen clock. 'Who on earth is that? It's not the milkman's day for his money, is it?' She plopped a huge slab of cake on Mikey's plate and went to open the door.

'Good evening, Daisy. How are you?' Babs sounded bright, but her tone seemed to be forced.

Daisy frowned as she looked from Babs to Lorraine. 'I'm fine, thank you. What a lovely surprise. Er . . . what brings you here tonight?'

The two women glanced at each other, neither appearing to know what to say next. It was Lorraine who found her voice first. 'Can we come in please, Daisy?'

Daisy opened the door further and beckoned them inside. 'Please, go through to the kitchen. We were just having some cake. Would you like a slice?'

Mikey looked up as they entered, his face and hands smeared with gooey chocolate.

'You remember Mikey, don't you?'

Babs had not seen the little boy since the crash but

had enquired about his well-being on numerous occasions. 'Of course. How are you, Mikey?'

He shrugged and took another enormous bite of cake. 'All right,' he mumbled.

'He's a little belter, he is,' said Daisy. 'Aren't you, Mikey, a little belter?'

She put the kettle on the hob. 'You'll have a drink, won't you?' She didn't wait for an answer. 'How's Selwyn?'

'Still in rehabilitation, but possibly coming home in the next few weeks,' answered Babs. 'They had him in a chair the other day, which really was a milestone. He said he felt a bit dizzy after all those months lying down, but it's a start, I suppose.'

Daisy folded her arms under her bosom. 'I must say, that was a rum do, Trisha swanning off like that, just when Selwyn needed her most. I nearly dropped cork-legged when I heard.'

Babs placed her arm around Lorraine and pulled her close. 'He's got us two, Daisy: his family. We're all he needs now.'

Daisy nodded her agreement. 'He couldn't be in better hands, Babs.'

Mikey sucked noisily through his straw as he attempted to extract the last of his orange juice from the glass. Babs nodded towards him. 'He looks well. How's he coping, you know, *without his Dad*?' She mimed the last three words.

'He's getting there,' said Daisy. 'I'm helping Andrea out with him because she's so . . .' She searched for the right word, but Babs filled the gap.

'Useless?'

'Mmm, an understatement if ever I heard one, but yes, you get the gist.'

Mikey climbed down from his chair. 'Can I go and watch television, please, Aunt Daisy, then you can talk about me.'

The kettle began to emit its hollow whistle and Daisy lifted it off the stove before the noise became too shrill. 'Yes, you can, Mikey, and don't worry, we're not going to talk about you.'

When he'd gone, Babs said, 'Not daft, is he?'

'Oh aye, sharp as a tack,' agreed Daisy. 'He's such a clever lad too.'

'You know, I spent some time with Karl on the day of the crash,' began Babs, 'and he told me that first thing that Monday morning he was going to see his solicitor about going for full custody.'

Daisy shook her head, sadness suddenly overwhelming her. 'Oh dear, that's tragic, that is. The poor little lad had happiness just around the corner and then in one instant it's all swept away.' She pulled a tissue from her sleeve, mopped her eyes and attempted to regain some composure. 'Still, I do my best with him, and to be honest, he's a comfort to me too. It's nice to have a little lad about the place again. Anyway, I'm sure you didn't come here to talk about Mikey. Was there something else I can help you with?'

Lorraine, who'd been silent up till now, stepped forward. 'I have some news that my mum thinks . . . well, we both think we should share with you.'

Daisy raised her eyebrows. 'Go on then, let's hear it.'

Lorraine glanced at her mother, unsure how to continue, but Babs came to her rescue. 'Well, it's a bit of a long story, but in a nutshell it all boils down to . . .' She stopped and indicated a chair. 'Er . . . perhaps you should sit down.'

Daisy planted her hands on her hips. 'I'm fine standing, thank you, so if you'd just come out with it.'

'Okay, if you're sure,' continued Babs. 'It appears that Petula had a sort of . . . well, I suppose you could call it a . . . fling with someone, which resulted in her becoming pregnant. They weren't in a relationship or anything but she wrote about it in her diary, and it seems that the father was . . .' She took a step forward and touched Daisy's arm. 'It seems the father was your Jerry.'

Daisy opened her mouth to speak but no words came. Babs must be mistaken, surely. Jerry wasn't the sort to have a one-night stand; it couldn't be his baby. But even as she tried to deny it to herself, the truth hit her like a cannon ball to the chest and she grabbed the table for support. Had she really abandoned her own flesh and blood, her only granddaughter, on the doorstep of a stranger's house?

Babs pulled out a chair. 'Have a seat, Daisy, you've had a shock. We'll finish off the brew.' She turned to her daughter. 'Lorraine, three sugars for Daisy.'

Daisy placed her elbows on the table and massaged her temples. 'Oh my God, what've I done?'

'Where d'yer keep your tea bags, Daisy?' asked Lorraine, opening doors and ferreting around in the cupboards.

Daisy looked up but it was obvious her mind was elsewhere. 'Oh, er, I don't use them, too expensive, I just have tea leaves. They're in that blue and white striped whatsit over there.'

Babs rubbed Daisy's back. 'What are you going to do now?'

'I honestly don't know, Babs. I mean, are you sure she's Jerry's baby?'

Lorraine placed the teapot in the middle of the table and popped on the knitted tea cosy. 'Well, Petula wrote about it in her diary in shorthand, while all the other entries were in longhand, and there was no mention of any other . . . er . . . episodes with boys. And the dates add up, too.'

'That's hardly conclusive, is it?'

'No, Daisy, it's not, but it is likely and we really thought you ought to know.'

Later, when Mikey was tucked up in bed, cocooned in his electric blanket, Daisy took Jerry's photograph off the mantelpiece and blew away the fine layer of dust that had accumulated on its surface, inwardly chastising herself for such uncharacteristic sloppiness. She ran her fingers over his beaming face. 'Oh, Jerry lad, what were you thinking?'

36

Daisy was determined to do something special for Mikey for his seventh birthday. It would be another milestone to overcome since his father's passing. They had already survived the first Christmas without Karl and Jerry, and though it had not exactly been uneventful, they had come through it together. It was now June, and the anniversary of the crash was fast approaching, along with her grand-daughter's first birthday.

Ever since Babs had told her that Jerry was the little girl's father, she'd harboured the secret, too afraid of the repercussions and the can of worms it would inevi-tably open. Despite the trauma of the discovery, there was no doubt in Daisy's mind that they had done the right thing. After all, the baby probably would not have survived the crash. She wasn't sure the authorities would see it that way, though. But now, as the child's first birthday loomed, she felt an overwhelming need to put her mind at rest that she was at least with loving adop-tive parents.

When she'd first suggested a weekend in Blackpool to Mikey, he'd been completely against the idea and said he never wanted to go back there ever again. Daisy could perfectly understand his reaction, though she'd pointed out that it was where he'd spent his last happy day with his dad, and that he might find some comfort from revisiting the town. Over the following months, Mikey had gradually come round to her way of thinking, and when she suggested that they go for his seventh birthday, he'd embraced the idea with an enthusiasm that Daisy thought had been lacking for a while. Andrea was more than happy to see the back of him for the weekend; when Daisy reminded her that it would be his birthday, she'd merely shrugged indifferently and said, 'Oh, is it?'

The streets of Manchester looked resplendent with yards of red, white and blue bunting strung between lamp posts and Union Jacks plastered to the front of buildings. One office window proudly displayed a home-made banner with the words 'Betty Rules OK' daubed in red paint.

Mikey cuddled up beside Daisy on the coach, Galen squashed between them. Daisy pulled the stuffed monkey out and placed it on her knee. 'He needs a seat of his own, he's that big.' She sniffed the top of the soft toy's head. 'Hmm, could do with a wash as well.'

Mikey rubbed the grime off the coach window with his sleeve and peered out. 'Why are there flags everywhere, Aunt Daisy?'

'It's for the Queen, love. It's her Silver Jubilee, which means she's been our queen for twenty-five years.'

Mikey chewed silently on his thumbnail. 'Oh, right. What do you have to do to become a queen then?'

'You have to be the daughter of a king.' This answer seemed to satisfy him, and he fell silent as he continued to gaze out of the window.

'Is there something the matter, Mikey love?'

He looked up at her and wrinkled his nose. 'This bus won't crash, will it, Aunt Daisy?'

'Oh Mikey, is that why you look so worried? Of course it won't.' She delved into her bag beneath the seat and pulled out a gift-wrapped package. 'I was saving this until we got to Blackpool, but you might as well have it now.' She passed it over to him. 'Happy birthday, Mikey.'

'Thank you,' he breathed as he took the parcel and tore off the paper. It was an artist's kit in a beautiful mahogany case, filled with pencils, crayons, paintbrushes and lots of tiny tubes of paint all neatly lined up in the lid. There was a pad of thick paper and an instruction book on how to draw landscapes, people and animals. Mikey's eyes were wide with wonder as he fingered the numerous brushes. He pulled one out and stroked its soft bristles across his cheek.

'Do you like it?' Daisy asked.

Mikey nodded his head. 'It's the best present I've ever had. I'm going to do you a picture for your wall, Aunt Daisy. Thank you.'

'You're welcome. I'm glad you like it. I know how good you are at drawing and painting already, so this will make you even better.'

It was only a short walk from the bus stop to Claremont Villas, and Mikey walked along beside her, proudly carrying his new artist's case, Galen tucked under his other arm. 'I could paint a picture of the beach,' he declared. 'Or of a donkey, or of that tower over there.' Daisy smiled at his infectious enthusiasm, relieved that he seemed to have put his reservations about Blackpool out of his mind.

They stopped as they arrived at the gate of the guest house, and Daisy took a deep breath to steady her nerves. She glanced across the road towards the bus shelter where she had crouched almost a year ago, willing someone to answer the door and find the baby.

She adopted a cheerful tone. 'Here we are then, this is where we're staying.' She pushed the gate open and Mikey followed her up the path to the front door. Daisy glanced down at the spot where she'd left the infant, hardly believing now that she had done so. The step had been freshly polished and a basket of purple petunias hung above her head.

The door opened and the landlady smiled down at the two of them. 'Good morning, welcome to Claremont Villas. You must be Mrs Duggan.' She bent down and held her hand out to Mikey. 'And you are?'

'I'm Mikey.' He held aloft his new case. 'Look what Aunt Daisy got me for my birthday. It's today.'

'Well isn't that just grand? It's your birthday today, is it? I wish I'd known, I'd have baked you a cake.'

Daisy scrutinised the landlady's face. Although she'd only caught a brief glimpse of her last year, she was as sure as she could be that this was the same woman who had scooped up her granddaughter. Mrs Roberts seemed so kind and genuine, maternal even, that Daisy just wanted to blurt out there and then that it was she who had left the baby on her doorstep. She couldn't wait a moment longer to find out where Mary Roberts had taken the child, but reasoned she had to tread carefully. She'd waited almost a year; a few more hours wouldn't hurt.

After unpacking, Daisy and Mikey took a stroll along the prom. Last summer's heatwave was a distant memory, and although the sky was cloudless, they battled against the onshore wind as it whipped across their faces. Mikey suddenly stopped and pointed across the road. 'Look, that's the pub where we had our chicken in a basket.'

Daisy glanced across at the Ferryman, where she had delivered her own granddaughter on the toilet floor. The paint was peeling off the whitewashed walls and a group of noisy bikers was assembled outside the front door, revving their engines. Even at this distance she could smell the rancid fat from the kitchen. She covered her nose with her hand and turned away, pulling at Mikey's arm. 'Come on, love, let's get back to the guest house and have our meal.'

The dining room of the Claremont Villas was laid out

with four separate tables, each with a lace tablecloth and a vase of plastic freesias. The bone-handled cutlery sparkled, and though the bold patterned carpet might have been worn down in places, it was freshly vacuumed and confirmed to Daisy that Mary could match her for fastidiousness in the cleaning department. The room began to fill up and Daisy nodded politely to the other guests as they filed in. Mary brought out the starter and placed glass dishes in front of Mikey and Daisy. 'Prawn cocktail, I hope that's okay.'

Daisy nodded. 'Perfect, and it looks wonderful.' She picked up the zigzag-cut lemon and squeezed it over the prawns.

Mary backed out of the room as they tucked into their meal. Daisy had been pondering for days about how she was going to broach the subject of the baby, and she was no nearer a solution now. She'd tried the opening gambit in her head numerous times, but it always sounded ridiculous even to her own ears. *I wonder, do you remember a baby being left on your doorstep?* See, ridiculous: how could anybody forget that? *You know the baby that you found on your doorstep last year? Can you tell me what you did with her?* Daisy shook her head and dabbed at the corner of her mouth with her napkin. 'How were the prawns, Mikey?' He'd guzzled the whole dishful, so it was a rhetorical question.

'I enjoyed them, Aunt Daisy, but what was that red dust on the top?'

Daisy laughed. 'It was paprika, Mikey. I don't suppose your mum uses it that much.'

Mary returned to collect their bowls, her face ruddy with the heat of the kitchen. At the doorway, she seemed to change her mind and retreated into the back, returning a few seconds later with a baby perched on her hip. 'Sorry about that, I could hear her crying in the back. She's teething, you see.' The baby's cheeks were bright red and shiny with tears. Mary bounced the child up and down and kissed her wet cheeks, and a small smile creased the wide-eyed infant's face. She lifted the baby's hand and jiggled it towards Daisy. 'Say hello.' The baby turned and buried her face in Mary's neck. Mary laughed. 'She's just shy.'

Daisy's mouth hung open. 'Is this . . . is this your baby?'

'Yes, it is. This is my daughter.' She lifted the baby's hand again. 'Say hello, Beth.'

37

Daisy gazed at the blue-eyed baby, who was now giggling as Mary tickled the sole of her foot. It couldn't possibly be the same child; it had to be a coincidence. It was a few moments before Daisy found her voice. 'She's beautiful, how old is she?' The baby wrapped her chubby arms round Mary's neck.

'She'll be one next month.'

As the hairs on the back of Daisy's neck lifted, she reached for her glass and took a calming swig of water. Just one more question was all it would take. 'Next month? How lovely.' She paused before casually adding, 'What date?'

Mary was distracted by Beth dribbling a long thread of drool, which landed on the floor. 'Oh my goodness, I'll just fetch a cloth.' She handed the baby to Daisy. 'Would you mind?'

Daisy reached up and pulled the little girl on to her knee. She searched her face for a family resemblance and it didn't take long to find it. It was all in the eyes. This baby had the same blue-green eyes that her son had been born with, but it was more than that; it was the shape of them, and the way her eyebrows formed a perfect arch above. She gingerly lifted the little girl's fringe and peered underneath. A cowlick, just like Jerry's. This really was Jerry's baby she was cradling. Her own granddaughter.

Mary returned and began to scrub away at the carpet. Daisy addressed her hunched form. 'What date did you say her birthday was?'

Mary straightened up and placed her hands in the small of her back. 'What? Oh, yes, it's the twenty-fourth.'

A wave of nausea rolled in and broke in Daisy's stomach. She placed her hand over her mouth and struggled to remain composed as the truth became clear. Mary had kept the baby and was bringing her up as her own. This was one scenario that Daisy had not bargained for, and she had no idea how she was going to deal with it. Her initial reaction was one of resentment. Mary was raising Daisy's granddaughter as her own flesh and blood, when Daisy could have taken her in herself had she known she was Jerry's daughter. As Mary took the baby back and the little girl beamed up at her, a small stab of jealousy pricked at Daisy's heart. But Mary was clearly besotted with Beth, and there could be no doubt that the little girl was thriving.

'She has your eyes,' Daisy ventured.

Mary did not miss a beat. 'Yes, I think she does.' She smoothed Beth's fair hair to one side and tickled her under her chin. Beth giggled, her gummy smile showing her delight. 'Come on, you, let's get you in that bath.' She turned to Daisy. 'If you'll excuse me, Ruth will serve you with the rest of your meal.'

The young waitress placed their main course of chicken pie and mash on the table. Several peas rolled off and landed in Daisy's lap. 'Oops, sorry about that,' apologised Ruth, casting a nervous glance towards the kitchen.

Daisy scooped them up with her dessert spoon. 'It's all right. No harm done.'

Mikey was already tucking in greedily but Daisy's appetite had completely vanished; she felt as though she'd swallowed an inflated balloon.

Mikey noticed immediately. 'Aren't you hungry, Aunt Daisy?'

'Well, that starter was quite filling, wasn't it? I knew I shouldn't have eaten all that brown bread.' She watched as Mikey shovelled mash into his mouth. 'I don't know where you put it all,' she laughed.

After tea, Daisy took Mikey out again to the Pleasure Beach. The little boy was excited to be up so late, but Daisy insisted that he deserved a special treat on his birthday. They wandered hand in hand, snaking their way through the rides, lights flashing and music pounding. Crowds of people were clamouring for a ride on the dodgems.

Mikey was unimpressed. 'Who wants to go on a ride where cars crash into each other? That doesn't sound like fun.'

Daisy steered him away, inwardly agreeing. 'Come on, let's go where it's a bit quieter. What about hoop-la or hook-a-duck, eh?'

As they rounded the bend, they were confronted by a stall surrounded by stuffed monkeys, all grotesquely suspended by their necks.

'Look!' Mikey exclaimed. 'This is where me dad won Galen for me.'

'So it is.' Daisy guided him away from the spectacle and into an arcade. 'Let's have a go on the penny falls, shall we?' She rummaged around in her purse and handed Mikey a fistful of coppers. She was beginning to wonder if it had been wise to bring Mikey back to Blackpool so soon. There seemed to be reminders of Karl everywhere.

Later, with Mikey tucked up in bed, Daisy sat in the guest lounge and sipped a port and lemon. She turned as she heard the door brush across the carpet and Mary stuck her head round. 'Mind if I join you? I usually have a little snifter of something before turning in.'

Daisy gestured to the chair opposite. 'Of course, please, it's your house.'

Mary poured herself a schooner of sweet sherry and slumped in the chair. 'Ooh, it's good to take the weight off.' She kicked off her slippers and tucked her legs beneath her. 'Beth's been waking up most nights with her teeth lately. It really takes it out of you, I can tell you.' She leaned her head back and closed her eyes.

Daisy took the opportunity to study Mary's face. She estimated she must be a good decade younger than Daisy herself, certainly no more than thirty-five. There was no doubt she was an attractive young woman, with flawless skin and a strong bone structure. Her hair was neatly curled, apart from one stray strand hanging down the middle of her forehead, which she had a habit of flicking away with a quick swivel of her head. Daisy studied the younger woman's hands and concluded that she was definitely a grafter, unafraid of hard work.

She nodded towards the wedding photo in the middle of the mantelpiece. 'Where's your husband, Mrs Roberts?' As soon as she had asked the question, she regretted her inquisitive tone, which had come across as just plain nosy.

Mary opened her eyes and spoke matter-of-factly. 'Thomas was killed in a mining accident two years ago. I'm a widow.'

'Oh dear, that is tragic, I'm terribly sorry.' Daisy fiddled with the buttons on her cardigan as she tried to think. She was afraid of upsetting Mary with further questions about her dead husband but had a desperate need to fill the uncomfortable silence. She looked across at the sash window. 'Er . . . how . . . how often do you have to wash your net curtains then?'

Mary sighed. 'Is that what you really want to know or are you wondering about Beth's father?'

Daisy felt her cheeks redden. 'Well, it's really none of

279

my business, Mrs Roberts,' she answered, even though nothing could be further from the truth.

'It's all right, Mrs Duggan. I'm not embarrassed about it any more.' She cleared her throat, lifted her chin and spoke defiantly and without shame. 'Beth was conceived as the result of an ill-advised one-night stand, but it's not something I regret. I mean, how could I? You've seen how adorable she is; she really is my world.' She paused to take another sip of sherry. 'We're doing okay, just the two of us, and I wouldn't change what happened for anything.'

Daisy was aghast at how easily the lie tripped off her tongue. She must have told it so many times that she had come to believe it herself. 'Yes,' she agreed. 'She's a lovely little thing, that's for sure.'

Mary cast her eyes downwards then and spoke in soft tones that made it difficult for Daisy to hear her properly. 'It took me a long, long time to accept that Thomas was dead. He was trapped down the mine, you see, and they sealed it with bodies still inside. Can you imagine anything more horrific?' She lifted her eyes and looked across at her dead husband's photograph. 'I realise now that I was deluding myself, but without a body I just couldn't believe that he was never coming back. The grief was all-consuming, and it was only when Beth came along that I realised there was a point to life after all, and that maybe I could carry on.' She pulled absently on the errant strand of hair as she continued. 'I still miss Thomas every day, and I know I'll never love another man in the way I loved him, but Beth makes the pain more bearable.' She shrugged. 'I suppose you could say she saved me. I'm happy again, and that's something I thought would never happen.'

Even though Daisy knew she was being lied to, she felt an unexpected mixture of grief and pity as she listened to Mary's story. She studied the younger woman, searching her face for any signs that might reveal her duplicity, but her features were a mask of composure that gave nothing away. Lost for words, Daisy drummed her fingers on the arm of the chair and merely nodded.

Mary drained her sherry and stood up to leave. 'Once a month.'

Daisy frowned. 'I'm sorry?'

'You asked how often I wash the net curtains. The answer's once a month. Goodnight, Mrs Duggan.'

Daisy slept fitfully that night, thrashing around so much she became entwined in the nylon sheets, making sparks fly off her nightdress. Mikey slept soundly in the bed next to her, the sea air having apparently knocked him out. She smiled fondly at his sleeping frame, his arm slumped over Galen. It was certainly possible to love a child who wasn't your own flesh and blood. Mary had given Beth a wonderful home here; she was clearly an attentive, doting mother, and to wrench the child away from all that would be cruel to both of them.

Daisy heaved herself out of bed and crept over to the window. She parted the curtains and looked out over the bay, the moonlight shimmering on the choppy surface of the black sea. She heard a faint thump behind her and turned to see that Galen had fallen to the floor. Mikey stirred and felt around absently for his soft toy. Daisy picked it up and tucked it back into the crook of his elbow.

She didn't know how long she had continued to stare out of the window, but by the time she crawled back into bed, her feet aching with the cold that had crept up from the wooden floor, she had made a decision. The first time she had held her granddaughter, she'd been a mere scrap of a thing that even her own mother had been unable to love. The baby's future had seemed bleak, but with Mary's dedicated care over the past year she had blossomed, and now her life was filled with promise. Mary had proved herself to be a more than adequate substitute for Beth's birth mother, and Daisy was going to reward that devotion in the only way she could. She was going to give Mary the peace of mind she deserved.

38

Michael folded the newspaper cutting and laid it on the granite countertop. Most of the time he managed to keep the events of that dreadful day buried deep enough so they could not hurt him. Forty years might have passed, but if he allowed himself to dwell on what had happened, he could relive with every sinew the terror he'd felt as a six-year-old boy. When they'd pulled his father from the wreckage, Michael had been sitting at the roadside with a scratchy blanket wrapped around his shivering body, Babs beside him with her one good arm placed firmly around his shoulders. Karl had been brought out and manoeuvred on to a stretcher, but Babs had grabbed Michael's head and pulled it into her chest so he was unable to see. He remembered the kisses she'd planted on the top of his head as she'd rocked him back and forth.

Beth's voice brought him back to the present. 'Michael, I'm sorry.' She rubbed his forearm, up and down. 'I know this must bring back some painful memories for you.'

'It's a long time ago now, Beth,' he said. 'You're my family now, you and Jake.' At the sound of his name, Jake looked up from his book. 'Daddy, are you coming back to carry on reading to me?'

'In a minute, son.' He turned to Beth. 'You said something about a letter?'

'It's in the envelope.' She pulled out a stool from under the breakfast bar. 'I think you'd better sit down.'

Michael eased himself on to the stool as he took out the letter and began to read.

4 June 1977

Dear Mrs Roberts,

I am writing to thank you for a lovely stay at Claremont Villas. Blackpool has always been very dear to me as it was where my late husband Jim and I had our honeymoon. However, it wasn't just fond memories that drew me back this weekend. Almost a year ago, I did something that I was not proud of at the time but have been able to come to terms with since. Your daughter truly is adorable and is obviously thriving on the love and affection you have for her, and I think you deserve some peace of mind. I imagine that even now, a year later, you dread every knock on your door, but let me assure you, Beth's mother will never come back to claim her. She was killed that same day in a bus crash. I have

*enclosed the newspaper cutting with this letter. It
was me who left Beth on your doorstep that day.
Had I not done so, she would surely have perished
in her mother's arms.*

*The young girl who gave birth did not even
know she was pregnant and was terrified of her
father finding out. I don't think any of us were
thinking straight when we decided to leave the
baby somewhere she would be found and looked
after.*

*I also think that perhaps both you and I broke
the law that day, and no good can come of going
to the authorities now that almost a year has
passed. I hope you can now rest easy in the knowledge that you are able to bring Beth up as your
own daughter without fear of anyone coming back
to claim her.*

Yours sincerely,
Daisy Duggan

Beth took the letter from Michael when he'd finished
reading it and scanned it once more, even though she
knew every treacherous word by heart. 'Can you believe
it?' she whispered. 'All my life I've thought the identity
of my father was some great big secret, when all along
my mother was harbouring the biggest secret of all.
She wasn't even my bloody mother. How could she do
that?'

Michael shook his head. 'I can't believe Aunt Daisy was in on this either.'

Beth snorted. 'Oh, I'll be having a word with her when she gets back, don't you worry.'

'Daddy, are you coming?'

'Sorry, Jake, can we finish the story another time? Switch the telly on for now.'

Jake stared at his father as though he couldn't believe his luck. He was usually being told to turn the television off.

Beth took hold of her husband's hand and brought it to her lips. 'You were on that bus, Michael. Who was my mother?'

Michael scratched his head. 'God, it was forty years ago, Beth. I was only six years old.'

'It's not something you'd forget, surely.'

Michael stared at his wife. 'I try not to think about it too deeply, actually.'

Beth relented. 'I'm sorry, you're right. I'll talk to Daisy about it.' She blew out her cheeks and scanned the letter once more before crossing the kitchen and reaching for the phone.

'No, I'm sorry,' Michael apologised. 'You deserve to know.' He gently took the phone from her and glanced at the kitchen clock. 'Not now, Beth, please. The telephone is not the right medium for something as big as this. Daisy'll be back soon, it'll wait till then.' He pinched the bridge of his nose and squeezed his eyes shut before continuing. 'Well the letter says your mother was killed on the way home. Only one girl died in the crash and her name was . . . er . . . Petula, I think. I didn't really know any of the other passengers; they were just friends of my dad's from the pub. I wasn't even supposed to be going on the trip but Andrea dumped me on Dad at the last minute. Anyway, I had no idea this Petula had had a baby. I can't even think when it might have happened.' He tapped his chin with his forefinger and frowned in concentration. 'Unless it was in the pub at the end of the day. Come to think of it, she was taken ill and had to lie down on the bus whilst we finished our meal. Perhaps it was then.'

'The poor girl. I wonder why she was so terrified of her father finding out. How old was she?'

Michael shook his head. 'I'm not sure. She seemed old to me, but then again, I was only six; everybody seemed old to me.'

'What a terrible decision for a young girl to have to make. And just think, if Petula hadn't died, then I might have been able to find out who my father is. Or maybe it wouldn't have mattered; she herself might have been a match for Jake.'

She glanced over at her son, now sitting cross-legged in front of the television with his thumb in his mouth. 'We need to focus on why that's important. It's not morbid curiosity, but a matter of life and death, *our son's* life and death,' she emphasised. She grabbed a pad and pen from the kitchen drawer. 'Right, think, Michael. Did Petula have any brothers or sisters?'

Michael shook his head. 'No, I'm pretty sure she didn't. I only found out years later that her father had taken his own life. There was only the two of them, and he just couldn't see a way forward on his own.'

Beth paused for a moment, pen hovering expectantly. 'How tragic this whole thing is. Another avenue closes, then.' She chewed the end of the pen. 'Who else knew about the baby?' She paused and jabbed the pen into her own chest. 'About me?'

Michael was studying the letter again. 'I think someone else did know something,' he said slowly. He turned the letter round so Beth could read it. 'Look, Daisy says, *I don't think any of us were thinking straight when we decided to leave the baby somewhere she would be found and looked after.* "Any of us". That means more than two people, doesn't it? If Daisy was referring to just herself and Petula, she would have written "either of us".'

'Surely if Daisy knew who my father was, though, she would have put it in the letter, but there's just no mention of him.'

'Daisy didn't know Petula well at all. I think it's highly unlikely she would have confided in her. There is someone who might know, though,' Michael pondered. 'She was close to her friend Lorraine, who was also on that bus. I think that's a good place to start, don't you?'

Beth had turned away and was staring out of the window, Daisy's letter in her hand. 'I wonder why she didn't want to keep me really.'

'Who?'

'Petula, my real mum. I know Daisy says she was terrified of her father, but to abandon your own baby . . .'

Michael pulled her into his embrace. 'Mary was your real mum, Beth, and you couldn't have had a better one.' He kissed her on the cheek and tucked her hair behind her ears. 'And think about it, if Petula had taken you home, you would've been on that bus.'

Beth shivered. 'God, you're right, I hadn't thought about that.'

At the sound of Jake's laughter, they both turned and stared at their son. He was in fits of giggles at his favourite cartoon, his cheeks glowing from the heat of the fire.

Michael gave her a smile of reassurance. 'We're going to get him better, Beth, you'll see.'

Half an hour later, Michael leaned back in his desk chair as Beth massaged his shoulders. A quick search on the internet had not thrown up anybody called Lorraine Pryce who would fit the bill. Lorraine would be in her late fifties now, probably married and, without her new surname, almost impossible to locate. He sighed and turned to Beth.

'There's only one thing for it,' he declared. 'I'll just have to go back.'

'Where to?'

He took her hands in his and kissed her fingers. 'Back to where it all began.'

39

The streets where Michael had grown up had changed little in forty years. The cobbles might have been buried beneath a layer of tarmac, but the red-brick terraced houses remained resolutely erect.

He stopped outside his old front door in Bagot Street, smiling as he noticed that the present owners had painted over the hideous mustard yellow and gone for a much more tasteful pale blue instead. He had no desire to knock on the door and ask to take a peek inside. This house did not hold happy memories for him, and he wasn't even sure what had drawn him back. The little hole in the pavement into which he had spent many hours rolling his marbles had long since been filled in. He'd whiled away most of his childhood on such simple pleasures, and he wondered briefly how today's kids would cope without all their electronic gadgetry to keep them amused and connected to their friends. He couldn't help feeling they were missing out on the priceless camaraderie that came with playing out in the street with your mates. Hopscotch for the girls and conkers for the boys.

He turned and looked across the street at Kevin's old

house. Kevin had always had the best conker – an unbeatable boulder that Michael only found out years later had been baked in the oven and covered with a layer of clear nail varnish. He laughed to himself at the memory. No wonder he'd been unable to beat Kevin, and had bruised knuckles for most of the autumn into the bargain. The kids today did not know what they were missing.

As the March wind began to sting his cheeks, Michael turned his collar up and quickened his pace, leaving the street where he had grown up without a backward glance. He would not be returning again. It took him only five minutes to walk to Daisy's old house in Lilac Avenue, which held much sweeter memories for him. Not for the first time he wondered what would have happened to him if Daisy had not taken him under her wing and shaped his life. As far back as his seventh birthday, when she'd given him the artist's kit, her influence had been far-reaching. With her encouragement and never-ending praise, she had made him believe that he could become an architect, and of course she was right. She always was. Without Daisy, he would not have a successful career and a practice of his own, and without Daisy he would never have met Beth.

After that first visit, they'd returned to Claremont Villas in Blackpool every year, always his birthday weekend, and he'd played with little Beth on the beach. At first he'd thought she was a pain; being six years his junior, she really wasn't much fun at all. But as the years passed and they both grew up, the age gap became irrelevant, and eventually they acknowledged that their friendship had grown into something more. Daisy and Beth's mother, Mary, had become great friends, and they really were like a little family.

Michael marvelled once more at how Daisy and Mary had colluded over the years to keep the identity of Beth's birth mother a secret. He glanced at his watch and screwed his eyes up as he tried to make out the date. Daisy would be back before the end of the month, and she certainly had some explaining to do.

It was late afternoon by the time he arrived at the Taverners. He was relieved to see that the pub had undergone a considerable transformation since the seventies; he was feeling a little peckish, and it was possible there would be some decent food on offer. Gone was the green and white tiled porch that resembled a public lavatory, and in its place was a wooden-beamed portico with a glass front door embossed with the name of the pub in a fancy swirling script. A spotlight shone down on the silver-flecked black tiles beneath his feet as he grabbed the brass handle and pushed the door open. The Saturday-afternoon crowd were eagerly tucking into their gastronomic delights, all served up on grey slate tiles instead of plates. The place had certainly come a long way since the days when Selwyn would offer a curled-up cheese sandwich on white bread, with an overripe tomato if you were lucky. The bar area was all open-plan now, with the snug confined to a bygone era.

A young girl dressed in black livery smiled in his direction and raised her eyebrows. 'What can I get you?'

'A pint of Boddies, please.'

'Coming up.' She pulled down on the handle, and the swirling foam filled the glass and sloshed over the top. 'Anything else?'

Michael stared at the blackboard behind the barmaid's head and smiled to himself. One of his pet hates was the pretentious way in which restaurants described food on their menus. Why couldn't they just say 'gravy' instead of 'jus', or 'sauce' instead of 'reduction'? Back in the seventies, he remembered his father, Karl, wearing a medallion round his neck. Now a medallion appeared to be a piece of pork. And as for cod goujons, why they couldn't just come out with it and call them fish fingers was a mystery. Of course Beth did not agree with him. As a food stylist, it was her job to arrange dishes in the most appealing way, and the same went for the description as far as she was concerned.

He was tempted by the beer-battered cod with twice-cooked hand-cut chips. He pointed to the blackboard. 'What on earth is Manchester caviar when it's at home?'

The barmaid frowned and answered as though he were an idiot. 'Mushy peas.'

Michael nodded. 'Of course, silly me. In that case I'll have the steak and ale pie, please.'

She punched the screen on the till. 'Do you want that with chips or salad?'

At this point he would usually look across at his wife and reluctantly order salad, but Beth wasn't here. 'Chips, please.'

He carried his pint over to a vacant table that had been wedged into a corner. Another barmaid appeared with a lighter and lit a candle. Then she fished in the front pocket of her apron and placed a set of napkin-wrapped cutlery on the table. 'Just one, is it?'

Michael nodded. 'Yes, just me.' He couldn't remember the last time he had eaten a meal alone in a pub; in fact he couldn't remember the last time they had eaten out as a family either. Their lives revolved around the hospital now, and simple pleasures such as this were a distant memory. He suddenly felt guilty and indulgent taking this time out for himself when Beth was at home with their poorly son. He should have just come in and asked what he needed to know and then carried on with his search for information.

He was impatient for his food to arrive now and stared expectantly at the double swing doors with their portholes through to the kitchen. He put down his half-supped pint and approached the bar again. The same young girl was serving another customer. 'Excuse me, is the landlord in?'

'Barry, you mean, the manager?'

'Er, well, yes, he'll do.'

'He's out back shifting barrels. I'll send him over when he's finished.'

Michael returned to the table and picked at the wax that was dripping down the side of the candle. When his food arrived, he did have to admit that it looked a bit special. The puff-pastry crust on the pie had risen about two inches and was a glossy golden brown, and his chips had been presented in a little Jenga-style stack. As he tucked in, a man appeared by his side. 'Everything all right with your food?'

It was another pet hate of his. Restaurant staff asking you a question about the food when they could clearly see that you had just stuffed a forkful into your mouth.

He nodded and wiped his mouth with his napkin, then swallowed quickly and took a sip of his beer. 'Yes, very good, thank you.'

'Alex behind the bar said you wanted a word.'

'Ah, yes, you must be Barry. I'm looking for the Pryce family. Selwyn was the landlord here about forty years ago and I was hoping that someone here might remember them. This is the last known address I have for them, you see.'

Barry rubbed his chin. 'Selwyn Pryce? And he was the landlord, you say?'

Michael nodded and bit the end off a chip.

'Forty years is a long time ago.' Barry chuckled. 'I wasn't born meself then.'

'I know – I realise there's only a remote chance that

someone will remember them, but I don't have any other options, so however unlikely—'

'Actually, hang on a minute,' Barry interrupted. 'We did a sixtieth birthday party once for someone who used to be the landlady here.'

Michael's heart quickened, but he refused to let himself get carried away.

Barry called over to the girl behind the bar. 'Alex, what time's Doreen due in?'

'Not till tomorrow now, Barry.' She continued to roll napkins around cutlery.

'Doreen makes all our desserts,' Barry explained. 'She's been here donkey's years. I'll give her a ring if you like.'

Michael stood up and shook his hand. 'I would be very grateful, thank you.'

It had been a long shot, but by the time Michael left the pub, he was armed with a piece of paper bearing the name and address of someone who knew the Pryce family and might just be able to tell him Lorraine's whereabouts.

He sat on the bus, diesel fumes invading his nostrils and making him feel slightly sick. He wished he'd brought the car, even though parking fees were extortionate in town and spaces were at a premium on a Saturday afternoon. The wet streets glistened under the street lights and a group of girls jumped back in alarm as the bus drove through a swollen puddle, soaking them. As it continued to hiss and bounce along the tree-lined streets on the outskirts of the city, Michael fingered the piece of paper in his hand and prepared a speech in his head.

The large three-storey Victorian semi looked well maintained, with a neatly mowed front lawn and weed-free borders. Like all the houses in this neighbourhood, it was marred only by the abundance of wheelie bins each household was forced to keep: brown, grey, green and blue, each crudely daubed with a number in thick white paint.

Every Thursday morning, Michael's own household was thrown into chaos as he and Beth tried to recall which bin was due for collection that day. 'Bin panic', Beth called it. Michael still had a smile on his face when the front door was opened by a rather striking blonde woman he guessed to be in her sixties, who gazed down at him from her vantage point on the top step.

'You'd better not be selling anything,' she warned as she began to close the door.

'No, no, nothing like that.' He took the piece of paper from his pocket. 'I'm looking for Patricia Atkins.'

She narrowed her eyes. 'That's me, who wants to know?'

Michael held out his hand. 'My name's Michael McKinnon. I wonder if you could spare a few minutes.'

She ignored the hand. 'What's this all about?' Her voice was throaty and thick with smoke.

It was obvious she was in no mood for pussyfooting about, so he decided to take the plunge. 'Do you know a girl called Lorraine Pryce?'

Her features clouded for a second as she took hold of the door jamb. As the silence dragged on, Michael feared he'd reached a dead end. He felt awkward imposing himself and was about to apologise and leave when she spoke again. 'I certainly do know her. Lorraine Pryce was my stepdaughter.'

40

Michael followed Trisha into her kitchen and accepted her offer of a seat at the huge pine table. 'Do you want a brew?'

He shook his head. 'No thanks, I've just had a pint in the Taverners.'

'Did Barry give you my address, then?'

Michael nodded. 'Yes, he rang one of his staff members who's worked at the Taverners a long time and she was able to—'

She cut him off. 'Do you mind if I smoke?' She fumbled around in her cigarette packet.

'Please, it's your house, go ahead.'

As she lit up and inflated her lungs with smoke, Michael could see her visibly relax, and he felt a fleeting sympathy for her obvious dependence on tobacco.

She noticed him watching and smiled apologetically. 'Filthy habit, I know.' She shrugged and took another long, calming drag. 'So why do you want to know about Lorraine?'

Michael shuffled in his seat. 'Look, I'd better start at the beginning. You don't remember me, do you?'

She frowned. 'No, should I?'

'It was a long time ago, but I'm sure you've not forgotten that bus crash.' He paused for a second. 'I know I haven't.'

Trisha flicked ash off the end of her cigarette, her interest piqued. 'How do you know about that?'

'I was on the bus.' He let his words sink in as Trisha tried to place him.

'Michael McKinnon, you say?' It only took a few seconds more for the penny to drop. 'Bloody hell, you're not little Mikey, are you? Karl's son?'

'The very same.'

She leaned back in her chair and regarded him across the table. 'My God, I've often wondered what happened to you.' She reached across and took his hand. 'How've you been?'

It was difficult to sum up the past forty years. 'Not bad. Married now, got a little boy of my own, Jake, he's five.' He didn't feel like expanding on his situation to a near-stranger. He just wanted the information, and then he would be on his way.

'Well I'm pleased for you, I really am. Tragic for you losing your dad like that.'

Michael was touched by her apparent concern and felt he had to ask Trisha about her own situation, even though he was anxious to be on his way. 'What about you?'

'Well, as you probably heard, I left Selwyn a few months after the crash.' She said it so matter-of-factly that Michael guessed she had long since given up feeling any remorse at the decision. 'I couldn't have coped with him like that and he was much better off with Barbara. Then I married Lenny when he got out of Strangeways. I'd always said I'd wait for him, just didn't think I'd have to wait twenty years.' She gave a hoarse laugh, which turned into a lung-wrenching cough. Eyes watering, she thumped her chest and grabbed the packet of cigarettes. 'Dear God, I've got to give these things up.'

Michael waited for her to compose herself before continuing. 'Anyway, Barry at the pub said you might know where I can find Lorraine. Do you?'

Trisha continued as though she hadn't heard the question. 'I didn't go in the Taverners for years after, certainly not while Selwyn and Barbara were still there, but when they left and the next people did the place up, I started dropping in again. It's been bought by a chain now, and Barry's the manager. I had my sixtieth there a few years back.' She glanced at Michael as if to check he was still listening. 'It's proper posh in there now, isn't it?'

Michael nodded and leaned across the table. 'And Lorraine, do you know where she is now?'

'Well, as you can imagine, we're not that close, but yes, as it happens, I do know where she can be contacted.' She rose from her seat and rummaged through a drawer full of odds and sods, fishing out a plastic telephone index. She slid the tab down the side to 'F' and pressed a button to make the lid pop up. 'Here it is, Lorraine Fenton.'

301

Michael craned to see for himself. 'That's smashing. Do you have her telephone number?'

'Telephone number? Good God, no. She lives in America; even if we did have anything to talk about, I couldn't afford to call her.' Trisha shrugged. 'I still send her a Christmas card, though.'

Michael's shoulders dropped a little and Trisha was quick to pick up on his body language.

'I can see that's not the answer you wanted, but directory enquiries will probably give you the number. Why do you want to contact her anyway?'

'Oh, it's a long story and I've taken up too much of your time already. I'll just write the address down if I may.' He reached into his pocket and pulled out a pen. 'Do you have a scrap of paper?'

'Her mum would have her telephone number.'

Michael looked up, a glimmer of hope causing his heart to beat faster. 'Her mother?'

'Sure. You must remember Barbara . . . you know, Babs, as they all called her.'

'Of course I remember her. You mean she's still . . .'

'Alive? Oh yeah, she lives in an old folk's home in Didsbury.'

The rain had turned to sleet by the time Michael left Trisha's house, and he pulled out his mobile to call for a taxi. As he stepped out of the cab fifteen minutes later, he surveyed the Pinewood Residential Home and gave a low appreciative whistle. It was a double-fronted property with a sweeping gravelled driveway leading up to the front steps, a huge bay window on either side. A smoked-glass door automatically slid across to allow Michael to enter the reception area. A chandelier hung from the domed ceiling, and his feet sank into the thick pile of the pale green carpet. He had seen five-star hotels that were less well-appointed.

The receptionist was pristine and polished, with a smart navy uniform and a blue and pink silk scarf tied at her throat. She reminded Michael of cabin crew as she beamed a welcome to him. 'Good evening, how may I help you?' He was sure her face muscles must be aching.

Michael cleared his throat. 'Yes, I wonder if I might have a word with one of your residents, Barbara Pryce.'

'Is she expecting you?'

'Er . . . no, but I won't keep her long.'

The receptionist smiled. 'If there's one thing our residents have, it's time.' She offered him a pen and pushed the visitors' book across the desk. 'I'll have someone go and find her, if you'll just sign in here.'

Babs was sitting alone in the communal lounge, a newspaper folded on her knee, her eyes closed and her hands clasped together on her lap. Michael crept up beside her and knelt down. Not wishing to startle her awake, he took hold of one of her hands and gently smoothed his thumb over the papery skin. She didn't stir, and he took the opportunity to study her. Her features were still strong and pretty, not too withered by her advancing years, though her once-dark locks were now completely white and he could see her pale pink scalp beneath her curls. He remembered how fond his father had been of her, and what a great time they had had at the fair, until he got lost and Babs had found him again. She'd looked after him in the immediate aftermath of the crash too, and he felt a rush of affection for the old woman, suddenly wanting to tell her how grateful he'd been.

He stood up and heard his knees crack. Babs's eyelids fluttered open and she gazed up at him, confusion ingrained on her face.

He spoke first, his voice just a whisper. 'Babs, sorry to wake you. It's Michael McKinnon. Er . . . you know, Mikey.'

Babs attempted to speak. She opened and closed her mouth a few times before anything came out. 'Mikey?' she managed eventually.

He crouched down by her side again so she could get a better look at him. 'You remember me, don't you?' The scent of lily of the valley wafted between them.

A faint smile spread across her lips and she reached out and stroked his cheek. 'As if I could forget you.' She placed her hands on the arms of the chair and braced herself.

'Oh, please don't get up, Babs.'

She brushed him aside and drew herself up to her full

height. 'I'm not that old and decrepit that I can't stand to greet my guests.'

Michael felt humbled, inwardly chastising himself. 'I'm sorry.' He leaned forward and gave her an awkward hug. 'It's good to see you.'

She gestured to another chair. 'Drag that over here, will you, and we can have a proper chat.'

Her sleep-filled features of a few moments ago were now animated; Michael found that he was glad he'd made this journey, even if it turned out to be fruitless in the long run.

'Er . . . well, how've you been?' he began.

Babs waited a few seconds before answering, a smile lingering on her lips. 'Oh, little Mikey. You haven't sought me out after all these years to ask me that, have you?'

She had a twinkle in her eye and Michael knew she was toying with him, still as sharp as ever. He held his palms aloft. 'You got me.'

Babs leaned forward and patted his knee, as though he was still the small boy he had been the last time she saw him. 'What can I do for you, Mikey?'

A lifetime had passed since anybody other than Aunt Daisy had called him that, and his mind went to his own son, who, truth be told, was rarely from his thoughts. Little Jake, so vulnerable and yet so full of life. A life that would simply ebb away were it not for a machine. People had always called Michael brave, but that was nothing compared to what his own son had to suffer day after day. That was the true definition of bravery. Michael tugged at his collar to let some of the heat out, the lump in his throat making it near impossible to speak. Unshed tears stood in his eyes, perilously close to spilling over. 'I need your help, Babs.'

Babs reached across to a table and pulled a tissue out of a box, handing it to Michael. The sight of it caused the tears to spill down his cheeks, and he flicked them away in embarrassment. 'I'm sorry,' he sniffed. 'Sometimes it's hard to hold it all in.'

He felt safe here, cocooned in this leather wing-backed chair, with nobody making any demands on him. He took a deep breath and continued. 'It's difficult to know where to start, so please bear with me. I hate bringing up the past, especially when it's so traumatic, but you remember the bus crash?'

Babs raised her eyebrows and stared in disbelief.

'I'm sorry, of course you do. I mean, how could we ever forget that night? Our lives changed for ever, and . . .' He realised he was rambling and could have kicked himself when he remembered what had happened to Selwyn. He knew it sounded like the afterthought it was, but he couldn't help himself asking anyway. 'Where's Selwyn? I mean, is he still . . . with us?' He cringed at his own excruciating clumsiness, wishing that Beth was by his side to dig him out of his hole.

Babs shook her head. 'He died in 2000, pneumonia; he was sixty-nine. Twenty-four years he lived with those injuries, and I don't think there was a day when he felt sorry for himself. He really was an incredible man, and I was lucky to be married to him.'

'He was lucky to have you, more like,' asserted Michael.

Babs wafted her hand in dismissal. 'That's love, Mikey. It's what you do.'

This was turning into a humbling experience for Michael. 'And your daughter, Lorraine?'

Babs's face immediately brightened. 'She lives in the States now, California, married a surgeon she did, but they're both retired now. They have a nice life.' She gazed around the plush day room. 'Who do you think pays for all this?'

'That's nice,' Michael said, wondering how he could turn the conversation round once more to the crash. He could hear the clattering of crockery in the kitchen, and the smell of roast chicken seeped into the day room. 'Well, you'll be having your tea soon, so I'd better press on.' Her expectant face gave him the confidence to continue. 'This is going to sound a bit crazy, but were you aware that Petula gave birth to a baby that day?'

There, it was out, he'd said it; there was no going back now. Babs's eyes darkened and she seemed to choose her words carefully. 'As a matter of fact, I was aware of that. I helped to deliver her.' She held her head high. 'I'm not ashamed of what we did, if that's what you're thinking. We did the right thing, you know. She would have been killed if Petula had taken her home.'

Michael nodded his agreement. 'Yes, I realise that. Do you ever wonder what happened to her, though? The baby, I mean?'

'Not for years, but I did think about her a lot, especially in that first year.'

'Daisy was involved in this too, wasn't she?'

Babs nodded. 'I couldn't have done it without her help. She was brilliant at the birth, so kind towards Petula, and she was the one who took the baby and left her somewhere she would be found.'

'The Claremont Villas guest house.'

Babs frowned. 'Yes, that name sounds familiar. I didn't go with Daisy. I was too busy clearing up the mess and looking after Petula.'

'Well, it seems Daisy was struck by an overwhelming desire to find out what had happened to that baby. She took me with her to Blackpool nearly a year later, and the baby was still there. Mary Roberts had named her Beth, and was bringing her up as her own daughter.'

Babs's mouth fell open. 'Daisy never told me she'd been back, but I suppose it makes sense. And the baby was all right, was she?'

'Thriving, actually. It was the reason Aunt Daisy didn't take it any further. We went back to Blackpool every year after that . . . and Beth and I are now married.'

Michael leaned back in his chair and waited for his words to sink in. The old lady's brain might be as sharp as it ever was, but this was going to take some computing.

Babs pursed her lips, ready to ask a question, but then appeared to change her mind. She gave a quick shake of her head as though she was trying to clear it, then placed her forefingers on her temples and closed her eyes.

'Why are you telling me all this now?' she asked eventually.

Quietly Michael explained about Jake and their desperate need to find blood relatives. 'Our last hope was finding Beth's father, but Mary would never tell Beth anything about him. Of course, we know why now: she didn't know herself. Mary had her stroke before Jake deteriorated, so even she didn't realise how important this was to us.' Michael gently took hold of Babs's hand, as though he could squeeze the information out of her. 'Babs, did Petula tell Lorraine who the baby's father was?'

She reached for another tissue and blew her nose softly. 'I'm so sorry about your son, Mikey. I can't imagine how hard it must be for you all. Petula didn't tell us about the father, but we did find out from her diary some months afterwards.'

Michael edged forward in his chair. 'Really? Do you have a name?'

Babs spoke as though it was obvious and he was a fool for even having to ask. 'Why, it was Jerry, of course, Jerry Duggan.'

Michael slumped back as the implications of Babs's words hit home. 'You mean, Jerry as in Daisy's son?'

Babs nodded. 'Exactly. But I'm surprised you don't already—'

Michael cut her off as he stood up and paced a tight circle, running his hand through his hair. 'You mean Daisy is Beth's grandmother?'

'Yes, she is, but—'

He glanced at his watch as he tried to calculate the time difference. He needed to ring Daisy immediately. 'This is unbelievable news. Just wait until I tell her.'

Babs heaved herself out of her chair and placed her hand on Michael's arm. 'But she already knows, love. She's always known.'

41

As soon as he was out on the street again, Michael pulled his phone from his pocket. The screen came to life and he groaned inwardly at the symbol in the top left corner showing he'd had a missed call. He dragged the symbol down and saw there were six missed calls in total, four from home and two from Beth's mobile.

A feeling of dread settled into his stomach like an undigested suet pudding as his fingers slid across the screen. Beth's mobile went straight to voicemail. His palms began to tingle and his fingers felt as useless as sausages as he scrolled down his list of contacts in search of a taxi firm. He told himself everything was fine, Beth was just impatient to find out if he had any news; that was bound to be it. It would be just like her to pester him for information instead of waiting for him to call her.

He was in the back of a taxi heading for home by the time Beth finally picked up. She sounded hoarse and tired and he knew instantly that his initial fears had been correct. After a brief, tense conversation he rang off and leaned across to speak to the driver. 'Change of plan, mate. Manchester Children's Hospital, please, as quickly as you can.'

Michael burst through the doors of the hospital, his raincoat flying behind him, as though he was in a medical drama. He ran his hands through his wet hair as he approached the front desk. 'My son was brought in about an hour ago, Jake McKinnon.'

The nurse tapped her keyboard and scanned the list of names. 'He's been moved to the ward. I'll have a porter escort you.' For someone who dealt with this kind of situation every day, her expression was grave, and he was grateful to her for not treating his son as just another patient.

'Thank you,' he managed.

He saw Beth before she saw him. She was standing outside Jake's room, staring through the window, her palm stroking the glass, Galen hanging down by her side. Michael quickened his pace, calling her name as he got closer. She turned as she heard him approaching, took a step forward and collapsed into his arms like a puppet who'd had its strings cut, her sobs muffled by the collar of his coat.

'I came as soon as I could. How is he?' He pushed her gently away so he too could gaze through the window at his son, as though he was a zoo specimen. Jake lay on the bed, almost totally obscured by wires. Several machines bleeped and flashed and three nurses buzzed around adjusting dials and checking readings.

'He's stable now, but they've sent for Dr Appleby,' Beth said. She held up Galen and attempted a smile. 'He's been asking for this.'

Michael took the monkey and sniffed the head of his favourite childhood toy. He watched as a nurse tenderly stroked Jake's forehead before picking up his wrist and studying her watch. 'Tell me what happened.'

'It's all my fault, Michael.'

'Come on, Beth.' He tightened his grip around her shoulders. 'You've got to stop blaming yourself.'

His reassurance seemed to give her the confidence to continue. 'He was upstairs, playing with his Lego in his bedroom. I know he likes to play with it in front of the fire, but I wanted to hoover the place and get it looking tidy for once. It's ages since I've felt able to do anything as mundane as housework, but I noticed the carpet was encrusted with bits of cereal and half-eaten biscuits. The dust on the mantelpiece was an inch thick, and I had this impulse to go around with the Mr Sheen. Jake didn't protest much when I said we had to take his Lego box upstairs; he even helped me put it all back in the box.' She smiled up at Michael. 'He's such a good boy.'

'You don't need to tell me that. Go on,' he urged.

'Well as soon as he got upstairs, he tipped the box out on his bedroom floor and carried on with his building. I said I would bring him some warm milk in a few minutes. Then I heard the doorbell and turned to leave before he could answer.' She shuddered, and her voice faltered. 'It was Elaine from next door, just checking to see how Jake was, and I asked her in for a cup of tea.' She looked up at Michael for confirmation that she'd done the right thing. 'I mean, how could I not?'

'Of course, it was only polite. Then what happened?'

'Michael, I swear he can't have been alone for more than ten minutes, but when I took his milk up, he was lying on his back on the floor, his eyes half closed, and completely still.' She gave way to a huge sob. 'I thought he was dead, Michael. I'm so sorry, it's all my fault.'

He pulled her into a fierce embrace, his response firm and emphatic. 'Beth, it's not your fault. I don't know how many times I've got to tell you to stop blaming yourself for everything that happens.'

He stared down at the moth-eaten monkey. His fur had worn away and one eye was missing, but his rictus grin was still plastered reassuringly on his face. Michael stroked the monkey's head and thought about his own father. Galen was his only link to Karl, and a poignant reminder of his father's last tragic day.

'My dad was determined to win this for me at the fair. I was upset because I'd got lost and thought I would never see him again. I'll never forget the look of relief on his face when Babs took me back to him. He squeezed me until I could hardly breathe and held me for ages, not saying anything. I think he was too overcome to speak and didn't want me to see him crying.' He stared at Jake, lying motionless on the bed. 'I know how he felt now. He thought he'd lost his son and he was terrified.'

'You still miss him, don't you?'

'He died when I was six, Beth. Forty years is a long time, but yes, I wish I could have had him for longer.'

They both turned as they heard Dr Appleby approaching. 'Good evening, Beth, Michael.' He dispensed with further niceties as he apprised them of Jake's condition. 'I'm afraid tests confirm that Jake has lost ninety per cent of his kidney function, which means he's now reached end-stage renal failure.' He waited for his words to sink in. 'Now, I know that sounds pretty awful, but please be assured that he can continue on dialysis, which will adequately perform the job of the kidneys. We'll keep him in here for a couple of days to monitor his progress, and then there's no reason why he won't be able to go home and continue with his overnight dialysis there until a suitable donor is found.'

'How long will that take, though, Doctor?' asked Beth.

Dr Appleby raised his eyebrows. 'To find a donor? I'll be honest with you, it could take years, or we might be lucky and find one next week. It really is a lottery.'

Michael took Beth's arm and nodded towards Jake's window. 'When can we go in and see him?'

Dr Appleby managed a smile. 'I'll have a word with the nurse and we'll see what we can do.' He patted Beth's shoulder. 'Don't be too alarmed by all the machines; we're just monitoring him for now, and the signs are encouraging.'

Beth took hold of her son's small hand, comforted by the warmth it delivered. His eyes were closed and he looked peaceful in spite of the spaghetti of wires surrounding his frail body. 'Do you know, only a third of the population is on the organ donor register.'

'Well, I suppose it's not something people think about until they're directly affected,' Michael answered. 'I mean, we weren't registered until all this happened, were we?'

'The worst thing is, I know I'll be ecstatic when a donor is found, but that won't happen unless somebody dies first. How can we be happy when another family has just lost someone they care deeply about?'

'It's difficult,' Michael agreed. 'But maybe it's a comfort to the relatives if they know that their loved one will live on in someone else.' He shrugged. 'I don't know, it means they didn't die for nothing, perhaps.'

'No, I suppose not.' She glanced across at him. 'Anyway, you've not told me how you got on with your search. No news, I take it?' She caught the barely perceptible flicker of his eyelid. 'Michael?'

'Not here, let's step outside.'

Beth placed a tender kiss on Jake's forehead, slipped Galen under the sheet next to him and followed Michael out into the corridor.

'Let's get a coffee,' he suggested.

She grabbed his arm to pull him back. 'No, tell me now, what do you know?'

Michael glanced furtively up and down the corridor as though he was going to reveal top-secret classified information. 'I did find out something.'

Beth felt her knees weaken. 'Go on.'

'I've found out the name of your father.' He paused momentarily. 'But you're not going to like it.'

She didn't bother to hide her impatience. 'For God's sake, Michael, just tell me.'

He placed his hands under her elbows as she stared expectantly into his face. 'It's Daisy's son, Jerry.'

She stared at him open-mouthed for several seconds before she found her voice. 'What? No, that's not possible. Daisy would have said something.'

Michael agreed. 'I know, it's incredible that she's kept this to herself all these years. I mean, she's your grandmother, Beth.'

As Michael's words sank in, Beth's thoughts turned to Daisy and the part she had played in their lives. She'd taken the six-year-old Michael under her wing, introduced them to each other and kept Mary's secret all these years. They both loved her as though she was one of the family, and now it appeared she really was. 'But why didn't she say anything? I don't understand.'

'She's been away for three months, Beth. She has no idea that Jake's condition has worsened, remember. She'd obviously made some sort of promise to your mother . . . to Mary, not to divulge who your parents were.'

Beth delved into her handbag. 'I'm calling her right now.'

Michael gently took hold of her phone. 'Please, Beth. I know you've had a shock, but now's not the time to go in all guns blazing. She'll be back the day after tomorrow; we'll talk to her then and see what she's got to say for herself.'

'But . . .'

Michael placed his finger on her lips. 'You heard Dr Appleby. Jake's stable, the machine's working and he's out of immediate danger. We've waited this long; we can wait a couple more days.'

42

'Can I get you another glass of champagne, Mrs Duggan?'

Daisy glanced up at the smiling air stewardess, marvelling that her immaculate make-up was still fresh and dewy even after several hours in the air. She nodded and raised her glass. The business-class ticket was costing a fortune; she might as well make the most of it. 'Yes, please, that would be lovely.' The air stewardess expertly refilled her champagne flute and addressed the passenger behind her with the same question.

After three months away, Daisy always looked forward to returning home to Lilac Avenue. The worst of the winter weather was sure to be over, and she relished the thought of the warm spring days to come, which she planned to spend pottering in her garden. She pressed the button on the side of her seat and it slowly moved into a horizontal position, like a dentist's chair. She stretched out her muscles gratefully and wondered how long her old bones would allow her to make such an arduous journey.

Once she had drained the champagne, she pulled the complimentary comfort pack out of the seat pocket in front of her. She slathered moisturiser over her face and positioned the eye mask. If she could spend the last few hours of the flight asleep, she would hopefully arrive feeling somewhat refreshed. Mikey would be waiting for her at the airport, and she felt a flutter of excitement at the thought of seeing him again. He was like a son to her and she had missed him terribly. His life hadn't turned out so badly after all, and Daisy knew she was in no small way responsible for that. The truth was, though, he'd saved her life too, giving her a reason to get up in the morning, someone to cook for, to knit for and lavish affection on, and she would always be grateful for that. Now he was happily married with a family of his own, and Daisy had played her part in that too. At eighty-five years of age, she knew she would probably not be around for many more years, but she could die with the knowledge that the frightened little boy who had lost the father he adored and then been neglected by his mother had turned out all right.

She thought about little Jake, who was so like his father in many ways: quiet, contemplative and so brave. He'd been in and out of hospital all his short life and his resilience was remarkable for one so young. Then there was Beth. Daisy had been the architect of her life too, though of course Beth was not aware of that fact. It saddened Daisy deeply that she'd been away when Mary died, because she knew how close Beth had been to her mother. She had wanted to return the minute she heard the news, but Mikey had persuaded her to remain where she was and enjoy the rest of her holiday. He was right; there would be plenty of time to pay her respects to Mary when she got back. If there was one person who would have understood why she did not return, it would have been Mary herself. There was absolutely no doubt in Daisy's mind that she had done the right thing all those years ago when she left the vulnerable towel-wrapped bundle on Mary's doorstep.

Daisy felt the plane judder as it began its descent through the thick clouds. She yawned theatrically to try and clear her ears as the stewardess gently asked her to put her seat back in the upright position. Daisy started to pack away her belongings into her flight bag and slipped her swollen feet back into her shoes. She plonked the stuffed teddy she had bought for Jake at the airport on top of the bag and settled in for the final minutes of the journey.

The plane bounced around in the cloud, the high winds buffeting it left and right, making Daisy's palms moist with anxiety. She squeezed her eyes shut as she felt the jolt of the wheels descending and waited for them to connect with the runway. It was only when she heard the reassuring bump confirming the plane's safe landing that she let go of her breath and stared out of the window. It was grey and dull, even though a watery sun tried valiantly to shine through the clouds. It wasn't quite raining, but there was mizzle in the early morning air. Daisy smiled. She was home.

Michael and Beth stood in the arrivals hall, the silence between them born of nerves and apprehension. Michael glanced up at the board again and scanned the list for Daisy's flight number. 'Look, it's landed.' He pointed. 'She'll be through soon.'

'I'll think I'll just ring Elaine again to check on Jake.'

Michael stared at her.

'I'm sorry, you're right. I only rang ten minutes ago, didn't I?'

Jake had been discharged from hospital the day before, and Beth had naturally been uneasy about leaving him. But she was also desperate to see Daisy. Jake was stable now, having his dialysis at home overnight, and they were all trying to be positive and just getting on with their lives in the best way they could. They didn't have any other choice. Elaine had been armed with Beth's mobile number, Michael's number, the direct number to Ward 36 at the hospital and Dr Appleby's number. An overnight bag lived in the hallway, ready for the joyous day when the call would come to say a donor had been found.

It was Michael who spotted her first, coming through the double doors, pushing her trolley laden with cases and trying her best to keep it travelling in a straight line. Although she looked tired, she radiated health, her silver hair contrasting with her tanned skin. When she spotted

322

them, she beamed and raised her arm to wave, causing the trolley to veer sharply to the left and catching the foot of a disgruntled passenger. 'Sorry,' she muttered.

Michael came to her assistance and greeted her with an affectionate embrace and a kiss on the cheek. Beth hovered behind, still not sure how she was going to handle the situation. Michael had forbidden her from just blurting everything out in her usual fashion.

'How are you, Aunt Daisy? You look well.'

She squeezed his arm. 'Ooh, I've had a grand time, I have, but it's good to be back. There's no place like home, you know.' She spotted Beth then. 'And Beth, how lovely of you both to come.' She pulled the younger woman towards her and cupped her face in her hands. 'You look tired, and you've lost weight. Losing your mum must have taken its toll.' She stopped and looked around. 'Where's Jake?'

The arrivals hall at Manchester airport was certainly not the place for a lifetime of secrets to be aired. Michael guided Daisy towards the exit. 'He's fine, he's at home with Elaine. He's had a couple of spells in hospital whilst you've been away, but he's settled now.'

Daisy stopped in her tracks. 'Hospital? Mikey, why on earth didn't you ring me?'

'He's fine, Aunt Daisy. Look, let's get you home. We'll put the kettle on and we can have a chat over a cup of tea.'

As Michael took charge of the trolley, Daisy linked her

arm through Beth's. 'I was so sorry to hear about your mother, Beth.'

'Oh, were you? Which—'

Michael shot her a warning look over his shoulder. He was right. It would wait.

The smell of Daisy's home in Lilac Avenue always transported Michael back to his childhood. The beeswax she used to polish her mahogany sideboard was ingrained into both the wood and the very fabric of her house. 'I've had the heating on for you,' he announced as Daisy turned the key in the lock.

'That's kind of you, Mikey love.'

'And I've got you some bread and milk in too.'

Daisy reached up and ruffled his hair. 'You're still a good lad.' She turned to Beth. 'I say, he's a good lad isn't he? You hang on to him, Beth.'

Beth offered a weak smile that had no hope of reaching her eyes.

Daisy frowned. 'You're awfully quiet, Beth. Is everything all right?' She grabbed hold of her arm. 'It's Jake, isn't it? There something you're not telling me. Mikey . . . what's going on?'

'Why don't we go and sit in the lounge,' suggested Michael, 'and we can fill you in on what's been happening here.'

'All right,' said Daisy warily. 'Can I just pop a wash on first. I need—'

Beth could stand it no longer and interjected more fiercely than she had intended. 'For God's sake, Daisy, will you please come and sit down. There's something we need to talk to you about.'

In spite of her tan, the colour seeped from Daisy's face. 'I knew something was wrong, I could feel it my water. What's happened?'

Michael gestured towards the door. 'In the lounge, Aunt Daisy . . . please.'

Daisy plonked herself down in the middle of the three-seater couch and Michael and Beth stood in front of the fireplace. Beth folded her arms and stared at her.

'I feel like I'm on trial here.' Daisy tried to laugh, but it came out as a nervous giggle.

'We know everything,' said Beth flatly.

Daisy shuffled to the edge of the couch. She had always feared this day would come, but she'd hoped to be the one to control it. It was a secret she'd intended to take to her grave, but it seemed events had caught up with her. She took a deep breath and braced herself for the barrage of questions.

43

The silence between the three of them seemed to drag on endlessly. It was Michael who spoke first. He tried to keep the anger out of his voice; after all, Daisy had acted in the best interests of both Beth and Mary throughout everything. 'Remember this?' He whipped an envelope out of his inside pocket.

Daisy reached up and studied her own familiar handwriting. 'I suppose it's the letter I wrote to Mary, is it?' She spoke quietly. 'Where did you find it?'

'At Mum's,' said Beth. 'Well, when I say Mum's . . .'

'Don't be like that, Beth.' Daisy sounded weary. 'Mary *was* your mum, nothing's changed there.'

'Except she wasn't really, was she?' Beth countered.

'In every way that mattered she was.' Daisy reached out for Beth's hand. 'Look, I know this is a terrible shock for you, but Mary could not have loved you any more if she had given birth to you herself. I had no way of knowing for sure at the time, but when I left you on her doorstep, I could not have chosen a more caring, loving person to bring you up.' She paused and rubbed the back of Beth's hand. 'Of course, I didn't know then that she wasn't going to hand you over to the authorities, but thank heavens she didn't. It was almost a year later that I found out she'd kept you, and you were both so happy, I couldn't just wrench you away, could I? It was the most difficult decision I've ever had to make. With every fibre of my being I wanted to scoop you up and bring you home, but it was too late. It would have been cruel and I just couldn't do that to Mary.' She paused. 'Or to you.'

Beth did not look convinced and withdrew her hand. 'And would you like to tell us why you went back to Blackpool to see if you could find out what had happened to me?' She was conscious she sounded like a particularly aggressive barrister.

'Well . . . I . . . I was just curious. I mean—'

'So it was nothing to do with me being your granddaughter?'

Daisy stared at Beth and then stole a glance at Michael. His face was stony and his cheeks pulsed as he clenched and unclenched his jaw. She longed for him to break out into his usual reassuring smile, but he remained silent. She ploughed on. 'By the time I found out Jerry was your father, you were settled with Mary. What could I do? I mean, it's not as if he could have looked after you, is it? I kept in touch with you after that, though I never told Mary who I was. I didn't want her to live in fear of you being taken away. We ended up becoming great friends, as you know, but believe me, Beth, if I'd known when you were born that you were my granddaughter, I would have taken you in, of course I would; there's no question about it.'

Beth looked at Daisy's gnarled hands, the arthritic knuckles swollen and misshapen, bulging blue veins visible through her papery skin. Although she clasped them tightly together, it did little to disguise the fact that her hands were shaking, and Beth felt ashamed that she was causing the old lady so much distress. She slumped on the settee beside her. 'I'm sorry we're being so hard on you. It's just that there's something we've not told you yet.' She glanced over at Michael, who nodded his reassurance. 'Jake's condition has deteriorated whilst you've been away.'

Daisy began to speak, but Beth raised her palm to stop her. 'We didn't tell you because there was nothing you could have done, and we knew you'd probably come rushing back.' Daisy tried again, but Beth interrupted her. 'Please, Daisy, just let me finish. Jake's kidneys have now all but failed, and he needs a transplant.'

Daisy laid her palm flat across her own chest. 'Oh no, the poor little mite, that's just terrible news.' She wafted her hand in front of her face. 'You're right, you should have told me. I would've come straight back.'

Beth managed a small smile. 'He's started dialysis and that will keep him . . . going, but he's on the waiting list for a kidney now.'

Michael joined them on the settee. 'Both Beth and I have been tested, but neither of us is a match, so that's why we've been trying to find other relatives. You know how small our family is, though, so it isn't looking good. That's why tracing Beth's father was so important. He's our only hope.'

Daisy struggled to get out of her seat.

'Where're you going, Aunt Daisy?'

She turned and stared at him. 'Where do you think? To get the phone.'

Daisy dialled the number carefully and cleared her throat. The ringtone sounded muffled and distant, and after a series of clicks she was connected with the familiar voice on the other side of the world.

'Hello, it's Daisy,' she began.

'Oh, you're back then. Did you have a good journey?'

'Not too bad, thank you.'

'What's the weather like there? Not too cold and miserable, I hope.'

Daisy ignored the question. 'Is he there?'

'What? Oh . . . sure, I'll just get him.'

She heard her place the phone down on the huge smoked-glass table where Daisy had spent the previous three months eating her meals. Then her disembodied voice rang out round the kitchen, the sound echoing off the tiled walls.

'Jerry, your mum's on the phone.'

44

Jerry replaced the phone in its cradle on the wall and leaned his forehead against the front of the huge mirrored fridge, welcoming its coolness. He rubbed the resulting greasy mark away with his sleeve, reached for a glass off the draining board and thrust it under the water dispenser, his hand trembling as he raised the glass to his lips and swilled out his parched mouth. Through the window he watched his wife out on the patio as she scrubbed away at the barbecue grill. He opened the fridge and pulled out a chilled bottle of rosé, then grabbed two glasses from the dresser and headed out to join her.

'Lydia love, can you leave that for a minute and come and sit down.'

She looked up and frowned. 'It won't take me a minute to finish it. I want to do it whilst the water's still hot.' She dunked her scourer into the bowl of frothy water and carried on scrubbing.

After thirty-five years of marriage, he knew her well enough to know that arguing would be a futile exercise. He would have to wait until he had her full attention.

The Melbourne summer was slowly transitioning into

autumn, and there was a nip in the evening air that heralded the cooler temperatures to come. Jerry sat himself on the padded swing seat and took a gulp of wine, resting his head back and succumbing to the calming motion of the swing. He closed his eyes and allowed his mother's news to penetrate the dark recesses of his memory. He hadn't thought about the accident for years, because when he did, the overriding sensation of guilt was too much to bear. He'd let everybody down that day and some people had paid with their lives. He knew what everybody had thought of him back in those days: an oddity with no real friends and some questionable hobbies, with his plane spotting and bell ringing. Lydia was the only person who had truly understood him and loved him for who he was. If he'd followed her to Australia in the first place, then that dreadful crash would never have happened.

He thought about Petula and felt his cheeks colour with embarrassment. His mother would no doubt be under the impression that her granddaughter had been conceived during an act of tenderness and love rather than a spontaneous outpouring of frustration culminating in that fateful tryst in Petula's hall. For months afterwards Jerry had gone out of his way to avoid Petula, such was the extent of his mortification at his appalling behaviour. It didn't matter that she was complicit; he should have controlled himself. Instead he'd let his feelings for Lydia cloud the situation and had been unable to think straight.

He opened his eyes as he felt his wife plonk herself next to him on the swing seat, sloshing wine over his hand. 'Do you want a refill?' she asked.

Jerry nodded and held his glass up. 'Thanks, love.'

'Your mum got back all right then?' She stripped off her yellow rubber gloves and let them fall to the floor. 'I must say, she seemed a bit distant on the phone. Perhaps she was tired.'

Jerry twirled the stem of his glass between his fingers, wondering where on earth he was going to start. Lydia would have made a wonderful mother, but each time she'd miscarried, the agony had intensified. The crushing disappointment and devastation became harder to bear, and after the seventh attempt to carry a baby to full term failed, she finally accepted that she would never be blessed with children. Now Jerry was about to tell the person he loved most that he was a father.

She patted his thigh. 'You're quiet, Jerry. Is something wrong?'

His wife had always been unnervingly perceptive, and he knew she deserved nothing less than the whole truth, no matter how painful it would be for him to recount and for her to hear. He was thankful they were sitting side by side and he did not have to look into her eyes. He stared directly ahead as he spoke.

'Lydia, I've got something to tell you.' He paused and took a breath. 'Some of it you know already, about the crash and that . . .'

332

She turned to face him. 'What crash? What are you talking about?'

'The crash I was involved in just before I came out to join you in Australia.'

'Good God, why are you bringing that up now? That must be, what, nearly forty years ago?'

'You're right,' he confirmed. 'It will be forty years this July.' He turned to look at her face then, bare of make-up and with only a few lines around her eyes and mouth. She'd always been fastidious about applying sun cream, and despite the fact that her hair was shot through with silver, she looked at least a decade younger than her fifty-eight years. In her youth she'd never been conventionally pretty, but she had matured into a handsome woman, and her figure – gangly and boyish in her teenage years – was still enviably trim.

'Lydia, I need to talk about what happened that day, and then you can ask me as many questions as you want. I promise I will answer them truthfully.'

'You're frightening me now, Jerry. Why are you being so mysterious?'

He stood up and faced her as though he was on a stage and she was the audience. He would need to deliver the performance of his life. He cradled his glass as he spoke, glad to have something to hold on to.

'I was never supposed to be driving that day, but the chap Selwyn had asked to take us was ill and he was looking for volunteers. Nobody could believe it when I

333

offered because they had no idea I even had a driving licence. Anyway, I got us all there safely and we had a reasonable day out. We met at a pub before driving home; they'd all been drinking, of course, but I'd only had the one pint. I was absolutely fine to drive, no question.'

Lydia stared intently at him and tucked her legs underneath her as she settled into a more comfortable position. 'Go on, I'm listening.'

'Well, we set off up the motorway and they were all in good spirits, singing and that. After a while I needed to use the bathroom. Everybody was eager to get home, so they all groaned when I pulled into the service station, but I was desperate. It must have been the pint I had with my tea.'

'So you were driving when you left . . . where was it again, Blackpool?'

Jerry nodded. 'The rest of them waited on the bus whilst I went inside. There were two lads in the toilets when I went in and I didn't like the look of them, so I decided to use the cubicle instead of the urinal. They were rough-looking blokes, skinheads, with tattoos, the lot. When I came out of the cubicle, they started taking the mickey, wanting to know what I'd got that they hadn't and why I hadn't used the urinal.' He gave a small laugh. 'You remember what a magnet I was for bullies back then. I just ignored them, but they shoved me against the wall and took hold of my collar. I mean, it was totally unprovoked but they could see I was an easy target. Then one of them took my glasses off and crunched them beneath his feet before they both ran out laughing.'

'You poor thing, Jerry. What did you do then?'

'Well, you know how blind I am without my glasses; there was no way I could drive the rest of the way. I went back to the bus and told them I'd dropped my specs and couldn't see well enough to drive. I couldn't tell them what had really happened; I felt such a fool.'

'You should have told Daisy, she would have sorted them out.'

Jerry managed a chuckle. 'You're probably right, she would.' He lowered his voice. 'Anyway, Michael's father, Karl, offered to drive the rest of the way. We weren't that far from home and he hadn't had much to drink so I thought it would be all right. He took the wheel and I sat in the back with Mum and the others. It was shortly after that that we crashed.'

He noticed Lydia give an involuntary shudder. 'It must've been terrible.'

He stared over the garden fence at the water in the bay beyond, shimmering in the evening sun. 'It was, but don't you see, it's all my fault. If I'd stood up to those bullies, they wouldn't have crushed my glasses and it would have been me in the driver's seat, not Karl. It should have been me who died. Michael lost his father because of me. Imagine that, seeing your own father killed.'

Lydia heaved herself off the swing seat and embraced

him. 'Don't talk like that, Jerry. Of course it's not your fault.'

She stroked his cheek and planted a kiss on his lips. Her voice was weary but filled with concern. 'Why are you going over all this again now?'

'There were two other people who died as well as Karl. An old man called Harry, a lovely chap who Mum and I had spent the day with; and a young girl called Petula, who went through the windscreen.'

'I remember you telling me that. How dreadful, the poor girl.'

Jerry took both of Lydia's hands in his own and squeezed them firmly. 'The reason I'm telling you all this now is that Daisy's just told me Petula was pregnant.'

'Oh no, so the baby died too. How far gone was she, do you know?'

'She was full-term. She gave birth to a baby girl just before we set off home.' He shook his head as he pictured how the scene must have unfolded, the distaste evident in his puckered features. 'In the pub toilet, on the floor.'

He watched as confusion spread across his wife's face, her pupils darting left and right as she tried to focus.

'I'm the father of that little girl, Lydia.' He brought her hands up to his lips and kissed them. 'I have a daughter. It's Beth.' He exhaled with relief that he'd managed to get the words out, and then added more emphatically, 'Beth is my daughter.'

Without a word, Lydia let go of his hands and turned

towards the fence, staring out across the water. He left her alone with her thoughts for a few moments until he could stand it no longer. He crept up behind her and placed his hands on her shoulders. She didn't say a word but merely let her head rest against his chest. It was only a small gesture but one that told him she understood. He braced himself to deliver the final bombshell.

'I have to go back to England, Lydia, and I really need you to come with me.'

45

Michael and Beth were huddled together in quiet conversation when Daisy returned to the lounge. They stopped talking when she entered the room.

'It's all sorted,' she announced. 'Jerry'll be back within the next few days, depending on how quickly he can sort out a flight.'

'How did he take the news?' asked Beth. 'About having a daughter, I mean.'

'Hard to say, really. It's not something I thought I would have to tell him over the phone; in fact I never really thought I would have to tell him at all.'

'Don't you think he has a right to know he has a daughter?' asked Michael.

Daisy didn't care for his accusatory tone and immediately went on the defensive. Years of pent-up emotion threatened to spill over in a torrent of self-justification. She fought to keep her composure as she tried to explain her actions.

'You didn't know my Jerry back then, Mikey. He was heartbroken when Lydia's family took her to Australia. I knew he would never find another girl to love him like

338

she did, and I was right about that at least. I know the only reason he didn't go with her in the first place was because of me. He didn't want to leave me on my own, that's how caring he was. He was badly injured in the crash and was actually in a coma for a few days, but he made a really good recovery, and when he was strong enough I insisted he visit Lydia in Oz. He needed a change; he was really quite depressed after the accident, not himself at all. He and Lydia had kept in touch for the couple of years she'd been away. She wrote to him every week, you know. That's how devoted she was to him.' She shook her head. 'He'd tried to move on with his life, he'd been promoted at Williams and Glyn's, but he had no real friends here and certainly no sign of a girlfriend. He was lonely and he felt overwhelmed with guilt that Karl had had to take the wheel.'

Michael bowed his head at the mention of his father's name.

'So, with my blessing, off he went to Australia,' continued Daisy. 'It really was the making of him. Lydia, true to her word, had never stopped loving him, and he managed to get a great job in a bank and made a success of his life there.' She emphasised her point. 'You've seen the pictures of their house in Melbourne; he could never have achieved that kind of success if he'd stayed here in Manchester. They have a nice retirement, no money worries or anything. He buys my plane ticket for me every year; really, both of them are so generous.' She paused for a moment. 'Anyway,

I'm getting ahead of myself here. Mikey, would you please fetch me a glass of water, I'm parched.'

She could hear him in the kitchen, turning the tap on full blast until it ran cold. She turned to Beth. 'I didn't abandon you, Beth, and I'm sorry Jake is so poorly, but I'm going to fix it, you'll see.'

Michael returned with the water and she took a long, grateful gulp. 'It was almost a year after you were born, Beth, that I found out Jerry was your father. Well, it was a total shock, I can tell you. I hadn't even known he was in a relationship with this Petula. By the time I found out, he'd decided to stay in Australia; he was doing well with his job and was engaged to Lydia. He'd been transformed from an awkward, socially inept youth – and as his mother I can say these things – into a confident man with everything to look forward to. If I had told him he had a baby, there was a risk he would have come straight back to England, leaving Lydia and all his prospects behind. I couldn't do that to him, could I?'

She stared at Michael and Beth, searching their faces for confirmation that she had made the right decision. It was Beth who spoke first. 'Don't you think it should have been up to him, though, Daisy?'

'It's easy to say that now, but think about the effect it would have had on both you and Mary. It would have devastated her and been callous in the extreme to wrench you away when you'd bonded with each other for almost a year.'

340

'But all these years you denied me the chance to know my father.'

'I realise that, love, but I was in a quandary. I just did what I thought was for the best.' She turned to Michael. 'You're quiet, Mikey. What have you got to say about all this?'

'To be honest, Aunt Daisy, I've bigger things to worry about.' His weariness cloaked every word. 'My son's desperately ill and all I'm concerned with is finding him a donor, getting him better and rebuilding his life. He's five years old and hasn't even had the chance to live yet. Everything else is in the past and can't be undone, so there's no point in going over it.' He pulled his handkerchief out of his pocket and mopped his brow. 'Did you tell Jerry about Jake?'

Daisy nodded. 'That's why he's coming over: he wants to meet his daughter and his grandson. You must understand, it's all been a big shock for him too. He's completely blameless in all this, but he didn't hesitate when I told him about Jake's illness.' She paused and allowed herself a cautious smile. 'He's willing to be tested, Mikey.'

She tilted her head towards the ceiling in an effort to contain the tears now standing in her eyes. 'I just hope that one day you will find it in your hearts to forgive me.'

Michael took a step towards her and pulled her into his arms. It was all the reassurance she needed.

46

'What do you think I should wear?' Beth held up yet another outfit in front of the mirror; a pile of discarded clothes lay on the bed beside her. 'I can't decide on whether to go smart or casual. I mean, you never see it in magazines, do you? There are suggestions for weddings, how to dress for the office, for a casual dinner date, but never any advice on what to wear when you meet your father for the first time.' She turned to her husband, who was lying back on their bed, his hands clasped behind his head, watching her with quiet amusement. 'What do you think?' She held up a grey trouser suit she had not worn for months.

'I think that's too formal. In any case, it'll drown you now, I expect.'

She held the trousers against her slender frame. 'Mmm, I suppose you're right.' She had spent most of her adult life on one diet or another, trying to lose that extra half-stone. From Atkins to Dukan to cabbage soup, she'd tried them all, but none was as effective as the 'Worried Sick About Your Desperately Ill Child Diet'. She did not recommend it. 'I'm just going to go with jeans then, and this cashmere jumper.'

'I think that will be perfect. Jerry's going to love you whatever you decide to wear.'

'Mmm,' she mused. 'I hope so. Is Jake still asleep?'

'Yes, I've just checked on him. The machine has about another hour to run, so hopefully he'll stay asleep until then.'

Beth checked her wristwatch. 'That's fine, we'll have plenty of time to check the dialysis fluid, take his temperature and get him dressed before we have to leave. I said I'd ring Elaine when we're ready to go.'

'Whatever would we do without her?'

'She's a good neighbour, that's for sure, and she's wonderful with Jake, isn't she? He's become quite fond of her, actually.'

She took the brush to her hair and pulled it into a ponytail. The style emphasised her high cheekbones and made her face look thinner, but with a coat of mascara and a slick of lip gloss she would look presentable.

Down in the kitchen, Michael popped bread into the toaster. 'One slice or two?'

She knew she would have to force down some breakfast, but the thought of putting anything in her mouth made her want to retch. Butterflies had taken up residence in her stomach and there was no room for anything else. 'Er, just the one, please.'

She gazed down at the photo of Jerry that Daisy had given her. 'Do you remember him, Michael?'

'Who, Jerry? No, not really. I used to play in his room

when I was kid. Daisy had kept all his old toys and I remember he had this brilliant geometry set that I used to draw stuff with.' Michael flicked the switch on the kettle as he smiled at the memory. 'And he had this globe that lit up. I used to love looking at Australia and couldn't believe that he lived on the other side of the world.'

Beth ran her thumb over the photo. 'He looks like a nice bloke, though, doesn't he? I wonder what sort of father he would have been.' She shook her head. 'I just can't imagine what it must be like to have a dad.'

The toaster spat out three slices and Michael began to spread them with butter. 'Well all I can say is, my dad was the most important person in my life. I idolised him actually. I can still remember them telling me he'd died. I know it was a long time ago, but I'll never forget lying in that hospital bed willing him to walk through the door and tell me they'd made a mistake. I just couldn't believe I was never going to see him again.'

'It must be worse for you, Michael. You knew what you were missing. I've never had a dad to miss.'

Michael handed her a slice of toast. 'Let's look forward now, Beth. It's the future that matters, not the past.'

The twenty-minute drive to the airport seemed interminable. Daisy sat in the back seat, staring silently out of the window. The runway came into view, the lights shimmering on the rain-soaked surface, and Beth attempted to swallow her non-existent saliva.

She recognised him the instant she saw him come through the double doors of the arrivals hall. As well as the photo Daisy had given her, she'd seen numerous others of him over the years and could easily have picked him out of a crowd. His hair was still thick and dark, with only a few flecks of grey, but the black-rimmed glasses, so familiar to Beth from the photo on Daisy's sideboard, had been replaced with a more modern, frameless pair. His face was spangled with five o'clock shadow and he looked exhausted. Lydia was by his side, cutting a surprisingly elegant figure, a pale pink pashmina slung about her shoulders. He waved as he spotted them waiting by the tape barrier and quickened his pace.

Daisy moved forward to greet them. 'Welcome home, son.'

As he embraced his mother, Beth caught his eye over Daisy's shoulder. He smiled and moved his mother gently away. 'You must be Beth.' He held out his hand. 'Jerry Duggan. I'm pleased to meet you.' His Manchester accent was still in there somewhere, but the Australian lilt now dominated his vowels, her name coming out as more of a 'Bith'.

She took hold of his hand and smiled. 'I'm pleased to meet you too . . . er . . . Jerry.' She'd wondered whether she should call him Dad, but when the moment came, she realised she had never called anybody that before, and the word lodged in her throat.

Michael made his way forward and thrust his hand out.

'Jerry, it's good to meet you at last, thank you so much for coming.'

'Don't mention it, nothing could have stopped me making this journey. Please, meet my wife, Lydia.'

The car ride back to Daisy's house was somewhat strained, with nobody wanting to bring up the subject of Jake and why Jerry and Lydia had travelled over ten thousand miles to see them. They made small talk about the flight and the weather, and by the time they arrived at Daisy's house, Beth couldn't wait to get out of the car.

'Who wants a proper brew, then?' Daisy enquired as she filled the kettle. She turned to her daughter-in-law. 'No offence, Lydia, but there's no place like home when you want a proper cup of tea.'

Lydia laughed. 'None taken, Daisy. As a matter of fact, I agree with you. I think it's all about the water as much as anything.'

Crowded into the small lounge, with cups of tea in hand, they all sat in silence. Typically, it was Daisy who was brave enough to wrestle the elephant in the room to the ground in her no-nonsense fashion. 'Now, Jerry, you've discussed this kidney donation thing with Lydia, have you?'

'Naturally, and she's in full agreement. We'll do whatever's necessary.'

Beth's throat immediately tightened and she fiddled nervously with her necklace. 'Jerry, we can't thank you enough . . . I mean, for even considering this. It's such a huge thing and we are so grateful.'

'It's the least I can do. I haven't been around for you all these years, and if I can do anything to help Jake, then it will be my privilege to do so.' He paused and took hold of Lydia's hand. 'He is our grandson, after all.'

'Words of thanks seem inadequate,' said Michael, 'but as Beth says, we are grateful you're willing to be tested. We've made an appointment with Dr Appleby – he's Jake's nephrologist – for the day after tomorrow. We thought we'd give you the chance to get over your jet lag first.'

'When can I meet Jake?' asked Jerry. 'I'd like to get to know the little chap.'

Beth smiled at Michael. 'We were hoping you'd say that. Please come for your evening meal tomorrow night, about five. Jake goes to bed at seven, so that'll give you a couple of hours with him.'

She noticed Daisy staring down into her lap, pulling at a loose thread on her cardigan. 'What's up, Daisy?'

The old woman sighed. 'Oh, nothing really. I'm just sad that it's such terrible circumstances that have brought us all together, and I'm sorry I had to wait a lifetime to tell you the truth about your father.'

'Daisy, it's all right. I know you were thinking of Mary, and I can understand your reasons, so there's no point in fretting about it. All that matters now is Jake.' She folded her arms around her grandmother and let her head rest on her shoulder, finding comfort in the familiar scent

347

of Daisy's face powder. It was true: Daisy had not abandoned her but had been a comforting presence in her life since she was a baby, and Beth knew she had to let go of any lingering resentment.

'Thank you, love. That means a lot. I want you to get to know Jerry and Lydia too. You need some time with them on your own, so don't worry about me. I won't be coming for dinner tomorrow.'

Beth went to protest, but Daisy stopped her. 'I insist. You don't need me there getting in the way.'

Jake was kneeling at the coffee table, a crayon in his hand, his tongue sticking out to the side in concentration. 'Who's coming to see me, Mummy?'

Beth stopped scraping the carrots for a second. 'I told you, your grandad, my daddy.'

He looked up from his drawing. 'But I didn't think you had a daddy. Why have I never seen him before?'

'Because he lives in Australia, on the other side of the world.'

'Well how did Nana meet him then?'

Beth had not prepared herself for such penetrating questions, but her son was evidently not daft. 'It's a bit complicated, Jake. Nana was my adoptive mother, you see. My birth mother died in an accident just after I was born.'

'Oh, right. That's sad.' He changed his red crayon for a yellow one and asked, 'Please can I have a carrot stick, Mummy?'

Beth opened the oven and basted the joint of beef. She'd asked Daisy what Jerry's favourite meal growing up had been, and the answer was a roast with all the trimmings, especially Yorkshire puddings. Unfortunately, Yorkshire puddings were the one thing she was no good at. It didn't matter whose recipe she used – Delia's, Nigella's – the result was always a flat disc with uncooked dough in the middle. She called over to her husband, who was ensconced by the fire reading his paper. 'Michael, have you opened the red wine? It needs to breathe.'

'Yes, love, I did it the first time you asked me.'

'And have you put a jug of water on the table?' He didn't look up from his paper. 'Again, all done.'

She caught a glimpse of her reflection in the window. 'Look at the state of me, my face is all shiny and red.' She hurriedly untied her apron. 'I'm just going upstairs to powder my nose.'

Michael rested the paper on his lap. 'You look fine to me, Beth.'

'I'll be the judge of that. Keep a listen out for the doorbell.'

When she came downstairs again, she looked fresher but no more relaxed. She brandished her hairbrush at Jake. 'Come here, you. Let's tidy that mop up.'

'Aww, do you have to?' Jake looked across at his father, hoping to garner some support.

'I wouldn't bother arguing, son, you know she's going to win.'

Beth smoothed the brush over Jake's hair, creating a parting and sweeping his fringe to one side. 'There, that's better. Doesn't he look smart, Michael?'

The doorbell rang before Michael could answer and Beth jumped to her feet. 'Oh God, they're here. Shall I answer it?'

'Well one of us should.' He smiled and kissed her on the cheek. 'Calm down, Beth, you're so jumpy.'

'I know, I can't help it,' she whispered. 'I just want him to like Jake. I mean, what if he doesn't like him? He might change his mind.'

'Beth, you're being ridiculous. Look at him.'

They both turned to stare at Jake. He was engrossed once more in his colouring, having run his fingers through his hair, which was now sporting its usual tousled look. Beth laughed. 'You're right, how could anybody not love Jake?'

47

It was awkward in the narrow hallway, with the five of them crammed into such a small space. Jake clung to the back of Beth's legs and peered round, his thumb stuck firmly in his mouth. Beth bent down and peeled him away. 'Jerry, Lydia, this is Jake.' She smoothed his hair. 'Say hello, Jake.'

He removed his thumb, leaving a slimy film of saliva down his chin. 'Hello.' Then he turned and scuttled back into the kitchen.

'I'm sorry, he's just shy,' Beth apologised.

Jerry laughed. 'It's quite all right. I'm sure I was just the same.'

'Can I take your coat, Lydia?' offered Michael. He slipped the garment off Lydia's shoulders and hung it on the banister. 'Come through to the kitchen, please.'

Lydia gazed round at the cavernous room, kitchen at one end and a comfy living space filled with squashy sofas and a log fire at the other. Patio doors looked out on to the walled garden. 'What a lovely room.'

'We like it,' said Beth. 'We practically live in it. I can get on with the cooking, and Jake is near enough for me to keep my eye on him. We're eating in the dining room tonight, though, as it's a special occasion.' She turned to Michael. 'You did turn the radiator on in there, didn't you?'

He raised his eyes to the ceiling. 'Yes, Beth, I did.' He clapped his hands together. 'Now, who wants a drink?'

Jerry proffered a bottle of red wine. 'I hope this is all right. I didn't know what you would be serving.'

Beth reached for the bottle. 'Oh, there was no need, but thank you, Jerry, it's perfect. We're having roast beef.'

'Excellent, my favourite.'

Jake approached them with a piece of paper pressed to his chest. 'I've done a drawing for you, Grandad.'

Jerry bent down and took the picture. 'Is this you and me, Jake?'

Jake nodded and returned to his sanctuary behind Beth's legs.

'Well I must say, I think that's the best drawing I've ever seen.' Jerry ran his fingers over the crayoning. 'You are clever. Thank you, I will treasure it.'

He passed the picture over to Lydia, a wide grin splitting his face. He touched Beth's forearm. 'It seems I've missed out on quite a lot.'

She nodded. 'We both have.'

'We've certainly got a lot of catching-up to do,' confirmed Michael as he finished pouring four glasses of Prosecco. 'I think we should drink a toast.' He passed the glasses round and held his own aloft. 'To family.'

'To family,' they chorused, the following silence deafening as they all took a sip.

'Can I have one of those, please?' asked Jake.

'You certainly cannot,' replied Beth. 'You can have a glass of orange juice, just a small one.'

She turned to Jerry. 'We have to be careful with his intake of fluids, you see.'

Jerry cleared his throat, more out of nerves than necessity. 'Of course.'

'He's a gorgeous little boy,' ventured Lydia. 'You must be so proud of him.'

'Oh, we are,' confirmed Michael. 'He has to put up with a lot, but he always has a smile on his face. I'm in awe of him actually.'

'Let's go and sit in the lounge, shall we?' Beth ushered them all towards the door, Jake clinging to his glass of juice with both hands.

'Am I allowed to take this into the best room then, Mummy?' His eyes were wide with astonishment.

Beth nodded solemnly. 'Just this once, but be careful not to spill any.'

'What is it that you do exactly, Beth?' asked Lydia as they gathered round the dining room table.

'For a job? I'm a food stylist, which basically means I make food look pretty for photos. I'm freelance, so I work for all sorts of publications, but mainly magazines, and I've done a few cookbooks.'

'How interesting.'

'Yes, it can be. I enjoy it anyway.'

The red wine had made her mellow and she found herself relaxed and actually enjoying the evening rather than enduring it. Jake chatted away, his initial shyness long forgotten. He turned to Lydia on his left side and whispered in her ear. 'Are you my nana now, then?'

Lydia looked at Beth and raised her eyebrows before answering. Beth confirmed Jake's question with a slight nod of her head.

'Er, well yes, Jake, I suppose I am.'

'Oh, that's good, because I had a nana, you see, but she died.'

'I heard, and I'm really sorry about that, Jake. But you know, I wouldn't want to take her place.' She patted the back of his hand. 'Why don't you call me Grandma instead?' She looked across at Michael. 'Would that be all right with you? I mean, what does he call your mother?'

Michael shrugged. 'We don't see her much. It's a long story. She wasn't a great mother and she's an even worse grandmother. Don't worry about it.'

'I don't like her,' announced Jake. 'She's got no teeth and her breath smells.'

Lydia was taken aback. 'Oh my goodness, well that's too bad.'

'She's an alcoholic,' explained Michael. 'It's a miracle she's still here, to be honest.' He drained the rest of his wine and gazed at his son, now scooping his finger round his bowl and licking off the last traces of cream and meringue. 'Still, nobody said life was fair.'

Beth reached under the table and rested her hand on Michael's thigh. 'Daisy fills the role of grandmother to Jake, just as she became a surrogate mum for Michael.'

'She loves you like a son, Michael,' said Jerry. 'I can certainly vouch for that.'

Beth stood up and began to collect the bowls. 'It's time for Jake's bath now. Why don't we have coffee in the lounge afterwards?'

Jake slid off his chair. 'Can Grandma read my story tonight?'

Lydia cocked her head to one side and smiled fondly. 'I would love to, Jake, thank you.'

Once Jake was snuggled up under his Minions duvet, smelling of bubble bath and Johnson's baby talc, his face still glowing from the warm water, Beth called Jerry and Lydia up to his bedroom.

'Wow, what a special room you've got, Jake,' commented Lydia. 'And just look at all those soft toys on your bed. I'm surprised there's any room for you.'

Jake picked up Galen and thrust it towards her. 'This is my favourite. It was my daddy's when he was a little boy.'

Lydia took the moth-eaten monkey and held it close. 'Well I think he's just gorgeous.'

Jerry nodded towards the machine on Jake's bedside cabinet. 'Is that his . . . you know . . .'

'Dialysis machine,' confirmed Beth. 'We'll let him have his story first and then we'll hook him up afterwards.'

'Hooked up to a machine all night. That sounds tough,' Jerry whispered.

Jake reached up to his shelf and pulled a book down. '*Five Go to Mystery Moor*. We're on chapter five.'

'He loves these books. I was worried he was bit young, but he can't get enough of them,' Beth said. 'You've finished *Smuggler's Top*, then?' She could hear Michael downstairs stacking the dishwasher. 'The bedtime story is his dad's department, so you are honoured, Lydia.'

'I'd like to stay too, if that's all right with Jake,' said Jerry.

'Hooray,' exclaimed Jake. 'You can both read a chapter.'

Beth left them to it and joined Michael in the kitchen. He was scraping the plates and running them under the tap before loading them into the machine. 'How do you think it's going?' she asked.

'They seem like lovely people. I can see now why Daisy was so keen for Jerry to stay with Lydia. She's delightful.'

'Jake seems to have taken to them as well.' She filled the kettle and set out the cups and saucers. 'Do you think we dare hope that he's a match?'

Michael exhaled, the rush of air causing a paper napkin to flutter to the floor. He gripped the edge of the sink. 'I can hardly bear to think of the alternative if he isn't, to be honest.' He turned to face Beth, the strain clearly visible in his eyes.

'Oh Michael, come here.' She reached around his broad shoulders and squeezed him tight. 'I'm the worrier, remember. You're the strong one.'

They were still standing in their contemplative embrace when Lydia appeared in the kitchen.

'We're finished with the story and Jake says he's ready for his tube.'

'Thank you, Lydia,' replied Beth.

Michael picked up a tea towel and began to polish glasses. 'Tell him I'll be up in a while.'

'Sure.' She climbed the stairs two at a time as she returned to hook her son up to the machine that was keeping him alive.

Lydia took the towel off Michael. 'Why don't you let me do those?' She indicated the stool by the island. 'Perch yourself there, you look shattered.'

Michael regarded her with gratitude, a small guffaw escaping his lips. 'Beth thinks I'm the strong one, but she's way more practical than I am. I'm useless at seeing to Jake's tube and all that. It makes me feel queasy, to be honest, but she's brilliant at it. She's like a nurse.'

Lydia smiled. 'She's like a mum, you mean.'

'You're right, she's a great mum. I always knew she would be. It took us a long time to have Jake and she was elated when he was born, we both were. It didn't last, though; within a few weeks it was apparent that his kidneys weren't functioning properly. We always hoped it wouldn't come to this, but a transplant is now his last hope.'

Lydia replaced the clean glass on the worktop. 'Jerry will do all he can, I promise you that.'

'It's such a massive thing to ask of anyone, though, let alone someone we hardly know.'

'He's family and he wants to make up for all the years he's lost. Imagine finding out you have a daughter almost forty years later. It came as such a shock to him. He was mad with Daisy at first for concealing the truth, but he can appreciate her reasons now.'

'I could never be mad at Aunt Daisy for long. I would've had a pretty awful childhood after my dad died if it wasn't for her.'

Lydia put down the tea towel and pulled another stool up close to him. 'Jerry and I asked Daisy to come and live with us in Australia many, many times. Do you know why she always refused?'

Michael thought about the question only for a second. He already knew the answer. 'You're going to say it was because of me, aren't you?'

Lydia nodded. 'She knew Jerry was happy with me, knew I would take the same care of him that she had. The last thing she said to him before he flew out to join me was "Tell Lydia she must air your vests".' She shook her head. 'Only Daisy would think of that. And do you know what? I still air them to this day.'

Michael looked quizzical. 'I didn't know people still

wore vests. Especially in hot countries like Australia.'

Lydia gave a small laugh. 'This is Jerry Duggan we're talking about.'

Jerry stood by Jake's bedroom door, hands clasped behind his back, as he watched Beth fill the machine with dialysate fluid. She worked with the precision and expertise of a skilled physician as Jake lay back on his pillow, his hands lifting up his pyjama top to expose the end of the catheter. It already looked like a well-rehearsed procedure even though he knew Jake had only been having the treatment for a short while.

'This fluid will pass through the catheter into Jake's abdomen and will stay there for a few hours. That's called the dwell stage,' explained Beth. 'The machine then drains this fluid away along with all the toxins from Jake's body and replaces it with fresh fluid.'

Jerry winced and shook his head.

'Don't worry, Grandad. It doesn't hurt.'

'Several fluid exchanges occur overnight, using the lining of his abdomen as a filter, effectively doing the job of his kidneys.'

'Amazing what they can do these days,' observed Jerry. 'It's completely safe, I take it.'

Beth stole a glance at Jake. 'Oh yes, perfectly. We just have to watch out for infections, don't we, Jake?'

Jake nodded. 'I've not to touch this.' He pointed to the dark blue end of the catheter protruding from his tummy.

'And we're really careful about washing our hands, aren't we, Jake?'

She fastened the tubes to the catheter, one for the dialysate fluid and one for the waste products to drain away. 'There we are, all done.' She planted a kiss on his tummy and pulled down his pyjama top. 'Daddy'll be up in a minute.'

'Okay, Mummy.' He snuggled under the duvet and arranged Galen next to him, ensuring the monkey's head was comfortably on the pillow.

'Goodnight, Jake. It was a pleasure to meet you.' Jerry held out his hand as though he were concluding a business meeting. Unlike Lydia, he was not a natural around children. Jake wrestled his arms from under the duvet and held them wide. Jerry leaned forward, and Jake grabbed him round the neck and gave him a clumsy hug.

Jerry backed out of the door as Beth switched off the main light. The room was plunged into darkness, with only the night light providing a warm, comforting glow.

'He's a smashing little chap,' he whispered when they were out on the landing. 'I do hope I can help him.'

48

'Dr Appleby, this is my father, Jerry Duggan,' announced Beth.

This is my father: how strange it felt to say those words. Strange, but wonderful.

'I'm pleased to meet you, Mr Duggan, thank you for coming. Please, take a seat.'

Beth, Michael and Jerry pulled up chairs as Dr Appleby took his place behind his desk, wasting no time in coming straight to the point. 'Mr Duggan, donating an organ is the greatest gift you can ever give to another human being, a truly altruistic and selfless act, and I'm sure both Beth and Michael here are grateful you are even considering it.'

'I'm more than just considering it, Dr Appleby, I am going to do it.'

'I appreciate your commitment, but there's a long way to go before anything is decided. Anyway, as I was saying, this gift of one of your kidneys will enable Jake to lead the active normal life he has so far been denied, and will prolong his life expectancy. However, it is a decision not to be taken lightly. I understand emotions are running high, but you owe it to yourself and your family to consider the impact this donation will have on your own life.'

Beth took a sideways look at Jerry, whilst willing Dr Appleby to stop putting doubts in his head.

'At the risk of sounding flippant, Dr Appleby, I have two kidneys but I have only one grandson.'

'That may well be the case, but I wouldn't be doing my job if I didn't apprise you of all the risks. You will of course undergo a full medical examination within the next few days if the initial blood test proves your blood group is compatible with Jake's.'

'This is where Michael and I failed, at the first hurdle,' added Beth.

Dr Appleby tapped his pen on his pad. 'Beth, please don't think of it in terms of failure. I agree it was bad luck that neither of you were compatible, but try not to see it as some sort of inadequacy on your part.'

He cleared his throat and continued in his firm but reassuring tone. 'I'll try to keep it simple, Mr Duggan. Your blood type needs to be compatible with Jake's. If it is, then we can proceed to the tissue typing test and then finally a crossmatch, but I'll come to all that later in the process. Jake is type O, which means he can only receive from a donor who is also type O.'

Jerry leaned forward in his chair and beat a little tune on the desk with his fingers, making no effort to conceal his excitement. 'I know I'm type O, Dr Appleby, the universal donor, I believe.' He grinned at Beth and Michael. 'I've donated blood before, so I know my type.'

'If the blood test you've already undertaken confirms that, then we can proceed to the next stage. Your blood will be compatible with Jake's.'

Beth's heart shifted a little as hope began to creep in.

'When will we know for sure?' asked Michael.

Dr Appleby glanced at the clock on his wall. 'I've asked for it to be given priority, so I'm hoping to know by five. I will give you a call at home as soon as the result comes in.'

Beth beamed at Michael. 'That's good news, isn't it?'

He reached for her hand. 'It's certainly a cause for optimism, but let's not get carried away. As Dr Appleby says, there's a long way to go.'

The doctor turned once more to Jerry. 'Are you fit and well, and as far as you know, do you have two working kidneys?'

Jerry nodded. 'Absolutely, no health problems at all. But what about my age? I'm sixty-one.'

'As long as you're in good health, your age is not a barrier. We removed a kidney from a seventy-year-old last week, and both he and the recipient, his wife, are doing fine.'

'Good heavens, that's wonderful,' remarked Jerry. 'And very encouraging.'

'Yes, a living donation is always preferable to one from a cadaver, for several reasons,' continued Dr Appleby.

'Firstly, the kidney is removed under optimum conditions; in other words, it's a planned operation, not an emergency one, and the kidney can be transplanted into the recipient without delay. Secondly, we don't have to be as stringent with the tissue typing. A poorly matched live donor transplant will still do better than a well-matched kidney from a cadaver, because the kidney will have suffered less damage.'

'There must be some risks to the donor, though? Can you explain what those are?' asked Michael.

Beth glared at her husband. The last thing they needed was Jerry changing his mind.

'Well, as with any operation, there are some risks, but they are minimal. I'll explain them all in greater detail at the next consultation.' The doctor stood up, indicating that he was bringing the meeting to an end. 'I will have to leave it there for the time being if you don't mind, but thank you all for coming. I'll telephone you later with the blood test result and we'll take it from there.'

Jake was snuggled up under a blanket on the sofa with Lydia when they returned home. His entire soft toy collection was lined up in front of the fire, with a piece of paper and a pencil in front of each of them. 'We've been playing schools,' explained Lydia.

Beth looked at the blackboard that Lydia had obviously heaved downstairs from Jake's bedroom. There were some simple spellings on it: CAT, DOG and DRAF.

'What on earth is a draf, Jake?'

'Mummy, don't be silly. It's that animal with the very long neck.'

Lydia suppressed a laugh. 'I didn't have the heart to correct him, and to be honest I wasn't sure how to spell it myself. Is it one r and two f's, or the other way round?'

'One r, I think, Lydia. Anyway, thanks for looking after him. How's he been?'

'Absolutely perfect. We've had a super time, haven't we, Jake?'

'Grandma,' piped Jake. 'Can I come to your house sometime?'

'Blimey,' exclaimed Michael. 'The furthest I got when I was your age was Butlin's in Minehead.'

Lydia laughed. 'Well, our house is a very long way away, but when you're feeling better, of course you can come.'

Jake picked up his colouring book and began to colour in the sun. 'How far away is your house?'

Jerry crouched down beside his grandson. 'It's 10,552 miles from Melbourne to Manchester.'

Lydia cast her eyes skywards. 'Trust you to know the exact mileage, Jerry.'

'Wow,' exclaimed Jake. 'That must be as far as the moon.'

'Not quite, Jake. The moon's 238,000 miles away.'

Jake's eyes widened in wonder. 'That's as far away as heaven.'

Jerry gave a little chortle. 'Well, heaven doesn't really ex—'

'Jerry,' interrupted Lydia. 'That's enough.'

'I was only trying to educate the boy.'

Beth swooped in between them and started collecting up the soft toys. 'Come on now, let's get tidied away and we can think about tea.'

'Can I suggest we order a takeaway tonight?' announced Jerry. 'My treat. Chinese or Indian?'

'That's kind of you, Jerry, thank you, but it will have to be Chinese. Jake's not very good with the spices and what have you, but he adores his egg-fried rice.'

'Well that's settled then,' said Jerry. 'Do you have a takeaway menu to hand?'

With the meal ordered for six o'clock, Beth watched the hands of the big station clock over the fireplace crawl round agonisingly slowly. She kept glancing towards the hall, willing the phone to ring whilst knowing she would be afraid to answer it when it finally did. Jerry and Lydia were playing dominoes with Jake, and Michael was reading the newspaper, although she could tell by the way he was bouncing his left leg up and down that he was not taking the words in, and his corrugated forehead confirmed that he was just as anxious as she was.

'Shall I put the kettle on?' she asked, jumping up from her seat. She was desperate for something to do, something to make the minutes tick by a little quicker.

By the time the call finally came, she found her shaking legs would not cooperate.

'Oh . . . will you get it, please, Michael?' she asked, but he was already halfway there.

She crept along the hallway to try and see his face, but he had his back to her and she could only hear his side of the conversation. 'Hmm . . . ah ha . . . I understand. Well what does that mean? . . . I see, I see . . .'

Beth moved in front of him and raised her eyebrows, miming *Tell me, tell me.*

After the longest goodbye known to man, Michael finally replaced the phone in the base station and raised both thumbs, a wide smile lifting his careworn features. Then he stretched his arms out and she flung herself against him. He stroked her hair, pulling her long ponytail through his fingers as he kissed the top of her head. 'Definitely type O, Beth. The blood's compatible; we can move to the next stage.'

49

She'd been tossing around in bed for the past hour, turning her pillow over to the cool side, plumping it up and bashing it with her fist, and getting her legs knotted in the duvet cover, but still sleep had eluded her. She didn't know which was worse: trying to stay awake when you were shattered and craving sleep, or lying there with your eyes closed willing yourself to drift off into oblivion.

She peeped in on Jake and noticed his left leg hanging out of the bed. His bare foot was freezing and she held it in her hands for a few seconds before tucking it back under the duvet. He didn't wake; merely stirred and rolled on to his side. The machine still had another couple of hours to run, and it was always preferable for him to sleep through the entire cycle. She made her way downstairs and pulled out the cafetière, her trembling hands causing her to catch the scoop on the rim of the glass jug. Brown speckles of coffee scattered across the white surface, and she cursed as she reached for the kitchen roll.

Over two weeks had passed since Jerry and Lydia had arrived from Australia, and now the day had come when they would finally find out if the transplant could go ahead. Jerry had been subjected to a battery of exhaustive tests in the past fortnight, and everything hinged on the final crossmatch. He had borne the prodding and poking, the endless questions about his health, the psychological analysis, urine tests, X-rays – the lot – with admirable patience and good humour. He was also steadfast in his belief that he would be a match, and would not entertain any other opinion.

And in between it all he had relished his new-found role as a grandfather. Little Jake had never had a grandad, and all his expectations of what one should be like came from the television or story books. But Jerry was nothing like those stereotypical depictions. He did not sit around all day stuffing his pipe with tobacco and handing out Werther's Originals. In the short time he'd been here, he'd taken Jake to Jodrell Bank and the Science Museum, and had awakened in him an inquisitive mind that had hitherto only been interested in Lego and toy cars. Now Jake was able to name all the planets in the correct order, and together he and Jerry had begun a project that would result in a model of the solar system made out of papier mâché. Whenever Beth watched the two of them together, she was all too aware what a wonderful father she had missed out on. She was already dreading the day when he and Lydia would return to Australia, even though she hoped they would be leaving behind the greatest gift it was possible to give another human being.

She poured the water on the ground beans and inhaled the sharp smell as a plume of steam filtered up her nose. They were due at the hospital at ten, another four hours away, and Beth needed a way to pass the time. She noticed a ring of grime around the base of the tap and began to chisel it away with her fingernail. It must have taken years for it to build up, and she was surprised and a little ashamed that it had taken her this long to notice it. She jumped as her mobile phone vibrated and travelled a short distance across the worktop. *Are you awake? I can't sleep. Jx*

She texted straight back. They might as well fret together.

Michael was still in bed when Jerry tapped on the back door. 'Morning, love,' he said as Beth beckoned him inside. His glasses steamed up as they met the warm air of the kitchen.

She poured him a coffee and they sat side by side in the chairs overlooking the garden.

'There's a nip in the air,' commented Jerry.

'Do you think we can dispense with the small talk?' She pulled her dressing gown together and tightened the belt. 'I feel like we've never had a proper chat – you know, about things other than kidney donations and that. I want a normal conversation. I want to know more about you.'

'Okay, what exactly do you want to know?'

'Well, er . . .' Momentarily stumped, she groped around for the right words. 'My mother, what was she like?'

She'd obviously caught him off guard. 'Oh, Petula? Hmm, well now, let me see.' He rubbed his chin and gazed out across the lawn. 'You look nothing like her, for starters. She was rather . . . big-boned, shall we say; tomboyish even.'

'Did you love her?'

Jerry shook his head. 'I'm not going to lie to you, Beth. I didn't love her; in fact I'm ashamed to say I didn't really know her all that well. I'm not going to sugar-coat it; you deserve to know the truth. I won't say I wasn't upset when I heard she'd died in the accident, but no more upset than I would have been if it was the other girl, Lorraine, or even Trisha.'

Beth tucked her legs beneath her, settling in for the long haul. It was taking her mind off Jake at any rate. 'So how did you come to get her pregnant, then?'

Jerry laughed. 'You don't beat about the bush, do you?'

She smiled. 'Nope, I call a spade a shovel, me.'

He drew his palm slowly across his forehead. 'It was forty years ago, Beth. I haven't thought about her much since. I didn't know she was pregnant, remember? She was quite a surly girl in many ways, not like Lorraine, who was much more outgoing.' He guffawed. 'Lorraine wouldn't have looked twice at me, that's for sure. Anyway, Lorraine introduced us and we hung around the pub a bit. They both thought I was a bit of an oddity, and I suppose in a way they were right. I did have trouble fitting in.'

Beth smiled and patted his knee. 'It would be a dull world if we were all the same, Jerry.'

He nodded. 'One night, after a lock-in at the pub—'

'A lock-in? Like drinking illegally, you mean?'

'Well, I wouldn't put it quite like that. In those days, they called last orders at ten thirty and you had half an hour to drink up. Sometimes Selwyn – he was the landlord – would close the curtains, dim the lights and let us carry on for a while. That night I left with Daisy and Petula, and when we got back to our house, Mum said I should walk Petula the rest of the way home. I was mad, I can tell you, I wanted to get to bed, but she insisted and then Petula invited me in for a coffee.' Jerry lowered his voice to barely a whisper. 'I'm not proud of myself, but it happened in her hallway. I wasn't thinking straight. I missed Lydia so much and I let myself down.'

Beth thought about her sleeping child upstairs, attached to a machine, a gruelling routine that defined his life, all of their lives. 'I'm very glad you did, Jerry.'

He rummaged around in his jacket pocket. 'Would you like to see a photo of her?'

'Really? You have one?'

He passed over a washed-out colour photograph. 'It was taken on the day of the crash, when we all arrived in Blackpool. I'm not in it, of course. Predictably, I was the only one with a camera.'

Beth peered at the nine figures standing side by side, leaning on the railings. 'Which one is she?'

'The tall one with short brown hair.' He pointed to Petula, who was standing with her arm around the girl next to her, her head tilted to one side as she squinted into the sun.

'Gosh, that was my mother? She looks so young, and she definitely doesn't look pregnant. How awful it must have been for her to take the decision to abandon her baby. I just can't imagine anybody doing that.'

'It doesn't bear thinking about what might have happened to you if she had taken you home, though,' said Jerry.

'I know. Not only might I have been killed, but I would never have had Mary as my mother. Petula had no way of knowing it, but by sacrificing her own chance to be a mother, she gave Mary the greatest gift of all.'

'And you too,' confirmed Jerry.

She snuggled up to him and laid her head on his shoulder as they both studied the photograph. 'Do you know what happened to the others?'

Jerry pointed to an old man with a straggly white beard. 'That was Harry – he died in the crash too – and this here is Karl, Michael's father.'

Beth took the photo and peered more closely at the handsome young man with longish dark hair, sunglasses perched on top of his head, his narrow hips accentuated by his ridiculously wide flares. He was leaning back, one elbow propped on the railings and his other hand placed on the shoulder of a little boy standing between his legs.

'Oh my God, Jerry. You have no idea what this will mean to Michael. He has no photos of his father whatsoever.'

'What, none at all, seriously?'

'He said his mother burned them all.'

'How awful. Why would she do that?'

'Believe me, we've long since given up trying to understand Andrea.'

Jerry shook his head and turned his attention back to the photograph. 'And of course you know that little chap.'

'Michael,' whispered Beth. She sniffed loudly as she rummaged around in her pocket for a tissue. 'I'm sorry, it's just such a poignant picture. To think that three of them would not live to see the end of the day is just heartbreaking. They all look so happy, not a care in the world, with no clue that they were posing for their last ever photograph.' She shuddered. 'Just wait until Michael sees this!'

'Wait until I see what?'

They both turned as Michael entered the kitchen, rubbing the sleep out of his eyes, dressed only in a pair of boxer shorts.

'Michael, where's your dressing gown? We've got a guest.'

'Oh, hello, Jerry.' He glanced at the clock. 'You're early, it's only six thirty.'

'I couldn't sleep so I thought I'd come round and keep Beth company. Neither of us can settle.'

'Any coffee left?'

'I think you may be able to squeeze a cup out. Pop it in the microwave if it's not warm enough.'

She passed the photo over to Michael. 'We were just looking at this.'

Michael frowned as he took the picture. He held it at arm's length and squinted. 'Oh my God, is this . . . ?' He ferreted around under a pile of newspapers and retrieved his glasses, bringing the photo closer to his face. 'I've never seen this picture before.'

'It came as a bit of a shock to me,' said Jerry. 'The film was still in my camera a year later, when Lydia and I went up to Sydney. I finished it off, and when I got the pictures back, the Blackpool ones were still on there.'

'Look at Dad,' said Michael. 'He looks so happy. I remember he was squeezing my neck. That's why my shoulders are hunched up and I'm giggling.' He fell silent as he stared at the photo. An image of his six-year-old self filled his head. His mother sprawled on the rug in front of the fire, the empty photo album by her side. He had never hated her more than at that moment. He remembered how he'd wanted to scald her with the hot tea, to hurt her as much as she'd hurt him.

'Are you all right, love?' asked Beth.

He choked on his words. 'Yes . . . yes I'm fine.' He attempted a thin smile. 'It's good to see him again. I thought I'd forgotten what he looked like, but this has brought him back to me as clearly as anything. It's like looking through a window to the past. None of us could have imagined how that day was going to end. We all look so happy, don't we? Look at Daisy with her arm linked through Harry's.' He paused and shook his head. 'Poor bloke. And look at Trisha, with her leg across Selwyn's body. You can tell he's loving it, the way he's gazing down her top.'

'Jerry was just showing me Petula.'

'Of course, your mother.' He pointed to the photo. 'There she is, you can't really miss her. I didn't know her, but she seemed nice enough. I've no idea where you get your good looks from, though, Beth.'

Jerry cleared his throat. 'Maybe from her father?'

They both looked at him, and Michael laughed as he placed the photo on the table. 'Definitely from you, Jerry.'

Beth linked her arm through her husband's. 'Come on, I'll make you some fresh coffee.'

The nurse ushered them all into Dr Appleby's office, indicating the three chairs. 'Please take a seat, the doctor will be along shortly.'

Beth scrutinised the young woman's face for a clue as to what the outcome of this meeting would be. She noticed that the nurse looked at the floor a lot; did this mean she couldn't meet her eye? It must be bad news, then. Beth felt moisture in her armpits and had the urge to start shedding layers. She looked across at Michael. 'Is it hot in here or is it just me?' She could feel beads of perspiration on her top lip.

'It's a bit warm, I suppose,' Michael conceded. 'Do you want me to fetch you a glass of water?'

Beth draped her jacket over the back of her chair. 'No, I'll be all right. He'll be here in a minute.'

Jerry reached across and gave her hand a reassuring squeeze. 'The waiting's almost over. Just a few more minutes and then we'll know.'

The crossmatch was the final test prior to the transplant surgery and was carried out to see whether Jake had developed any antibodies that would attack the donated kidney. Their blood had been mixed together, and if Jake's cells attacked and killed Jerry's, then the crossmatch would be considered positive and the transplant would not be able to go ahead. Jake would have to wait for a donor from some poor soul who had lost their life. If the crossmatch proved negative, however, surgery would take place within forty-eight hours.

None of them spoke, the silence broken only by Jerry clicking his pen and Michael bouncing his knee up and down, causing his chair to squeak rhythmically in time to the motion. Beth placed her hand on his thigh.

He smiled apologetically. 'Sorry, love. I can't help it.'

She turned to Jerry and gently took the pen from his hands. 'Oh, I'm sorry.' He stood up and paced a tight circle around the room.

'Jerry,' Beth began. 'I just want you to know that whatever the result of this final test, we'll always be indebted to you for even allowing yourself to be tested. The fact that you're willing to give one of your kidneys to a little boy you barely know is one of the most selfless things I've ever heard.' She reached down to her handbag, pulled out a tissue and dabbed at her moist palms. 'It crucifies Michael and me that we aren't able to help our son, but knowing that you were willing to even try means the world.'

Jerry stopped pacing and stood facing both of them. 'He's my flesh and blood, Beth.' He spread his arms and shrugged as though all he had offered to do was give Jake his last Rolo. 'I would do anything for him. He's my grandson.'

Michael stood up and shook his hand. 'Thank you, Jerry.'

'What is keeping Dr Appleby?' Beth glanced at the clock on the wall for the tenth time in as many minutes. 'It's quarter past already.'

Before anybody could say anything else, the door opened and Dr Appleby entered, flanked by two junior doctors. This was it then; all their hopes were pinned on the next words to come out of Dr Appleby's mouth.

He studied the clipboard in his hands, then turned over the next sheet. Once he had digested all the information, he looked up at the expectant faces assembled before him. Beth stared directly into his eyes and he met her gaze but didn't say anything. He didn't need to.

Epilogue

Beth had always been a nervous flyer, and this mid-air turbulence was not doing anything to convince her that air travel was the safest mode of transport. She looked across at Michael, plugged into the entertainment system, oblivious to the imminent threat to their lives. She tugged at his sleeve. 'Michael.'

He pushed the headphones back from his ears. 'What?'

'All this bouncing round, do you think we're safe?'

'Of course we are. Aircraft are hardly ever brought down by clear air turbulence.'

'*Hardly* ever?'

Michael laughed. '*Never*, then. Aircraft nowadays are built to sustain this kind of stress. We'll be through it soon, stop worrying.' He gave her arm a reassuring squeeze before he clamped the headphones back on to his ears, leaving her to fret alone.

'Can I get you anything more to drink?'

Beth smiled at the pretty young stewardess leaning over her seat, admiring her flawless skin and doll-like features.

'I could use another gin and tonic, please, a large one.'

'Certainly, madam.'

Beth settled herself into her seat once more. Surely if the crew were still allowed to walk around the cabin serving drinks, then this turbulence couldn't be all that serious? She downed the gin and tonic, reclined her seat and tried to sleep.

Jerry reached into his cavernous fridge and pulled out the little bottle of live yoghurt. He peeled back the foil lid and drained the contents in one go before lining up his vitamins along the countertop. He picked them up one by one and chugged them down with a glass of water. He knew it was important these days more than ever to take care of himself, and while he might not be rippling with muscle, his body was lean and his heart was strong. His old seventies bicycle might have looked like something the vicar would ride, and he'd been subject to plenty of ridicule back then, but it had kept him fit, saved him a fortune on fuel and nurtured a love of cycling that remained to this day. He'd lived with just one kidney for almost four years now, and this had only made him more determined to stay healthy. It was fortunate that the Melbourne climate suited him just fine; it was seldom unbearably hot or unbearably cold, and its reputation for lots of rain was unfounded. He surmised this was just a rumour put about by jealous natives of Brisbane or Sydney.

He called up to his wife. 'Are you coming, Lydia?'

She appeared at the top of the stairs in a pair of pale

grey jogging trousers and a lime-green vest. She'd piled her hair into a bun, stretching the skin around her eyes. With her toned brown arms on show, she looked nowhere near her sixty-two years. 'I'm just looking for my runners, I'll be right down.'

Every morning at seven, the pair of them power-walked the length of the beach, stopping for a cappuccino in the café at the end before completing the return leg. Sometimes they would come again in the evening to watch the colony of little penguins return home to the St Kilda breakwater at twilight. Jerry volunteered as a penguin guide and was always happy to answer visitors' questions, although he spent most of his time telling tourists not to use flash photography or shove their selfie sticks into the penguins' nesting sites.

He called up to his wife again. 'Lydia, I'll wait for you outside. I'm just going to do some stretches.'

Lydia bounded down the stairs. 'I'm here now. Do we really need to do this today? I've still got loads to do.'

'I'll help you, and we've got plenty of time; they don't land until this afternoon.'

She stood on tiptoe and kissed him on the cheek. 'You're such a creature of habit, Jerry Duggan.'

As they entered the arrivals hall, Michael making a valiant effort to keep their overloaded trolley steady, Beth's eyes scanned the throng of people waiting to greet the passengers. They mostly consisted of bored-looking taxi drivers holding up name placards, and it didn't take her long to spot Jerry and Lydia, who were both waving enthusiastically.

'Welcome to Australia,' beamed Jerry. 'Did you have a good flight?' Beth eased her sleeping daughter on to her shoulder and embraced her father with one arm, his familiar lemony-fresh scent bringing on a rush of affection. She gave him an extra squeeze. 'A bit bumpy, but we came through unscathed.'

She held him at arm's length and looked him up and down. 'You look well, Dad; a bit too trim maybe. I hope you've not been overdoing things.'

Jerry tutted and turned to Lydia. 'She's only been here thirty seconds and she's telling me what to do.' He stroked the back of his granddaughter's blond hair, and the little girl stirred and turned to face him, rubbing the sleep out of her eyes.

Jerry pushed her fringe to the side. 'Hello, sweetheart.'

She turned away again and buried her head in her mother's neck. It had been an arduous journey for the three-year-old.

Beth laughed. 'She's tired, that's all, Dad. She'll come round in a bit.'

Jerry clapped his hands together. 'Now, where's that grandson of mine.' He spotted Jake hovering behind the trolley full of cases. 'My goodness, look how much you've grown. I hardly recognised you.' He held his arms wide. 'Got a hug for your old grandad, then?'

Jake rushed forward and almost knocked Jerry off his feet.

'It's good to see you, lad.' He dropped a kiss on the top of the boy's head. 'Come on then, let's get you back to our house and we'll have a nice cool glass of Grandma's home-made lemonade.'

The yellow and white striped awning shielded the patio from the heat of the sun. Lydia placed the huge jug of lemonade stuffed with lemon slices and mint on the table and set out the glasses. A cloud of blue smoke wafted over the garden fence.

'That's Bruce next door, barbecuing his shrimp,' explained Jerry.

Michael snorted on his lemonade, the liquid coming out of his nose. 'Bruce is barbecuing his shrimp? Please tell me he's married to Sheila and then we'll have a hat trick of Australian clichés.'

Jerry frowned. 'No, his wife's called Maisie, actually.'

'Michael's just teasing you, Dad,' Beth explained.

'What . . . Oh, I see, yes, Bruce and Sheila, very funny.'

They fell into a comfortable silence as they sipped their drinks. Although they Skyped regularly, Beth had not seen Jerry and Lydia since they'd come over to England last year for Daisy's funeral. Even at eighty-eight years of age, Daisy had continued to live alone, fiercely resisting all attempts to shoehorn her into assisted housing. *That's for old people*, she had insisted. When Michael had found her sitting in her favourite armchair, knitting still in her lap, he had assumed she was just asleep; nothing had prepared him for the fact that she was serenely dead. She might have had a long and largely happy life, but this was not much consolation to Michael, and the grief had remained etched into his face for months afterwards. The only crumb of comfort was that she had lived long enough to get to know her great-granddaughter.

Beth let her head loll back on the lounger as she watched Jake kick a football against the garage wall on the other side of the garden. He was just a normal kid with bags of excess energy and a zest for life that she'd never thought she would see.

'Can I play too?'

Jake bent down and placed the ball at his little sister's feet. She aimed a huge kick but her foot skimmed over the top of the ball and she landed with a thump on her bottom. Beth immediately sprang up from her chair, but Michael placed his hand on her arm. 'I think big brother's got this.'

Jake pulled his sister to her feet and wiped her tears with the hem of his T-shirt. 'There you are, Daisy, you're all right now.'

Beth reached across and squeezed Michael's hand as they watched their children playing on the sun-baked grass. Daisy Duggan had made an impossible decision all those years ago when she'd left a newborn baby on a stranger's doorstep, and every day Beth was grateful that

Daisy had been brave enough to follow her heart. She took a sip of the long, cool drink in front of her and thought back to the journey that had brought her to this moment, to this faraway place they would now call home. She had come so close to losing all that was dear to her but the shadow of her past had been lifted. It was time to live in the light.

Acknowledgements

Thanks to my agent, Anne Williams, who always gives me good counsel, to the talented team at Headline and especially my editor, Sherise Hobbs, who is wise beyond words and steers me in the right direction.

Thanks to those who read early drafts and were brave enough to give their honest opinion. They include my husband Rob Hughes, my parents Audrey and Gordon Watkin and good friend, Grace Higgins.

Thanks to Caroline Ramsay for her help with all matters concerning childbirth and to Rick McCabe at the General Register Office in Southport for his generous assistance regarding the procedure for registering births in the seventies.

Finally, thank you to everybody who read my debut novel *The Letter*. Your enthusiasm and love for that book helped inspire me to write this one.

THE SECRET

Kathryn Hughes

Bonus Material

The Gresford Mining Disaster

Although Thomas Roberts worked in a fictional colliery somewhere in the Lancashire Coalfield, my inspiration for what happened to him and his colleagues was based on fact.

On Saturday 22nd September 1934 at around 2.08A.M., one of the worst British mining disasters occurred at the Gresford Colliery, near Wrexham in North Wales. A violent explosion ripped through the Dennis shaft, 2,264 feet below the surface. Working conditions had always been poor in the shaft; the ventilation was inadequate, the air hot and humid and the shaft was prone to firedamp (methane gas). Fires broke out and blocked the main access road and only six miners who were taking a mid-shift break managed to escape. For two days, rescuers battled with the flames but eventually they were forced to withdraw as conditions were deemed too hazardous. In total, 262 miners working in the Dennis section were killed, along with three members of the rescue team. Only eleven bodies were ever recovered and the remains of the other victims were left entombed within the permanently sealed damaged shaft. The disaster claimed its final victim a few days later, when the shaft blew off its seal and a surface worker was killed by flying debris.

The cause of the explosion was never proved but the inquiry found a number of factors which contributed to the disaster, including failure of safety procedures and poor mine management. Over half a million pounds was raised for the disaster fund but, in spite of this, miners suffered untold hardship due to the temporary closure of the mine and their subsequent loss of income.

The mine was reopened for coal production in January 1936, excluding the Dennis section, and finally closed for good on economic grounds on 10th November 1973. 266 miners lost their lives in the Gresford Disaster and they must never be forgotten.

Many thanks to my good friend, Dave Haslam, for telling me about this disaster, which tragically claimed the life of his great-grandfather, Edward Jones.

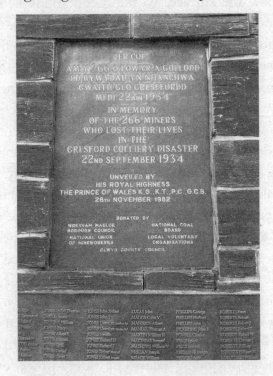

The Gresford Memorial Photograph © Dave Haslam

A message from the NHS Blood and Transplant Department

Every day three people in the UK die in need of a transplant because we're not all willing to donate our organs. NHS Blood and Transplant is asking more people to agree to donation. One day it could be someone you love, or even you in need of a transplant.

Make sure your family know you want to be an organ donor. Register to donate and tell them your decisions. Letting your family know your organ donation decision will make it much easier for them to support what you want.

Joining the NHS Organ Donor Register really is a simple process – it takes two minutes. Visit www.organdonation. nhs.uk or call 0300 123 23 23.

Discover Kathryn's bestselling first novel

THE LETTER

Read on for an extract . . .

March 1973

This time she was going to die, of that she was certain. She knew she must only have a few seconds left and she silently prayed for the end to come quickly. She could feel the warm, sticky blood as it ran down the back of her neck. She had heard the sickening sound of her skull cracking as her husband slammed her head into the wall. There was something in her mouth that felt like a piece of gravel; she knew it was a tooth and she desperately tried to spit it out. His hands were gripped so tightly around her throat that it was impossible for her to draw breath or make any kind of sound. Her lungs screamed out for oxygen and the pressure on the back of her eyeballs was so intense she was sure they were going to pop out. Her head began to swim, and then, mercifully, she started to black out.

She heard the long-forgotten sound of the school bell and suddenly she was five years old again. The chatter of the other children was almost drowned out by the incessant ringing. As she screamed at them to stop, she realised she had a voice after all.

She stared up at the bedroom ceiling for a second and then squinted at the alarm clock that had just roused her from her sleep. Cold sweat trickled down her spine and she tugged at the bedclothes, pulling them up to her chin in an effort to savour the warmth for a few seconds longer. Her heart was still pounding after the nightmare and she blew out gently through her mouth. Her warm breath hung in the frigid air of the bedroom. With an enormous effort she heaved herself out of bed and winced as her bare feet found the icy roughness of the wooden floor. She glanced over at Rick, who thankfully was still sound asleep, snoring off the effects of the bottle of whisky he had drunk the night before. She checked that his cigarettes were still on the bedside table where she had carefully positioned them. If there was one thing guaranteed to put Rick in a foul mood, it was not being able to find his fags in the morning.

She crept quietly into the bathroom and eased the door shut. It would probably take an explosion not seen since Hiroshima to wake him, but Tina wasn't taking any chances. She ran a basin for a wash, the water freezing as usual. Sometimes it was a choice between feeding themselves and feeding the meter. Rick had lost his job on the buses, so there was little money for heat. Enough to drink, smoke and gamble, though, she noted in the silence of her brain.

She went downstairs, filled the kettle and placed it on the stove. The paper boy had been and she absently pulled the newspapers through the letter box: *The Sun* for her and *The Sporting Life* for Rick. The headline caught her attention. It was Grand National day. Her shoulders sagged and she shuddered at the thought of all the money Rick would squander on the race. There was little doubt he would be too drunk by lunchtime to venture out to the bookmaker's, and it would be left to Tina to put the bet on. The betting shop was next door to the charity shop where she helped out on Saturdays, and the bookie, Graham, had become a close friend over the years. Despite working all week as a shorthand typist in an insurance office, Tina looked forward to her day in the charity shop. Rick had told her it was ridiculous for her to spend the day voluntarily sorting through dead people's clothes when she could work in a proper shop and contribute even more to the family coffers. For Tina, it was an excuse to spend the day out of Rick's way, and she enjoyed chatting to the customers and having normal conversations where she didn't have to watch every word she said.

She switched on the radio and turned the volume down a touch. Tony Blackburn always managed to make her smile with his corny jokes. He was just announcing Donny Osmond's new single, 'The Twelfth of Never', when the kettle began to give its hollow whistle. She snatched it up before the noise became too shrill, and put two spoonfuls of tea leaves into the old stained pot. She sat down at the kitchen table while she waited for the tea to brew, and opened her paper. She held her breath as the toilet flushed upstairs. She heard the floorboards creak as Rick padded back to bed, and exhaled with relief. Then she froze as he called:

'Tina! Where are my fags?'

Jesus. He smokes like a beagle.

She jumped up immediately and belted up the stairs two at a time.

'On your bedside table where I put them last night,' she replied, arriving breathlessly at his side.

She ran her hand over the table in the gloom but could not feel them. She swallowed her rising panic.

'I'll have to pull the curtains a little. I can't see.'

'For God's sake, woman! Is it too much to ask for a man to be able to have a fag when he wakes up? I'm gagging here.'

His sour morning breath stank of stale whisky.

She finally found the cigarettes on the floor between the bed and the table.

'Here they are. You must have knocked them off in your sleep.'

Rick stared at her for a moment before he reached up and snatched the packet from her. She flinched and instinctively covered her face with her hands. He grabbed her wrist and their eyes met for a second before Tina closed hers and fought back the tears.

She could recall the first time Rick had hit her like it had happened only yesterday. Even the memory of it caused her cheek to sting and burn. It wasn't just the physical pain, though, but the sudden stark reality that things were never going to be the same again. The fact that it was also their wedding night made it harder to take. Up until that moment the day had been perfect. Rick looked so handsome in his new brown suit, cream shirt and silk tie. The white carnation in his buttonhole confirmed him as the groom and Tina thought it was impossible to love anybody more than she loved him. Everyone had told her she looked stunning. Her long dark hair was swept up into a loose bun and woven through with tiny flowers. Her pale blue eyes shone out from beneath thick false eyelashes and her complexion radiated a natural beauty that needed no help from cosmetics. The party after the wedding was a lively affair at an inexpensive local hotel, and the happy couple and their guests had danced the night away.

As they were preparing for bed that night in their hotel room, Tina noticed that Rick was unusually quiet.

'Are you all right, love?' she asked. She put her arms around his neck. 'It was a wonderful day, wasn't it? I can't believe I'm Mrs Craig at last.' She pulled away from him suddenly. 'Hey, I'll have to practise my new signature.' She picked up a pen and paper from the bedside table and wrote *Mrs Tina Craig* with a flourish.

Still Rick said nothing; just stared at her. He lit a cigarette and poured himself a glass of cheap champagne. He swigged it down in one gulp and walked over to where Tina was sitting on the bed.

'Stand up,' he commanded.

Tina was puzzled by his tone but did as she was asked.

Rick raised his hand and whipped it sharply across her face.

'Don't ever make a fool of me again.' With that he stormed out of the bedroom.

He spent the night slumped in the hotel lounge surrounded by empty glasses, and it was days before he would tell Tina exactly what her transgression had been. Apparently he hadn't liked the way she had danced with one of his work colleagues. She had looked at him too provocatively and flirted with him in front of their guests. Tina couldn't even remember the guy, let alone the incident, but it was the start of Rick's paranoid fixation that she was coming on to every man she met. She often wondered if she should have left him the very next day. But she was a romantic at heart and wanted to give her fledgling marriage every chance to succeed. She was sure the incident was a one-off, and Rick allayed any niggling doubts when he presented her with a bouquet by way of an apology. Such was his remorse and contrition that Tina had no hesitation in forgiving him immediately. It was only a few days later that she noticed a card buried amongst the flowers. She smiled to herself as she pulled it out. *With fond memories of our beloved Nan*, she read. The bugger had stolen the flowers from a grave in the churchyard!

*   *   *

Now, four years later, they stared at each other for a second longer before Rick released his grip.

'Thanks, love.' He smiled. 'Now be a good girl and fetch me a brew.'

Tina exhaled with relief and rubbed her crimson wrist. Ever since that wedding night incident, she had vowed she was not going to be a victim. No way was she going to be one of those battered wives who made excuses for their husbands' vile behaviour. There had been many times when she had threatened to leave, but she always backed out at the last minute. Rick was so repentant and humble and, of course, promised never to raise his hand to her again. These days, though, he was drinking a lot more heavily and his outbursts were more frequent. The time had finally come when she could stand it no longer.

The problem was, she had nowhere to go. She had no family, and although she did have a couple of close friends, she could never impose on them to the extent of asking them to take her in. It was her wages that paid the rent, but there was no way Rick would leave voluntarily. So she had started an escape fund. She needed enough money for a deposit and a month's rent on a new place, and then she would be free. That was a lot more difficult than it sounded. She rarely had any spare money left to save, but no matter how long it took, she was determined to leave. The old coffee jar she kept hidden at the back of the kitchen cupboard was filling up nicely, and she now had just over fifty pounds. But with rent on even the most basic bedsit commanding eight pounds per week, plus a deposit of at least thirty, she would need to save a lot more before she could make the break. For the time being she would make the best of it, staying out of Rick's way as much as possible and trying not to get him riled.

She carried Rick's tea upstairs, together with *The Sporting Life* tucked under her arm.

'Here you are,' she said, trying to sound breezy.

There was no reply. He was fast asleep again, propped up on the pillow, mouth open, a cigarette balanced precariously on his dry, cracked bottom lip. Tina picked it off and stubbed it out.

'For Christ's sake! You'll kill us both,' she muttered.

She set the mug down and pondered what to do. Should she wake him and incur his wrath? Or should she just leave the tea on the bedside table? When he woke up it would no doubt be stone cold, which would be sure to send him into a rage, but by then she would hopefully be at the shop and out of harm's way. The decision was taken out of her hands as he stirred and forced his eyes open.

'Your tea's there,' she said. 'I'm going to the shop now. Will you be OK?'

Rick pushed himself up on to his elbows.

'My mouth's as dry as a camel's,' he sniffed. 'Thanks for the tea, love.'

He patted the quilt, indicating for her to sit down.

'Come here.'

That was what life was like with Rick. He was an evil, spiteful bully one minute and an angelic choirboy the next.

'Sorry about before. You know, about the ciggies? I wouldn't hurt you, Tina, you know that.'

Tina could scarcely believe her ears, but it was never a good idea to contradict Rick so she merely nodded.

'Look,' he continued. 'Could you do me a favour?'

She let out a small, inaudible sigh and raised her eyes to the ceiling. *Here we go.*

'Could you put a bet on for me?'

She could bite her tongue no longer.

'Do you think that's a good idea, Rick? You know how tight things are. With only me earning, there's not much spare cash for things like gambling.'

'*With only me earning,*' Rick mimicked. 'You never miss a chance to get that in, do you, you sanctimonious cow?' Tina was momentarily startled by his vicious reaction, but he was not finished. 'It's the Grand National, for Christ's sake! Everybody has a bet today.'

He reached down to the floor, picked up his trousers from where he had discarded them the night before and pulled out a roll of banknotes.

'There's fifty quid here.' He tore off the lid of his cigarette packet and wrote the name of a horse on the back. 'Fifty pounds to win.'

He handed her the money and the scrap of cardboard. Tina was stunned.

'Where did you get this?' She held up the roll of notes.

'Well it's not really any of your business, but since you ask, I won it on the horses. There, you see, who says it's a mug's game?'

Liar.

Her head was swirling and she felt her neck begin to flush.

'This is more than a week's wages for me, Rick.'

'I know. Aren't I clever?' he replied smugly.

She clasped her hands together as though in prayer and brought them up to her lips. She tried to remain calm as she blew gently through her fingers. 'But this money could pay our electricity bill or our food bill for a whole month.'

'Christ, Tina! You're so boring.'

She fanned out the notes in her trembling hands. She knew then that she was not physically capable of handing over such a large amount to a bookie.

'Can't you put it on?' she begged.

'You work next door to the bloody betting shop, I'm hardly putting you out.'

Tina could feel the tears starting to sting but she had made up her mind. She would take the money and discuss with Graham what to do. She had taken money from Rick before for a bet and not put it on. The horse had inevitably lost and he had been none the wiser. However, Tina felt she had aged about ten years during the course of that race, and this time it was different. The stakes were so much higher. *Fifty pounds, for heaven's sake.*

Suddenly and inexplicably she found herself in the grip of panic. She felt the heat rise from her toes to the back of her neck and she found it difficult to breathe. She backed out of the bedroom, muttering excuses about having left the toast under the grill, and ran downstairs to the kitchen. She climbed up on to a stool and reached into the back of the cupboard, feeling around for the coffee jar containing her escape fund. Her fingers found the familiar shape and she pulled the jar out and clutched it to her chest. Her hands shook as she tried to unscrew the lid. Her sweaty palms could not get the grip she needed and she groped around for the tea towel. Finally the lid yielded and she peered inside. There was nothing but a few coppers left. She shook the jar and looked again, as though her eyes had deceived her the first time.

'Bastard!' she cried out. 'Bastard, bastard, bastard!'

She started to weep, the huge sobs making her shoulders heave.

'Thought you could pull the wool over my eyes, did you?'

She jumped and spun round to see Rick leaning in the doorway, another cigarette hanging from his lips and wearing only his greying tea-stained vest and grubby underpants.

'You took it! How could you? I've worked all hours to save that money. It's taken me months.'

She slumped down on to the floor and rocked back and forth, still clutching the almost-empty jar. Rick strode over and dragged her roughly to her feet.

'Pull yourself together. What do you expect when you hide money from your own husband? What are you saving for anyway?'

To get away from you, you drunken, manipulative waste of space.

'It was supposed to be a . . . surprise, you know, a little holiday for us. I thought a break would do us both good.'

Rick pondered this for a second and then relaxed his grip on Tina's arm. He frowned doubtfully.

'A nice idea. Tell you what, when that horse romps home, we'll have a belting holiday, maybe even go abroad.'

Tina nodded miserably and wiped her eyes.

'Go and get yourself cleaned up. You're going to be late for work. I'm off back to bed. I'm knackered.'

He dropped a kiss on the top of her head and headed back upstairs.

Tina stood alone in the middle of the kitchen. She had never felt so wretched or desperate in her life, but she was determined she was not going to put that bet on. That fifty pounds was hers, and no way was it going to be wasted on a horse race, Grand National or not. She took the money and stuffed it into her purse, then took a cursory look at the name Rick had written on the cigarette packet.

Red Rum.

You'd better not win, you bugger.